R. GARLAND GRAY

DARKSCAPE

REDEMPTION

Medallion Press, Inc.
Printed in USA

DEDICATION

For Dov, my real-life hero.
And for those who deserve a second chance.

Published 2009 by Medallion Press, Inc.

The MEDALLION PRESS LOGO
is a registered trademark of Medallion Press, Inc.

Printed in the United States of America
Typeset in Adobe Garamond Pro

ISBN# 978-193383655-3

10 9 8 7 6 5 4 3 2 1
First Edition

R. GARLAND GRAY

DARKSCAPE

REDEMPTION

"The gods visit the sins of the fathers upon the children."
~ Euripides, Ancient Earth

PROLOGUE

Braemar Keep of Clan Douglas
Planet Mars
Standard Year 3187

DECLAN STUFFED THE book reader into his back pocket and made his way down the muddy banks of the crater lake. He stood at the edge of the water, his child's heart heavy with longing. A northerly breeze ruffled strands of black hair into his eyes and he glanced at the shawl of lavender light across the horizon. The twilight sky of his new home was beautiful, but it did not lift his spirits. At ten years old, he was more aware of life's unfairness then other children his age and because of this, kept mostly to himself. He scooped up a silvery rock, the size of his palm. It was cool, wet, and smooth, and the fingers of his right hand tightened around it.

"Declan?"

Looking over his shoulder, he squinted up the grassy embankment. His guardian stood above him wearing a pristine, high-collared black uniform. In the setting light, Second Commander Winn de Douglas looked almost godlike, the Clan Douglas coat of arms sparkling on his left shoulder.

Inside his heart, he vowed silently that he would wear the uniform one day, too.

"I must leave now, Declan."

"Yes, sir," he replied in a flat tone, his emotions carefully contained.

"Why are you out here?"

"I like to read by the waters, sometimes."

His guardian scanned the horizon. "You had wanted to ask me a question before I left."

"Yes, sir. Will the Dragon Comet come here, too, sir?"

His guardian frowned. "Why do you ask about the old comet?"

"Before we left, the boys at my old school said the Dragon Comet would come again into our solar system and destroy Mars."

"They are misinformed. The planet fragments after the impact attest to that. Do you know the story of Ancient Earth and the Dragon Comet, boy?"

"No, sir," Declan replied, wishing the second commander would stay with him. But that was never possible. His guardian had too many responsibilities and left him in the care of a governess who smelled like green soap. But today was different. As the commander walked down the embankment, Declan struggled to hide his surprise.

"Declan, come and sit with me on this rock ledge. There is room for both of us and I will share the story with you. It is important that you know it."

Declan scrambled up the embankment, sat down on the slanted ledge, and waited.

Winn de Douglas propped an arm upon a raised knee, rubbed his chin and began slowly. "Long ago, Ancient Earth's astronomers had thought Halley's comet had returned in its seventy-six-year orbit. But they soon found out that it was not Halley. The cometary astronomers named the new comet Dragon, for its drag-on-shaped nucleus. At first, there was much excitement at this new cosmic wonder but when they calculated the comet's path, everything changed for the worse. Do you know what happened next?"

Declan shook his head.

"They learned that the Dragon Comet was going to pass dangerously close to Earth. Life as they knew it was going to end. Governments were informed of the terrible news and met in secret. Bases were built on other planets. It took time and resources, but they did it. When the Dragon passed by Earth, it rained catastrophic ice and darkness for many long months, as had been anticipated, killing most everything. Then it moved away and collided with the planet . . ."

"Mercury."

"Yes." His guardian glanced at him with a raised brow. "I thought you did not know the history of the Dragon comet."

Declan shrugged, his gaze settling on the sweeping lines of Braemar Keep, the base fortress of his guardian's powerful clan. "I know parts of the story, sir."

"Knowing part of something is never enough. Information is power, Declan."

"Yes, sir."

The second commander squinted at the setting sun. "I have some time, yet. I will finish your history lesson, if you like."

"Yes, sir."

"When the comet collided with Mercury, it changed our solar system forever. Those who survived the event are our ancestors."

"Is that when the red nebula formed?" Declan asked, wondering about the infamous space cloud of death. He had heard several boys talk about it the other day.

"Yes, the collision spewed hot planetary material into space. It formed into the huge gas cloud and dark star lanes we know as the Moukad Nebula. It is my belief that someday that material will coalesce into an infant planet but neither you nor I will be around to see it. Do you have any more questions?"

"No, sir."

The second commander stood, ready to report back to his command. "Come and walk with me."

Declan tossed his rock into the black waters of the lake and stood. "The nebula is a very dangerous place, isn't it?"

"If you know the risk, there is no danger."

Declan nodded and joined his guardian. He would forever remember that particular lie.

CHAPTER ONE

MacKendrick Castle Keep of Clan MacKendrick
Planet Forest
Standard Year 3211

DECLAN DE DOUGLAS despised waiting, especially when it was associated with stupidity. With the arrival of the eighteenth month of the peace, he had come to Clan MacKendrick to negotiate a trade treaty. With ten fruitless days under his belt, nothing had been accomplished, except for a temper brewing deep in his gut.

Standing alone in the Hall of Entrance of the MacKendrick Castle Keep, he struggled with a brutal urge to return to the negotiation table and punch Lord Tomaidh Henderson in his cherubic face. All morning he had listened to the man's faultfinding arguments about the trade agreement proposed by Clan Douglas.

"Arrogant imbecile," Declan muttered, raking a hand through his black hair. To say he disliked the wealth and snobbery of men like Lord Henderson would be an incredible understatement.

Declan exhaled loudly and walked over to the north end windows, his booted heels echoing in the massive and fancy hall. Folding his arms across his chest, he gazed out upon the rain-soaked terraces, the familiar feelings of distrust echoing inside him. Since the war, he trusted only two others. It was more than enough for a simple commander turned master trader. He swiped at the tickle in his right ear, his fingers coming away damp with blood. It was getting worse, this wrongness inside him. He would have to deal with it at some point, deal with the genetic transference that had saved his life at the war's end. Perhaps when he got back he would visit with the doctor. His moody gaze returned to the false tranquility of the outside and the drenched gorges and forests in the distance.

Unwanted memories tightened in his chest. He had become unknowing even to himself. His instinctual responses were swinging more often to aggressive dominance and violence rather than quiet restraint thanks to the matrix transference. He managed to cage the rage, just barely, by guarding his every thought, his every emotion. What he felt, he kept to himself, an old skill he had developed during his years of growing up as the outsider.

His right hand rested on the window frame. The MacKendrick chieftain had asked him to wait in the hall. He had no choice but to do so. This clan followed the old Scottish ways of Ancient Earth. He needed to respect that, if he wanted the trade treaty signed, but he did not have to like it.

Out of the corner of his eye, he saw a gray cat limp under the long table and across the hall. At the sight of the small, encumbered beast, the anger in him eased.

"Meow," he breathed.

The cat paused, twitching its right ear toward the sound.

"Hello, little gray. Are you one of the princess's orphans?" He had heard Princess MacKendrick rescued hurt and unwanted animals and found good homes for them.

The cat glanced at him, beige eyes uncertain.

"I'll not hurt you, kitty."

The animal took a step toward him, tail swaying, then thought better of it, and disappeared around a corner.

"Sense danger, do you?" Declan chuckled. "Smart kitty." The animal was probably searching for its mistress. During his short stay, he had glimpsed Princess Fallon MacKendrick on two occasions. That flowing mass of flame-colored hair was unmistakable. She looked exactly what she was, a spoiled and aloof young woman. Declan returned to his study of the landscape and pushed her from his mind. He had more important things to deal with than a pretty face.

At his back, tartans of the clans of Henderson, MacHendry, MacNaughton, Gunn, and other close kinships hung like flags on a smooth whitewashed wall. MacKendrick was the leader of a group of multiple clans with similar genealogical origins from Ancient Earth.

That was why he had come to this distant planet. Their agreement to trade with Clan Douglas would lead to others.

If they agree, Declan mused darkly. The war had severed old alliances, causing a uniform distrust of Clan Douglas. Peace returned only eighteen months ago. Clan Kinsale and Clan States were the first to sign trade treaties, becoming new allies. He vowed there would be more. He needed time to reclaim Clan Douglas's honor and rebuild the important trade treaties ruined by the conflict. He needed . . .

Soft footfalls echoed in the hall and Declan pushed off the window frame.

"*Dia duit ar maidin*," a silky voice purred in welcome from behind him.

Clasping his hands behind his back, and keeping his profile to her, he nodded respectfully. "Good morning, Princess." The matrix coldness inside him shifted, black mist clinging to blood, body, and soul, a constant awareness of what he was, and was no longer. The father would probably castrate him if he dared to touch her.

"You understand the old Irish?"

"*Beagán*," he replied. A little.

"You pronounce the word correctly for one who only speaks *a little* of the ancient language."

"I am a quick learner."

"I am not," she said, and he could feel her smile. "My mother had a great fondness for the Old Irish language of her ancestors and taught me. I try to speak it in order to keep her close to me."

"I am sorry for your loss." He continued to study the outside.

"She died many years ago, but thank you."

Declan felt uncomfortable with her near him. He had heard rumors of her telekinetic ability, the ability to move objects by psychic force, and planted his feet more firmly.

"Have you seen our 1450 manuscript cataloging our clan's descent from the Scottish tribe of Loarn?" she asked, by way of polite conversation.

He was in no mood to converse in a civilized manner and glanced at the far corner, where a crystal pedestal stood with a clear protective dome. "Yes, your father showed it to me earlier."

"But you are not impressed?"

"Every clan has their history. Some are more impressive than others."

"True," she replied. "Are we one of those you consider to be impressive?"

A loaded question, he thought. "Yes, you are among those with notable ancestries."

"An acceptable answer, Master Trader, and most diplomatic."

"Thank you." He bowed his head and fervently wished to be anywhere but here.

She laughed softly. "My father shall be but a moment.

He signs the trade agreement, as do the others."

"Am I that transparent?"

"No, not really."

"Your father and his kinships have finally agreed among themselves?" He kept the contemptuous note for the kinships from his tone.

"Yes, finally."

"I will wait." He made a brief nod, lowered his lids, and glanced at her.

Princess Fallon MacKendrick had been born to privilege. Dark auburn brows curved delicately over luminous brown eyes laced with red-tipped lashes. Nary a freckle marred her perfect white skin. Her face was oval. A slender nose drew his gaze downward to moist lips, the color of ripe peaches. He knew she was studying him with a dangerous curiosity.

"May I offer you something to drink, Master Trader?"

"No, thank you, Princess," he said flatly, his gaze returning to the veranda outside. He was familiar with her ancestry, which blended ancient Irish and Scottish blood. He also knew she was twenty-four years old. He had just turned thirty-four. A ten-year difference separated them.

"Would you like to sit down and rest while you wait for them to finish up?"

"No, thank you."

She stepped into his peripheral vision and glanced

out the window. "Do you like the rain, Master Trader?"

"Do you, Princess?"

"Yes, the rain is a wild thing."

"And you like wild things?" he inquired.

"Yes, I do."

"'In wildness is the preservation of the world,'" Declan quoted, unable to help himself. "Henry David Thoreau, *Walking*, 1862, Ancient Earth."

She looked up at him in surprise. "You are well-read."

"Yes."

"But you are a trader."

"I gather from your inflection that you find traders to be less educated. How many have you met?"

"Not many. The few my father introduced me to were rather unrefined."

"Some are unrefined, some are not."

"You are not . . . unrefined."

It was a statement, but he answered it anyway. "If you consider a person who is well-read to be refined, then I suppose I am."

"I love to read. I like to learn about the days that came before me and the people, ideas, and worlds outside of my home. Why do you read?"

"To escape."

"Escape?"

"Yes." He knew she wanted him to elaborate, but he would not. To open that door, was to open a realm of hurt.

She smiled sweetly at his continued silence and he allowed a slight smile to curve his lips.

"You seem tall to me."

He blinked. This princess switched subjects rather spontaneously. "I am one hundred and ninety-three centimeters, to be exact."

"Oh."

"Anything else you wish to know?" he prompted with amusement.

"Most others who wear uniforms display their rank when they visit my father. I noticed that you do not."

Declan glanced down at the unmarked Clan Douglas uniform he wore. "Very observant, but I am not like most master traders."

"I have gathered that."

Princess Fallon MacKendrick was a bold one and he felt slightly ambushed by her directness. He needed to get out of here before he said, or did, something he would regret.

"I've been told the sound of rain is soothing to those with a weary heart."

"I know not, Princess." Declan looked over his shoulder into the fancy empty hall for a chaperone or one of the princess's handmaidens.

"Know not," she repeated quietly.

"Princess, you really should not be here."

"You mean I should not be here, alone with you, a handsome off-world clansman who knows more about life than I ever will."

She blindsided him into speechlessness.

"Are you familiar with *Henderson the Rain King*, 1959, Ancient Earth?" she inserted quickly—and thank goodness she did, because he did not know what to say.

It took him a moment to recover and he added the author's name. "Saul Bellow, Nobel Prize winning writer."

"'There was a disturbance . . . '"

He finished the quote, for he knew it well, "'. . . in my heart, a voice that spoke there and said, I want, I want, I want!'"

The princess whispered the rest of it. "'It happened every afternoon, and when I tried to suppress it, it got even stronger . . . It never said a thing except I want, I want, I want.'"

"It is dangerous to want, Princess." A muscle began to tick in his jaw.

"Why?"

"It can be your destroyer."

"Is it yours?"

"It is no longer," Declan answered carefully. He glanced at the closed doors, behind which the clan leaders where taking their damned sweet time.

The princess took a quick look over her shoulder, too. "I apologize for the delay."

"No apology is needed." He turned back and studied the confounded rain.

"May I ask you something?"

"This question is different than the others?"

She blushed, a surprising pink shade he saw out of the corner of his eye.

"My father says I am too bold sometimes."

A small smile tucked at the corner of his lips. "Ask your question, Princess."

"I have heard many opinions about the war."

Everything inside him went still. He did not want to talk about the war. "There are always opinions with war."

"I know this, but from the perspective of Clan Douglas, will you tell me how the war started?"

"Why would you want to know our perspective?"

"Indulge me."

"Know thy enemy?" he voiced his thoughts aloud without realizing it.

"Are you our enemy, Master Trader?"

"No, Princess. I am not."

"Then indulge me with your viewpoint. Consider it a diplomatic request."

"Very well." Declan took a moment to craft an impartial response in his mind. "I cannot speak for Clan Douglas," he stated softly, memories colliding inside him. "But I will tell you what I know. Before the war, Clan Douglas discovered an alternate resource of power in the deep caverns on their home world. It was a small cache of energy crystals. The finding created a stir among the clans of Ancient Earth. Representatives from each clan met aboard the Clan Douglas starship *Edinburgh* to discuss how best to share in this significant discovery." Declan shifted on his feet. "Unknown to anyone at the time, Clan Ramayan's representative, Commander Lin Jacob Rama, harbored a personal vendetta against the Clan Douglas lord commander."

"That would be Lord Commander Drum de Douglas?"

The princess was obviously trying to keep the players straight in her own mind. "Yes," Declan replied. "Commander Rama secretly killed the leaders aboard the *Edinburgh*."

"And Clan Douglas was blamed?"

"Yes. A war began and many good men and women died."

"And then the war ended," she murmured, "with Clan Douglas exonerated of the sins of one man. One man who killed so many. Commander Lin Jacob Rama. Why did he do it?"

"Rama wanted a woman he had no right to want," Declan answered, trying to keep it simple. *Like father, like son*. He wanted, too. Desire consumed him like living flames, but he was no longer human.

"Commander Rama wanted a woman?" The princess's voice beguiled him, touching deep down inside where some semblance of the human part of him lingered.

"Yes," he answered.

"They say he was maddened."

Declan thought she would have asked about the woman. "Yes, that is what they say."

"Did you know him?"

My father. "Yes," he replied easily, despite the turmoil inside him.

"What was he like?"

His gaze targeted the curved stairs and decorative railings of the veranda outside. "Brilliant, driven, and maddened."

"Did you know the woman, the one he wanted but could not have?"

My mother. "Lady Saph-ire de Douglas was Lord Drum's wife." *Forbidden, as this princess is to me.*

"Thank you for answering my questions."

Declan bowed his head in acknowledgment, hoping this piece of the conversation had ended. The wounds within him were too fresh.

"Maybe society and culture should be feminized. Women fight less often."

His lips curved. How very wise of her to sense his unease and change the subject. "Maybe," he echoed, trying to at least appear optimistic.

She said nothing more and his gaze dropped to the

bottom of the window frame for a moment. He felt peculiar. This inquisitive princess made him feel alive in a way he had not felt in a very long time.

They stood together in silence, looking out the window, watching the rain, listening to the splatter echo on the tile roof of the castle keep.

The matrix aggression faded within him and he felt his body becoming attuned to her quiet. He did not understand his response to her but was grateful for this simple moment of shared peace. His senses reached out, the loneliness of his existence becoming transparent in a way that gave him discord. He felt momentarily lost. But this gift of harmony and silence was not to last, and he should have known better.

"*Jamais Arrière,*" she whispered, seeking to breach the calm he could ill afford.

The Douglas clan motto splintered his quiet, a reminder of loyalty and vows long ago shattered. And she so clearly said it seeking a reaction from him—and by God, he'd give this inquisitive starfire one she would not soon forget.

"What?" He turned fully and faced her.

In that wonderful and terrible instant, Fallon's world abruptly changed. "*Never Behind* is the Clan Douglas motto," she said, held in the currents of a corporeal blast of awareness, the likes of which she never encountered before in her entire life.

"I know what *Jamais Arrière* means, Princess."

"You do?" Fallon's voice faltered at the quicksilver flash of heat in his gaze. "Of course, you must know," she remarked, barely regaining her composure. He had the most unusual eyes she had ever seen. Framed by long black lashes, the irises of his eyes appeared larger than normal. The silvery-blue color, rimmed with black, reminded her of moonbeams on a winter's night. But they were not cold, never that. Fallon stood spellbound, captured by their black fiery intensity.

She had once heard about the conspicuously large irises of the lord chieftain of Clan Douglas. She had not heard of another Douglas bearing this infamous trait, but reasoned he must be kin of the royal house. Fallon stared at him, caught by his dark good looks. His features were aristocratic but crafted in a primitive sort of way, as if the genes that formed him were in constant battle. Beard shadow darkened a strong jaw and corded neck. He wore his long hair in a single piratical braid, which fell between impossibly wide shoulders. The slope and design of him, outlined by the uniform, gave her little cause to doubt his lean, rugged power. Her gaze returned to a handsome face set with watchfulness.

"Agreeable, Princess?" he asked in a voice laced with amusement.

A pink blush stained her cheeks.

"You are one of the Douglas royals," Fallon murmured very seriously.

"Why do you say that?"

"Your eyes. The irises are larger than normal."

Black eyelashes swept low, hiding his thoughts. "A fallacy," he replied with measured softness.

Fallon folded her hands together in front of her. Her heart beat in her ears so loudly she could barely hear him. "Pardon?"

He tilted his head and an uneasy sensation settled in the pit of her stomach. "Master Trader?" she whispered, feeling her voice go all shaky.

"Princess," he rejoined with a voice woven from night's temptation.

Every molecule inside her body responded, humming with physical alertness. She felt the perfection of his masculine strength, coiled and waiting, vibrating with life. His gaze slowly drifted down to her breasts, igniting a terrible rush of need and desire. She felt dizzy from it, her heart fluttering wildly in her chest. She took a step closer, drawn by the extraordinary tempest of him, and his jaw tightened.

Behind them, the sounds of heavy footfalls echoed in the great hall and the darkly handsome trader moved around her to greet her father.

Fallon took a recovering breath. Never in her life had she reacted to a man in such a primitive fashion. She could only compare it to an adrenaline rush, as if she had run the paths around her home numerous times. Pasting a pleasant smile on her face, she turned to properly greet her father.

"I see you have met my daughter."

"Yes, sir, I have." Declan grasped the hand of Lord Dughall MacKendrick in a firm handshake while attempting to lock down his responses to the vivacious daughter. He did not like having the essence of his control nearly breached but it had almost come to that.

He focused on the MacKendrick chieftain, a man in his late fifties with shocking red hair and icy blue eyes. Despite the simple white shirt and black breeches, the older man wore authority in every pore of his being.

Declan released the hand of the renowned clan leader and stepped back, careful to not look at the daughter. He knew Lord Dughall had discovered alien jump gates bordering Ancient Earth's solar system many years before. The ancient jump gates allowed ships to teleport to predefined coordinates in space. Perhaps someday the creators of the jump gates would contact the descendants of Earth, then again, perhaps not. For now, they enjoyed and benefited from the alien travel-ways that opened to new worlds like the MacKendricks' beautiful planet.

"You have your trade treaty, sir." Lord MacKendrick smiled warmly.

Unable to help himself, Declan's gaze flickered to the princess. "So your daughter has told me."

"Ah, the lass has stolen my thunder once again."

In response, the princess rolled her eyes and Declan battled back a smile, faintly uncomfortable with the way she so easily elicited responses from him.

"Come here, daughter, and let me introduce you properly."

She glided to her father's side, a beautiful flame-haired creature; whose charm he was struggling to ignore, and failing miserably.

"Lord Declan de Douglas of Clan Douglas, may I present my daughter, Princess Fallon MacKendrick of Clan MacKendrick."

Declan bowed from the waist. "I am honored, sir. But I am no lord." He looked at the princess, his emotions in full lockdown. "I am a simple trader for Clan Douglas. You may call me Declan."

"Declan." She pronounced his name like some delectable dessert. "I am honored, sir."

"Thank you. Some would not be." Declan wished she were a plain and unmemorable woman. Her ethereal beauty would haunt his dreams long after he left this planet.

"You are the brother of Lord Lachlan de Douglas?" she inquired with just the right note of stately interest. But she was definitely snooping, the inquisitive peach.

Declan nodded. *Half brother.* He did not wish to discuss Lachlan and turned to the father. "Have the treaty and signatures been downloaded to my freighter's onboard computer?"

"Done." Lord MacKendrick nodded. "I expect my first textile shipment within a month."

"Agreed."

"That black ship is classed as a freighter?" the princess asked, an insatiable curiosity lighting up her lustrous brown eyes.

It was very different from the unwelcome stares he often received. "The *Black Ghost* is a small armored freighter," Declan answered, letting a little of his pride slip into his voice.

"It looks more like a gigantic black wing to me."

Declan felt his lips curve at her challenging tone. "Stealth and precision produce dominance. I like to own the battlefield."

She arched a delicate brow at him. "And what battlefield is that, sir?"

"Whatever battlefield there is," he answered decisively. "I do not like to lose, Princess."

"Fallon," her father gently scolded. "You must forgive my daughter, sir. She can be a bit too inquisitive for her own good."

Declan did not doubt it. However, he found her interest oddly refreshing. He did not like people with hidden agendas. "I would enjoy a discussion on aerodynamic agility, innovations in avionics," he gave her a direct look while keeping his voice neutral, "and thrust vectoring technology."

"Would you offer instead a tour of your ship, Lord de Douglas?" she countered without missing a beat.

In her face, Declan saw confidence and spirit, mingled with a beguiling sense of humor. "Just Declan, Princess."

"Declan," she repeated his name. "Would you offer a tour of your ship?"

Though he knew he should not, he found himself responding positively. "Yes, I would be happy to offer you a tour of my ship, if it is agreeable with your father."

The instant he offered, he regretted it.

"You may give the lass a brief tour," Lord MacKendrick conceded. "Five minutes worth and no more. I need to check on two freighters in the ship bays anyway. I will have my guardsmen escort you the rest of the way."

Declan gestured before him. "After you, Princess."

As if by royal decree, the golden rain stopped when they left the pavilion. Declan walked beside Lord MacKendrick through the last gated arch in the castle wall. In front of them, the MacKendrick princess led the way, her shapely form flanked by two guardsmen. A cascade of shiny hair tumbled down her back to gently swaying hips.

Declan grimaced and looked away. This gut attraction was becoming annoying, and he focused on keeping pace with the older lord. They left the perimeter walls and entered the open ship bays beyond. Streams of amber biochemical luminescent lights, also known as BLUs, lit the gray walkways. To the left were the clan ships. All other ships were berthed in the bays on the right.

Poor defense strategy, Declan mused as he scanned the area. Being located in one place made the clan ships vulnerable to attack. If they were under his command, he'd disperse the ships, thereby making it harder for the enemy to destroy all of them in a single strike. But they were not under his command. Nothing was under his command anymore. He had resigned his commission as second commander on the High Council warship *Necromancer* long ago.

Out of habit, he continued to take in his the surroundings until their group paused in front of two gray freighters. Lord MacKendrick stopped to speak with one of the freighter pilots who were waiting and motioned for them to continue on without him.

The princess glanced over her shoulder. "Walk beside me."

A royal command, Declan thought and moved beside her as the guards dropped in behind them.

"My father does not trust you." She lifted her skirts and walked around a small puddle. "Why do you think that is, Master Trader?"

Declan locked his hands behind his back and shrugged. *Your father senses danger.* She smelled of roses and rain and all things good in the world.

"Are you a threat to me?" she inquired.

"Do you sense danger, Princess?"

"You answer questions with questions. How very safe."

"I am not safe," he rejoined.

"I think you are."

"You would be wrong, Princess."

"Maybe, but I have always been a fairly good judge of character."

They came to a stop in front of his armored ship.

The princess walked under a black wing and ran a finger along clean fluid lines. "She stands larger than I thought she would."

"The design of the *Black Ghost* is meant to be misleading. She is aerodynamic. The wings sweep back for interstellar travel and sweep forward for travel in planetary atmospheres."

"The *Black Ghost* appears to be more of a fighter than a freighter with all these closed ports." She glanced back at him and he gave her a silent smile.

"Is she powered by the Delta One system designed by the late Lord Drumlanrig de Douglas?"

He was impressed. "Possibly." He stood several

paces away from her, flanked by her father's guards.

"How many energy crystals does she carry?"

"Three small," he replied, unwilling to share any more detailed information.

"For a fighter more than a freighter?"

"Yes, other Clan Douglas ships carry larger freight when needed and require more power."

"What exactly do you do, Master Trader?"

"I am the negotiator in charge of root and branch restructuring, in order to see Clan Douglas trade operations resurrected."

Her brows knitted together. "Three crystals do not seem enough to meet the power requirements of this ship."

"You are an expert on ship power systems?"

"No, of course not. Three crystals just seem inadequate to me."

"Three are enough for my needs."

She nodded and he hoped the subject was closed. "May I go inside, Master Trader?" she inquired sweetly. A princess used to getting her own way.

"I think not."

"I thought I would be given a tour." Her tone had taken on a definite edge.

My foolhardy invitation, he thought, angry with himself. "Of the outside."

Her eyes narrowed and Declan saw a flash of temper, but then she did something most unexpected. Instead of displaying displeasure at his refusal, she looked back at his ship and offered genuine praise. "And a fine outside she has."

"Thank you. *The Black Ghost* was designed for catastrophic success and can engage in combat while carrying medium cargo loads."

"Catastrophic success?" She looked back at him in bewilderment.

"My apologies. It is an old military term meaning quick victory," he explained.

"Sounds like an oxymoron to me."

A chuckle burst out of him. "I suppose."

"I still would like to go inside."

"I know."

"But I am not going to, am I?"

He shook his head. "No, Princess."

"And why not?"

Good question. "Details," Declan drawled, unable to help but enjoy their verbal bantering.

"As in a stealth ship's secrets?"

Very astute, he thought. "Yes."

"May I remind you, sir, the war is over."

"For you," he agreed.

"What do you mean?"

Keep it simple, he thought, and after a small silence, replied, "There are always secrets to uncover, Princess, as there are always battles to be fought."

"How pessimistic of you. The war has ended."

"I do not speak only of war."

She searched his face, seeking answers he was not able to give to himself. "In what battlefield do you still fight?" she prompted.

Declan felt the matrix darkness churning inside him. He took a mental step back from her straightforward manner and quickly steered the conversation away from himself. "I speak only of aerodynamic agility, innovations in avionics, and thrust vectoring."

"I think you speak of other things."

This conversation was becoming dangerous. "What do you think I speak of, Princess?"

She gave him a strong and uncomfortable study. "I am not sure. I suspect beneath the armor you present to the world lies a man who distrusts the future."

He had stepped into that one and *wham*, a direct hit. He gave her a cocky grin to hide his discomfort.

"Princess MacKendrick, it is time to go," the lead guardsman interrupted, stepping between them.

The princess dropped her gaze to the floor and Declan wanted to wring the guard's neck.

"I am sorry, Master Trader. I spoke improperly."

"Don't be, Princess. Around me you may speak as you will." He stepped around the guard and she looked up.

The guard whispered in her ear and she nodded. "I must go, Master Trader."

"So it seems." He saw reluctance in her posture and keenness in her gaze. The MacKendrick princess was not at all what he had expected.

"So, daughter, have you seen enough?" Lord Mac-Kendrick called out before rejoining them.

"No, father."

"We must not detain the Master Trader for any longer. I am sure he is a busy man."

The princess showed signs of a strong disagreement and Declan decided to diffuse the situation before it got out of hand. He did not want to be the center of an argument between father and daughter. Stepping forward, he drew their attention, and bowed from the waist. "*Slán agat*," he said, knowing the princess's fondness for the olden language. Farewell.

Her lips curved with an appreciative smile. She dropped into a small curtsy, offering a gesture of respect. "*Slán leat*," she replied softly. "You know the meaning of the two gestures?"

Declan straightened with a gentle smile. "Yes, *Slán leat* means farewell to the person leaving. *Slán agat* means farewell to the person staying behind."

"I am most impressed, sir."

"Thank you, Princess." He turned to the father. "Sir, I must take my leave. Our business is concluded?"

The father nodded and reached for his daughter's arm. "Come, Fallon."

Declan watched the MacKendrick party leave. When they finally disappeared behind the castle keep walls, he blew air out of his lungs, glad to have them gone. He turned to his ship. Above his head, a crack of thunder sounded. He stared out upon the vast beautiful landscape of the planet named Forest. Rain began to fall. Behind the exposed ship bays, silvery grasses dotted the walls of the steep gorge. To the west, craggy peaks rose in the distance beyond the forests.

The rain cooled his heated skin.

I want. I want. I want.

He inhaled deeply of the crisp air, hearing the princess's musical voice in his head.

He wanted, too.

An intimacy he would never allow himself.

He had spoken only a partial truth to her. Wanting was a destroyer, but also a redeemer. It depended on what you wanted and if you had the right to it.

He looked around. Someday he'd settle on a planet such as this. A vision of milk-white softness and silken flames burned brightly in his mind. Declan muttered an oath and turned to his ship. "*Ghost*, open hatch." The ship, equipped with the latest in voice recognition technology, responded to his command. Behind the right wing, the black hatch clicked and swung open.

He did not have the right to want her. Her Royal Highness Princess Fallon MacKendrick was off limits to the likes of him, a matrix abomination, a lowly trader for a clan struggling to reclaim its honor.

Damn the clans for their prejudice. Clan Douglas had not started the war, yet they were blamed for it. Reaching out, he caressed the rain-slicked hull of the *Black Ghost*. He must remember his place and his vow. He wanted forgiveness and redemption from Lachlan. He wanted to sleep at night. He wanted peace in his soul. The guilt in his heart left no room for a pampered princess.

A tiny bark erupted from inside the ship.

A smile curved his lips and he glanced inside the open hatch.

"Impatient, Thorn?" he asked his wee-gadhar companion.

A skinny white poodlefly, no bigger than a man's index finger, hovered just inside the ship. Gossamer wings of silver beat in rapid tempo while iridescent eyes blinked at him.

"Just rain, silly pup," Declan explained. "Do you wish to come out?"

Thorn snarled, baring pearly white teeth.

Declan chuckled softly. "You are bigger than the raindrops."

The wee-gadhars, or wee-dogs, were genetic hybrids from Ancient Earth and he enjoyed their loyalty and playfulness. But more importantly, he saw no judgment in his pet's eyes.

Thorn let out a loud woof.

"Suit yourself." With a final look at the MacKendrick Castle, he whispered, "*Slán a fhágáil ag duine*, Princess." I bid you farewell, Princess.

It felt like a lifetime ago when he had learned a few of the Old Irish phrases from a friend during his tour of duty as second commander on the warship *Necromancer*. Thinking about today's events, he felt satisfaction for having taken the time to memorize them.

He grabbed the handholds and swung himself up into the cool dark interior of his ship.

Thorn barked, her tail wagging with joy.

Time to leave.

Fallon stood stiffly under her father's glare. They were in the Hall of Entrance and the humid air felt cool upon her heated cheeks. Her hand caressed the smooth rose stone of the fireplace mantle while she waited for her father to say his piece.

"Daughter, that man is not for you."

"Father," she began softly. A treacherous longing welled up inside her heart. She walked over to one of the engraved armchairs and held on with damp hands. "He stirs me in ways no man ever has."

"Stirs you? Impossible, you just met him."

Fallon could not explain how her heart had bloomed with the trader's slightest regard. "Please explain why he is not for me?"

"For one thing, violence and darkness resides in him. They do not call him the Douglas Savage for nothing. I will not have a union with an uncultivated Douglas, especially with your undisciplined gift. It would be a disaster waiting to happen."

"My gift? What does my gift have to do with anything?"

Her father walked to the side of the table, two chairs away from her. "Fallon, you have led a sheltered life and would not understand. The low five rating of your telekinesis is false. You and I both know it. When in high emotion, as you often are, your talent multiplies, and becomes dangerous."

"I can control it."

"You never *had* to control it. You never had to face a crisis situation." Her father's eyes lit with anger. "The only way to deal with this cursed gift was to shelter you from the harsh realities of life, and your mother and I did just that. We made sure this thing inside you never developed." He exhaled loudly. "Do I need to mention those precognitive flashes you have experienced every few years or so? Knowing how this or that will happen? This is not a gift, but a burden."

Fallon bit her lip with frustration. "In my entire

lifetime, I've only had three of those episodes."

"Three episodes are more than enough for a glimpse of doom: a ship crashing in the fields, your mother falling down the staircase, the stillborn death of a friend's child."

"I should have been trained."

Her father clasped his fists behind his back and shook his head. "If you had been trained, you would have led a different kind of life."

"I do not understand."

He exhaled loudly and his lips thinned. "I will not discuss this any further. There are other and more important matters on my mind."

"Yes, father," she murmured dutifully and bit her bottom lip. How could he dismiss her desires so cruelly?

"I assumed you heard about the rumors of Clan Douglas unearthing a new horde of energy crystals on their home world."

"Yes, that is why I imagined you accepted their invitation to re-establish trade relations."

"Though it discomforts me to associate with them, I did accept their invitation. An alliance with them could possibly ensure our future energy needs."

"I see," she replied in a caustic tone.

"I wonder if you do, Daughter."

"Yes, I understand all too clearly. They are good enough to trade with, but not good enough to sit at your table beside your daughter!"

In a sudden glint, the table's massive centerpiece exploded into pieces, startling both of them into ducking and covering their heads.

Fallon was aghast at her actions and ran to her father. "Are you all right?"

Lord MacKendrick straightened and wiped off his jacket with jerky movements. "That was your mother's favorite centerpiece," he stated.

"Yes, I am so sorry." Shamefaced, Fallon turned and saw the scattered silver pieces all over the table and floor. It was a miracle she and her father had not been cut by the broken crystal. She would never forgive herself if he had been hurt and buried her trembling hands in her skirts.

"That is precisely what I meant by control, Daughter. When in high emotion, things around you explode, implode, or nothing happens at all. I do not know when to duck, run, or simply ignore and go about my business."

"I am so sorry."

He grunted and she was not sure if he accepted her apology.

"If I strive to do better, would you consider the Master Trader to be my consort?"

"Declan de Douglas is as unpredictable and dangerous as your blasted abilities. As I said before, it would be a disaster waiting to happen. Enough of this. The issue is moot. I have arranged for your engagement to Lord Tomaidh Henderson."

Fallon blinked in momentary shock. "My engagement? To Thomas?" Outrage took over. "He cannot see beyond his stomach!"

"I have waited long enough for you to choose a proper mate, bless your mother's soul. And Tomaidh holds no idiotic fascination for your telekinetic and precognitive gifts."

Fallon felt sick to her stomach. "Please do not do this."

"Fallon, I cannot take the time to explain to you the importance of this match for our clan. Will you honor my choice and fulfill your duty?"

She wished she had never been born with these horrible gifts. But she was the MacKendrick princess and knew her duty well. "Yes." She gave her father a curt nod, though her heart recoiled.

"Good lass." Lord Dughall nodded, greatly missing the counsel of his beloved Irish wife where his willful daughter was concerned. He turned and left the hall, ordering his daughter to have what was left of the centerpiece cleaned up.

Fallon stared after him with a burgeoning rebellion. The blood of her warrior ancestors flowed hotly through her veins. She would not surrender so easily. Not now, not when she finally knew what she wanted. She would find a way out of the betrothal contract without detriment to her clan and she would have Declan de Douglas for her consort.

CHAPTER
TWO

Io's Space Station
Two Standard Months Later

Situated above jupiter's moon Io, the space station looked like a giant silver bicycle wheel with a very large hub. The hub contained the working areas, power plant, air and waste systems. The rim contained visitor and staff living quarters, meeting rooms, food and trade shops, an emergency trauma center, and extensive docking facilities that were in a constant state of maintenance.

From an oval window inside the space station, Declan de Douglas watched the Clan Douglas flagship *Claymore* slide alongside one of the tubular spokes into Space Dock One. The one hundred and fifty men and women serving aboard her had long ago restored the hull to its former sleek gray. He adjusted the dark glasses hiding his eyes and thought of his own ship. The *Black Ghost's* unique design always drew unwanted attention, so he had left it behind, berthed at Braemar Keep on Planet Mars, the Clan Douglas home world. He also left Thorn, his wee-gadhar companion with Dr. William de

Douglas. Declan knew that the matrix doctor who had saved his life would take good care of Thorn.

His gaze slid to the unremarkable and small Clan Douglas ship he had used to arrive at the space station a few days ago. He wanted to blend in, to be a ghost among the many travelers here. His gaze slid once more across the dock. Thick silver docking arms clanked loudly, then extended from the spokes to the warship's hull. Once in place, they would allow the smooth exchange of cargo, personnel, and the Douglas royal family. Declan pushed his hands through his recently clipped hair. The tips of the black silken strands fell to his collar instead of the cumbersome length down his back.

Rumors of a kidnap plot were what brought him here. With a calm certainty, he knew the would-be kidnappers would try to grab the Douglas twin heirs here, on Io's space station. In his estimation, the space station presented the weakest link in the journey, and if anything was going to happen, it would happen here. Security was too tight on Io's silver base to make a kidnapping plan feasible.

"Bloody hell," he muttered.

"I agree. Most of us don't trust the Douglas clan."

Declan turned from the window to the balding man standing beside him. The brown business suit was much older than him and he spoke with an accent.

"Why is that?" he prompted, keeping a sharp edge

to his tone.

"Everyone knows they killed the leaders and started the war."

Declan chose his words carefully. "Commander Lin Jacob Rama killed the leaders and started the war." His right hand slid to the sheath hidden under his coat arm. Weapons were not allowed on the space station, but that did not stop him. He fingered the handle of his onyx-jeweled dagger, struggling to control the matrix tempest inside him. "High Council's ruling declared Clan Douglas innocent."

"Pah."

Declan glowered behind his black glasses. "The High Council is a learned group of men and women who govern the clans of Ancient Earth. Do you question their authority?"

The suit bristled slightly. "I do not question our High Council, but Commander Rama is dead and cannot defend himself."

"Do you call the High Council liars then?"

"No, of course not. But if Clan Douglas had shared their energy crystal discovery none of this would have happened."

"There were no crystals to share," Declan retorted.

"We heard that, too. They said there was only one small discovery. All other crystals were worthless. But what about this new horde they've found? I have heard these crystals are more powerful than any of the others. I doubt those conniving earthscots will share them with us."

Declan spoke slowly so each word would be carefully understood. "Do you and the others deserve to reap the rewards for Clan Douglas's labor? What clan are you from, old man?"

"I am Master Balan, and my clan is of little importance."

Balan? The name sounded familiar. "Any relation to the Balan Slave Auction House?"

"My cousin."

Declan had a deep loathing of slavers.

"Do you know the auction house, sir?" the idiot asked, with a proud tilt of his chin.

He looked back out the window. "I have heard of them. They are the ones who use those goddamn slave collars."

"It is legal in certain sectors, sir."

"It would not be legal for long if I had any say about it," he said tightly.

"And who might you be, sir?"

He turned back to the annoyance and slid the dark glasses down his nose. Fear flickered in the man's brown eyes for just a moment and then, a curious flash of interest.

Declan's gaze narrowed. "I see you know who I am."

"Yes, your reputation precedes you, Douglas Savage. Are you going to kill me?"

"Kill you?" Declan chuckled low and shoved the glasses back up the bridge of his nose. "Do you deserve to die for the falsehoods you spread?"

Balan's left eyelid twitched, giving away his discomfort and Declan muttered an oath. "Go away, old man, and do not speak ill of Clan Douglas again."

The suit walked away and he returned his attention to the space dock. "What am I doing, bullying old men now?" he muttered in disgust.

A twinge of pain shot through his right ear. It was familiar, a festering wound refusing to heal, and for a moment, he flashed back to the matrix science lab of Dr. William.

Something's at fault, something's not right, the good doctor had mumbled under his breath, his face buried in notebooks and computer printouts.

Declan swiped at his ear, and his finger came away with a bright crimson smear. That day at the science lab, he had gotten a good look at the doctor's scribbled notes.

Until Declan accepts what he is, there may be a distinct possibility that his soul will reject this new body. The bleeding right ear might be a first indicator of the rejection. I must . . .

For some reason, Declan could not bring himself to care. The memory slipped away and he looked back to where the brown suit had disappeared.

Stupid to let my anger rule, he mused. Hopefully his reputation had frightened the old man enough so he would say nothing of the Douglas Savage being on the space station.

Declan focused back on the *Claymore* in Space Dock One and dismissed Balan from his mind. By coming to the High Council with a plan to share the new energy crystal discovery, Lachlan would end the grumbling distrust of Clan Douglas in one swift move. It was a brilliant strategy.

All Declan had to do was keep the Clan Douglas first family safe from harm. He turned on his heel and made his way to Space Dock One.

Staying far enough back not to be noticed, Master Balan followed. After all, the purpose of his trip was to locate and collar a new stud to save his ailing brothel business. The Douglas Savage, a man who lived in shadows, would hardly be missed, he reasoned. Besides, it would be a shame to let that aggressive and masculine perfection waste away behind dark glasses and a long gray coat.

Declan's steps took on a sense of urgency. Inside the space station, the sweaty smells of humanity permeated the artificial air. Trade merchants were busily attending to their booths while travelers moved through gray corridors on their way to rebuilding lives that had been lost in the war.

He passed by a slanted window. In the cold darkness of space, white shuttles were transporting people between the space station and the silver base located on the surface of the Io moon. Over the past year, the base had become the judicial seat of the High Council and a booming place of trade. It was really odd because the base was also reputed to be the birthplace of the outlawed matrix robots and should be in a security lockdown. But what did he know, he was just a simple trader.

Declan rounded a corner and stopped just inside the entranceway to Space Dock One. Each space dock consisted of wide gray walkways for personnel, a circular loading dock for cargo, and a large maintenance area, able to provide equipment and technical support when needed.

Arrival crews were already engaged in bustling activity. Their dark orange overalls swarmed over the entire area. A wide tube connected the Clan Douglas flagship to the station.

At the bottom of the tube's open doors, the space station greeter paced nervously. He was a man in his late sixties, in a polished white suit with the station's red badge proudly pinned to his chest. The greeter posed no threat in Declan's estimation but he swore under his breath when he saw the Douglas lord and lady depart from the ship, each carrying a twin in their arms. Only two guards trailed behind them. *Where the hell are the rest of the security guards?* he wondered angrily.

From the shadows, Declan watched his half brother stop and talk with the greeter. Though Lachlan was younger by almost two years, he wore the mantle of chieftain with calm authority and . . .

His half brother looked up and scanned the docking bay, seemingly sensing . . .

Declan dropped back into the shadows. There was no way in hell that Lachlan could know he was here. Pain sliced through his right ear and memories washed over him, pulling him back in time.

Back to . . .

. . . his death.

He had fought on the wrong side of the war.

The last decisive battle had taken place within the damaged, ice-encrusted walls of Braemar Keep on planet Mars.

Driven by madness and a lust for revenge, Commander Rama had pledged to destroy Clan Douglas.

And he, like a fool, had stupidly helped.

Until . . .

His mind flashed back to that one defining moment.

Time slowed.

In his mind, he saw flames engulfing the reflective chamber of the energy crystals.

He saw Commander Rama's gory hands shaking with the effort of aiming the pulsar gun at Lachlan and Kimberly.

He had stepped in front of Rama, his insane and diabolically driven father.

Guilt and shame tightened his chest.

He remembered extending his hand, trying to help, to end it. "Father. It is over. Please don't . . ."

"You dare defy me?" His father had bellowed and fired the weapon.

Pain exploded in his chest, red beams ripping out a hole. He could still taste the coppery burn of blood shooting up into his throat. He could still hear the echo of Lachlan's roar behind him. Then darkness had seeped into his vision and he could no longer feel anything but pain.

The next thing he recalled was a great gush of black rage and cold shackles holding him down on an examination table. He swallowed hard, the images coming fast and furious. Based on matrix robot technology, the secret Genetic Transference Process Dr. William developed had cheated death.

His death.

He was reborn. Dr. William had recovered two men: first Lachlan, then himself.

Adjustment was an understatement.

Later he had learned how Rama lied to the High Council; secretly murdered the clan leaders; murdered Lord Drum, Lachlan's father; murdered Winn, the man who raised him; murdered so many people in his vengeance.

The pain in his ear receded and his half brother turned away. The dark past evaporated into steam and mist. Declan blew air out of his lungs and pushed aside the horrid memories. He forced himself to return to the present and channeled all his energies upon the scene unfolding before him. He had given his vow of loyalty to Lachlan after the war and pledged to protect and defend the Clan Douglas first family from harm, no matter the personal cost. That was one vow he would never break.

Next to Lachlan's tall frame, the old greeter looked like a round white mouse with a bent nose. Lady Kimberly's black uniform mirrored her husband's, except hers outlined a feminine slenderness. He had met Kimberly in pilot training and had always thought her lovely. Back then she had been involved with another cadet named Declan and so he had kept his distance.

A new feminine form came to mind, one with flame-colored hair and dark brown eyes. Heat pulsed through his blood and Declan mentally shook himself. He did not want to think about a spirited princess who could disrupt his center with a single look. Instead, he moved silently behind a payload of orange cargo containers and waited. There were too many places for an ambush on the space station, so he had to stay close and out of sight.

The station greeter bowed and led the Clan Douglas first family down the corridor out of Space Dock One. Two Douglas guards brought up the rear. They each carried pulsar rifles and Declan silently approved. The *no weapon* rule on the station had been set aside in this instance. He shadowed them through the corridors, staying close but hidden. *Too crowded in here to do a snatch-and-grab operation*, he mused, *but dangerous nonetheless.*

The transport shuttle area, located on the other side of the space station, shared a forked entranceway with Space Dock Twenty-four. They took the left walkway and Declan discreetly followed. The corridor opened up to a wide, cavernous landing bay. A stream of amber lights in the floor lit the single walkway leading down in front of ten shuttle berths. The first seven shuttle berths were empty and dark.

"They would have to be empty," Declan muttered, trying to stay out of sight. He ducked behind orange cargo bins in the maintenance area. White puffs of steam clouded visibility and he could just make out the gray fuel lines snaking across the floor. The space station greeter stopped in front of Shuttle Berth Eight.

Two representatives from the High Council exited the shuttle in Berth Eight and extended a greeting to Lachlan.

Just then three masked men slipped out of the steam into Shuttle Berth Six. Declan had no time to warn Lachlan and Kimberly. He had to stop the threat now. Tossing the dark glasses, he unsheathed the dagger and moved in with deadly determination. He jumped over two yellow maintenance trams and dropped down on all fours, listening for the sounds of the intruders. Since the matrix had altered his humanity, his hearing went beyond excellent.

A heavy breath.

He bolted forward, struck with an inhuman swiftness and opened a man's jugular with his dagger. His left hand covered the man's mouth, blocking his scream, and he eased him down to the floor in a soundless death.

One down.

Stunned by the surprise attack, the other two masked men disappeared into the false safety of the white steam. Declan tracked the intruders to the first empty shuttle berth. In the background, he heard the engines of Lachlan's shuttle come on line.

Pain shot through his right arm.

Declan pivoted and rolled to his left, but did not drop the dagger. He came to his feet instantly and met the second gray-clad man one on one. Despite his injury, he killed the second man in seconds.

Two down.

Behind him, the whirring sound of the shuttle rising

from the deck echoed in the vastness of the landing bay.

Warm blood streamed down Declan's right arm. His nostrils flared, senses searching outward for the location of the third man.

A bright beam of red pulsar light sliced open Declan's right shoulder.

Pain blazed through his muscles, spewing red blood. How the men had gotten pulsar weapons past security, he did not know. He dropped to his knees in agony. The matrix in his genetic makeup gave him an almost inhuman tolerance to pain and he maintained his grip on the dagger.

"You cannot fight a pulsar gun," the male voice taunted coldly.

Declan looked up into the eyes of his gray-clad attacker and smiled. "You think not?"

He flung the dagger.

The blade embedded itself between the man's startled eyes. The pulsar gun slipped from his attacker's fingers, clattering to the floor, and the man crumpled into a lifeless heap in front of him.

"Three down." Declan's watery gaze slid to the exiting shuttle as it left the dock and slipped out into the blackness of space.

Safe. They are safe.

It was his last thought before white pain exploded inside his head.

Declan fell to the floor, barely conscious. Blood streamed from a deep laceration down his right temple.

There were two more attackers. He had been sloppy.

"I should kill him."

Through a red blur, Declan saw a fat masked man gripping a pipe above him.

"What for?" another said, exiting the white steam.

Declan struggled to roll to his side.

"I have never seen a man move so fast."

They were talking about him.

"I'll hit him on the head again, and then we'll see who moves fast."

The fat one swung the pipe high and he could barely lift an arm to defend himself.

"Why bother? He looks about dead already. Besides, we don't have the Douglas twins. How are we going to get our money now? Tom Henderson won't pay."

The name Henderson flashed through the pain in Declan's mind. *Henderson wanted the twins. Thomas Henderson.* In his mind he saw tartans hanging like flags in a large hall opposite a rose brick hearth. In the center hung the Henderson green. He needed to remain conscious, needed to listen, but darkness was crowding the terrible hurt. Bloodstained lashes fluttered closed and he lost the battle to remain awake.

"If I may be of assistance." Master Balan came forward and held up his hands to show he posed no threat to these thugs. "Is that all of you?" he asked diplomatically.

"Who the hell are you?" a fat gray-clad man demanded as he gripped a pipe.

"It does not matter who I am." Balan lowered his hands and straightened his brown suit jacket. "I understand you are in need of money. As a business man, I'm prepared to offer you a tidy sum for the merchandise."

"What merchandise?" the man standing near the steam asked suspiciously.

Balan nodded toward the bleeding man at their feet. "How much do you want for him? I'm prepared to pay handsomely."

"Him?" The fat one chuckled with disbelief. "You want to pay us for him?"

"Yes, and for your silence," Balan urged softly. "No one needs to know of this deal. Let it be between us . . . business associates."

The two thugs looked at each other, then back at Balan.

The masked man near the steam stepped forward. "Silence goes both ways."

"Agreed."

"How much?" the fat one asked.

"Whatever your original deal for the Douglas twins was."

"Twenty thousand credits."

"Done," Balan said. He wanted the Douglas Savage

in his stable, no matter the cost. "If he is alive."

"Oh, he's alive all right." The fat one nudged the Douglas Savage in the ribs with the pipe. "See? He's moaning."

A smile of deep pleasure crossed Balan's lips. "Done and done." He watched the blood seeping from the right ear of his new pleasurer and assumed it came from the beating.

CHAPTER THREE

Dove Inn
Orrin, First Moon of Planet Forest

AN EARLY TWILIGHT had reluctantly waned with the coming of night. Fallon laid her older gray cloak on the flowery bedspread. In those quiet moments, when she listened to naught but her own heart, she thought of the Douglas Savage.

The velvety quality of his voice . . .

The clean male scent of him . . .

The way he moved with muscular grace.

She slipped the emerald engagement ring from her third finger and placed it on the imitation polished cherry nightstand beside the bed.

Straightening, she pushed thoughts of the Douglas Savage aside, and glanced around at her plush surroundings. The Dove Inn had been designed to imitate the old hotels of Ancient Earth. The bedroom walls and floor were the color of butternut milk and the fishnet canopy above the four-poster bed gave the large room a warm, cozy feel. She ran fingertips across the tops of the two armchairs, which were soft and woven in delicate checker patterns of peach and pink. The scarflike swag at the top of the three-panel window, when combined with the lace curtains, added a level of privacy. The curtains blocked out the sounds and scents of resident life.

Pulling the curtains aside, she opened a slender window, and looked out upon the tops of buildings. Behind her, Clare fussed with the clothing at the dresser yet again.

"Lord Henderson said he be escorting you when he returns from tending his business," her maid said conversationally.

Fallon nodded. The only thing she knew about Lord Henderson's business was his mentioning of a DNA synthesis, to which she had paid as little attention as possible. "Clare, since we have come to this place, Lord Henderson has attended three days worth of business interests. Has he ever escorted me anywhere that he had promised?"

The maid frowned. "Nay."

"Well then, we are in agreement," Fallon said softly and thought the matter closed when Clare turned back to her folding, but that was not the case.

"You should not be givin' your new things away."

"They were hungry," Fallon answered quietly.

"Wild and unruly, to my way of thinking."

When she had walked the windy path of the inn's back gardens after breakfast, she saw a small family huddled in the shelter of the corner arches of the garden. The hollow eyes of the youngest boy tugged at her compassion. Shedding her new blue travel cloak, she had approached them and handed the warm cloak to the terrified young mother. The father, only a few years older than Fallon herself, had asked if she would turn them in. Fallon had reassured him she would not. She had bought the family a warm meal and with a private word to the innkeeper, had been assured that the man would be given a job, and a warm place found for his family.

It pleased her to help those in need, especially the wild creatures who called to her soul.

Fallon sighed, her thoughts turning to her own problems. In one month's time, she'd speak her marriage vows to Lord Henderson at MacKendrick Castle. She'd been unable to find a way out of the betrothal contract without risking damage to clan relations and her father's reputation. She was resigned to a fate not of her making and plucked at the bodice of her peach gown. Sometimes she detested the olden ways.

"One of the maids said the food be verra good here although we should stay away from the local wines. The inn has a fine art gallery on the lower level with some old watercolors. We could visit the library restaurant, too, if you like."

"Gossiping with the local maids again, Clare?" she teased gently.

"How else would I be hearing things about the Douglas Savage?"

Fallon stared aghast at her gray-haired maid. "Clare, how . . ."

The older woman grinned, then nonchalantly placed white undergarments in the top drawer of the dresser. "I know your heart yearns for the man they be calling the Douglas Savage. You have not been the same since meeting him. And I disagree with your father giving you over to the fatling lord."

Fallon walked over and took the other woman's warm hands in hers. Drawing her to the bed, they both sat on the edge, like infatuated schoolgirls. "Tell me what you hear of him," Fallon said with hushed enthusiasm.

"Well, it not be precisely him."

She searched Clare's flushed face. "I do not understand."

"Remember when you spilled satinleaf juice on your blue gown yesterday?"

"Yes."

"Though I tried, the stain stuck so I brought the gown downstairs to the maid's quarters to see what could be done."

"And?"

"Three of the inn maids be talking with a maid of a lady who be staying on the floor below us."

"Clare, all of the floors are below us."

"Well, this lady's maid said her mistress be verra rich and bored. And she said, her mistress likes to frequent the male brothels."

"Please say what you mean to say."

"This lady's maid said her mistress had just returned to Orrin because she had heard rumors of a new male pleasurer resembling the Douglas Savage in one of the local brothels here."

Fallon sat back, too stunned to speak.

"The lady's maid said she dinna know which brothel kept the pleasurer, but her mistress be planning to go out tonight and visit it. Your handsome Douglas Savage be of interest to many of the ladies." Clare giggled.

"He is not mine." Fallon stood up. "Help me get ready."

"Ready?"

"Yes, I want you to point out this lady's maid to me."

"You canna be doing what I think you be doing!"

"I do not know what you are thinking but I plan on following this lady tonight." She was not going to spend another day and night in this suffocating room.

"Oh, Princess Fallon," Clare whined, but hurried to assist. "What will I tell Lord Henderson when he be returning later and calls you for dinner?"

"Tell him I have a headache and went to bed early." Fallon's pulse quickened with growing excitement. She kicked off her peach slippers and put on her comfortable gray walking boots. "Get my dagger."

Clare retrieved the small weapon from the dresser for her and Fallon tied the dagger and sheath to the inside of her right thigh. "I need untraceable currency. I do not want to use my account."

Clare pulled out a handful of the local currency Lord Henderson had left for them to use. "Mistress, some of these notes are large amounts."

"They will do." She put some in her purse and wrapped the rest in two handkerchiefs. Leaning over, she tucked the handkerchiefs securely in her shin-high boots.

"There." Straightening, she smoothed her hands down the peach folds of her dress. "How do I look?"

When the maid frowned, Fallon looked down at herself. "It is my simplest gown." The gown had embroidered detail along the line of the bust and the sleeves, which gathered close to her arms and scrunched at her wrists.

"Princess Fallon, I doona think you should do this. Please reconsider."

"You did not think I should have helped that family, either." Fallon reached for the dark gray cloak lying on the bedspread. "Help me with this." She flipped her braid over her shoulder and handed the cloak to Clare, who whined, "I am sorry I mentioned anything."

"But you did." Fallon slipped her arms into the smooth folds of the cloak. Since the betrothal announcement, she had struggled to find some redeeming qualities in her overbearing, overweight betrothed. She had found only one. Lord Henderson would be a good provider. She would want for nothing, locked away in his cold castle base, a pretty ornament to be shown on special occasions, and on others, a broodmare for his children. Her heart coveted so much more.

"I shall be gone for a little while." Fallon adjusted the cloak's black clasp under her chin.

"I doona agree with this."

"I know."

"Well then, since I canna change your mind, keep the hood up to cover your hair and face."

Fallon made the adjustment and her maid nodded with approval.

"Keep the cloak closed to hide the light color of the dress. Aye, and stay in the shadows when you go out. Do you have the commlink?"

"In my bag." Fallon reached into her small bag and held up the tiny communication device. "Staying in the shadows should be easy. Night fell an hour ago."

"Please reconsider."

Fallon shook her head and took Clare's arm. "Come, show me this lady's maid."

"If I do, will you promise to take the guards with you?"

"Yes." Fallon opened the door and led Clare out into the pale green corridor.

"How many guards will you be taking?"

Her eyes twinkled with amusement. "Two," she replied.

"From Lord Henderson's ship?"

"From the inn. Now, show me this maid."

Clare reluctantly led the way. "If you go a-missing, I will never hear the end of it."

A small smile curved Fallon's lips. *Gone a-missing. If only it were so.*

He was unable to remember a thing and felt a distorted perception of himself, as if the world and he existed in two different realities. In his dreams, he saw a rose stone castle standing on a wooded gorge and a flame-haired, faceless woman calling his name—Declan.

So he was Declan.

Declan.

It was as good a name as any. He touched the area of painful throbbing at his right temple. He remembered the word his captor called him. It had been upon his awakening in an emulsion tank yesterday. At first he thought he had misunderstood—but he had not.

Whore.

That is what his captor had called him.

He was not a whore.

He knew this deep inside his soul, despite what his

captor had said. He hated slavers.

He crawled unsteadily to his feet, feeling trapped and uncertain. Declan tested the chain connecting the neck collar to the thick link embedded in the shiny black stone floor. Yellow lights kept the small room in shadows. He looked down at the shiny floor that reflected his image. He wore two things: a slim neck collar, and weightless, black gauze pants with a drawstring at the waist.

For a second, he frowned down at the healing scar creasing his right forearm, unable to remember how he got hurt. It was the strangest sensation to not know your own self.

"Are you thirsty?"

Declan looked up. A blond man held a tall glass of purified water to him in offering. Around his neck, he too wore a collar.

"You should drink." The man gestured to the glass.

Declan walked over with the chain clanking behind him. He took the glass and sniffed it.

"It is safe."

He looked into the younger man's slanted blue eyes and quenched his thirst.

"Drink slowly, your stomach is empty."

Handing the empty glass back to the younger man, he muttered his thanks then touched the offending device around his neck. "What is this?"

"The collar of a pleasurer."

"My collar is different than yours." Brothels or private patrons kept pleasurers. For the most part, they were willing whores. He definitely was not willing.

"How do you know your collar is different?"

Declan pointed at the shiny floor. "My reflection shows a collar with two lights. Your collar has only one light."

"Yes. You wear the new collar." The blond man's skin turned as white as the gauze shirt and pants he wore.

"What kind of new collar?" Declan asked carefully.

"This is the first time I have seen it. The rest of us . . . we all wear the single lust stage collar to enhance the act."

"We?"

"The pleasurers of Balan's Brothel."

"How do I remove the collar?"

"Only the master can remove our collars. I have said too much. I must go. I should not be here."

Declan watched the younger man retreat without saying a word. The glass of water had rejuvenated him. Except for the shiny black floor, the room felt like a holding cell aboard a warship. *How do I know that?*

He looked up at the gray ceiling. Above him, the low sounds of a woman's husky laughter floated in the air. This might be a whorehouse, but he was not a whore.

He was not a whore.

He knew it, as he knew his hair was black and his eyes were blue.

His right hand fisted on the thick chain. There was a wrongness inside his mind, something missing.

"How do you feel, my defiant one?"

Declan pivoted and glared at an older man in a black business suit.

"I see Snow gave you water. He shows too much empathy, that one, but I will deal with him later. Tell me, how do you feel?"

Declan did not answer.

"Any aftereffects from the emulsion tank healing?"

"No." He felt an instinctive aversion and focused on the man's familiar-sounding voice.

The suit pushed off from the doorjamb and said, "Lights at eighty percent." The room flooded with bright yellow light, blinding Declan. He raised his left forearm to shield his eyes.

"I'm glad you've recovered from your head injuries."

The suit came into the room, his hands casually locked behind him. "Do you remember me, my defiant one?"

Declan lowered his arm. "No."

"Unfortunate. I had hoped we were able to reverse it."

"Reverse what?" A sickly feeling settled in the pit of his stomach.

"I am Master Balan and you are my prized pleasurer. Two nights ago, my competition stole you and performed an identity wash procedure. To my great chagrin, we arrived too late to stop them. In our rescue attempt, you were injured." Master Balan tapped his temple to show the location of the injury. "Do you remember?"

"No."

"Unfortunate. Once we returned home, I had you placed in an emulsion tank for healing. Our technicians noted a couple of low-level problems, odd DNA strands, some abnormal cell structure, but nothing to concern yourself with. Physically, you are healed. We'll just have to replace the old memories with new ones."

Declan stood still. *Identity wash.* They had stolen his memories. *Goddamn bastards.* He had nothing to go on now but instincts—and the alarms inside him were going off. Master Balan was lying. Declan did not doubt it.

The idiot suit mistook his silence for ignorance. "Do you remember the emulsion tank you were in yesterday?"

"Some."

"Do you know the purpose of such a tank, my defiant one?"

Declan answered the question with a touch of impatience. "The emulsion tank's solution helps stimulate hypercritical healing. It is based on ancient hydropathy."

Master Balan held up his hands and chuckled. "Good. Obviously, some memories remained intact. I am glad. I had to purchase a small, inexpensive emulsion tank because of this unfortunate incident. I cannot have my whores injured."

"I am not a whore." Declan's hands fisted at his sides. The cold chain slid down his chest. His forearm and right shoulder ached. He was practically deaf in his right ear. A throbbing pounded inside his head and his legs felt shaky. These were the aftereffects of an emulsion tank healing, an unfinished healing. He did not know how he knew this, but he did.

"Forgive me for the use of the word whore. It is an archaic term, my pleasurer."

"I am not a pleasurer."

"But you are, my defiant one. Your body was made to give patronesses pleasure and you have taken great pride in it. That unusual sword tattoo scaling down your back has often been a great source for gossip."

Tattoo? Declan glanced down at his right shoulder in momentary confusion. There was a single black spike creeping just over his shoulder. A sword image materialized in his mind then dispersed into vapor. Yes, he had a tattoo.

Balan smiled tolerantly. "Do you remember the name your patronesses call you?"

"No." The only patroness Declan remembered was the flame-haired, faceless woman in his dreams, the one who called him Declan.

"Your patronesses call you Savage."

That name also felt familiar to him.

"Do not worry about the lost memories, my defiant one. They were inconsequential."

"Memories are never inconsequential."

"In this case, they are. After all, it is only an identity wash, a partial loss of your memories. Let me review them for you. You were stolen, identity washed, and received a substantial blow to the head."

"From you," Declan stated with icy conviction.

"No." Balan shook his head, a secret smile playing about his lips. "Not from me. My emulsion tank, regrettably, is not equipped with all the bells and whistles for a complete restorative healing."

"Your tank is grossly inadequate," Declan answered.

"Yes, well." Balan's face turned a slight shade of red. He slid his right hand into his pocket. "Do you remember anything?" he asked cautiously. "Anything at all?"

"Not at the moment." Declan clamped down on his growing frustration and watched the older man finger something in his pocket. "Where the hell am I?"

"We are on the lower floors of my brothel, an exclusive pleasure house." Balan touched his chest. "I am your master."

"Not likely," Declan declared with quiet fury.

"I see you have returned to your old defiant self. Perhaps I have been too lenient with you."

"I doubt it."

"Did you notice I gave you the new collar? Do you

remember how it works?"

"No." Declan fought a losing battle with his temper. "But I'm goddamn sure you'll remind me."

Balan held up a palm-sized black device with tiny buttons.

"This is your collar's controller. I believe it best we go through its operation and refresh your memory, before your next patroness arrives. I decided to maintain touch button technology instead of voice recognition, at least for now."

Declan glared at the device and glared at the man. "What patroness?"

"You rested long enough, my defiant one. It is time to reap the harvest that I have set in motion. Rumors have already begun to spread of the new collar and of the defiant new pleasurer who wears it. It is time to earn riches for your master."

Defiant NEW pleasurer? Declan picked up on the suit's mistake. "I'll not perform for you or any other. This is a holding cell," Declan growled low.

Balan's left eyelid twitched.

The tick caught Declan's attention. A faint memory of this man's unease appeared, then evaporated into the black fissure in his mind.

"You speak falsely, old man." He was convinced now, beyond a doubt. Despite his stolen identity he knew all this was a lie.

"I do not lie," Balan countered.

"Release me, damn you."

"No. You see, I am very greedy and I plan on charging inconceivable amounts of credits for your use."

Declan jerked at the chain.

"You display superior strength, excellent stamina, and a fine defiant spirit. It is one of the reasons why I chose the new collar for you. Some of the wealthy patronesses requested a unique change in their pleasure. Something darker—more dangerous."

"Bastard." Declan stepped forward and was brought up short by the chain.

"I believe I will start my explanation of the controller with this little black button near the bottom. I press this," his finger paused above the button, "and five seconds later you are dead."

Declan stilled.

"A wise choice. Let us continue." He held up the controller. "The top row consists of three red buttons. These are the pain modes and they activate the tiny red light in your collar. The first red button induces a strong discomfort, Pain Stage One." He pointed to the second red button. "This second button sends a disobedient pleasurer to his knees and, if maintained, brings on unconsciousness. We call it Pain Stage Two. The third red button induces convulsions and can only be maintained for a short period of time before death. This is Pain Stage Three. Do not worry, the black button and the second and third pain stages are deactivated when we give you to a patroness. Now, on to the lust modes."

Declan's features hardened. "I am not a piece of meat."

Balan only smiled and tapped his finger on the controller. "Pay attention. The blue buttons on the next row are the lust modes and they activate the blue light in the collar. The first blue button, Lust Stage One, induces lust. The second button, Lust Stage Two, creates a possessive lover." He paused, his finger lingering above the third button. "The third blue button, Lust Stage Three, is the new rape mode."

"Rape mode?" Declan was not sure he had heard the last part correctly.

Balan's finger pressed the first red button. "Let me demonstrate a pain mode for you so you understand who is the master here. Then I think we shall rinse your mouth with one of my mint washes so you will taste fresh for your patroness."

Gone a-missing and lost my mind too, Fallon thought. They had found the maid flirting with the cook's assistant in the inn's kitchen. Coaxing the young woman into the gardens had proven difficult, until Fallon mentioned payment. Once out among the green bushes, the maid described her mistress for a considerable sum of currency. Clare had grumbled about untrustworthy and greedy servants and Fallon agreed. But in this case, it had worked in her favor. She now had a name and a description of the woman. Madam Florence Lorraine Meir was a blonde in her mid-fifties with purple streaks of dye in her hair and a penchant for bright yellow clothes.

Fallon thought Madam Meir would be easy to locate and follow. Contracting a two-guard escort from the inn, she left a grumbling Clare behind in their suite and took up position in the lounge downstairs. The guards stood near the checkout desk, waiting for her signal, looking bored. They did not have to wait long. Madam Meir appeared in a canary yellow dress with a matching cloak of equal brightness. Gem combs glittered in her piles of purple-streaked blonde hair. An image of a lemonquake beetle, which was common at home, flashed in Fallon's mind before she rose and trailed Madam Meir out the double doors of the inn into the streets beyond.

Halfway into town, however, Fallon decided to release the two Dove Inn guards from their charge. Duly lining their pockets, she extracted a promise from each of them not to return to the inn until the morning. In this way, Clare would not have cause to become alarmed and she would have the rest of the night to herself. Freedom was calling exhilaratingly.

On her own now, she continued to follow the tower of blonde hair to Lombardi Terrace, a fine gem and gift shop in the middle of the well-lit town. Upon entering the shop rimmed with tiny glittering lights, Fallon ducked behind a pair of gray planters. She watched Madam Meir greet three middle-aged matrons near the checkout counter. They were obviously old friends. By their expensive clothes and cloisonné jewelry, Fallon could tell they were all of the wealthy class.

She moved closer, pretending interest in a corner tub with fake brown vines curling over the edges.

Fashionable veils covered the other women's faces. They spoke in whispers of Balan's expensive new pleasurer who greatly resembled the infamous Douglas Savage. Fallon reached for a small white vase above the tub. Carrying it close to keep her nervous hands busy, she did something she had never done before. She walked over and introduced herself.

Hours later, she entered Balan's Brothel with her new acquaintance, Madam Florence Lorraine Meir. The other women from the gift shop had made alternate plans for the evening and could not join them. Thank goodness, Fallon thought, giving serious consideration to having lost her sanity.

Balan's brothel was a white-bricked building perched on a narrow, side-sloping lot. It overlooked a large pond and private gardens with roaming rock walls. It was near midnight and they were the only ones seated in the fragrant waiting room.

Madam Meir straightened her yellow cloak with plump hands. "This is a place where a lady can take her pleasure in private," she whispered.

Fallon simply nodded, not knowing how to respond. A large fireplace, flanked by wood columns, anchored the high ceilings and tall windows. The brick walls, couches, chairs, and plush carpets wore luxurious patterns of white upon gold.

"Have you ever met the Douglas Savage?" Meir asked.

"Once."

"Once is all you need," the older woman breathed. "I did not exactly meet him in person, you understand. But I passed him in a crowd. Heavens above, when he glanced at me I thought I would faint."

"Your hair probably blinded him," Fallon replied, smiling sweetly to tame her remark.

"Yes, well. I'm sure he recognizes good taste when he sees it."

"Yes," Fallon appeased, trying to keep a straight face.

"We'll draw straws to see who gets the pleasurer first. Don't worry, the collar keeps him willing. We should get our money's worth. I just hope this pleasurer really looks like the Douglas Savage."

Fallon had a terrible urge to smack the woman.

A small musical beep came from inside the madam's

yellow cloak.

"Excuse me," Madam Meir said, reaching for her commlink and stepping away.

Inhaling deeply, Fallon struggled to steady her nerves. This was not the Douglas Savage, but some look-alike pleasurer. She knew she should return to the inn, but could not make her legs move. She needed to see what this man looked like.

Madam Meir returned. "I must leave you, my dear."

"Leave me?" Fallon echoed in surprise.

"Yes, I can see you are not too disappointed with having the pleasurer all to yourself this evening." Meir giggled like a child.

"May I help you?" A slender brunette approached.

Fallon turned around to face a young woman dressed in a sleek ankle-length red dress. A slim gray collar with a single tiny light rested around her neck.

"Yes, please," Madam Meir responded. "My young friend here would like to purchase the services of Balan's new male pleasurer. The one with the odd eyes who resembles the Douglas Savage."

"He is very expensive," the woman purred.

"How much?" Fallon asked.

"One thousand credits for the first hour, five hundred credits thereafter."

"One thousand credits?" Meir sputtered. "I should go into this business myself."

Fallon held up her hand to quiet the whining madam. "What do his eyes look like?"

"I do not know, mistress," the girl replied. "Only a paying patroness may see his eyes."

Fallon looked from Madam Meir to the girl and back again. "I'll take him for one hour." She opened her purse.

CHAPTER
FOUR

"THIS WAY, MISTRESS."

Fallon followed the collared girl in the red slinky dress up a main stairwell to a big white room on the third floor. Before leaving, Madam Meir promised to remain silent if anyone inquired about her. Fallon hoped the older woman would keep her word. At this point, she had no choice but to trust her.

Stopping just inside the room, Fallon's small booted feet sank into a luxurious white carpet. The room smelled of many perfumes, scents layered upon scents.

"What is behind the door?" Fallon inquired and pointed to the closed door on the opposite wall.

"Servants' corridor, mistress."

Fallon looked to her left. Two ceiling spotlights bathed a white bed in a soft pink glow. An elaborately carved headboard stood at the head of the bed. Rose petals had been sprinkled upon white sheets like spots of blood. Matching nightstands stood under the round windows on either side of the large bed.

Her collared escort moved into the room and gestured to the right.

A roaring fire crackled in a white-brick hearth. At either corner of the fireplace, armchairs in flowery patterns of white on white added to the room's comfortable ambience. A small round table near the second armchair supported a gold tray of white cherries and a pitcher of purified water.

"Will this do?" the girl inquired.

Fallon nodded.

"I will leave you then."

"Thank you." Fallon moved to the nearest armchair. Alone now, she dropped her peach bag in the seat of the first chair. With trembling fingers, she unclasped her cloak and laid it across the arm.

Fallon sat in the second white armchair and stared into the orange flames. *I must be mad*, she mused, feeling both uncertain and excited. Chilled hands twisted in her lap and she silently thought once again, *What am I doing here? Am I so infatuated with the Douglas Savage that I would ruin my honor with a male double?*

"This is wrong," she whispered, and stood, intent upon leaving.

"There is nothing wrong with taking your pleasure, mistress."

Fallon turned and faced an older man in a high-collared

suit. "You have a quiet step," she accused.

"Forgive me. I am Master Balan, proprietor of Balan's Brothel."

She gave a curt nod. The man smelled of too many indulgences and she fought the impulse to back away from him.

"You are very young, mistress."

"Not so young that I do not know what I want," Fallon countered, trying to appear casual.

"Very well, then." He gestured to the open servants' doorway. "Bring her pleasurer in."

Fallon turned to the doorway.

This was it.

She could not back out now.

A man in a gray jumpsuit appeared first. He led a taller, half-naked man into the room.

Fallon stared in horror at the silver shackles binding the taller man's wrists in front of him. Muscles bunched in his upper arms as if he fought some invisible battle.

A red visor covered half the pleasurer's face, hiding his eyes and most of his features. His lips appeared pale and thin, delineating the strain within. Shiny black hair fell in waves to his nape, and a slim gray collar rested on his collarbone. A tiny light lit the collar in ominous red.

Fallon's heart pounded in her throat. Never had she imagined it would be like this.

The pleasurer's upper body gleamed with sweat. A

triangle of glistening black hair arrowed down his chest to a sculpted stomach and disappeared below the waistband of black gauze pants. The drawstring pants slung low on lean hips and the muscular length of his long legs were clearly outlined. His feet were bare and narrow.

"Your pleasurer, mistress." The proprietor signaled his guard who then pushed the pleasurer to his knees. "He is in Pain Stage One. I thought you might want me to explain the new controller."

Fallon glanced at the palm-sized device in the man's hand. *The pleasurer is in pain?* She did not understand any of this.

"Proceed," she said, hoping her voice sounded strong.

"The control is touch activated, not voice. I will explain the buttons you may use. The other buttons are deactivated and of no importance to you."

Fallon nodded.

"The first red button activates the red light in his collar to tell you he is in Pain Stage One. This mode induces a strong discomfort and may be used if he displeases you."

In dismay, Fallon glanced at the slim gray collar around the pleasurer's corded neck. "I thought pleasurers were willing."

"Some are. Some need incentive."

"How do I stop the pain?"

"Toggle the first red button to free him from the collar mode or press one of the blue buttons to deactivate it."

"What are the other two red buttons for?" she prompted.

"They are deactivated and not available for our patrons." The proprietor tapped the device with his thumb. "The blue buttons on the second row are the lust modes. When you press one of these buttons the blue light in the collar activates with Lust Stages One, Two, or Three."

Fallon frowned. "I understood there to be only one lust stage."

"This is the new collar. It has three lust stages that I will explain to you."

"Proceed, Master Balan."

"Stage One induces lust. Stage Two creates a possessive lover." He paused, his finger lingering on the third blue button. "Stage Three is recommended for those with particular tastes."

"Particular tastes?" Fallon repeated, unable to think of what these particular tastes might be.

The proprietor cleared his throat. "Stage Three is the new rape mode."

"Rape?" she sputtered with horror.

"Yes, it is a specialty item newly coded into the collars and offered in our male pleasurers. Some of our wealthy patronesses requested a more dangerous thrill. You are the first to have the opportunity to try it, mistress."

"How awful."

The proprietor's patient smile faded. "To some," he remarked. "As I noted before, it is for particular tastes and has a twenty-minute safety window. After twenty minutes, Stage Three deactivates automatically."

Fallon rubbed her forehead. She had no idea such horrors existed.

Balan tapped the device again, drawing her attention. "As a warning, the blue light blinks in Stage Three. There are no restrictions on the other lust stages."

"What is the black button?" she asked.

"Deactivated and unimportant. Shall we review? How do you stop or change stages?"

"Toggle the button to free him from a collar mode or press another button."

The proprietor nodded his approval.

She repeated the directions without prompting: "The first red button activates the red light on his collar with Pain Stage One." She could only surmise the other red buttons were severer forms of pain punishment and that is why they were not available to patrons. "The blue buttons in the second row activate the blue light in his collar with Lust Stages One, Two, or Three. Lust Stage Three is a rape stage with a twenty-minute safety window. Did I restate the directions correctly, Master Balan?"

"Yes, well done, mistress."

Fallon took the controller from his hand. She immediately pressed the first red button to free the pleasurer from pain.

Click.

The pleasurer flinched.

The red light in the collar went dark, reassuring Fallon that the pleasurer was now free from the collar's horrible influence.

"Let me check the controller for you one last time." Master Balan took the controller back firmly. He made a big deal about turning it this way and that, which Fallon found exceedingly odd. She did not see him press the first blue button for Lust Stage One when he handed the controller back to her.

Fallon gripped the black controller in cold hands and pasted a smile on her face. "Thank you, Master Balan. You may leave."

"As you wish." The proprietor signaled to his guard. "Remove the shackles."

Master Balan then followed his guard out, closing the door behind him, confident in his pleasurer's upcoming performance.

All at once, Fallon found herself alone with the dark-haired pleasurer. Clutching the controller, she looked down at him. He continued to kneel, his head bowed, black hair spilling forward. She could not see the collar and wished he would say something to break the silence.

But he did not.

It was up to her to tell him of her mistake. "I am so sorry." She found herself speaking softly as if he might suddenly jump up and grab her. Yet, whoever this man might be, he did not deserve the collar's pain. She set the controller on the seat of the nearest armchair and warily approached him.

"This is all a misunderstanding." She tried to peek under the visor.

"Misunderstanding," he murmured.

"Yes," she said, startled by the familiar voice. "I made a mistake. I should not be here."

He raised his head, reached for the red visor, and tossed it aside. It landed silently on the white carpet in front of the bed, a splash of red. But Fallon did not notice.

All she could do was gape at him with her mouth hanging open.

Declan de Douglas watched her in heated silence, his silvery-blue gaze brimming with black fire.

"There is no misunderstanding," he said silkily and Fallon stepped back, vaguely alarmed. A new thin white scar speared his right temple all the way down to his cheek. The mark added another layer of primitively to his chiseled features. His raven-black hair was shorter and tousled, falling to his nape. She did not know if she liked it as much as the longer length. It framed his beautiful face, but with a harsher reality.

"Am I agreeable?" Black lashes lowered, releasing her from his hypnotic hold.

"What are you doing here?" Her voice came out with high-pitched concern.

"Whatever you want me to do, Peaches."

Fallon cleared her throat. "That is not what I mean."

"What did you mean then?" The corner of his lips curved in seductive amusement as his gaze lowered. "You are small. Do you think you can take all of me?"

Heat burned in her cheeks at his implication. "Take all of you?" she echoed dimly. Something felt terribly wrong here. His pupils were dilated. "I do not think I understand you."

"Don't you?" he urged gently.

His gaze targeted the bed then swept back to her, his intent frighteningly clear. Rocking back to his feet, he stood in one fluid motion. "Perhaps I should show you."

Fallon glanced at the bed. "It is not necessary." When she looked back, a masculine chest filled her vision. She looked up. He was bigger and more threatening than she remembered.

She took another step back.

He followed. "Do not fear me."

"Of course, I do not fear you."

"Little liar." He reached out and touched the silken braid lying across her shoulder. "Your hair feels soft," he murmured. "It is the color of hot flames."

Fallon watched long fingers play with the silver ribbons interwoven in her hair. Suddenly a strange discord slashed across his features.

"Are you all right?" she prompted, torn between her own fear and concern for him.

He closed his eyes and inhaled deeply. "That depends on your definition of all right."

"You look discomforted."

He chuckled darkly and looked down at her from beneath lowered lids. "I can have you out of the gown before you take your next breath." His hand locked around her wrist like a strip of titanium. "But I think we will go slow for you." He guided her palm to rest upon his warm chest, her fingers buried in crisp black hair. "Can you feel my heart beating?"

"Yes," she choked.

He leaned close, his breath scorching her temple. "I'm hungry, Peaches. Feed me."

Fallon didn't know what to do. She supposed she was in danger of losing her maidenhead, but Declan so consumed her senses she could not think clearly.

"What do you need from me? I know many ways to pleasure a woman. Tell me what you need."

"Need? Nothing . . . I need nothing." Fallon backed up and collided with a white brick wall.

He continued to hold her wrist and moved to invade her private space.

"Please stop." Fallon brought her other hand to his chest and pushed, but to no avail.

"I have stopped," he replied softly. His right forearm braced on the brick wall above her head while his other hand released her wrist. "You must know I'll not hurt you, Peaches."

When he no longer seemed to be stalking her, Fallon let go a bated breath, and pulled her head back to look up at him. "Why do you call me Peaches?"

He smiled in response. His head dipped low. "I'll call you whatever you want, honey."

"What are you doing?" she demanded.

"*Péitseog agus uachtar.*" Peaches and cream. He sipped at her temple, sending shards of excitement into her bloodstream.

"Let me give you pleasure."

She couldn't seem to breathe. A large hand slipped behind her head.

"Taste me," he urged, his mouth lowering to hers.

Fallon closed her eyes. His supple lips were gentle, coaxing, applying a tender pressure. Her hands fisted against his hot skin.

"Open for me," he breathed, kissing the corner of her mouth. His tongue moistened her bottom lip, sliding along the crease. "Do you not wish to taste me, Peaches?"

"Taste you?" Her dreams had overflowed with images of him since they had parted on her home planet of Forest. But never like this. Most definitely never like this.

"How? Show me."

He pulled back, his gaze searching her face in wonder. "You have not tasted a man before?"

Fallon swallowed nervously. "Not like this."

"You are a virgin?"

"I am," she admitted in a halting whisper.

For a moment, his gaze vacillated from blue to a dilated black and Fallon had a slight impression of threat.

"I shall teach you. Do not worry, I will treat you with gentleness."

Hands locked around her shoulders with power. His head lowered, his tongue delving into her mouth, forcing compliance. He tasted slightly of lemongrass and mint as if he had freshly cleaned his mouth. Fallon drank of him, her body humming like a musical instrument.

He made a rough sound in his throat and pulled back, lips caressing hers. "I promise to go slowly and coax you into taking me fully."

Fallon could only nod helplessly, caught in his allure. Reaching up, her arms encircled his neck. The slave collar pressed into the tender flesh of her forearm.

"Want me, Peaches?"

"Yes," she said with an uneven voice.

His body visibly tightened and his mouth lowered with a new and menacing quality. The collar pressed into her arm again and a terrible thought fixated in Fallon's mind.

The collar.

Declan had shown little interest in her when they first met at her father's castle. Why did he now want her? Fallon yanked her mouth free and pushed against his chest.

A snarl of warning erupted in the back of his throat and he grabbed her jaw with one hand. He held her firmly place while his mouth feasted forcibly on her, his tongue thrusting in and out mimicking what was to come.

She became frightened. And when his right hand cupped her breast, she sank her teeth into his bottom lip and immediately gained her release. But in the next instant, Fallon found herself pinned against the wall, a powerful left hand locked around her throat.

He stared down at her in black rage, his tongue sliding along the cut in his bottom lip. A dangerous smile played about the aggressive sweep of his mouth.

"Rough, Peaches?"

Alarms shrilled inside her. Fallon held on to his thick wrist and stared at the collar around his neck. A blue light was lit but it did not blink. He was not in the rape stage but in one of the other lust stages. But was it stage one or two?

"The controller," she blurted out and pointed to the armchair where she had laid the device.

"Declan, please, the controller. It is over there on the armchair. You are in a lust stage. We must turn it off."

His face went blank. "What did you call me?"

"Declan."

"You!" he said with stunned amazement, his gaze searching her face. "You are the one who calls me Declan in my dreams."

"It is your name, is it not?"

Their gazes locked and . . .

. . . Declan found a piece of the puzzle that was maiming his mind.

The image of a flame-haired woman formed, except now the image had a face—this young woman's face. He took in the color of her hair and the whiteness of her skin, the brown eyes . . . In his arms, he held the woman who could help him uncover his stolen past.

He looked over at the small black device resting on the seat of the white armchair. Deep inside, he understood her words. Understood *something*.

He dropped his hand and released her. Stepping back, his entire body shook with the force of his restraint.

"Declan?"

"I cannot." He turned away, his body trembling and battling the slavery hold of the collar.

Fallon found herself staring at a black sword tattoo descending down the slope of his back, the tip of the blade ending just below his lean waist. She had never seen anything remotely like the ancestral design and found herself engaged despite the situation. There were black scrolls across the back of his shoulders as well. But before she could peer closer at the intriguing body artwork, he abruptly faced her.

It was then that her threatening situation became suddenly more real.

With a pinprick of fear, Fallon lifted her gaze to harsh features wavering in turmoil.

"I am done waiting," he growled, then stepped forward, and lifted her roughly in his arms, his intent clear.

Even as her arms locked around his neck, she cried. "Stop, Declan!"

He stopped, part of him responding to the fear and alarm in her voice.

"You do not wish to mate with me?" he asked vehemently.

Yes, but not like this. "No, put me down."

He swallowed hard then set her down on the white carpet, and stepped back. "As you request."

Fallon stumbled away from him, her eyes wide with astonishment. Her back smacked the hard brick wall again. Never did she expect him to release her, especially when controlled by the collar. She rushed over to the armchair, grabbed the controller, and pushed the button for Lust Stage One.

Click.

He flinched.

"There," she said with relief and peered up at his collar. It was dark. But he stood with a peculiar quiver, his eyes closed. "Declan? Are you all right? How do you feel?"

He stood so still, a raging tempest smoldering and waiting to explode.

"Declan?"

His eyes cracked open with a quicksilver flash of rage and Fallon sucked in her breath.

Declan opened his eyes fully. The driving lust was gone but in its wake resided a blazing hot fury. He stepped away from the young woman, and with a frustrated growl, punched the wall. In his peripheral, he saw her jump back in surprise. Droplets of blood splattered the white brick where his knuckles had connected. But strangely, no pain did he feel.

"Declan, please," she called softly in concern. "It's all right now."

He chuckled scornfully. Nothing was all right. He braced his forearms against the wall and rested his head there. He felt ill, as if his humanity collided with . . . A lost memory slipped free from the resident darkness in his mind. He recalled an unbearable pain in his chest, a sudden struggling for breath. As if from a great distance, he saw himself resting upon a diagnostic bed with an older man leaning over him. He tried to see the white-haired man's face, but the memory was already dimming.

He let it go, unable to understand it.

"Declan, are you all right?"

No, he was not all right. "Do you take pleasure in using a man against his will?" At this moment, he hated her as much as he hated Balan.

"How could you think that?"

"You came here," he sneered at her.

"I came here because of you!" she shouted back at him.

Her zealous response surprised him. "Who are you?"

Delicate brows curved in a slight frown. "You do not remember me?"

"No, damn you." He pushed away from the wall, staggered, and braced his hand against the wall once more for balance.

"Declan, your right ear is bleeding."

He touched the lobe and stared at crimson fingertips in surprise.

"Perhaps you should sit down."

She touched his arm and he pulled away as if burned. "Answer my question, damn you."

"Maybe you should sit down first. You look white as a ghost."

"I don't care what I look like. Answer me. Who are you?"

She looked up at him, clearly disappointed. "I am Princess Fallon MacKendrick of Clan MacKendrick."

Declan shut his eyes, flung his head back, and gave into the absurd laughter. He didn't know why her answer struck him as funny, but it did. "A pampered princess in a brothel. I don't believe it."

She bit her lip. "Yes, well."

In the next instant, he felt the wash of weakness and his legs collapsed out from under him. His shoulder struck the wall and his knees hit the floor hard. "Bloody hell."

She rushed forward and caught him around the shoulders, her arms surprisingly strong for one so small. He gripped her slender hips and buried his face in her sweet-smelling waist, wanting to disappear.

"What is wrong with you?" she demanded.

"What the hell is a pampered princess doing in a male brothel?" he mumbled insolently into the folds of her rose-scented gown. "Don't men beg for your attentions?" He felt himself drifting away, a strange calling coming in to claim him.

Small capable hands buried themselves in his hair and pulled his head back. He stared up into eyes that were wide with alarm.

"What is wrong with you?" she demanded.

"Matrix." The word slipped free from his lips without conscious thought.

"Matrix?" the princess repeated, not understanding.

Neither did he.

"The outlawed matrix robots?" she asked warily, obviously feeling her way. "The ones from the moon Io? I don't understand. What do they have to do with you?"

"Damned if I know." Declan's vision began to gray around the edges.

She cupped the back of his head and pressed him back into her soft stomach. He clung to her with his ebbing strength, feeling strangely comforted.

"Did Master Balan hurt you, Declan?"

He chuckled low with remembrance of the pain.

Fingers touched his bloody right ear. "I do not see any injury to your ear, yet it bleeds."

"I need to rest." A great darkness was rising.

"How long?"

"A few hours," he barely managed, before succumbing to the pull of oblivion.

Fallon felt his body go lax. He slipped silently from her arms to the carpeted floor and rolled over onto his back.

"Declan?" She dropped down to her knees beside him. Reaching over, she turned his head and inspected his ear. Dark crimson crusted the pink shell. She checked again for a wound and found none. Strangely, it appeared to have stopped bleeding in the same manner that it had started. Leaning forward, she pressed her lips to his forehead and tasted the warm, salty essence of him. "You do not feel like you have a fever." She sat back on her heels, at a loss for how to deal with a half-naked, unconscious clan trader posing as a pleasurer. She brushed damp hair from his forehead. Sweat soaked his body, making the black gauze pants almost transparent.

Fallon clasped her hands in her lap. His chest rose and fell at a slow rate. "Master Balan did hurt you, I know it." She looked at his bloody right hand. Lifting it into her lap, she inspected his bruised knuckles. "No bones broken. You must learn to control your temper."

She placed his hand gently down on the carpet. Blood seeped from the scrapes on his knuckle, quickly staining the white weave near her knee.

"Declan. Tell me what to do."

He did not answer.

Lifting the hem of her gown, Fallon reached for the small dagger sheathed at her thigh and walked over to the bed. She freed the corner of the white sheet. With a few quick cuts, she had what she needed.

Returning to his side, she knelt, placed his hand in her lap and bandaged his knuckles. Next, she checked his lip. The tiny wound where she nipped him had closed.

She returned the dagger to its sheath and sat back on her heels, her brows drawing together in a deep frown. Pulling her gown aside, she rechecked the amount of currency in her boots. It was just enough to purchase four more hours with him. Pushing to her feet, she stepped over Declan's prone form, went to the commlink on the wall, and pressed the white button.

A woman's voice answered. "Yes, mistress."

"I wish to purchase four additional hours with him." If he were ill or exhausted, she'd give him time to sleep.

The girl hesitated. "Let me check with the master."

Fallon rested her forehead against the cool brick wall and prayed.

The commlink on the wall crackled. "The master agreed. You must pay first. I'll come up."

Fallon straightened with relief. "I shall leave payment outside my door. I do not wish to be disturbed."

"I will be right up."

The commlink went silent.

Fallon pulled her gown up again and retrieved the currency hidden inside her boots. Thank goodness she had the foresight to bring extra. Opening the door, she placed it on the floor just as the girl in the red dress came up the stairs. She nodded to the girl then quickly closed the door.

Would these four more hours be enough time for Declan to regain his strength? She returned to his side and knelt. Curling her legs under her, she kept a silent watch.

Declan came to his feet in a detonation of raw power then stilled, waiting for the world to right itself. Pain shot through his right ear. It took him a moment to recognize his surroundings and the impending danger.

A lovely creature with brown eyes and red tipped lashes stared up at him in open-jaw astonishment.

Thirst parched his throat. He needed liquid and nodded to her. "Princess."

Moving to the table near the hearth, Declan grabbed the pitcher of water and drank deeply.

In his peripheral vision, the princess came slowly to her feet. "How do you feel?"

He placed the empty pitcher back on the table, wiped his mouth with the back of his hand and popped a succulent white cherry into his mouth. "Better." He glanced around the room. "How long have I been out?"

"You slept almost five standard hours."

He looked at her with disbelief. "You let me sleep five hours?"

The princess straightened her skirts. "I originally paid for one hour with you then I purchased an additional four hours."

Declan raised a dark brow in skepticism. "Why would you do that?"

She shrugged. "You collapsed in my arms. You needed to rest."

He glanced down at his throbbing right hand and bloodstained bandage. He did not remember the bandage, but he remembered quite clearly punching the wall to vent his frustration and rage.

From beneath lowered lids, he peered at her, noting the familiar red hair and feminine shape of her. She was the woman in his dreams and he needed her. Struggling through his stubborn pride, he roughly whispered, "Thank you."

"Declan, how did you become a pleasurer?"

He looked away, feeling a faint emptiness inside him. "I don't remember."

The commlink crackled, followed by three distinctive sound alerts.

Beep. Beep. Beep.

The princess paled. "We are out of time."

"Master Balan wants his pleasurer back," Declan snarled.

"I do not have any more currency."

"Don't worry, you won't need it." He picked up one of the armchairs and jammed it into the hearth. Orange flames instantly licked at fabric.

"What are you doing?"

"Creating a diversion, Princess." Declan moved in front of the servants' door and kicked. The white door swung open with a bang.

She came up beside him. "They'll hear us downstairs."

He grabbed her arm and pushed her out the door into the servant's corridor. "Time to leave."

"Wait!" She struggled against his firm grip.

"No," he argued. "We need to leave now."

"Stop!" She shoved hard against his chest. "The controller!"

He looked back into the smoky room. "Damn it." He'd forgotten about the collar's controller.

"Stay here."

He ran back into the bedroom. Smoke billowed from the flame-engulfed chair in the hearth and he recalled Balan's earlier speech. Destroying the controller, without first deactivating it, enabled Pain Stage Three, giving the wearer a painful death. Coughing, his eyes burning, he dropped down on all fours. He had to keep the blasted thing with him and find another way to deactivate the damn collar. The controller lay on the smoldering carpet near the fire and he reached for it. Hot white pain seared the flesh of his fingers. He jerked his hand back. "Bloody hell, I can't touch it."

"What is it?"

"A goddamn automatic safety prevents me from holding my own controller!"

"Here, let me." The princess touched his shoulder, held out her right hand and . . . the controller jumped into her palm as if on springs.

"What the hell?" Declan pulled back with surprise.

"Come on." His princess disappeared out the servants' door.

Declan came to his feet and bolted after her.

CHAPTER
FIVE

THREE STONE STEPS led to the private back garden of the brothel. In the distance, star clusters faded behind a purple-splashed dawn.

Fallon hiked up her skirts. Her feet hit the white walkway at a run; gravel crunched beneath her boots.

"Declan." His name came out in a breathless rush, mingling with the scents of the genetically altered thyme and mint plants.

In front of her, he checked his long stride so she could keep up. He said something sharply, but she could not hear above her heart pounding in her ears.

Fallon could only imagine how the tiny stones in the path cut into his bare feet.

She ran on, praying they would not be found.

All around them, dark shapes morphed into decadent statues—reclining, leaning, standing—all in various stages of copulation.

On either side of the gravel pathway, plants with

grassy leaves flowered with multiple blooms of white and cream. Fallon saw everything as she rushed by. Smaller faerie sculptures, antiqued with ash and wax, peeped through flower petals. Trees shaped like graceful domes overhung the winding pathway. White lace leaves dangled in mounds of tears. Tiny birds with multiple pairs of gold and blue wings glided through the air in their search for food.

Fallon struggled to keep up with the pace Declan set. They had just rounded a corner of black boulders, sprinkled with fragrant white phlox, when Declan stopped short.

She crashed into his strong back with a muffled oath, her nose plastered to sweaty skin and the tattooed image of a blade. His hand shot back, his fingers digging into her arm to steady her.

She felt him tense. Grasping his lean waist, she peered around him.

An exotic-looking blond stranger stood in the morning shadows. He was sunlight to Declan's darkness.

Fallon stared at the gray collar resting on his collarbone. With only one light, it was thinner than Declan's.

"Here, take these." The stranger thrust a pile of dark clothes into Declan's arms, then stepped back and pointed. "Follow the path around the pond to the rocky wall and turn right."

Fallon looked to where he indicated. Dwarf bearded

irises of some hybrid variety stretched to the edge of the pond's black waters, hiding the path from the naked eye.

She turned back to the stranger. Beneath her palms, Declan's body was taut with tension.

"Go through the gate and head west," the stranger continued with his directions. "In the black light district is the Bloodgood bar. I have friends there who can help you."

"What are the names of these friends?" Declan inquired, his tone less then friendly.

"Names are too dangerous. When they see the collar, they will approach you."

"How far to the Bloodgood bar from here?" he asked, shifting in front of her.

"It'll take you most of the day. Once you leave the main part of town, houses are sparse until you reach the black light district. The Bloodgood bar is at the farthest end.

"Why do you help us?" Fallon asked in a small voice.

Slanted blue eyes slid to Declan. "Because he is not one of us. He needs to be free," the stranger replied.

"You are a pleasurer?" Fallon asked.

"Yes, mistress."

Fallon stepped around Declan and wiped her sweaty hands in her skirts. "Come with us," she offered.

The pleasurer shook his head. "No, mistress."

"Why not?" Fallon persisted. She could feel Declan's

displeasure digging holes in her back.

"Freedom is not for everyone, mistress. I am happy here."

"To be kept and used?" Fallon murmured incredulously.

"Yes, mistress." He bowed his head and smiled. "To be kept and used. Not all of us wear the new rape collar."

Shouts rose behind them, coming from the brothel.

Declan muttered an oath.

Fallon turned back, only to discover the blond pleasurer had disappeared behind tall green hedges before she could thank him.

Declan grabbed her wrist.

"What about him?" she asked.

"He made his choice."

Her own pleasurer leaped forward, dragging her to the path leading to the black pond.

Lord Tomaidh Henderson of Clan Henderson stared at the small patch of dried blood on the carpet, now soiled and grubby with smoke, burn marks, and the water it had taken to stop the blaze. The stench the fire had left offended his sensitive nature.

"A virgin's blood, Tommy?"

Stiffening at the familiar voice, Lord Henderson

glanced behind him. Normally, he did not associate with brutal and insane personalities, but business was business.

Commander Lin Derek Ramayan relaxed against the doorjamb, arms casually folded across his chest. He wore the prestigious black uniform of the warship *Shadowkeep*. His blond hair was cropped short and his eyes, like those of the legendary father before him, were of the palest blue. They watched him with a glittering and uncomfortable intensity.

"Blood from your bride-to-be, Tommy?"

"Yes," Lord Henderson replied, looking down at the bloodstain. No other explanation could be found in his own mind. His hands fisted at his sides.

"Are you sure, Tommy? DNA testing . . ."

"I do not need a test to know what happened here, and do not call me Tommy." Lord Henderson pulled at his red frock coat. An ancient symbol of the aristocracy, it barely hid a bulging stomach born of indulgences. He was a man in his middle thirties, accustomed to obedience from those around him.

"If she were mine, I would have kept a tighter leash."

"She is not yours," he said low and forcefully. Why his bride-to-be had gone to a brothel to purchase the services of a male pleasurer, he could not fathom. It had taken his men most of the night to track her to this place of soiled virtue, but he'd arrived at Balan's Brothel too late.

"What are you doing here?" Lord Henderson prompted with a sneer, not turning around. He rolled his shoulders to relieve the tension. "I thought you'd be off playing with your space pirates."

Ramayan's lips curved in a sinister smile. "For shame, Tommy. You and I both know I don't play with space pirates. For your information, the warship *Shadowkeep* of Clan Ramayan delivered the Spanish ambassador to the MacKendrick Castle. Renewing old trade negotiations, I suppose. It seems to be the thing to do since the war ended. Anyway, I contacted your ship, *Pict*. Her captain said you were here." His voice lowered. "I expected more than a single vial of the virus."

"That was a sample." Lord Henderson's voice shook with anger. "I did not have the Douglas energy crystals to run the DNA synthesizers, damn you. You know their astronomical fuel consumption."

"I cannot wait much longer. The interceptor satellites are near completion. My window of opportunity is closing. I need to plant the virus soon."

"You'll have your virus. I've made other arrangements, do not worry." Lord Henderson turned his attention back to the scorched room. "Balan!" he called impatiently.

The proprietor walked back from the soiled bed, wiping the sweat from his brow, his shoes squishing in the white foam.

"That dark-haired pleasurer is worth a lot to me," Balan said in obvious upset. "I've lost much this night."

"You mean the Douglas Savage, do you not, Master Balan?" Commander Ramayan inquired knowingly.

"I'll handle this, Commander," Lord Henderson spoke with impatience.

"As you wish."

Henderson slapped pristine gray gloves in his hand to get Balan's attention. "How convenient for you that my men rendered the Douglas Savage unconscious at the space station."

Balan's left eyelid twitched. "I don't know what you are talking about."

"Is that so?" He gave the bloodstain near the tip of his left boot a final regard.

"No, I don't know anything about this Douglas Savage, my lord."

"Do not lie to me, Master Balan. I know you enslave young men against their will. Come now, tell me the truth, or it will go very badly for you."

The shorter man muttered under his breath. "I only enslave an uncommon few."

"What constitutes uncommon?" the commander inquired from behind him.

The proprietor shrugged. "Physical beauty. Virility. Stamina. Spirit. Intelligence. Few males possess all these traits."

Henderson scowled. It was quite true that he, himself, possessed all of these traits, so why did that bitch-whore run away? "Freeborn does not matter?" he asked.

"Not when there is a profit to be had."

Lord Henderson understood profit. "How long did the princess share this room with him?"

"She contracted for one standard hour then purchased four more."

His gaze slid to the scorched bed. "Five godforsaken hours? What the hell did he do with her?"

Behind him, Ramayan chuckled then moved up to join him. Henderson ignored him. "Was the pleasurer in a lust stage?" he demanded of the brothel owner.

The shorter man buried his fists in his pockets. "Yes, the pleasurers usually are in a lust stage. They perform better."

"Bastard. I'll make her watch when I slowly castrate him. Then I'll ship what's left of him back to his half brother." He slapped his gloves against his left thigh in high agitation.

"Master Balan, will you give us a moment?" Commander Ramayan asked.

The proprietor moved away and Ramayan turned his full attention to the fat lord.

"Damn the Douglas for not accepting my fair offer," Henderson muttered. "I only wanted to purchase a dozen of his clan's energy crystals, not the entire cache."

"Tommy, you need to listen to me."

"I am listening, damn you."

"The Douglas Savage belongs to me. I want him unharmed." Ramayan thought about the secrets of his past and what was owed him. Declan de Douglas was his younger half brother. They shared the same father. No one knew but him. No one would know until he wanted them to know.

The fat lord glared at him, anger overriding good sense. "Why?"

"My plans are my own, Tommy. I'll tell you this, though. If Declan is harmed, I'll kill you," he offered his promise of reality in a pleasant but menacing tone. "Do we understand each other, my fat friend?"

Lord Henderson's eyes narrowed with faint displeasure before he nodded. "Damn your secrets upon secrets, Ramayan. What is he to you? The bastard already destroyed my plans to kidnap the Douglas twins and force Lachlan into compliance."

"That's not my problem."

The commander's comment annoyed him greatly. "I told you. I require the Douglas energy crystals to run the DNA synthesizers to produce the oligos."

"Again, that is not my problem. I purchased the product and care not for the means by which you produce it."

Henderson gritted his teeth. The small DNA strands his scientists engineered were known as oligonucleotides or oligos. They could be customized to fit any client's design, be it deadly or benign. He cared little for the outcome of his cultivation of dangerous microorganisms, as long as he received his money. Ramayan was his first client. If the commander wanted a full-length, fast-acting poliovirus, then so be it. Based on human oligos, this poliovirus killed within days, instead of taking years to manifest.

"What are your plans, Tommy? I need to get back to my ship."

He hated being called Tommy. It was degrading. "They'll not defy me," he said and looked again at the remains of the scorched bed.

"I'm sure they will not," Commander Ramayan replied tolerantly. He watched as the fat lord gestured for the brothel proprietor to come near. With a kind of casual interest, he noted the little man's approach and the odd twitching above his left eye. It fascinated him in a malicious sort of way. Fear always fascinated him, making him hungry for more. "Your left eyelid twitches, Balan," he mocked, his lips twisting in a predator's interest. "A most exceedingly odd spasm."

Swallowing hard, the proprietor gave a faint tug on his eyelid, then turned to Henderson.

Ramayan locked his hands behind his back and

listened intently to his associate's dictate.

Lord Henderson exhaled sharply. His shoulders were tight with stress. He wanted the idiot princess back and was prepared to do what was needed. "Balan, I want you to post a reward for the whereabouts of your dark-haired pleasurer. Make it a large incentive. Say fifty thousand credits?"

"I cannot afford that," the man protested.

"But I can," he replied smugly. "I will provide the reward."

The proprietor's grimace turned into a grin. "I will see to it, my lord."

"Do not use the name Douglas Savage in your reward notice," the commander warned silkily. "We would not want to alert Clan Douglas."

"Agreed." Henderson gave a brief nod at the suggestion. All was falling back into place. He was in charge again.

"What about the princess?" the proprietor asked, showing the caution of one who was exceedingly wise when dealing with spoiled individuals.

The feeling of control deserted Henderson. "The bitch-whore is none of your concern, Balan." He waved the bothersome little man away.

"Lower class individual," the commander muttered after Balan left.

"Yes."

"I am curious, Tommy. What is your plan?"

"I will tell her father that the pleasurer kidnapped her from the Dove Inn. When the Douglas Savage tires of her, she'll probably crawl back to me anyway, begging for my forgiveness." His lips curved into a cruel smile, relishing the thought.

Ramayan knew that look well. "Contemplating a princess's punishment, Tommy?"

"Looking forward to it, Commander. Looking forward to it."

Ramayan patted his associate on the back, feeling the thick layers of fat beneath the expensive clothes. "I will be in touch, Tommy." Turning on his heel, he walked out, leaving the stench of the fire behind. He had much to do. Upon receipt of the completed infectious agents, he needed to get them into the Douglas's planetary satellites before their launch. He turned a corner, his mood turning darker. It would be the final act of retribution for the death of a father he had never known. The past drifted into his soul and he remembered his mother, a favored whore of Commander Lin Jacob Rama . . . until the Lady Saph-ire Townshend came into the picture. Pregnant and abandoned by her benefactor, his mother had birthed him in a brothel. She had raised him spouting stories of his proud Clan Ramayan lineage and his kinship to the warrior clan. At an early age, he had learned to hate her. He hated her simplicity and her poverty, and had run away and joined the military. All of that was behind him, locked safely in the past. He was in his late thirties now, the commander of *Shadowkeep*, his father's warship.

The time for vengeance was almost upon him. He suspected his father would have been proud.

CHAPTER
SIX

THE SHORT DAYS of the planet favored their escape. By the time they had reached the black light district and located the shack called the Bloodgood bar, twilight stretched across the flat land. The foul smells of poverty and sweat rode the warm air currents of the narrow alleys and dirt paths.

In the new night sky, densely crowded star clusters shone in a strange, red luminescence.

Fallon desired food, a bath, and a place to rest. She supposed Declan desired only the darkness of night. He seemed to become one with it.

"Why do we wait out here?" she asked, contemplating the shadowed alley before them. He did not answer.

"Declan, must you pin me against the wall?"

"Yes, and I'm not exactly pinning you. I need to know where you are." He surveyed the narrow alley outside the bar for danger.

"I am here, behind you."

He glanced over his shoulder and studied her up-turned face. "Telekinesis?" he asked slowly.

Fallon looked away. "Yes." In the past, people had often reacted strangely when witnessing her gift. She now found herself hesitating, wondering if Declan would find her strange, too.

"What rating?" he asked.

"I rate five, very limited."

"But enough to whip a palm-sized device from the floor to your hand."

"The power of my gift increases with strong emotions, and I felt a little agitated."

"A little agitated?" Declan chuckled, looking back down the alley. "I wonder what happens when you become very agitated."

Fallon frowned at him. "Do you laugh at me?"

"No, Princess." He looked back at her, all laughter gone. "Where is the controller?"

"In my bodice. You can trust me to keep it safe."

His gaze dropped to her bodice then slowly returned to her face. "I believe you."

"You are not disconcerted by my gift?" Fallon asked quietly.

"Should I be?"

"I would never use it against you."

"I know."

"You do?" She searched his face for confirmation.

"Yes."

Fallon moistened her lips and changed the subject, before she reached up and kissed him. "Must we wait out here?"

"Yes, I think it best for the moment." His gaze slid back down the alley. "I want to see the type of patrons who frequent the Bloodgood bar, before we enter."

"Why? We can tell the type of people when we go into the bar." It did not make sense to stand out here in the smelly alley. "Let us go in."

"No, my instincts say to wait. Now be quiet for a moment."

Fallon sighed. Standing there in silence in the cramped corner, she became acutely aware of the larger size of his body compared to hers, the slope and strength of his back, and the tantalizing scent of male in her lungs . . .

She shifted sideways, trying to move around him but there was little room and her hip rubbed against him.

He glanced down at her then, silvery-blue eyes watching from beneath lowered lids. Fallon stared openly at him in fascination. Strands of black hair fell into his odd eyes. His black lashes were indecently long and thick. In the dim light, his eyes appeared eerily silver and alien, not quite human.

"Princess?" His voice sounded low and caressing in the quiet of the alleyway.

"Silver moonlight lives in your eyes." His gaze made her feel as if she belonged to him, body and soul.

He let go a harsh laugh and turned away. "You're serious, aren't you?"

"I meant no disrespect," she said into his shoulder. "They are beautiful, like the rest of you."

He looked back at her. "No one has ever called me beautiful, Princess, not that I can remember."

"Maybe you have not listened, Declan."

"Princess, I am not—"

"I know what you are."

"You do?" He watched her face for some recognizable sign, something to hold on to.

Fallon grew warm under his scrutiny and suddenly found herself facing him. "I think it more important we turn our efforts to removing the slave collar from around your neck." She touched the collar.

He nodded in agreement. "Trust a princess to keep priorities in order." He glanced back down the alley's darkness again.

"After we remove the collar, we must escape this planet. It would be best if we steal a proper ship."

"A proper ship?" he echoed faintly, looking back at her.

"Yes," Fallon replied, "'so we can own the battle-field.'" She proudly mimicked his words from when they had first met.

He looked at her oddly. "Battlefield?"

"Something with agile aerodynamics, innovative avionics and . . ." She paused.

"Thrust vectoring." The words were out of Declan's mouth before he knew it. "You're talking about the flying capability of a ship?" He frowned. "Princess, have we had this conversation before?"

"Yes, at Clan MacKendrick castle. You must remember the . . ."

"MacKendrick what?"

She frowned up at him. "I may not be memorable, sir, but I assure you Clan MacKendrick Castle is."

"Wait." He held his hands up. "I assure you, Princess, you are memorable. Very memorable."

"I am?"

He looked at her sideways before turning away. "Yes, exceedingly memorable, exceptionally memorable, superbly memorable." He raked a hand through his hair, attempting to turn his mind back to contemplating the alley and bar, a hopeless task.

Fallon regarded him quietly. If he considered her memorable, then why didn't he remember her? Her eyelashes lowered. Why did the master trader of Clan Douglas wear a slave collar? She had so many questions. She looked at his handsome profile, at the white scar trailing down his temple. He must have endured a grave injury, to leave such a ragged scar. And why did blood seep from his right ear? The words *identity theft* and *amnesia* popped into her head.

"Declan?"

"Quiet."

"Is the *Black Ghost* near?" she asked, wondering if he remembered his stealth ship.

"*Black Ghost*?" His voice sounded strange and uncertain to her. "No, not near."

"Where is it then?" she inquired.

He stared off into the distance. "I don't know. Look, Princess," he glanced back at her, "let's just concentrate on the task at hand."

"All right," she agreed softly. But one did not misplace their ship, she thought. "Since the *Ghost* is not near, may I suggest we make do with another proper ship?"

"Yes, a proper ship," he restated with a sense of detachment.

Fallon turned back to the alley and listened to the voices floating up from the bar.

"It sounds crowded with people."

"Yes, this seems to be a hot spot for the adventurous."

She gripped his arm. "We should go in and find this person who can help us remove your collar." She pointed to the entranceway of the bar. "Shall we go in?"

"Eventually," he said quietly, watching the entrance with a powerful concentration.

"I believe it prudent we go currently, rather than eventually. I suspect Master Balan must be looking for you by now."

"I don't trust the information that Snow gave us. However, since our options are limited, we'll go in and keep a low profile." He took her hand. "You are Peaches and . . ."

"You are my pleasurer. I understand."

He led her to the bar's entrance then moved behind her, feigning servitude.

"Ready?" Declan whispered.

Fallon nodded. His hand gently pressed into her back, guiding her forward.

"Remember, you are the master here, Peaches. I am but your humble pleasurer."

She could feel his cocky smirk behind her as they entered the dimly lit bar.

"The back table in the corner, Peaches. To the right."

Lifting her skirts, Fallon led the way. She walked around a slender, ebony-skinned woman to the cluttered tables at the back.

Declan stepped around her and pulled out a chair for her to sit on.

Murmuring her thanks, Fallon sat down. Her pleasurer moved left, and seated himself with his back to the wall. She rested her hands in her lap. "It's a little dingy in here," she observed.

"It's a hellhole."

Looking around the shadowy bar, she saw dust everywhere. "It seems a bit untidy."

"Yes, typical for a hellhole."

"And hot," she added.

"Yes, it is warm. But at least the ceiling fans move the air around."

She shifted uncomfortably, looking up at the large ceiling fan to their right. It provided little comfort, she thought. Her gown clung to her sweat-dampened skin and she desperately wanted a bath. As a precaution, she had wrapped the controller in a white cloth to prevent the buttons from being pressed accidentally, and had placed it in her bodice. But the device now dug into the tender underside of her right breast.

She had fervently hoped for a delicately spiced cooked meal, a scented bath, and a private room to rest. But the Bloodgood bar did not look promising. Sordid men and women spoke in hushed tones amongst themselves while they ate and drank.

"Is it safe?" She leaned forward, her fingers tracing the scars that marred the table's irregular surface.

"Safe is a relative term."

He did not look at her but continued to scan the bar and patrons. Fallon sat back in her seat, every one of her senses absorbed by him. She could not help it. He fascinated her. He sat quiet, but there was a predatory alertness in his posture.

"I never saw a tattoo before," she said by way of conversation.

He just gazed at her.

"Did it hurt?"

"No."

"Oh. Is the sword symbolic of something?" She could see that her question made him uncomfortable.

He looked away, and gave a hard tug on the collar of his shirt.

"Is the shirt uncomfortable?" She reached over and touched a straining seam at his shoulder. The pleasurer's borrowed clothes were snug on his big frame.

"Tight would be a better description."

Fallon noted the high neckline of the black shirt. It hid the control collar from all sides except for the lace-up front, which he kept undone so as not to tear the shirt's seams.

"Do the pants and shoes fit at least?" she inquired.

"The pants are snug. The shoes will not cripple me."

"Oh. That is good."

"Yes, not being crippled is good."

She nodded and not knowing what else to say, turned and looked around, listening to the drone of hushed voices.

"Can you not tie up that mane of flames you call hair?"

She did not understand his displeasure. "I lost my

ribbons."

"Then pull the damn hood up and cover your hair."

"But it is warm in here." She unhooked the cloak's gold clasp under her chin.

Her pleasurer reached over the table and grabbed her wrist. Long fingers slid over hers and with one hand, he refastened the gold clasp. "Keep the cloak on. You will draw too much attention without it."

His touch sent curling warmth through her blood and Fallon stared into his handsome face, her heart pounding.

"Did you hear me?" he asked.

She nodded and he released her hand, leaning back in his chair. Maybe he was right, she mused. Her peach gown had a finely stitched bodice, much too fine for anybody frequenting the Bloodgood bar. She adjusted the heavy cloak and continued her quiet study of the surroundings. The ebony-skinned woman was moving from table to table, talking softly with the patrons. To their left, a man fell drunkenly out of his chair and was lifted back up by his amused companions. It was not a place of reassurance but of souls seeking to lose themselves in drink. Inevitably, Fallon's focus returned to her collared companion. Declan made her feel both safe and frightened at the same time. And despite the difficulty they were in, he was her living and breathing fantasy. She wished she could run her fingers through his beautiful hair and . . .

"Peaches, do not look at me in that way."

She blinked. "What way?"

"Innocent," he muttered but with a curve to his sensuous mouth.

"Hot-blooded, isn't he?" The ebony woman sauntered to the table with a drink in her hand.

Fallon met their new visitor's interested gaze and did not falter. "Very," she replied.

She felt Declan's hard silent regard and her palms grew moist and cold. Taking the lead in this conversation seemed imperative to her.

"May I join you?" the older woman asked and placed her drink on the table.

Declan went utterly motionless. "No, you may not."

"I was not talking to you, slave."

"Forgive the manners of my pleasurer. Please sit." Fallon gestured to the ladder-back chair next to her.

The ebony woman smiled. "I prefer this one." Grabbing the folds of her ankle-length black dress, she slid gracefully into the bench seat beside Declan, and immediately Fallon felt a stab of jealousy. This woman was both beautiful and worldly.

"We don't see his quality around here," the ebony woman said. "Certainly not with those blue eyes."

Her pleasurer lowered his lashes submissively, hiding his thoughts. But Fallon knew there was nothing submissive in the tenseness of his posture, nor the muscle tick in his jaw.

"Lordy," the ebony woman said in a very appreciative tone, "he is gorgeous." Their visitor placed three fingers under Declan's chin and lifted his head up.

Her pleasurer jerked out of her hand and glared at the woman from beneath lowered lids.

"I would appreciate it if you did not touch him," Fallon said firmly.

"He doesn't like it?"

"Would you?"

"Being kept as a private pleasurer has its rewards. If you decided to enter the profession, you could ask any price, with your fair coloring."

Declan's handsome features turned menacing.

"Possessive, isn't he?" The woman laughed and extended her hand. "I am Madam Cherry, proprietress of the Bloodgood bar."

Fallon grasped the woman's smooth hand, felt Declan's warning glare, and replied, "I am Peaches."

"Ah." The woman nodded in quiet amusement. "And your gorgeous pleasurer? By what name do you call him?" Fallon released the woman's hand and saw her focus on Declan once again.

"Savage," Declan answered through clenched teeth.

"Savage. How appropriate." The woman openly ogled his body. "Have you feasted this evening, Savage?"

"We have no money." Fallon knew she had blundered the moment Declan looked at her.

"Well, we have a meat stew this evening and purified water, if you mean to barter." The proprietress clasped her hands together on the table.

Fallon held Declan's gaze. A flicker of indecision crossed his face before he looked away.

"What would you take in payment for the food and drink?" he inquired, his voice sounding wrong.

In response, Madam Cherry reached up and touched the collar. "The new rape collar. I've heard rumors about it. Have you used it yet, Peaches?"

Fallon shook her head.

"Perhaps you will let me. In exchange for the meal, I'll take your pleasurer in my bed. Are we agreed?"

Fallon's eyes flashed with outrage. "*Bíodh an diabhal agat*!" she spat with venom, coming to her feet. You go to hell.

"Peaches," Declan warned.

"Is he not worth the meal?" the proprietress inquired sweetly.

Fallon balled her fists. "He is worth more than food, more than anything you could ever think to offer, you . . . you white-haired bitch!"

"All right," the proprietress held up her hands, "I did not mean to insult you. In exchange for the meal, I'll take one hour with him in Lust Stage Two."

"Not one minute!" Fallon's voice rose. "Not one second!" Her fist slammed down on the table with a loud smack. As if in reaction, the ceiling fan, circling above their heads and to the right, hit the floor with a terrible loud sound. It exploded into a thousand pieces and everyone ducked, covering their heads.

Fallon gasped, knowing what she had done. She straightened to make sure no one had been hurt by her gift and was amazed by what she saw. These people, in their dingy clothes, simply turned back to what they were doing, their heads bowed in private conversations as if nothing had happened. Two men with brooms appeared and began to clean up.

"Sit down, Peaches," Declan ordered gently.

Fallon sat and glared at Madam Cherry, who continued to look up at the hole in her ceiling.

"Weak ceiling," Fallon offered, and found Declan watching her closely. She gave him one of her brightest smiles.

"Very curious," Madam Cherry said quietly. "I'll have to notify the landlord. I cannot have ceiling fans falling for no reason and hitting my customers."

"Probably an old fan," Fallon said, and watched Madam Cherry speak with the men cleaning up. She refused to look at Declan.

The woman returned and sat down at their table once more. "You have quite a temper, Peaches, don't you?"

Fallon felt the anger rise up in her again.

"Bring the food," Declan interjected quietly. "You'll have your hour."

Fallon turned to Declan. "No, Savage."

He looked at her then, his gaze searching. "Peaches, are you not hungry?"

"I am neither hungry nor thirsty." Fallon fought back hot tears. "I shall not have you service another against your will." She leaned forward. "Never, Savage," she said hoarsely. "Do you hear me? Never." Her voice shook.

Declan raked a hand through his hair and muttered an oath.

"It appears the MacKendrick princess is very protective of you, Savage." A knowing smile curved the proprietress's shiny red lips.

Declan's hand shot out with lightning speed. He twisted the woman's arm behind her back and held her immobile against his side.

"One word," he said low in her ear, "and I'll break your arm in so many places, Madam Cherry, it'll never mend properly."

The woman nodded in understanding.

"What do you know of the MacKendrick princess?" Declan demanded in a hushed tone while scanning the bar for threats.

"You're hurting me."

"I'll do more than that if you don't answer my question."

"If you don't release me this instant, young man, I'll not help you."

Declan snorted. "A moment ago you wanted to use me like an animal. Now you want to help me?"

Fallon leaned across the table and squeezed Declan's arm. Muscles bunched under her fingers. "Maybe we should listen?"

"No." Her very angry pleasurer glanced at her for a full second before turning back to the proprietress.

"Tell me why I should believe you, Madam," he said with a slightly calmer tone.

"Snow alerted me."

"Snow?" Declan echoed. "The blond pleasurer with the slanted blue eyes from Balan's?"

"You're wearing his clothes. Clothes I bought for him, damn it. Release me now, Savage, or by the faith, I'll not help you remove the damn collar."

"Why should we believe you?" Fallon asked. Her arm pressed across Declan's chest as if she could curb the power and rage emanating from him.

"I hate slavers," Madam Cherry retorted.

Declan dropped his hands and released her.

The proprietress rubbed her arm. "Snow said Balan collared Savage against his will. Brought him in bloody and half dead. Had to use an emulsion tank to save his life." The older woman's eyes became misty with sadness. "My brother wasn't so lucky years ago. He didn't survive the capture."

Fallon sat back. "I'm sorry for your loss." A sudden chill ran down her spine. The mention of being in an emulsion tank still affected her after all these years. The familiar nightmare shifted in her mind, a memory willfully pushed aside. When she was four, she had almost died in an emulsion tank. In her memories, she once again relived it, the cold press of an oxygen coil, the whirring sound of a malfunction, blue fluid racing into her nose and mouth, the drowning terror . . .

The technician's delay in recognizing the system failure had almost cost her life. She had died that crisp morning long ago and had been brought back.

"If only my brother had been placed in an emulsion tank." The proprietress's voice shook a little with the remembered grief.

Fallon concealed her own terror and peered at Declan.

He watched her with a peculiar concentration, almost as if he sensed her agitation.

"Emulsion tank technology is no guarantee that your brother would have lived," Declan said, turning back to the proprietress.

"I know," Madam Cherry replied. "But he was not given that chance."

"I am truly sorry for your loss, Madam," Fallon offered again.

The proprietress's glazed eyes turned to her. "Thank

you." It took the woman a moment to compose herself. "Princess, your pleasurer wears the new rape collar. It is very bad. Be careful with him."

"I'd never hurt her," Declan said firmly.

"You might not, but the collar would." The proprietress stood and casually adjusted the belt on her dress.

"Can you help us, Madam Cherry?" Fallon looked up into the woman's face, trying to decide whether or not to trust her.

"I cannot remove the collar, but I know where you can go for help." She glanced at Declan. "I have never seen anyone with eyes such as his. Is he a mutation of some sort?"

"No," Fallon responded before her annoyed pleasurer could.

"Well then. I feel compelled to mention that Balan has posted a large reward for him."

Declan held up his hands to silence both of them. "How much of a reward?"

"The listing said fifty thousand credits to be rewarded for the whereabouts of a dark-haired pleasurer with odd blue eyes and a sword tattoo down his back."

Declan cursed under his breath. "I thought I would have more time."

"Apparently not. And I should also mention that a reward of one hundred thousand credits was posted for information leading to the safe recovery of the kidnapped MacKendrick princess."

Fallon choked. "I am not kidnapped."

"Peaches." Declan stood and held out his hand to her. "Madam Cherry, is there a private place where we may speak?"

The proprietress nodded.

"Lead on then, if you will. I dislike being the center of attention in your bar."

Fallon stood and slipped her hand into Declan's.

They followed the proprietress out a side door.

CHAPTER
SEVEN

THEY WERE IN a small room above the Bloodgood bar.

Declan stared into the bathroom's cracked mirror. The wild images in his mind went on. *The bloodletting, rapid pulsar fire, green tartans flowing like flags, twin boys, people dying . . .*

He felt isolated in a world where he no longer understood who he was.

He needed to warn somebody.

Protect.

Defend.

Guard against danger.

But who?

Hell. He could not remember his own name. *Declan. Savage. Declan. Savage. Bloody goddamn hell.* Why did he remember some things yet not others? It was like a piece of his mind had gone missing, leaving the rest of him unaffected. He had no answers, no goddamn answers, and it made him feel vulnerable in a way that not only angered him but planted the fear of the unknown in his gut as well. He glanced over his shoulder, noticing the silence for the first time. His princess was watching him with uncertainty. "Princess?"

"I cannot reach to unbutton the back of my gown."

He looked away a brief moment to steady himself. Pushing off the sink, he went to her.

"Turn around." He eyed the row of tiny cloth buttons warily. "Whoever invented gowns with buttons down the back?"

"It is an old style my mother favored." She lifted her hair out of the way. The fiery tresses fascinated him. He wanted to bury his hands in the silken length, bring the strands to his nose, and inhale the sweet fragrance.

"Declan?"

"You want to tell me what you were doing in a male brothel?" he queried.

"Mistress Meir said Balan's brothel had a look-alike. I did not expect you to be there."

Declan's fingers paused on the second button. "Perhaps you should start from the beginning. The reward post says you were kidnapped. Who is looking for you?"

"My maid Clare must have told Thomas when I did not return last eve to the Dove Inn. With all that has happened, I forgot about him. He must be looking for me."

"Who is Thomas?" Declan asked.

She hesitated. "Lord Tomaidh Henderson of Clan

Henderson, my betrothed."

"Your betrothed?" A dark fury formed in his blood. The name churned his stomach. "If you are betrothed," Declan said very carefully, "what, pray tell, were you doing in a brothel seeking a male pleasurer?"

"That is rather complicated."

"Try me." Declan's fingers had not moved from the second button.

"Well, if you must know, I went looking for you. Mistress Meir said Master Balan had a pleasurer who looked like you. I mean, I really did not expect *you* to be in a brothel."

"Let me see if I understand this." He leaned over her shoulder. "You went to a male brothel because this Madam Meir told you Master Balan possessed a pleasurer who looked like me?"

"Yes."

He lowered his dark head to hers. "Infatuation, Princess?" he teased, and heard her breath catch. Declan's fingers moved to caress her nape. "What did you plan to do with this double once you had purchased his services?"

"What do you mean?"

Her evasive answer did not sit well with him. Declan could feel jealousy building in his blood. He struggled to control his emotions and not do something impulsive he would later regret. "Would you have mated with him?"

The princess remained silent.

"Then why did you go there?" He pulled back, his gaze sliding down her slender body.

When she did not answer, his eyes darkened dangerously. "I ask again, Princess: why did you go there?" With his thumb, he stroked the curve of her ear then detected a trembling response in her small frame. "Have it your way, then." His hands returned to the tiny buttons—his fingers never felt so large and cumbersome. "Can't you use your gift to undo these buttons?"

"If I cannot see it, I make a mess of things."

He struggled on gallantly. "You will not go to a brothel again, Princess."

"I have no need."

"There are always needs, Princess."

"And wants," she added.

His hands paused. *I want. I want. I want.* "And wants," he agreed, feeling a sense of dislocation. "Do you love this Lord Henderson?"

"He is my father's choice. I do not love him."

The fury inside him slipped away, replaced by a new calm.

"Are you having difficulty with the buttons?" she asked.

Declan stared at the tiny row of buttons streaming down her slender back and ending just above the curve of her posterior. "No."

"Why do you stop then?"

He continued working. By his estimate, he was on button number twenty-three, not a quarter of the way finished.

"Will we remain long here?"

He shrugged. "An hour to clean up and rest, no more."

Declan glanced over Fallon's bright head at the small, square room. His princess did not seem used to hardships and he had quickly accepted Madam Cherry's offer of food and shelter.

The small room offered a place of rest, a momentary sanctuary from his feelings of confusion. He looked at the rough limestone walls and the faded blue drapes softening the old windows. A change of black, nondescript, military uniforms rested on the bed for each of them. Hidden underneath the clothes lay two pulsar guns and one small dagger.

"The meat stew tasted well enough," Fallon offered.

Declan's gaze slid to the empty yellow earthenware bowls atop the rickety table against the coarse white wall.

"Yes," he agreed. His fingers continued working on the buttons. Despite the shabby look of the room, Madam Cherry had assured them everything was sanitary.

"Do you trust Madam Cherry?"

Declan did not hesitate. "I don't trust, Princess."

"Anyone?" She glanced over her shoulder at him.

Within those soft brown depths, he saw sanctuary.

"You can trust me, Declan," she said very seriously,

her voice gentle and vulnerable.

For a moment he searched her face, then looked away. "Those brown eyes of yours see right through a man," he murmured with a troubled tone.

"Do they?"

He chuckled darkly. His lips tightened, marking his cynicism.

"I am loyal, honorable, and worthy of trust, Declan."

He detected affection in her voice, a need for him to believe her. "That's the problem, Princess. I am not." He tried to keep his voice casual.

"You are worthy and wish not to believe it. That is the real problem."

"Pampered Princess, don't you know danger when you see it?"

"I do not see danger."

"I do. Turn around and let me finish with these infernal buttons."

She turned around and kept the silence, but Declan could feel her mind working.

"I hope the water is hot."

He smiled at his princess's change of subject. "It's an air shower, Princess. They tend to be body temperature or cool."

"Air shower?" She glanced over her shoulder again. "How do you wash with air?"

"The same as you do with water. Turn around and

hold still."

She turned around and huffed with disappointment. "I shall pass on this air shower. I prefer water."

"You will not pass on the air shower."

She pivoted around, holding the loose gown to her breasts.

"Why will I not?" she demanded, obviously put out.

"Your scent," Declan said.

"My scent is offensive?" Brown eyes flashed at him in anger.

"No," he explained with a strange twist of his lips. "But a scent tracker could find you easily. Your rose-scented perfume is an easy marker."

"Oh. Well then, an air shower it shall be."

Declan's lips twitched. He could not help it.

"Is that a smile I detect?"

She got him. He broke out in a grin. Stepping aside, he bowed. "Your royal air shower awaits, Your Highness."

His princess laughed softly. "Thank you, good sir." As she moved forward, she tripped on the folds of her gown.

Declan reached out to steady her.

The controller slipped from where she had hidden it in her bodice. It landed on his foot, skidding sideways across the brown tile floor.

Click.

Declan flinched.

The blue light activated in the collar.

A black pool of primal lust sucked him in.

He fell back against the wall beside the sink.

A scorching heat violated his blood.

He struggled to think beyond the raging firestorm and choked on his own saliva.

Lust pounded in his veins with a compulsion to mate. Painful heaviness and desperate need settled between his legs. His lashes lowered, shutting out the world, shutting out all—except the sound and scent of the young woman.

Fallon checked her balance and turned back to Declan with a playful smile that soon faltered with uncertainty. His back was to the wall. His head was bowed, eyes closed, black lashes splayed against suddenly flushed cheeks. "Declan?" she called to him, clutching the gown to her breasts. "What's wrong?"

She moved closer and touched his wrist in concern. "Declan, are you all right?"

His lashes lifted.

Fallon stared up into sharp, dilated eyes glittering with lust. Her breath caught in her throat and her gaze moved instantly to his collar.

A blue light showed steady with no blinking. She bolted for the controller on the floor and tripped on her gown again. Hard hands caught and yanked her up. Her back slammed into an immovable chest.

"Easy," he breathed harshly in her ear.

"Oh, God," she voiced her fear aloud.

Large hands slid down her arms. Fingers clamped around her wrists and directed her arms across her breasts. With one hand, he locked both her wrists together, effectively dominating her. "You would not run from me, would you?"

"Declan. You are in a lust stage. I do not know which one."

He laughed, a hint of huskiness in his voice. "It does not matter." Warm lips brushed against her bare shoulder, sending shivers of fear and excitement into her blood. Sandwiched between these two emotions, she stood still.

"What do you need of me, Peaches?"

"To let me go," she whispered helpfully and looked over her shoulder at him.

He abruptly released her and Fallon stumbled from him in surprise, clutching at her gown.

Slowly, he backed her up against the wall and with a quick tug and shrug removed his shirt.

"Declan, what are you doing?"

"I am burning."

Pressing the gown to her breasts, Fallon gazed up at him in fear. "Please, Declan. You frighten me."

"Your body hungers for me. Let the gown drop." He tugged her hands free, stretched her arms above her head, and curled one hand around both her wrists, effectively pinning her.

Fallon stood quivering in her peach shift, the gown at her ankles and her arms pulled above her head. "Declan." Her voice shook. "I think you are in Lust Stage Two."

She felt him tense above her in momentary confusion, his eyes glittering.

"Yes," he murmured. "I want." His head lowered, his lips aggressively seeking hers.

Fallon twisted her head away. "Please, Declan. Release me, I must get the controller."

"No, no controller." His mouth fastened on hers hurtfully then gentled, seeking to tame her. Inside her core, pleasure bloomed at his command. Emotions surged wild and wanting, emotions she no longer understood, but felt. He was voracious in his need, calling to her passion, and she whimpered into his mouth, caught in the heat of his forcefulness. He released her hands.

Her arms dropped to his shoulders and encircled his neck. She held on to him, craving his fire, pressing closer, wanting his dominating kiss, his burning touch. She rubbed up against him, desperate to merge with his body, his soul, then . . .

The collar pressed into her forearm.

The collar.

Oh, God.

The collar!

Alarm spread through her. She tried pulling away, but he would have none of it. His hands cupped her head, tilting her face, his lips moving possessively over hers.

Fallon gripped his thick wrists, shifted, and brought her knee up hard into his groin. Immediately, she gained her release.

He bent over, cupped his manhood and stumbled back.

"I'm sorry," Fallon choked, dropping to her knees on the floor and snatching the controller.

In the next instant, she found herself caught underneath a hard muscled body. He pinned her to the floor, his breath harsh in her right ear.

"That hurt, Peaches."

With casual strength, he flipped her on her back, his hands buried in her hair.

Fallon stared up into features hardened with pain and lust. His mouth hovered a mere breath from her own.

"Why would you want to hurt me?" he demanded hoarsely.

Fallon could not answer, could not move, the controller momentarily forgotten in her hand. His eyes were almost completely black. Blood seeped out of his right ear and down his throat.

"I'd never hurt you," he rasped and gazed down at her body in stark ownership. "You are so beautiful. I need to be inside you." His right hand twisted in her shift. With a quick tug, he ripped it open down the center.

Fallon fought to cover herself. "Stop!"

"No. I want you." One hand caught her wrists again and held them above her head while the other shaped the swell of her breast. His gaze gleamed with warning.

Fallon intuitively changed tactics. Recognizing his need for dominance, she surrendered. The hardest thing she had ever had to do was to force her body to go limp under him. She clutched the controller in her hand, unable to reach any of the buttons, and waited.

"That's better." His hands slid down her arms, releasing her. Warm lips latched onto a nipple, eliciting a new fire to flame her body.

Fallon unwrapped the flimsy white cloth from around the controller. A knee forced her thighs apart. A finger slid into her, probing her core, testing the barrier.

"*Spéirbhean*," he murmured, his mouth working against her neck. Beautiful woman.

His finger probed deeper, causing a searing pain to cut through her.

"Please, stop." Fallon couldn't breathe. It hurt.

He lifted his head.

A dilated gaze met hers.

"Please?" he echoed, testing the fragile tissue of her virginity with his finger once again. "Hush, it will hurt only a moment, I promise."

He sat back to unfasten his pants.

Fallon hastily finished unwrapping the controller. With tears streaming down her cheeks, she pressed the first blue button on the controller to return him to Lust Stage One, and then again to free him from the collar's lust.

Click.

Click.

The light went dark in the collar and Fallon closed her eyes, sick and quivering down to her very core.

Declan stumbled back off her. His back hit a hard wall and he fell to his knees in a drowning heap of pain. Breathing with difficulty, he tried to regain his equilibrium. *Bloody hell*, his princess had kneed him hard. It felt like his balls were in his throat. He blinked back hot tears. Without the collar's influence, the pain was intense. He struggled through the nausea. His right hand splayed on a swaying floor. Pain rifled through his ear and blood splattered on his knuckles. He dropped his head down and waited for the world to right itself.

It was a long while before he could think clearly, before the pain in his ear dwindled . . . and then what had happened came back in a sickening rush.

The horrible lust.

The pain of want.

The luscious feel of her.

The sweet taste of her.

The fragrant scent of her.

Even now, the compulsion to mate flowed hotly in

his blood. It would take time for the collar to entirely release its beastly hold on him, though he doubted his manhood would ever work right again. He shuddered, a lessening ripple of pain and agony replaced by a slow, spreading dread.

From beneath lowered lids, he glanced at his unmoving princess.

"Princess." His chest tightened. "Did I hurt you?"

She was curled in a fetal position on the floor, the controller buried protectively against her breast.

"That monster is not me, Princess."

"I know," she whispered to the floor, then struggled to pull herself up. "I am sorry, I need to . . ." Grabbing her gown, she promptly threw up into the ripped folds. The vomit kept coming, followed by dry heaves, bruising and splintering her insides.

"Oh, God," she cried miserably. "Oh, God."

Declan crawled over to her and cradled her icy body in his lap. "Hush, Princess," he soothed, kissing her cheek. He suspected she felt fear and desire, all mixed up inside. "It's all right."

She raised her head and looked at him, eyes glazed with uncertainty.

"Is that all of it then?" Declan asked gently, keeping the weight of her on his thigh and away from his throbbing manhood.

She nodded, helplessly.

Wiping her mouth tenderly, he pushed the soiled gown aside.

"Princess." Declan's throat tightened. "I'm so sorry. I could not stop it. I need you to believe me."

Her eyes were a strange shade of brown. "I need a bath," she blurted. "I feel unclean."

"That's an understandable reaction."

She looked away.

"There is nothing for you to be ashamed of." He touched her cheek, intending to turn her face to him, but she flinched.

Declan froze. "You fear me. You fear my touch." The realization left a cold hurt inside and he dropped his hand away.

"Please release me," his princess said shakily.

"And then what? I cannot let you go."

"Please, I need to go."

"Go where?"

He held her gently on his lap, his hands resting on her slim waist.

"Breathe, Princess."

"I cannot seem to."

"Sure you can. In and out. Think of a stream of water flowing through woods. Always flowing, always moving. Breathe. That's it."

"Please release me."

"I know what you need," he said softly, wanting

to cuddle her so they could both heal from the collar's bruising.

"Please." She swayed away from him, fear in her eyes.

Declan swallowed hard. Despite weak legs, he lifted her in his arms, and carried her into the bath. She weighed next to nothing, a frightened princess that somehow had gotten under his skin.

"I'll not harm you," he said, an ache in his own chest. "Put the controller down on the sink."

She shook her head. Her right hand held the device in a death grip.

He rested his chin on the top of her head. "Princess, you cannot take it with you into the air shower."

She glanced down at herself, saw the vomit staining her shift, her skin, and cringed with disgust.

Declan pressed his chin to her chilled temple. "I've seen worse. Place the controller on the sink."

She looked at the black controller in her hand.

"It'll be all right," Declan coaxed. "Go ahead."

He saw her reluctance, but she leaned forward, placing the small controller very carefully on the sink. Her trust touched him deep inside.

"Good girl."

"Put me down. I wish to be alone."

"Do you know how to work an air shower?" he asked, feeling very protective of her.

"I do not know what an air shower is."

He barely heard her. "I will show you then."

"No."

"You said I could trust you, Princess." She refused to meet his gaze. "I ask the same in kind."

Without waiting for an answer, he turned around and opened the air shower's opaque door. "We both need to clean ourselves of the damn collar's lust." He stepped into purple shadows and into a sea of tiny, floating blue crystals. There were millions of them and she gasped with surprise, her hands locking around his neck in a death hold.

"What is this?" she cried out in alarm.

"Cleaning crystals," he barely managed beneath her stranglehold. The stall's door closed behind them with a firm click, locking them in an alien world of blue crystals, moving air, and soft whirring sounds.

Tiny blue diamonds began to attach to their skin.

"Get them off me!" She kicked out, causing him to lose balance.

Declan's back slammed against the shower wall. "Princess, stop." He pulled her tightly across his chest, careful to contain her flailing legs. "Listen to me." His lips pressed to her ear. "Listen to me," he whispered harshly. "The cleaning crystals will not harm you."

She stopped fighting, but her grip on his neck did not ease.

"Princess, loosen your hold, you're choking me."

She did, her initial panic giving way to curiosity.

"Thank you." He took a recovering breath. With his left shoulder, Declan pushed off the wall. He lowered her feet to the white tile floor, but could not straighten up.

"Princess," he said very patiently, "you need to let go of me."

They stood nose to nose. "Why?" she murmured.

"So I can straighten up, for one thing."

"Straighten?" she repeated. The tips of their noses touched.

"Yes, as in stand up straight."

"Oh."

Her arms slipped from his throat.

Declan stood up and took a half step back. She looked down, watching crystals attach to her soiled skin.

"They tickle, a little."

"Yes, turn around and face the other wall."

To his great surprise, she complied, presenting him with a flawless back.

"There is nothing to fear. Close your eyes."

She turned about, brown eyes shot daggers at him. "Are you daft?"

"Not at the moment." Declan chuckled low, glad to see her temper return. "The crystals remove dirt, but sometimes burn the eyes."

"Where is the waterfall sound coming from?"

"Just the sound of an air shower."

"It makes a peaceful sound."

"Yes." Declan closed his eyes and tilted his head back, letting the calming sound soothe him.

"Are you staying?"

"Yes." From beneath lowered lids, he watched her peruse his body. He knew what she saw.

"You are still aroused."

"Yes, it seems even a well-placed knee cannot dull my ardor." He chuckled in bitter resentment.

Her cheeks turned pink. "I am sorry about that."

"Don't be. The kick was deserved." He pushed his hands through his hair.

"I thought a man in an aroused state must mate, otherwise it's hurtful to him."

Declan took a deep breath. "That is a fallacy. It is, at most, uncomfortable. But regardless of a man's discomfort, if a woman says no, it is no."

"But, what happened before . . ."

"What happened before was the collar, Princess. I'd never take a woman against her will."

"I want to believe you."

"Good," he murmured. It was a first curative step.

"Do you intend to remove your pants?"

He bit back a grin at her swift change of subject. "Do you trust me to?" he inquired quietly.

"Can the crystals clean through clothes?"

"No."

Between them tiny crystals swirled. Guarded eyes watched him, a battle of curiosity and apprehension waging there.

"You can trust me, princess." He silently prayed she would.

"All right, Declan. I am just frightened."

"I know." Relief flooded through his blood.

Turning, she slipped out of her soiled shift and tossed it in the corner of the stall to his right.

He let out a long breath. Without her shift, she looked like a pale goddess surrounded by purple rain.

"I am undressed," she murmured with uncertainty.

"I noticed. Enjoy the air shower. You are safe."

The diamondlike crystals pressed coolly against their heated skin, nuzzling temple and hair in a soothing fashion.

Declan looked away from the tempting sight before him. He knelt, removing first one shoe then the next. The thick material of the shoes made them as heavy as ancient combat boots. He opened the shower door and tossed them outside.

"Are you unclothed?"

"Almost." His fingers made quick work of the waist laces. He almost sighed in relief when his painful erection sprang free. He'd give anything for an ice-cold water shower right now. He stepped out of the pants and tossed them in the corner over her peach shift.

"I understood pleasurers did not wear undergarments," she added nervously.

"I would not know. As to my own undergarments, I have none."

"Oh. You are unclothed then."

"Bare to the bone," he answered, keeping as far away from her as possible, which was complicated, given his aroused state.

Fallon swallowed. "Declan?"

"Yes."

"I do not blame you for what happened before. I know it was the collar's lust."

"Thank you." His eyes had already begun to tear, so Declan closed them. The dread inside his heart eased.

"Wash, Princess," he commanded softly. He rubbed the crystals into his own skin and hair, allowing the cool stillness to overtake the turbulence inside him. The crystals, though resembling hard diamonds, were composed of a cool, lighter-than-air gel. Purple light danced behind his eyelids, creating bizarre images of steamy geysers and shallow basins and adding to the detachment living inside him. He wanted to sink into the depths of the purple light with his princess and make love to her for all eternity. He wanted to remember and no longer feel like the observer of his own life. He kept his eyes closed and let the oblivion slowly take him.

Fallon glanced over her shoulder. She watched him

with growing attraction. Never had she seen a man in his full glory. Eyes closed, head thrown back, he presented her with an unprecedented invitation to observe him.

She stared openly. In the purple light of the air shower his pale golden skin looked smooth and flawless. Formed of muscular slopes and hard angles, his body seemed so very different from her own soft curves. As he washed his hair, muscles flexed in his arms and stomach. Fallon felt heat in her lower belly, but she continued her downward inspection, following the dark triangle of black chest hair, down the thin stream lining a rippling abdomen, down to the dark nest between his powerful legs. Her eyes burned from the crystals and tears trailed down her cheeks, but she could not look away from the male part of him, so hard and different.

"Are you washing, Princess?"

Fallon abruptly turned around, red staining her cheeks. "Yes." She quickly mimicked his movements. Closing her eyes, she took in great gulps of air. "Are you considered large?" The question came out of her mouth and she blushed with embarrassment. But having never seen a man's parts, it seemed a worthy question for an insatiably curious princess.

"Large?"

"Down there." She pointed over her shoulder.

"Down there?" His gaze cracked open and drifted down his own body to where she pointed. "Ah, *down there*," he said with quiet laughter. "I am almost twenty-two centimeters."

Fallon opened her eyes. She thought about it and faced him. "Is that size considered large?"

"So much for a man's fragile ego."

"What do you mean?"

"Pampered Princess." Declan shut his eyes. "I am considered well-endowed."

"A stallion, then?"

He choked and faced the tile wall behind him. "Where did you hear that?"

"I read it in one of my romance books."

"Ah. You like happy endings then?"

Fallon tilted her head, inspecting his rear half. The sword tattoo only enhanced the masculine angles of him. *What was it about this man?* she wondered distractedly. One moment, she was petrified of him, and in the next, she wanted to run her hands all over his body.

"Princess?"

"Mmmm." Her lashes lowered in observation.

Declan blew air out of his nostrils. "Turn around and finish washing."

She did not move.

"Now, Princess."

Fallon found herself smiling.

"Turn around and wash." He enunciated very clearly.

"If you wish." She presented her back to him. "Did

I offend you?"

"No," he ground out. "Just wash. Close your eyes and concentrate on the feel of the crystals against your skin."

"You can turn around now. My eyes are closed. I've seen everything there is to see."

"Yes, I know." He turned back around.

Fallon tried concentrating on the crystals, but it proved difficult. Her body felt alive. Beneath her hands, the gelatinous crystals felt warm and cool at the same time. Cleaning the dirt from her skin, they left behind a feeling of wellness. Soiled crystals disintegrated into tiny dust particles of light, only to be replaced by clearer diamonds.

"Declan?"

"Yes."

"I believe I may come to enjoy air showers."

"Keep your eyes closed. Feel the cleansing of the crystals. Listen to the whirring sounds of the shower, Princess, and let your mind and body calm."

From beneath lowered lids Declan watched her, unable to resist the temptation of her luminous, ivory form. She moved with a simple grace in the purple shadows, innocently flaunting luxurious curves. The cleaning crystals glittered in her red hair like blue diamonds.

Something substantial seared his heart, embedding itself in his soul. He felt lost in a maelstrom of emotions and realized suddenly that he cared greatly for his princess. His chest tightened. Burning tears spilled from black lashes.

"It feels glorious," she whispered in delight.

"Better than water?"

"Almost." She ran her fingers through her hair. "Please explain how it works."

"The crystals bond on a molecular level with grime, sweat, and blood and then disintegrate. You'll notice most are no longer attracted to you."

His princess opened her eyes and looked down at herself. Most crystals floated away from her skin. Only a few continued to attach, down near her private place.

She bent down to rub at the crystals.

"Spread your legs," Declan said.

She froze at the husky sound of his voice and glanced over her shoulder. He held her teary gaze.

"By spreading your legs, the crystals can clean there as well." He paused, a growing number of undeclared needs beating in his body. "I'm told," he softened his voice, "it is a pleasant sensation."

For a long moment she watched him then did as he suggested.

Declan lowered his eyes. "I'll await you outside." He turned and stepped quietly out of the air shower.

The door clicked closed behind him and he released a pent-up breath.

"Hello, my defiant one." Master Balan smiled in triumph. Veiny hands gripped the black controller.

"Balan," Declan said icily. He hoped the whirring sound of the air shower masked the presence of the princess.

His would-be master stood just inside the bathroom doorway. Two beefy guards in gray jumpsuits flanked him.

"Your patroness left you unmarked. Good. I do not like it when they score my property with their nails and teeth. It is so uncivilized. I'm glad I found you before my associate did. Off-world lords can be so violent in their vengeance." He caressed the controller. "We'll make good use of your obvious virility." He pointed to the soiled peach gown in the corner. "Where is the bitch-whore?"

Declan attacked. No thought, just instinct as old as time—*to protect his mate.*

His fist connected with Balan's face. There was a crunching of bone and a man's guttural scream. He jumped the two guards, forcing them back into the bedroom.

Fallon cracked open the stall door and peered out. With his back to her, Master Balan appeared to be holding the wall up beside the cracked mirror. Droplets of blood splattered the wall.

Grunts exploded in the bedroom beyond her eyesight.

Grabbing Declan's heavy shoe, she jumped out of the air shower and clobbered Balan over the head from behind.

Whack!

He grunted in pain and surprise, sliding down the wall and landing on his knees.

"Give me that controller." Fallon hit him again, really hard.

Whack!

The horrid man let out a yelp, dropped the controller, and fell flat on his face.

Fallon dropped the shoe and snatched the controller to her naked breast.

Cold fingers locked around her ankle.

She let out a surprised shriek, hopping on one foot. Declan was there, an explosion of speed and fury. Icy fingers released her ankle as Balan was dragged into the bedroom.

She stood beside the air shower naked, frozen by the violence of the last few seconds. Cold tremors racked her body. She held the controller protectively between her breasts, listening to the suddenly terrifying silence.

"Did he hurt you?"

Fallon looked up.

Declan stood in the doorway, unmindful of his nakedness. Rage and darkness stained his features.

Her gaze dropped to the floor. She shook her head. "I hit him with your shoe."

"Hard shoe," he said dryly.

Fallon's hands whitened on the controller. "Hard

head." She took a deep breath. "I never hurt anybody before."

"I know," he replied gently.

Fallon looked down at his perfect bare toes.

"There are no robes," she said in a voice sounding shrill to her own ears.

"Yes, no robes."

A long silence came and went between them.

Fallon did not look up. "Are they dead?" A quiet desperation crept into her voice.

"No, Princess. Look at me."

She raised her head.

He extended his hand. "Come. We must leave now."

She felt glued to the floor. Her lower lip began to tremble, adding to her turmoil and mortification.

"Princess?"

A whimper escaped her throat. Muscular arms locked around her, sinewy strength holding her, keeping her safe. She wanted to stay in his arms forever.

"You're not going to swoon on me, are you?" he asked against her temple.

"I am fine," she mumbled against warm skin. "I absolutely refuse to feel muddled like this."

His chin rested on top of her head. "Are you feeling better now?"

Fallon nodded.

"Even royal princesses can have a momentary upheaval."

"Momentary upheaval?" She looked up. For an agonizing moment, she thought he might kiss her. "You are being nice," she said, and realized that the moment became lost with her words.

The tenderness in his smile faded. "I'm not nice, Princess."

His arms tightened around her before releasing. "Come."

He took her hand and Fallon followed him into the bedroom.

Balan lay unmoving on the floor next to his two thugs. Their arms and legs were tied up behind them in strips of white bed sheets. They were unconscious and gagged. She looked at the upended table with broken legs pointing to the ceiling. One yellow earthenware bowl lay on the white bed, the other was shattered on the floor.

Declan tossed her clothes to her, keeping his eyes averted. "Get dressed."

Fallon caught the clothes. Placing them on the chair, she quickly began to dress, all the while watching Declan.

He grabbed the black pants off the bed and shoved his legs into them violently. He left the waist open because he couldn't seem to close it. Sitting on the bed, he pulled on dark socks, then shoved his feet into the same type of lightweight black combat boots she was laboring to lace up.

Standing, he quickly shrugged into the ribbed knit sweater, and with a painful grimace closed his pants. Next, he grabbed the uniform jacket and slipped it on. The small dagger went into the sheath in his boot, then he shoved the larger pulsar gun into his waistband.

Fallon pulled on her own thin sweater, tucked it in, closed her pants, and placed the controller in a thigh pocket. "Do I get a weapon?" she asked.

He looked at the second pulsar gun then back at her, skepticism clearly outlining his features. "Do you know how to use one?"

"Yes, my father instructed me."

He checked the safety and handed her the weapon. Fallon mimicked him and shoved the weapon into her waistband. "I have never worn military clothing." Reaching behind her, she made quick work of a braid, tying the end with a black ribbon. "Which clan's uniform is this?" she asked, shrugging into her own jacket.

The door to the room swung open.

"No markings, just battle issue, so you can move freely among the lower classes," Madam Cherry replied, coming into the room. "A surplus of military clothing makes it cheap and readily available to the common people. I heard the commotion downstairs in the bar." She glanced at the bound and unconscious men on the floor. "What happened here?"

"Unwanted visitors," Declan explained with a contemptuous tone.

"You both need to leave quickly." Madam Cherry motioned to the door. "There are men downstairs asking about the princess. One of my patrons must have informed Balan, hoping for the reward."

"So it seems," Declan replied, not thoroughly convinced.

The proprietress pulled a tiny folded paper from her waist belt and handed it to him. "I have the name of a collar master."

"What is a collar master?" Fallon asked curiously.

"A person who designs slave collars," Madam Cherry explained as Declan handed her the paper.

"Davi Li," Fallon read the funny sounding name aloud. She tucked the paper into her jacket's pocket. "We should go, Savage."

Taking her hand, Declan led her outside.

CHAPTER
EIGHT

Braemar Keep, Home of Clan Douglas
Planet Mars

DAWN ROSE ABOVE distant purple mountains and fissured cliff walls, spilling a thin spray of white mist down to Braemar Keep and the crater lake.

Dotting the planet's surface were atmosphere machines. They utilized water, light, heat, and other ingredients to alter a once hostile planet into a place of beauty and breathable atmosphere.

Lord Lachlan de Douglas stood in front of the floor-to-ceiling bow window of the lord's quarters, staring outward upon his changing planet. He wore blue cotton mark pants low on his hips, armguards on his forearms, and nothing else.

Behind him, the parlor room expanded in massive proportions. Chairs, couches, and tables were arranged for casual comfort. To the right, massive bookcases brimmed with books on military and clan history, star charts, and astrology. A wooden staircase led to a second landing where paintings depicted the rugged charm of

Ancient Earth's Scotland, Ireland, and England.

Lachlan's lips thinned in restless contemplation and he folded powerful arms across his chest. The deeply etched silver armguards hugging his forearms glinted in the light. Because of the war, he had become the Clan Douglas chieftain and lord commander at thirty years old. All his immediate blood kin were dead, except for Declan. "Bloody hell," he muttered.

A sleepy woof erupted to his right.

Lachlan glanced over his shoulder at the two white wee-gadhars, or poodleflys, as his wife named them. Kite and Thorn lay snuggled together on his blue couch, lifemated.

"Not you, Kite," he said with gruff tenderness. "Go back to sleep, pup." Kite's tiny tail thumped against the couch. Iridescent eyes closed. He placed his head gently beside Thorn, the skinniest poodlefly Lachlan had ever seen.

Declan would have to find another traveling companion, Lachlan mused. Thorn would be in the family way very soon. He turned back to the window. A deep unease settled in the pit of his stomach.

"Lachlan?"

Lachlan turned and smiled tenderly. His wife stood in the arched doorway of their bedroom.

"Here, Greeneyes." He held out his hand and she came to him, a graceful warrior wearing a simple lace nightdress.

He gathered her in his arms and kissed her forehead. "Morning, my love. How are the boys?"

"Sleeping."

He nodded. In the cool air of the room, she smelled of their sons' orange juice.

"What troubles you?" she whispered against his neck. "Is it the defense satellites?"

Lachlan rested his chin on the top of her silky head. "No, the trial deployment is on schedule. I think Declan is in trouble."

"How do you know?"

Lachlan held her close. "He has not checked in."

"Did Dr. William speak to you?"

"Yes, he was very insistent that I let him search for Declan."

"He feels responsible for you and Declan. I understand. Did you give him the *Stargazer*?"

"That ship isna verra friendly," Lachlan mimicked Dr. William's brogue.

Kimberly laughed softly. "His brogue only appears when he is agitated or excited. You and I both know Dr. William's piloting skills are, at best, erratic. That ship, thank heavens, can practically fly itself."

"The man is incorrigible." Lachlan's arms tightened around her. Kimberly was his sanctuary from the matrix.

"What else can we do?" Her lips touched his shoulder.

"We wait."

She pulled back to look up at him. Large green eyes met his. "I know you wish to look for Declan."

Lachlan shook his head. "I'm too visible right now. Negotiations with the High Council must come first."

"We wait then."

"Yes." Lachlan pulled her back into his embrace. "We wait. But not for goddamn long."

CHAPTER
NINE

A PALE NIGHT slipped down upon them. Heat engulfed the shadows, thickening the air with heavy humidity. They stood under white cliffs, eighty kilometers east of town.

Fallon looked around. "I do not like this." She wiped the sweat from her brow with the back of her sleeve. "The entrance of the cave looks menacing."

"Yeah, menacing works for me," Declan agreed.

A bizarre clutter of contorted rock forms in shades of gray and taupe framed the entrance of the underground community. They were many clicks from the Bloodgood bar, in a patch of land known as the Small Desert.

Fallon placed a hand on the warm rock face to steady herself. "I do not think this is the right cave."

"It's the right one, Princess." He knelt in front of her and adjusted the dagger in his boot's sheath.

"How do you know this?" she asked, leaning forward to watch him. His hair appeared blue-black in the retreating light.

"See the rock formation over there?" He pointed before straightening.

She looked up and squinted. "That tall gray rock shaped like a wedding cake?"

"Yes."

"But Madam Cherry said bridal slab." Fallon hadn't known what the woman meant at the time, but . . . "Ah, bridal slab."

"Exactly." He turned to her. "This is a new place, Princess, so stay close to me. I don't know what to expect."

She looked to the entrance. "It should be cooler inside."

"Yes," he granted. "Now follow me and be careful."

Fallon obediently followed him across a gray ledge of stone and black pebbles. White moths fluttered above a peculiarly shaped rock to their right. "This place feels ancient."

"Yes, it seems to be an old land."

They walked around several smaller rock formations. A black furry beetle scurried across their path and she froze.

"It's just a beetle, Princess."

"The size of my foot," she retorted, taken slightly aback.

He chuckled. "I've seen bigger."

"I have not." The cave opened into a subterranean world and Fallon peered in and frowned at the strange glowing. "Declan?" she said worriedly.

"It'll be all right. Follow me." A few steps into the cave and they were faced with a land bridge of narrow proportions, about fifteen meters in length. It was formed of natural arching black rocks and it spanned a deep chasm of blue sand and black mushrooms.

"I do not care much for heights," she said. The air in the cave felt dense to her, a suffocating layer upon her lungs.

"Then don't look down. Look at me." He took her hand and gently pulled her forward. "Remember, Princess, in this place I am Savage and you are Peaches. I said don't look down. Pay attention to me. As I wear the collar and a military uniform, we should get noticed quickly. If anyone should ask, I am your pleasurer for a debt owed. Offer them no further explanation. Do you understand?"

Fallon nodded.

"Keeping walking with me, Peaches. You are doing fine."

Calloused fingers held her hand, giving her a mantle of security.

"There seems to be a great distance from the bridge to the bottom," she offered.

"Yes, that is why they build bridges. Keep your gaze forward. We are near the end of it."

They crossed the long bridge and Fallon released a sigh of relief. She was not usually afraid of heights, but this deep abyss would challenge anyone, except Declan, of course. Ahead of them, strange breezes whispered in a tunnel of tawny lights, mounted high on the rocky walls.

"I have never been in an underground community," Fallon said, her heart full of both worry and anticipation.

"Underground dwellings have several advantages over surface dwellings."

"Such as?" She could not think of any.

"Safety and ecology for one," he answered.

"Well, I prefer sunshine."

His lips twitched at the corners. "So do I, Peaches. But this artificial light will have to suffice for now."

They continued walking toward the light and the murmur of life in the distance. They followed the path worn by endless passings, and after a couple hundred meters, turned right. Warm humid air graduated to coolness with a distinctive metallic scent. Silver doorways, arched entrances, and large burrows marked the sealed walls on either side of them.

"Are those the doors to underground homes?" Fallon asked, peering into the shadows.

"That would be my guess."

"I hear people." She tilted her head, cupping her ear. "Somewhere."

"Ahead of us."

She followed Declan into an open underground grotto filled with fifty or more people who were trading wares. Mechanical equipment, looking very much like old tunneling machines, lined the walls. White light spilled into the space from lamps embedded in the rock surface above.

"It feels like a dusty village." Fallon swiped at the coating of dust on her sleeve.

In front of her, Declan scanned the crowded area. "Don't bother swiping, Peaches." He glanced back at her over his shoulder. "It marks us as newcomers." His right hand rested lightly on his belt.

Fallon brought her hands to her sides and looked around. Dust coated everything and no one gave it a second thought. She brushed a stray strand of hair out of her eyes. "How shall we find him, this collar master?"

"He will find us."

"How do you know?"

He glanced over his shoulder at her again. "It is a small town, Peaches. And with most small towns, word travels quickly regarding newcomers, especially when one of them wears the uniform and collar."

Fallon scrutinized the crowd. Already, several merchants had glanced their way.

Declan held out his right hand to her. "Come, let us find a place to rest."

"Rest, here?" Joining him, Fallon slipped her hand into his once again. From beneath hooded lids, his silvery-blue eyes were wary, belying his soothing tone.

Danger stalked them.

"This is a town, Peaches. Surely they must have a hotel for weary travelers."

"You must mean a rock hole, Savage." They could not have a hotel here, could they?

He squeezed her hand in warning.

"The Rock Hole Hotel is on the other side of the square."

Both she and Declan turned to the blonde watching them. Adjusting her blue cloak, the woman pointed west. "That way."

"Rock Hole Hotel, how fitting," Declan murmured in Fallon's ear. He bowed his head to the woman. "Thank you, mistress."

The woman came closer and stopped before them. "You are clan warriors?" She indicated their unmarked clan uniforms.

"We seek only rest," Fallon reassured her. "We bring no harm."

The woman looked at Declan. "Since when does a clan warrior wear the collar?"

"Since now." Fallon stepped forward. "He belongs to me."

The woman's dark eyes turned to her for the first time.

"Clan warriors do not wear the collar."

"This one does," Fallon said firmly. "A debt owed."

"A debt owed?"

"Yes."

"Is he your private pleasurer?"

Fallon slowly nodded, wary of the next question. In her opinion, this cloaked woman showed too much interest in Declan.

"Will you share him?"

"Never."

The woman looked back to Declan. "He is most unusual."

The understatement of the millennium, Fallon thought. "He is unusual," she agreed, and pointed west. "You said the hotel is across the square?"

"You speak with a slight accent."

"So do you." Fallon pointed again. "The hotel?"

The woman nodded. "Yes. On the other side of the market."

"My thanks." Fallon turned away in a royal cut. "Come, Savage. I am weary."

Her pleasurer kept his face impassive and obediently followed her.

"Will the collar master find us now?" Fallon whispered over her shoulder, slightly annoyed.

"Yes, the stage is set. If the collar master does not know about our arrival, he will soon."

Her pleasurer followed her down the center of the market square like the proper slave he pretended to be. On either side of them, merchants offered their wares:

handcrafted wooden boxes, sugared fruit wreaths, peppermint-oil lamps, candle lanterns, gem trees, faith boxes, commlinks, and other items too numerous to name. The sugary scent of the candy filled the air. They entered the jewelry area of the market place. On these tables lay bracelets of opals and sterling links, garnets and charms, dune clan opal rings, golden translucent amber nuggets, personalized clan necklaces, and more.

Fallon saw none of it.

"Peaches, slow down."

"Why?" she called back.

He jogged to catch up with her and grabbed her arm. "Because you are creating a dust cloud in your wake and bringing unwanted attention."

Fallon dutifully slowed her pace and he released her.

"So you think me unusual?" he teased.

She was in no mood for it. "Yes," she replied sharply, jealousy prickling her. She was mad at him and mad at the woman for wanting him.

"Go left."

"Why?" She stopped and pointed. "West is this way."

"Look to your left. Do you see the black sign with white lettering over there?"

She did. Fallon glared at the sign, which said, Rock Hole Hotel. When she looked over her shoulder at him, his dark brow was arched with inquiry.

"Shall we?" he prompted.

She shoved hair out of her eyes and stomped under the black sign in a fit of dust and unreasonable anger. Several paces beyond the sign, ornate silver doors arched beneath a slab of jutting rock, shadowing the entryway to the hotel.

She stopped in front of the doors and he came up behind her. "Do not be angry, Peaches."

"I am not . . ." Fallon spun around and stopped, her chest tightening at the shadows reflected his face.

He looked down at her, a silent battle rising within him, graying the silver-blue of his eyes.

All her stupid jealousy was forgotten. "Are you all right?" she asked and touched his arm.

"Not really."

"What do you need? How can I help you?"

He shook his head in quick denial. "Need is a weakness," he replied in a voice full of cynicism. He turned away from her and faced a square teeming with strangers, a momentary respite from the surge of emotions between them. Then a sudden devil's laugh burst out of him. "What am I going to do with you?"

"You can let me in," Fallon replied quietly.

"Peaches, I cannot let *myself* in." He gave a mighty sigh. "Please go inside and get us a room."

"Are you coming in with me?"

"No, I must procure some method of payment for the room and the collar master."

Fallon watched him walk away, back to the merchant square.

Declan stayed away from the highly prized black opals and concentrated on the other stones on the merchants' long tables. The large quantities of rubies, garnets, and emeralds fit his needs. He moved on to another table, then another, choosing the brightest and clearest stones.

One hour later he returned to the hotel, his pockets lined with stolen bounty. Thick dust overtook the lobby of the hotel, offering a feeling of poor hygiene. Whether it was true or not, he did not know. With a slow stride, he followed the footprints on the dusty, red-tiled floor to the front desk. The clerk standing there had tattooed cheeks, bright eyes, and was of questionable gender.

"A young woman with red hair came in here a little while ago."

"Yes," the clerk confirmed. "Your woman is on the second floor, room two, on the right."

Declan nodded his thanks, turned, and climbed the narrow steps with infinite care. Pain lanced through his right ear and he braced his hand against a rough wall, giving himself the needed balance. Pausing at the top of the stairway, he took a deep breath and touched his ear.

A droplet of blood stained his fingers and the strange pain ended as soon as it had come. The deafness was worsening, but his other ear appeared to be compensating, at least for now. He knew he should be worried about . . . something, but strangely he did not seem to care. Forcing his legs to move, he walked down the dimly lit hallway to the second door on the right. Each step was measured and purposeful, for his balance left a lot to be desired. He felt as if pieces of himself were disintegrating with each passing day. Placing an open palm on the cool surface of the door, he pushed. The unlocked door swung open easily, revealing an agitated princess pacing in front of a small bed. His senses went on alert.

"The rooms do not have locks," she muttered with annoyance, folding slender arms across her breasts.

"I noticed." He closed the silver door and leaned back heavily upon it.

"The air shower does not work either."

"I'll look at it. They can be fickle."

She peered at him with a frown and he knew his weariness showed on his face.

"I cannot find the lights," she said in a tone no longer occupied with her own irritation.

He nodded. "I will find them, Peaches."

Her study of him was quite brief before she approached, her features lined with concern. "You look pale, Declan. Are you ill?"

"I am a little tired," he admitted and slowly scanned the small sleeping quarters. It was tolerable, at best. A black pitcher of purified water sat between three burning candles on the round table to his right. The bed itself was of a narrow frame. There was a dresser to the left with one chair propped up against the wall.

"Where did you go?" she prompted.

"Hold out your hand." Retrieving the stolen gems from his pocket, he dropped his glittering baubles into her open palm.

She looked down at them in awe. "Are these real?"

"Yes." He struggled to keep her in focus.

"You stole them?"

"For the record, Peaches, I skimmed from many, lightening the burden of our need."

"Stealing is not right."

"I'll not debate you. Hide the gems somewhere on your person." He pushed off from the door and walked over to contemplate the bed.

She joined him while stuffing the gems into her thigh pockets.

"The sheets look clean," he offered.

"It is a very small bed. When I inquired for a larger room, the hotel clerk said they are all like this."

"It will do."

"For what?" She looked up at him, her face a mixture of curiosity and wariness.

He grinned ruefully. "Rest, Peaches. That is all I am good for right now."

"I do not see how we both can fit on that narrow bed."

"We'll fit." He reached for her.

"What are you doing?"

"Time to rest. Stop squirming." He pulled her down beside him onto the soft bedsheets and spooned her. "You still have the weapon I gave you at the Bloodgood bar?"

"Yes."

"Check that the safety is set on your weapon and slide it under the pillow."

She pulled the weapon from out of her waistband and did as he requested before laying her head on the pillow.

Declan closed his eyes and buried his face in the sweet fragrance of her hair, seeking sanctuary.

"How will we know if anyone comes?" Fallon asked.

No answer.

"Savage?" She looked over her shoulder. He was out, his nose buried in her hair, and a strong arm resting around her waist possessively. She faced forward and closed her eyes. The single pillow they shared smelled musty. The bed felt hard and narrow and she would have preferred a bath before lying down on clean sheets. But life's little discomforts no longer affected her the way they once had. She was a woman in transition, no longer watching life, but participating in it. Sighing with contentment, Fallon snuggled closer, listening to Declan's rhythmic breathing. She smiled through her drowsiness and soon fell asleep in his arms.

CHAPTER
TEN

IT FELT LIKE dawn.

In an underground hotel without sunlight or moonlight, one could not easily tell the passing of time. But Fallon felt rested. In the darkness, she rose silently from the narrow bed so as not to disturb Declan and went over to the table to light a candle.

Turning around, she paused to study him. He slept in stillness, not a twitch or murmur of life to betray him.

It seemed unnatural to her, this deathlike sleep demanding total oblivion. She walked back to the bed. A small patch of dried blood caked the hair around his right ear.

Her gaze skimmed the length of him. He slept on his left side, one arm tucked under the pillow, the other outstretched, a knee extended in a relaxed slumberer's pose.

At his waist a pale strip of flesh caught her eye, a slope of rippled muscle, a thin stream of black hair arrowing beneath the waistband of his pants.

Fallon tilted her head and focused.

The top black button of his pants popped open.

Then the second.

Fallon clamped a hand over her eyes and shook her head, mortified! "Stop," she silently whispered and turned away, heading for the bathroom on unsteady legs. Once inside, she closed the bathroom's creaking door behind her and took a recovering breath.

"I cannot believe I just did that." She pushed off the door. On a narrow shelf above the red sink, two tiny light domes were lit. Fallon undressed and folded her pants carefully so the thigh pocket containing Declan's controller was on top. Walking over to the corner, she placed her clothes on the small black bench. With a final check on the controller, she turned to the shower's door and opened it.

The stall was a deep red color just like the sink.

"Please work this time." Leaning forward she jiggled the brown knobs gently. Jiggling was the scientific way to make things work, as any inept princess knew. Thousands of blue crystals materialized in the narrow stall, creating an artificial rain that did not fall, followed by a soft murmur in the confined space.

Grinning with delight, Fallon stepped into the shower stall and closed the door behind her with a firm click. Tilting her head back, she closed her eyes, sighed, and let the blue crystals cleanse her. Gelatinous crystals began to attach to her skin. It felt wonderful, but her mind would not calm. Declan was in trouble. Dark secrets lived in his soul, burdens too great to be shared. She wished he would let her in, let her help.

The sound of the bathroom door clicked.

Fallon opened her eyes. A fuzzy blue image stood outside the air shower. It was too short to be Declan.

"He did not satisfy you?" a woman's voice inquired.

Outrage coursed through her. "Who are you?"

The fuzzy image came closer and the shower door clicked open, revealing a woman in a hooded blue cloak. "It would have been better if you had ordered him to remove his clothes."

It was the blonde from the square; Fallon covered herself with her hands as best she could.

"His skin sliding against yours with heat and sweat enhances the mating."

For the first time in her life, Fallon was at a loss. "We slept only."

The woman held out a red robe. "Why would you do that?"

"He is tired." Fallon snatched the robe to her and stepped out of the red stall. She struggled into it while the small intruder moved around her and shut the shower.

"That must be the reason we cannot wake him. He is obviously an alpha male and they are always alert. I thought you wore him out with your sexual demands."

"My demands?" Fallon choked. "Who are you?

What are you doing here?"

"I am collar master Davi Li. I was led to believe you might be looking for my services. If I am mistaken, I will leave."

"No, please stay." Fallon could not hide her amazement. "You are the collar master?"

"I see you were expecting a man. Most do."

"But you are so young. You look like you are still in school."

Davi Li dropped her hood to her shoulders and Fallon saw a youthful face surrounded by a halo of hair more silver than yellow.

"If the pleasurer were mine, I would keep him collared. Males like him are uncommon, a perfection beyond price. And once they wear the collar for a long time it becomes almost an integral part of their nature to please. They no longer have any resolve of their own and perform always as the master or mistress wishes, even to their own injury, making them the perfect mating machines."

Fallon felt a strong urgency to have Declan's collar removed as soon as possible. "He is not mine," she said, and met the woman's black eyes.

"He is, if you own this." Davi Li held the controller up in the palm of her dwarflike right hand.

"Give it to me." Fallon made a grab for the controller.

The collar master stepped back, tucking the controller safely behind her. "I will. But there are conditions."

"What conditions?" Fallon moved to block the door. "You shall not leave with that controller."

"My conditions are for freeing the pleasurer."

The tension inside her eased. "You are talking about payment then?" Fallon asked cautiously.

"Yes."

"I have gems."

The woman hesitated before shaking her head. "I have many gems. I do not need more."

"You wish to barter?" Fallon inquired slowly. Many of her clansmen bartered for services, so it was possible these people would also.

"Yes, that is our way here."

"As you can see, I do not own much."

"You are a beautiful woman, Red Hair. I wish you to perform a service for me."

Fallon held out her right hand. "Give me the controller, then we talk."

The collar master walked over and placed the controller in her hand.

Fallon tucked the device into the front pocket of the robe while the shorter woman explained what services were required.

"Do we have an arrangement?"

Fallon swallowed, her stomach churning. "Yes, we have an arrangement."

"You will come to my home before I free him and

perform the service."

"Yes." Fallon thought only of how the collar would sap away Declan's extraordinary will and make him less than what he was. "What guarantee do you offer that you will fulfill your end of the bargain?"

"You have my word."

This community existed on a bartering system. Yet something about this woman with dwarflike hands unnerved her. "Your word is not acceptable."

"Then I will leave. Please step aside."

"Wait." Fallon gripped the doorknob tightly behind her back, her hands suddenly sweaty and cold.

"My time is precious, Red Hair. Do we have an agreement?"

"Yes, we have an agreement."

"Then let us open the door and try to wake your handsome pleasurer."

Fallon pulled the door open with a soft click. She followed the collar master into the small sleeping quarters and was startled to find two men standing on either side of the bed. In a hushed voice, she demanded, "Who are they?"

"They are my associates. Lights on," the collar master said, pitching her voice low.

Light flooded the room from circular recesses in the wall.

Although surprised by the influx of light, Fallon

peered at the bed, where Declan lay unconscious on his back. He did not move, did not respond, and she felt a slight trepidation in the pit of her stomach. They had stripped him of his jacket and sweater, exposing the upper half of his body. Fallon nibbled her bottom lip, wondering why he had not awakened.

Collar Master Davi Li clasped small hands in front of her, a woman getting ready to do business. "Red Hair, please wake your pleasurer."

With the collar master's authoritative words one of the men stepped aside, making way for her to move closer to the bed. Clutching the red robe under her chin, Fallon took two steps closer to the small bed. The slave collar gleamed ominously around his corded neck.

"Savage?"

He came off the bed in an explosion of speed and power, just like in the brothel. Except this time he attacked, punching the nearest man in the face.

"Savage, stop!" Fallon felt a surge of adrenaline, grabbed a sinewy forearm, and got dragged across the bed for her troubles. "Savage, listen to me. Listen to me!"

He stopped, his glance one of fire and fury.

"The collar master is here to help us," she blurted quickly.

"Collar master?" he echoed raggedly, seeking orientation in his surroundings. Fallon held on to his arm.

"We need to do a little work on your wakeup method,

Savage." A nervous laugh rose in her throat.

"My wakeup method is just fine," he muttered, eyeing the two men in the room.

Fallon let go of his arm and climbed off the bed to join him.

"He is even more elemental awake than asleep," the collar master said and Fallon heard admiration in the other woman's voice.

Yes, she thought with a rush of heat. *Definitely elemental.*

"But that bleeding ear must be attended to if he is to keep his value."

Declan's eyes met hers with a flicker of irritation.

She gave him a warning glance. "Savage, this is Collar Master Davi Li." With the sleeve of her oversized robe, she dabbed at the trickle of blood at his neck. "You remember, the woman from the merchant's square? She recommended the hotel to us."

Her pleasurer gently pushed her hand away. "I remember, mistress."

Fallon was startled by his use of the word *mistress*. It felt awkward coming from his lips.

"You gave my associate a bloody nose," Davi Li accused.

"I do not like strangers in my bedroom," Declan replied with bare civility and Fallon was grateful for small favors.

"We are not strangers in this place. You are the

strangers."

"Can we talk about the collar?" Fallon cut in. Beside her, Declan did a quick inventory of his person. The gun at his waist was missing, along with his sweater and jacket. He stood only in black military combat boots and pants, which were mysteriously open at the waist.

He gazed at her sideways as if he had inner knowledge of her decadent thoughts and Fallon felt heat creep into her cheeks. With a twist of his lips, he proceeded to secure his pants. "Where are my weapons?"

"Why would a pleasurer have weapons?" the collar master remarked, drawing both their attention. "Foolish mistress, I say."

Declan stepped forward in quick anger but Fallon grabbed his arm. "No, Savage."

He dropped his gaze to hers, nodded, then stepped back, offering a false submission.

"How gloriously primitive you are, Savage, and I do like the sword tattoo on your back. It is a shame your mistress wishes to free you." She gave a witch's soft cackle. "Ah, those amazing silvery-blue eyes of yours blaze at me with annoyance. I wonder if they flash hotly or lose focus when you spill your seed."

Declan snorted and glared at Fallon. "*This* is the collar master?"

"So she says."

Her pleasurer arched a scornful brow at her. "And

you believe her?"

Fallon studied the collar master, suddenly uncertain. Perhaps she wanted to believe too much. But for what reason would this woman seek them out, she wondered. Why would Davi Li lie?

"I am a collar master, Red Hair," Davi Li said matter-of-factly. "If you want that collar removed, I suggest you believe me."

Fallon nodded and the woman turned back to Declan.

"Now answer me, pleasurer. Do your eyes lose focus when you spill your seed?"

Declan glanced sharply at the woman, his exasperation plainly seen. "What does this have to do with . . ."

"Answer the question, pleasurer," the collar master inserted.

"Depends on the woman," he ground out.

"A noncommittal answer. For this young woman, then." Fallon saw the woman point at her. "Answer me, slave. Do your eyes lose focus when you take her?"

"None of your goddamn business," Declan snarled. "Can you remove the collar or not?"

"I can remove it," the collar master replied.

"Name your price, then."

"The collar master and I have already agreed upon a price, Savage," Fallon said. It was obvious Declan did not like her explanation, but he turned back to the collar master and said, "When and where?"

"My dwelling is four streets west of the hotel. It is in a development called Ledge Rock, number 128. We will leave you now." Davi Li gestured to her associates to precede her out the door. "Come in one standard hour. I must prepare."

Fallon met the collar master's black gaze and nodded. One hour. She would be there.

The door closed and they were alone again.

"It did not take long for her to find us. Word travels quicker than I expected."

"Yes," she replied, feeling numb.

"You're a bit pale, Peaches."

"Lack of food, I suspect."

"I'll find a way to remedy that soon. Come away from the door." He touched her shoulder and the warmth of his hand shot through her.

"Is there a chance she lied to us?" She held the robe closed at her waist, her body chilled.

"Yes."

"How will we know?"

He stood watching her, the thin trickle of blood dry and dark against his golden skin. "I don't know, at least not yet."

"Does your ear hurt?" she asked.

"Some. The pain comes and goes."

"Can you hear out of it?"

"The other compensates well enough for now. It is a nonissue."

Her gaze dropped to the collar. As long as he wore that horrible device, he was vulnerable. "We must get you to a doctor, Savage."

"Eventually." He went to the bed and tossed the pillow aside. "They took all the weapons, damn them." He blew air out of his lungs and glanced back at her. "Peaches, I need to use the facilities. Are you finished in there?"

"Yes."

The creaky door sounded as he closed it behind him. She was alone in the room for barely a breath before the grating door sounded again and heat closed in upon her back.

"Peaches?"

"Yes." She glanced down at the large palm holding twenty sparkling gems near her waist.

"What form of payment did you agree upon?"

She lifted her gaze to his and found him studying her. "Gems are plentiful and are not valued as highly as we thought."

"Wrong answer." He pocketed the gems then turned her in his arms.

Fallon flattened her palms upon his chest, her fingers delving into crisp hair. She found it impossible to look at him and stared at the dried blood smeared across his collarbone.

A finger lifted her chin. "Look at me."

She raised her eyes, a terrible ache taking hold of her.

"Peaches, what did you barter?"

"Myself."

His hold tightened, the strength reflecting a sudden wash of dangerous emotions.

"I bartered me . . . myself," she explained and tried not to think about what she had agreed to. "She thinks I am beautiful and wants me to perform a service for her in exchange for the freeing."

"I'll bet she does."

She lifted her chin determinedly. "She would not agree to the gems, Savage."

"I don't give a damn about the gems." He looked at her sharply. "Why did you agree to this? I don't understand you."

"It was the only payment she would accept to free you from the collar." She stared at him through a watery blur.

He searched her face, his features caught in deep turbulence. "Lord God, Peaches, you humble me."

Fallon saw it coming.

His kiss.

Large hands gently buried in her hair.

A shot of desire went through her bloodstream and his decadent mouth lowered to hers, all warmth and tender probing. It was unlike the savagery directed by the collar and so much more disturbing to her soul. The stubble of his beard scratched her chin.

He backed her against the door, his large body planted solidly in front of her. Fallon held on to his shoulders in desperation. He tasted of secrets and male hunger, a frightening and exciting combination to her feminine perception. She could feel him straining against her, his tongue skimming the roof of her mouth. Powerful muscles bunched, then stilled beneath her hands in a sudden withdrawal, and Fallon's hands locked in his hair, not understanding. Her tongue darted inside his mouth, mimicking his movements, tasting the dark essence of him, wanting to be part of him, wanting . . .

"Stop." He pulled his head back forcefully.

"Savage, I . . ."

"Don't." He rested his forehead against the door to the right of her temple.

Chill filled her, replacing all warmth and Fallon turned away, blinking back tears. "You don't want me."

A cynical laugh erupted from him. "Give me your hand."

She did. He guided her palm down his lower belly and against the hard shape of him. "Never doubt that I want you, Peaches." There was a husky tone to his voice and he pulled away from her, adding distance between them. "We will find another method of payment for the collar master."

Feeling troubled, Fallon watched him retrieve his

sweater and jacket from the floor where they had been carelessly tossed. "You do not know what Davi Li wants of me," she whispered.

With quick efficiency, he shrugged into his clothes. "I know exactly what she wants. Here take these gems."

She held out her hands. Glittering jewels, warmed by his body heat, tumbled into her palms. "Where are you going?" she asked with a frown.

"First, I'm going to find us something to eat then we'll go visit the collar master. Get dressed."

"Will you not need some of these gems for a method of payment?"

"I kept a couple of emeralds. You hold on to the rest."

She nodded. In an orderly daze, she dressed, tucked the controller and gems safely into her thigh pockets, and thought distantly that the military clothing provided an ease of motion that her other clothing did not.

"I will be back in a little while, Peaches. Will you be all right here while I am gone?"

"Yes."

He kissed her briefly on the cheek, then disappeared out the door, leaving her alone in the room.

Fallon took a deep breath to regain her composure. She wasn't sure what had just happened, but she knew what she had to do. When she was sure he had gone, she left their hotel room, hurried out into the lobby, and paused to speak to the clerk to get directions to the

Ledge Rock area. The aversion she felt about the service Davi Li had asked of her didn't matter. It was more important to free Declan of the collar. With that firmly in mind, she returned to the room and left him a note telling him where she had gone. She cringed a little when she thought of his fury upon reading it, but her mind was set.

Once out on the dusty road, she headed west, away from the market area. The dirt road veered right and she came to the multiple dwellings of Ledge Rock. Fallon took a moment to look around. Flat doors dotted the gray slopes of the walls on either side of her and she walked along the stone walkway, looking for number 128. Up ahead, she spotted a worn-down doorway marked with the number *128* in black lettering. Before she lost her nerve, she hurried to the door and was about to knock, when the door swung open on creaking hinges. "I have been waiting for you," Davi Li said.

Fallon nodded, her stomach tying in knots.

The collar master stepped back and motioned her to come in. "Your pleasurer will join us later?"

"Yes. I left him a note." Fallon stepped into a narrow, red-tiled hallway. The underground home felt terribly primitive, not at all what she expected from a collar master.

"This way." Davi Li gestured her forward.

"I wish to talk about this service you have requested

of me."

"We shall talk in a moment. Through here, if you will."

Fallon followed the woman to a door at the end of the long hallway, then into the shadows and the stink of sweat.

"Collar master?" Fallon called, suddenly wary. "I wish to discuss another method of payment."

"What payment would that be, my love?" prompted a familiar male voice.

Fallon spun around and the lights flashed on. "Thomas," she exclaimed, feeling a terrible sense of dread.

"In the flesh." Her betrothed bowed from the waist, a mockery of politeness in his red-coated finery. "Are you not surprised to see me?" he taunted in a menacing tone. Four clan guardsmen flanked him. The gray uniforms and ominous black visors sealed away their identities should they do any wrong.

"Thomas, please."

"Please what?" he shot back, his temper showing. "Did you think I could not find you? Did you think I would ever let you go?" His heavy cheeks flushed red, blond hair plastered to his sweaty forehead. "Should I forgive you for going to a brothel?"

Fallon could not answer.

"Well, my virtuous lady? Should I forgive you for running away with a pleasurer?"

"The pleasurer is in the hotel," Davi Li added from her right.

"He is not a pleasurer," Fallon responded fiercely.

"He wears the collar of a pleasurer," the woman countered.

"Enough, Lisa." Lord Henderson held up his hand. "You have been paid well for your services. Now answer me, did the pleasurer touch the princess?"

Fallon looked over at the other woman in bewilderment. "Lisa?"

"I was not able to discern that fact," Lisa answered. "But he wants her."

Lord Henderson's lips tightened in anger. "I asked a simple task of you, Lisa, and you have failed to find out what I needed. For that, do not expect the rest of your payment. You are worthless. Leave us."

The woman turned ashen, her shoulders curving inward as she moved to leave.

"Wait," Fallon said and came round to face the woman. "Lisa? Are you the collar master Davi Li?" She knew some people answered to more than one name. Her friend Garland did.

Henderson snickered. "Lisa?" He smiled in sick amusement. "She is but a whore I found on the streets outside the Bloodgood bar. I paid her to impersonate a collar master."

Fallon felt a wave of pity for Lisa and murmured, "I

am sorry."

"She is not worthy of your sympathy, Princess Fallon."

Fallon watched the woman leave before rounding on her betrothed in outrage. "Wealth cannot buy everything, Thomas."

"You are sadly mistaken, my dear." Beads of sweat rolled down his chubby cheeks. "I bought your father's acceptance, and with it, you. Now, where is the pleasurer?"

"I told you, he is not a pleasurer," she said hotly.

"Then what is he, Princess Fallon, that you shame your clan?"

"His name is Declan de Douglas and I do not shame my clan!"

"Do not raise your voice to me, you selfish bitch. You think I don't know how you despise my touch? Well, my dear, it matters little to me how you feel. You will bear my heirs, one after another. Feel my weight between your thighs every night of your life because I plan to use you well. I want royal blood flowing in my sons' veins. I want that extrasensory gift you never bothered to develop."

Fallon was appalled at his true nature. "How could my father ever have considered you for my husband?"

"Oh, I present myself well enough and there are profits to be had. Always profits in a new world. Always obligations. Now, where is the bastard?"

"Here." Her angry pleasurer barged into the room, punched Lord Henderson in the face, and knocked the fat lord back into the other men. There was a brief scuffle with Declan in the middle of it. He seemed so much quicker and stronger than the others, and then he was beside her, yanking her through the door.

"I should take you over my knee," he growled at her. "What the hell were you thinking, leaving the hotel without me?"

Regret heated her cheeks.

"Move, Princess. I bought us very little time."

He dragged her down the narrow hallway and they burst through the second door into the dusty open on the other side. He turned right, pulling her with him.

Fallon ran as fast as she could, trying to keep pace with him. His iron hold on her wrist tightened and he tugged her into an open doorway leading to a private backyard. They ran through a hanging sculpture of metallic junk clattering in the artificial breeze. Gray dust swirled around their ankles and Fallon coughed. "Is it time to steal a proper ship then?" she gagged.

"Stop talking and move." Declan jerked her around a water storage tank. "We have no weapons and they do. Here, through these air vents."

Fallon recoiled. "They are oily."

"I know." He released her, sank his fingers into the

black muck, which made her cringe, and jerked the mesh ring off the rim.

Click. Click.

She turned around and stared into the barrels of four pulsar weapons.

"Drop the vent, Savage," Lord Henderson spat, breathing heavily and holding his purpling cheek.

"Thomas, stop this insanity." Fallon stepped in front of Declan and found herself shoved into Lord Henderson's arms by one of his guardsmen.

"Don't you goddamn touch her," Declan snarled behind her.

"You don't give the orders here, Savage. I do." Her betrothed jerked her arms behind her and Fallon bit back a whimper.

Declan moved to defend her but Fallon shook her head. "I am not hurt."

"Drop the vent," one of Henderson's guardsmen warned.

Declan shot the guardsman a quick glance and tossed the vent aside.

Lord Henderson chuckled, confident in his superiority. "Good, little pleasurer. Now tell me, where is your controller?"

"Go play with yourself."

The butt of a gun slammed into Declan's jaw, briefly stunning him.

"Stop this, Thomas," Fallon commanded in her most royal tone, praying he would listen. But her betrothed was an arrogant and jealous man used to having his own way.

"Remember, Princess Fallon, what happens here is your doing. Stun him!"

"No!" she called out. A burst of red light momentarily blinded her. When she looked again, Declan lay on his back in a cloud of dust, unconscious.

"Why?" she cried, trying to wrestle herself free, tears streaming down her cheeks, but no one answered her.

CHAPTER
ELEVEN

Lord Henderson's ship, *Pict*

A SHIVER RACED through him and Declan awoke to foreign sounds and the smell of his own dried sweat. Grayness gave way to cool colors muted in shadow and gloom. He lay on a metal floor, freezing, grimy with dirt and oil. There was a sharp rending pain in his right shoulder and a dull twinge in his chest.

He shifted and his arm wrenched up behind him, and he looked up the blue wall. They had shackled his right wrist at an odd angle.

Getting his legs under him, Declan hauled himself up. It took all of his strength just to stand. Breathing hard, he straightened out his right arm and felt the blood flow back into the tingling limb. Regaining his equilibrium, he rubbed his bruised chest. The stun setting of the pulsar weapon would leave a spreading bruise.

"Good. The lazy savage finally awakens."

Declan glanced over his shoulder. The fat lord stood beyond the circle of amber light that marked his prison.

Instead of responding to the jeering, Declan gazed calmly at his surroundings, instincts taking over. He was in the cargo hold of a small ship. A damn freezer locker, if you asked him. Two white shuttles were berthed about six meters from him against the opposite wall.

His captor moved in front of the nearest shuttle. A heavy red coat bulged over the evidence of gluttony at his waist.

"Where am I?" Declan asked. Words frosted to mist in front of his face.

"We are in the cargo hold of my ship. I apologize for the cold accommodations, but I do not have holding cells for escaped pleasurers."

Declan ignored the taunt. Instead, his senses flared outward, registering the motion of the ship. They were under way, probably just leaving orbit.

His gaze slid left. Two orange shipping crates were firmly chained to the wall about ten paces to his right. The warning labels read: *Caution—Integrated Biomaterial—Caution*.

Declan didn't like the look of that. His gaze slid back to the fat lord. "Small ship," he muttered, pitching his voice to offend.

"The *Pict* is a top-of-the-line ambassador-class craft," the lord answered with indignation and Declan bit back a satisfied smile. He loved it when idiots took the bait.

"Accompaniment of twenty," Declan carefully calculated.

"Twenty, plus five of my personal guards and . . ." His captor nodded with sudden understanding, then chuckled. "Very good. Now you know the class of the ship and how many are onboard her."

"Plus one princess?"

"Yes."

Declan watched the opulent lord come forward, yet carefully stay outside the rim of his lit prison. "And you are?"

"I am surprised you do not remember me. I am Lord Tomaidh Henderson."

"Henderson." The name triggered a seething rage in his blood. His sixth sense clamored warnings he did not understand but responded to, deep down where there was nothing real but himself.

"Where is the princess?"

"Safe. That is all you need to know."

"If you were concerned for her safety, she would not be aboard a ship with crates bearing warnings of integrated biomaterial."

"Oligonucleotides," Lord Henderson explained with a cocky grin. He walked over to the crates. "Do you know what they are?" he prompted, so obviously confident in his superiority of the subject material.

"Small DNA strands," Declan answered, watching his captor warm to the subject.

"Ah, you know something of it. Oligos consist of

about twenty-five or thirty units of DNA, a tiny fraction of an entire genome. Scientists have used oligos as molecular tools to find genes in organisms."

"Or they can be used to manufacture infectious agents," Declan countered. It was amazing what his damaged memory chose to remember. It was like only part of his brain was functioning.

"Or that," the other man agreed with a dark grin. "But you need a DNA synthesizer and the High Council has banned them."

"Have they?" Declan challenged. "How inconvenient for you."

"Yes, but one must make do."

"Is that what you are doing? Making do?"

His captor chuckled in feigned amusement. "I do not manufacture viruses."

Declan scrutinized the biohazard containment crates. "Oligos are small enough to lack fingerprints to identify them."

"So?"

"After they are stitched into something dangerous, they cannot be traced." The fat lord looked suddenly uneasy and Declan knew he had come close to the truth.

"Are you suggesting I am a bioterrorist?"

"I'm not suggesting anything," Declan replied icily. "It's too damn obvious."

Lord Henderson's neck and cheeks flushed purple.

"I want to see the princess."

"No."

"Now, Henderson."

"Bastard. You do not give orders to me! I should let you freeze to death in here for what you did. Her maidenhead was promised to me by oath and bridal contract!"

Declan arched a brow at his ruddy adversary. Though he had not taken the princess's maidenhead, he made no attempt to deny it.

"Taking the princess's virginity was mine by right of promise, you blue-eyed bastard. I went to the brothel and saw the blood on the carpet. You cannot deny it."

Declan's lips curved into a taunting smile. "I deny nothing."

The man looked ready to pop a vein. "She will pay for this violation."

He considered ripping the shackle off the wall and shoving it down Henderson's throat. "Touch her and you die."

"You will be castrated for this dishonor."

His gaze narrowed to menacing slits of silver. "You can try."

Henderson shoved his hands into his pockets. "But it seems I must refrain from my intentions. Your half brother has other plans for you and I will not mix pleasure with business. But if there is anything left of you when he finishes, rest assured I will take great pleasure in removing your virility."

Half brother? he mused in revelation. *That means someone is looking for me.*

"Perhaps the cold will dampen your defiance."

Nothing would ever dampen his defiance. It was one of the few things remaining wholly to himself.

Lord Henderson leaned forward. "Where is the controller to your collar?"

Declan shrugged, feeling heartened. The princess had kept it out of Henderson's hands.

"Do you like the cold? I can make it colder."

"Do you?" He shot back. "Death can be a very cold companion."

"Do you threaten me?"

"Take it as you will."

"If you do not care to tell me the location of the controller, there are ways to make a stubborn princess talk."

"I will say this again, since you seem unable to comprehend it. Touch her and you are dead."

"Do not threaten me." Lord Henderson jerked at his jacket with a false dignity. "I'd never permanently hurt Princess Fallon. She is to be my bride. We will discuss the location of the controller at a later date when the cold has taken away some of that defiance." He turned away and called back over his shoulder. "Enjoy your arctic prison, Savage."

Declan watched his fat captor walk out of the cargo

hold. When the order came to secure the black cargo doors the lights switched off, putting him in total darkness. He closed his fingers around the shackle and let the rage consume him.

Fallon worried about Declan. She hoped he had recovered from the effects of the pulsar gun. She wished to see him, but she could not leave her betrothed's private quarters even if she knew where to look. The two guardsmen posted outside the gray doors wouldn't even speak to her.

Pushing a stray curl out of her eyes, she looked around. Lord Henderson's quarters were immaculate. He did not tolerate disorder in anything. She headed for the bedroom in the back. It was a square room with a crimson rug and a huge bed. Above the black headboard hung a lovely tapestry of two hawks in flight above a red lake. She had been there when a tradeswoman from her clan had presented the tapestry to Lord Henderson. He had accepted the gift with barely a nod of appreciation. That should have been her first clue to his self-indulgent nature.

Fallon reached behind the tapestry and opened the small safe. With quick efficiency, she retrieved the controller from her thigh pocket and placed it in the back of the safe so it would not be easily seen. She closed the safe door and straightened the tapestry. Trying to anticipate her portly betrothed's thoughts was like wading through muddy waters. But she felt almost certain that he would never think to look in his own safe for Declan's controller.

With a final look at the tapestry, she stepped back and bumped her hip on the bed. Fallon looked down at the pale pink gown spread atop red sheets. Except for the color, it looked like a bridal gown with lace panels and frills. At one time, not so long ago, she would have greatly admired the ancient design of the gown, but no longer. Her tastes had radically changed. She preferred the simple cloth of the unmarked military uniform she wore now.

Fallon returned to the front room to wait. She sat in a red chair beside a table and willed herself to wait patiently.

She did not have to wait long.

Whoosh.

The doors to her lavish prison slid open.

"Lord Henderson," Fallon greeted and stood.

"Princess Fallon." He frowned at her uniform. "Do you not like the pink gown?"

She followed him to the bedroom. "Where is Declan?"

He took off his red coat and stood beside the bed, fingering the lace bodice of the dress. "Do not worry, my love. Your pleasurer is unharmed. I have him shackled in the cargo hold."

"Thomas," Fallon spread her hands wide in entreaty, "I shall stay willingly with you if you release him."

"Willingly or not, you will stay. Besides, I have plans for the Douglas Savage."

He walked past her back to the front room.

"What plans?" she asked, following him. "Declan is not a part of this. Please let him go."

"Are you thirsty?" He opened an overhead compartment and pulled down two blue-tinted glasses with silver bottoms. "I have your favorite red wine, my love."

"Thomas. Please let him go. He has done nothing."

"Nothing?" He gripped the heavy glass in a display of anger. "The Douglas Savage has caused me hardship."

"Hardship?" she prompted with disbelief. "You do not know the meaning of the word."

"Neither do you," he snapped, all pleasantry gone. "Tell me, my love, what would you do to gain your pleasurer's release?"

Fallon took an involuntary step back.

"Come now, Princess Fallon," he sneered. "Here is your chance to free your pleasurer. And if you try to use your damn telekinesis on me, you'll pay dearly."

He stalked her, tossing the empty glass aside. It skidded across the black counter and landed silently on the gray floor to Fallon's right.

"I do not know how my father trusted you," Fallon

spat in anger, backing away from him.

"As I said before, I am profitable."

Unexpectedly, the ship lurched under them and her fat stalker fell against the table with an oath. Fire sirens screamed to life, the sound high-pitched and hurtful.

It was all the diversion she needed. Fallon covered her ears and focused with her psychic gift. Envisioning a missile, she commanded the glass on the floor to hit Lord Henderson in the head.

In a flash, it hit his temple, his eyes bulging with pain and outrage. "You bitch, I will make you pay for that." He came at her, his face contorted in fury, and took a hard swipe at her.

Fallon ducked and rolled to the floor.

The front door to the quarters whooshed open and she scrambled for it, colliding with a sturdy pair of black boots. Fear clawed at her belly. Never bothering to look up and identify the Henderson guardsman, she scurried around the table for protection.

"Easy, Peaches."

"You!" Lord Henderson bellowed.

Declan moved too fast for Fallon to follow. He was a blur, grabbing her betrothed around the neck and dragging him backward.

"Don't fight me, or I'll snap your neck," Declan warned low, blocking the fat lord's airways.

Her betrothed stopped struggling. His limbs went

lax and he collapsed to the floor right before Fallon's eyes. She peered over the tabletop. "Is he dead, Declan?"

"No. Should he be?"

Fallon shook her head. "No. I am unharmed."

"Good, otherwise I might have mistakenly snapped his neck."

She took in the steel-gray uniform fitting his tall frame. The black visor masking the top part of his face kept his identity hidden like the rest of the guardsmen of Clan Henderson. He had a rather offensive-looking pulsar gun strapped to a strong right thigh and she suspected he knew how to use it quite well.

Fallon stood up. "Is there a fire on board? Or have we been attacked?"

"I rigged the fire alarms. There is no fire. No attack. The ship is safe. Are you sure you are unhurt?"

"I am fine."

"All right." Leaning down, Declan grabbed Henderson's right wrist and dragged him to the bedroom. "What the bloody hell does this guy weigh?"

"A lot." She followed him into the bedroom and stood by the foot of the bed. "May I ask what you are doing?"

"Buying us some time." Scowling faintly at the pink dress, he pushed it aside and pulled the red sheet off the bed, then tore it into strips. "Is the controller safe?"

"Yes. I hid it in the place he was least likely to look."

Stepping around Declan, she opened the small safe be-hind the tapestry and retrieved the controller.

"Good thinking. I suggest you put it in your thigh pocket again." He handed her a strip of the red silk sheet to wrap the controller and used the other strips to tie Henderson's wrists and ankles. Then he took another piece and shoved it into Henderson's mouth.

Fallon placed the controller safely in her thigh pocket. "Thomas said he shackled you in the cargo hold. How did you escape?"

"Weak shackles, Peaches." He came around the bed and took her arm, guiding her back to the front room.

"I don't understand."

"I pulled. The shackle cracked. Can we talk about this later? I'm in a bit of a hurry." He steered her to the front door, pressed the button to open it, and peered out. The two guardsmen who had been posted outside were gone, leaving their escape route free from any kind of hindrance.

"How are we leaving?" she asked.

"Why, by stealing a shuttle, of course." He stepped out into the corridor and Fallon followed.

"Where is everyone?"

"Some should be in engineering trying to figure out what I did to alter the ship's course back to the Orrin moon. The rest are probably trying to find what tripped the fire alarms."

She gave him a slanted look sideways.

"Come." He held out his hand with a smug grin. "Time to go."

They ran through the ship's empty corridors and down two levels to the cargo hold. Declan pulled her through black doors and she got a face full of very cold air. To their right were two unconscious men. They were tied up with their hands behind their backs. One of them wore only his underwear.

"Are they . . ."

"Unconscious, yes. Wait here."

Grabbing the ankles of the men, he dragged them both out of the cargo hold and into the outside corridor. Returning, he locked the black door behind him.

"One more thing before we leave." He went over to the orange crates.

"Declan, what are you doing?"

"I need to set fire to these crates."

"Why?"

"They contain dangerous and illegal materials. I do not want them showing up unexpectedly where they should not."

Fallon could not see what he was doing, but suddenly flames shot out from one of the crates.

"Declan!"

He came back and grabbed her hand. "Time to go."

"What about the fire suppression systems? Should

they not turn on?" She pitched her voice high to be heard over the alarms.

"I set a five minute delay. Don't worry, the ship and crew will be all right."

He pulled her along with him to the first shuttle.

Fallon found his choice of ship extremely lacking. "These are planetary transport shuttles, Declan. You cannot use them for traveling in deep space. They are for short distance travel only."

"I know that. Get in." He pushed her toward the open hatch of the closest shuttle.

"Declan, I do not think this is a good choice." Fallon glanced at the fire with growing trepidation.

"Princess, please don't argue. Our choices are very limited here. Get in." Large hands snagged her by the waist and lifted. Fallon stumbled forward into the shuttle before catching her balance. He was right behind her. He grabbed the hatch holds, swung up into the small space, and landed on his feet. "Please move, Peaches." He gently pushed her aside and secured the hatch. "We are good. Take a seat."

"Where?"

He pointed to a bench seat attached to a bulkhead, then slid into the pilot seat and powered up the shuttle's engines. The shrill sound of the *Pict*'s fire alarms could still be heard in the enclosed space.

"Are you sure about the fire suppression systems?"

She raised her voice to be heard. "I do not want anyone to be hurt by the fire."

"I'm sure, Princess," he called over his shoulder. "The systems are on a delay. In the event there is a malfunction, they can always vent the cargo hold to space to put out the fire. That is why I put those men safely out in the corridor."

She nodded, feeling better with his explanation.

"Strap in, Princess."

Fallon slid back and strapped into the seat. All of this felt so unreal. She watched him pull back on the controls and the small shuttle began to lift from the deck.

"Damn thing handles like a crate."

Gripping the edge of her seat, she looked out the front window of the shuttle. Gray smoke filled the space. She could barely make out the red lights framing the closed cargo bay doors.

"Do you plan on ramming them?" she inquired, shivering a little from the cold temperature in the shuttle.

"Give me a minute."

In front of her, his hands played across the command console with ease. The red lights around the doors flashed green. The cargo bay doors opened, giving them access to freedom, and Declan guided the shuttle into the airlock. Moments later, they were in the vast blackness of space. Directly to port lay Orrin, the first moon of Planet Forest. From this close distance, Fallon saw the moon's furrowed landscape. It always reminded her of a green-skinned apple.

The shuttle moved away from the *Pict* just as the ambassador-class ship fired its engines and sped away from the moon.

"They are leaving without coming after us?"

"Not exactly."

"Not exactly?" She grew curious when he did not elaborate further. "Declan, what did you do?"

"I reprogrammed the ship's navigational computer. I seem to have a knack for this sort of thing."

He seemed to have a knack for a great many things, she thought, and looked past him to the rapidly approaching moon. Fallon rubbed her arms, fighting back a shudder. "Can we get a little heat in here, please?"

He reached to his left and warm air immediately whooshed out of the vents at their feet. "Better?" he asked.

"Yes, thank you." Outside the shuttle's window, she saw the fluorescent atmospheric swirls of blues and greens that always shone around the moon this time of year. "Once we land, then what?"

"We will steal a spaceworthy ship."

"And where might we find this ship?"

He tapped a screen on the console. "Down there. I did a quick scan and found some ship traffic."

"And how do you propose to land us, unannounced?"

"A little trick I know."

"Care to explain?" Fallon prompted when he said nothing more.

"We are going to follow in a big ship's draft so we are invisible to planetary scans. They should pick us up as hull shadow only. The trick is to avoid the engine back-wash so we don't burn."

"Have you ever done this before?"

He turned back to the console. "I think so."

"You think so?" She rocked back in her seat.

"Yes. Things are a little murky right now."

"I do not feel reassured, Declan."

"Neither am I, but I've picked out our target ship."

Fallon looked up, eyes widening. "That is a big freighter," she agreed.

"Yes. There are five freighters actually. We will snuggle up with the last one." He swooped in and snagged along the underbelly so fast she had to hold on for balance.

"Will the freighter's sensors pick us up?"

"We should look like hull shadow to them as well, and I'm hoping the crew is lax enough that they will not give the sensor reading a second thought."

Fallon nodded. She sat quietly as they entered the low rust-colored clouds of the moon. Declan flew only a breath away from the enormous freighter and although she trusted in his flying ability, she still felt anxious about the close proximity between the two ships. Never in her life had she done anything like this.

"Declan?"

"Don't worry. If they have not warned us off by now, we are nothing to them."

In the shuttle's window, the landing area was coming up fast. Fallon sat transfixed in her seat while Declan guided them expertly under the big white freighter then veered off at the last minute. Fallon breathed a sigh of relief, but her respite was short-lived. "Declan, something smells like it is burning in here." She looked around the interior of the shuttle, searching for signs of smoke.

"The engines are overheating. I had to push it to keep up with the freighter. I need to find a place to land this thing before the engines cut out."

"How about the clump of trees to the right?" She unstrapped from her seat, took a step forward, intent upon joining him, and caught her heel on the blue wires dangling from under the bench seat. Fallon fell forward and flung out her hands for balance. Unfortunately, she landed on an overheated vent. "Eeeek!" She let out a screech of pain and rolled right, but Declan was already lifting her.

With tears streaming down her face, she held her reddened palms to her chest protectively. "I am all right," she said shakily.

Declan took one look at her hands, glanced at the vent, and started cursing.

The shuttle's landing alarms went off and he planted her back on the bench seat. "Do not move," he ordered and bolted back to the pilot controls.

Fallon's hands hurt. She went in search of the medic kit and found one located in a compartment marked *Medical*.

"What are you doing now?" He called over his shoulder.

"I found the medical kit." Pulling the red container out carefully, she sat back down on the bench and opened it gingerly.

"How bad are your hands burned?"

"Not bad." She refused to admit to her own clumsiness. "I found some burn gel. It says it's for minor burns."

"The whole undercarriage is hot because the engines are overheated, which includes the blasted air vents."

"Understood. Have you found a place for us to land?"

"Yes," he grunted. "Behind the blasted trees. Will you please stay in your seat until I land this crate?"

"I will." Fallon smeared the green gel over her aching palms. The shuttle jarred a little under her as it landed, then came to an abrupt stop.

"Sorry about that." She heard him turning off ship systems, and then he was standing above her.

"Here, let me do that." He sat down on the bench. "You need a thicker gel covering for it to work." Gently, he applied another layer over her slightly singed flesh before wrapping her hands with a sterile bandage. The cooling relief was finally kicking in.

"Any better?" he prompted.

"Yes. The burning is less."

"The skin is red but I don't think you sustained any permanent damage. They might swell a little bit."

"As long as they do not blister, I will be happy."

"The gel should prevent any blistering, Princess." He put the gel back in the medic container and gave her a hard look of reprimand.

"Next time, I promise to be more careful."

CHAPTER
TWELVE

Orrin, First Moon of Planet Forest

DECLAN AND FALLON stood on the outside of a series of underground cave hangars. The horizon showed puffs of white with a wonderful backdrop of gold displays. They had landed on the outskirts of the hangers, behind a clump of trees, and walked to the underground docking area, which was a series of excavated caves.

Declan knew the princess's hands hurt her. Black circles under her eyes marked her fatigue, but she smiled brilliantly every time he looked in her direction. It confounded him. "How are you doing, Peaches?"

"All right," she replied and tucked her bandaged hands behind her.

He gauged her answer, which probably did not describe her hurt at all. "We need to get you to a doctor."

"I am all right, Savage."

"Unlikely," he muttered and turned back. Behind them, blue pillars of stalactites hung from soaring crystal ceilings. Light came from millions of tiny glowworms housed in sticky mucus tubes on the crystal and lime-stone walls. He quickly skimmed the docking area for a choice ship to steal. A gray working-class freighter stood in one of the berths, waiting for her cargo to be unloaded, but it was too large for his purpose.

He turned back to the landing strip. Beyond the ships, oceans of butter-hued grasses dominated the land-scape. Cool morning winds blew, creating rippling waves through the tall grasses and scenting the air with sweet-ness. The calm unnerved him for some reason.

In the distance, the sound of a faint engine could be heard. He stuffed the pulsar gun, another confiscation, in the waistband of his pants and searched the horizon for the incoming ship.

"You steal well."

He detected a note of royal disapproval. "Only when I have to, and this situation requires it."

As they watched, a white ship skipped and skidded to a halt across the well-lit landing strip. It came to rest several paces to the right of where they stood and a slow, satisfied smile curved his lips. This ship was exactly what he had in mind.

"Dear God," his princess gasped softly, gripping his arm much too tightly. "He almost landed the ship on its side."

"Yes. That is space dominance."

"More like space disturbance if you ask me."

"The ship, Princess. Not the pilot."

"The ship?"

"Gazer Class. First kill capability. Highly maneuverable. Highly sophisticated. Crew of five. Soon just two."

"You mean it owns the battlefield?"

He glanced at her with a frown. "Sort of."

"That is the one then."

"Yes, that's the one we steal." Placing his hand on her back, he guided her forward.

"How?" She looked back at him, her face pale and uncertain.

He walked around her. "Just follow my lead."

"Now? Do you not think this is rather impulsive? Perhaps we should wait until night falls?"

"Now, Princess." He didn't try to reassure her because he really didn't know what would happen. He just reacted to situations as they presented themselves.

"What about the pilot? I do not want you to hurt anyone."

He walked directly to the ship. "I'll deal with the pilot. You stay behind me." A sharp surge of adrenaline flowed in his blood, making him feel nearly invincible.

"You will not deal harshly with the pilot, Savage."

Declan laughed. "No."

"I mean it," she said firmly.

"I don't doubt it. Now stay behind me."

As they approached the front of the ship, the hatch swung slowly open.

Declan crept along the side, stopped just below the hatch, then crouched low in the ship's shadow. He heard grumbling inside then saw a large hand reach for the handholds.

"Move back into the ship," he commanded and leveled the pulsar gun at the pilot's stomach.

The pilot huffed in annoyance, not at all fearful. "I just landed this infernal ship and managed to release the cumbersome hatch. No one said anything about hostile encounters on this blasted moon."

The voice sounded familiar. "Move back into the ship."

"Bloody culprit, show yourself then."

From behind him, his princess tugged on his arm. "Not now," he said low.

"I willna be handing over the Clan Douglas *Stargazer* to you, whoever you are," the pilot said indignantly.

"Please do as he says," his princess pleaded, leaning around him. "We will not harm you, but we need the ship."

Declan pushed her back behind him just as the pilot leaned out of the hatch in a vain attempt to locate the owner of the lovely voice.

"'Tis not verra friendly of you, lassie, to steal a good man's ship."

Before he could grab her, she skirted around him and faced the pilot.

"Please, sir," she said with a note of anxiety in her voice. "We are in desperate need of your ship and do not want to harm you."

"Is that so, lassie?"

"Bloody hell," Declan growled. "Peaches, get back here."

"Bloody hell?" the pilot echoed with a strange note of interest. "I know that voice."

His princess turned to him and Declan wanted to strangle her. "Savage, the man will not harm us."

"Savage?" The pilot leaned further out of the ship trying to see him. "Would that be the Douglas Savage trying to steal my ship then?"

"Oh, hell." Declan grabbed the edge of the hatch with his free hand and swung up into the ship. In the next instant, he found himself facing an older man with white hair and a pair of highly intelligent brown eyes.

"Hello, laddie."

Laddie? "Are there others on this ship?" he demanded.

"Just myself. I have had a terrible time finding you."

Declan surveyed the pilot and felt a queer awareness. "Who the hell are you?"

"Who do you think I am?" The question was asked carefully like a doctor's inquiry and Declan felt a piece of memory flicker inside him.

"I don't know you."

"That is rather strange, as I know you." He frowned. "Why is your right ear bleeding?"

Declan ignored the tickle in his bad ear. "Answer me, who are you?"

The man puffed out his chest. "I am Dr. William de Douglas."

The name meant nothing to him and he could see the man's disappointment.

"Can you tell me where you got that nasty scar on your temple?"

"I don't remember."

"I see." The Douglas doctor rubbed his chin, the lines in his forehead deepening with thought. "It looks like you be needing an emulsion tank healing and some time in a sensory unit."

"Declan?" a soft voice called from below the hatch.

"In a minute, Peaches."

"I do not think we have a minute."

"What's wrong?" he called over his shoulder.

"There are five men near the entrance to the hangar and they are pointing their guns at us."

"Get in here." Backing up while keeping the older man in sight, Declan held his hand out to her just as a red stream of pulsar fire blinded him.

"Fallon, get down." He ducked but knew his warning

came too late.

His princess bounced off the edge of the hatch and landed below, out of his sight.

"Where are the goddamn ship shields?" he roared in fury. Hanging out of the hatch, he returned fire. "Fallon?"

No answer.

"Doctor, if you want this ship to remain in one piece, get the shields up now!" he bellowed over his shoulder. Without the ship shields to protect them, they were vulnerable.

Firing his gun with one hand, he jumped down and scrambled under the wing to his bleeding princess.

"Fallon! How badly are you hurt?"

She looked up at him with shadowed eyes and he dropped down beside her. "When I tell you to get into a ship, you move like there is a fire under your feet. Do you understand me?" he bellowed, fear for her clawing away at his insides.

She nodded.

Wrapping an arm around her waist, he dragged her to him. "Hang on."

A yellow film came over the ship as the shields activated. They were close enough to the hull to be protected. Above their heads, red beams of light crossed the air and bounced off the automated shields in a splintering spray of red sparks.

"Fallon, keep your eyes open. Where are you hit?"

"Under my arm," she mumbled into his shoulder.

A numb terror ran down Declan's spine. He jammed the pulsar gun into the waistband of his pants and carefully lifted her.

"Get her in here," the doctor called from above them.

Declan grabbed the edge of the hatch but her blood on his hand made the grip slippery.

"Here, let me help." The doctor's fingers locked around his wrist. With a powerful surge of strength, he swung them both up into the safety of the ship's interior.

"Lock the hatch," Declan commanded and swung her up in his arms.

The doctor slammed the hatch closed behind them and with two quick thrusts of the lever, locked it.

Declan carried her inside.

"Damn the bastards," the doctor muttered in anger. "Why are they firing? Who are they? Wretched bastards. Bring her back here, Declan."

Declan pressed his lips to Fallon's temple. "Hang on," he whispered.

"Here, let me pull out the sleeper. Now, put her down gently." The doctor grabbed the medic pack from the compartment.

"I am fine," his princess said weakly. "Savage is hurt."

"No, Peaches, that's your blood on me." In an effort to stem the flow of blood, Declan pressed his right hand over the wound under her left arm. She flinched back in pain.

"Easy." He brushed a few strands of hair from her pale cheek. A great anger began to beat in him for the men who had hurt her needlessly.

Her eyes fluttered closed. "I am cold."

"Fallon? Open your eyes for me. You need to stay awake, honey."

"My eyes are open."

He laughed shakily. "No, they are not. Open them for me. Come on."

Her eyes cracked open.

"Good girl."

"Hello, lassie," the doctor said gently and knelt beside Declan.

"*Dia duit.*"

"That means hello," Declan explained.

The doctor gave her a reassuring smile. "My name is Dr. William de Douglas and I am going to help you."

"Thank you." She began to shiver uncontrollably from shock.

"Let me see what I have here. Laddie, move your hand."

Declan's gaze locked with the doctor's unwavering brown eyes. A world of knowledge stared back at him. A black cylinder and examination table flashed in his mind. Feelings of pain and isolation flowed through him . . .

"Laddie?"

"Are you a medical doctor?"

"Among other things."

Declan removed his hand just as she whispered, "I cannot seem to c-c-catch my breath."

If he could, he would breathe for her. He felt powerless and desperate in a way he could not name.

"Everything will be fine." The doctor reached in to the medic kit for the slim ultrasonic cutter. He began to cut through the princess's scorched uniform to reveal a small slit in her flesh that was spewing blood.

Bile locked in the back of Declan's throat. He had to trust this man to help her, as he could not.

"How bad is it?" he asked.

The doctor gently probed the wound with knowledge. "Could be a collapsed lung."

The ship abruptly rocked under them.

"Laddie, I think it prudent you get us out of here."

He agreed and touched her cold cheek. "I must leave you for a little while, but you'll be all right. The doctor will take good care of you."

She nodded and his focus switched into defensive mode.

Suspecting their attackers had a pulsar cannon, he climbed to his feet. That was the only weapon possibly capable of penetrating the shields of this class ship. With a quick stride, he made his way to the control center. Once there, he slipped into the pilot seat with an odd familiarity and wiped his bloody hands on his thighs. Crimson stained his fingernails and fury consumed him, leaving only the red haze of vengeance and a lust to kill.

His fingers played about the black semicircular panel of controls in front of the seat. He had no idea who their attackers were. Some bounty hunters out for the reward, no doubt.

His body knew this ship, knew her capability. He did not question it. Engines powered up in a few clicks. Warm air pushed through the silver vents at his heels and along the walls.

The doctor had called this ship *Stargazer*. Under his hand, she rose from the landing strip and rolled to starboard. Like a predator poised over its intended prey, she hovered close. Gun ports slid open in a single whoosh. Declan's gaze moved to the tactical display near his right elbow. The screen showed the perimeter of the ship. The men on the ground continued to fire, stupidly unaware of the gazer class ship's destructive potential. Deep down in the dark reaches of his damaged mind, he knew what this ship could do. Bloodstained hands grasped the weapon controls. "Damn you for hurting her," he snarled and gave no quarter.

The *Stargazer* left the moon's atmosphere and sped into the cold blackness of space. Declan gazed out the window into the endless void. Planets and stars and distant galaxies glittered in the far darkness. He felt strange and all torn up inside.

When heavy footfalls sounded behind him, he glanced over his shoulder. "How is she?"

"Resting." Dr. William walked around the black railing of the pilot area. "I gave her a sedative, and cleaned and wrapped the minor burns on her hands." He shook his head. "She needs the healing of an emulsion tank for the internal injuries."

Declan turned to the small screen below his left wrist and punched in a set of search codes, trying to locate the nearest emulsion tank installation.

"I know where there be a fine emulsion healing tank," the doctor said.

"Where?"

"The *Claymore*. She be somewhere in this sector. I need to . . ."

Declan didn't let the older man finish, but grabbed his wrist. "Contact them."

"I will, if you unhand me. I canna reach the commlink this way."

Shame washed over him instantly and he jerked his hand away. With a muttered apology for his violent response, he stepped back from the control panel to make room for the doctor's larger frame.

"I see you have not mastered the matrix temper, yet."

Matrix?

"Learning patience is the key to overcoming the matrix influence and rage. It will come to you, laddie, give it time." The doctor peered down at the console and frowned. "Now, where is the blasted commlink again?"

"Here." Reaching around the doctor, Declan pressed a red button and activated the commlink.

Loud static screeched across the air.

"Ah, there it is then. *Claymore*, this is Dr. William de Douglas. Please respond. I have an emergency, over."

For a few moments, only the crackling noise of the open commlink filled the silence. "*Claymore*, please respond," the doctor called again.

The crackling cleared.

"This is the Clan Douglas warship *Claymore*," a male voice replied. "Please identify yourself, over."

When Dr. William didn't answer, Declan moved beside him and flattened his hand against the control panel. "What is wrong? Answer them."

"Give me a minute, laddie. I am trying to remember my private code. Do you remember yours?"

"No."

Dr. William frowned then pressed the red button to respond, "*Claymore*, this is W20 William, over."

"Doctor William de Douglas," the voice replied.

"How may we be of assistance?"

"I have an injured lassie and need *Claymore*'s emulsion tank immediately. Meet me here." The doctor sent the coordinates.

"Delay that order." Declan slid into the pilot seat, did a quick calculation, altered the coordinates, and resent them. When the doctor started to protest, he quickly explained. "It is faster if I go to them rather than have them just come to me."

"Coordinates received. Dr. William?" the voice over the commlink paused. "Who is with you?"

Declan stared at the commlink. What name should he give? But the Douglas doctor answered for him. "Declan de Douglas."

"You've found him then."

"More like he found me."

Declan's gaze dropped to the floor. He had a name, but it did not feel familiar.

"Doctor, we will inform Lord Lachlan so he may call off the search."

"Good," the doctor agreed.

The voice on the commlink reconfirmed the coordinates then said, "Our ETA is two hours."

"Make it one." Declan ordered.

The doctor nodded his approval. "The sooner the better."

"*Stargazer* out." Declan set the autopilot to bring the

ship to top speed. "Is the princess secure in the back?"

"Tucked tight in the sleeper."

"Then you'd better hold on to the railing, Doctor."

The ship lurched and banked toward a cluster of dimmer stars, her speed rapidly increasing.

As the ship leveled off, Declan stood and stared unseeingly at the control panel. "My name?"

"Declan de Douglas."

He lifted his gaze and looked out the ship's window. "You know me?"

"I do."

He turned and quietly regarded the older man. "I am of Clan Douglas?"

"Aye, by choice."

"By choice, not by lineage?"

"That, too."

His gaze narrowed. "Either you are being evasive or my mind is more damaged then I thought."

"What happened to you, laddie?"

"I have no answers. Just strange dreams."

The doctor folded his arms across his chest. "Tell me."

The black fissure in his mind wavered like something alive. "A rose-colored castle rising from a pool of blood. At the shore is a woman with fiery hair. After that, only a black void."

"A forced memory wipe or identity wash, be my way of thinking. The rose-colored castle should be the

MacKendrick Castle Keep." He nodded over his shoulder. "And back there, I'm assuming, the woman with red hair be the kidnapped MacKendrick princess."

"Why did you say forced?"

"Seeing the scar on your temple and you wearing a slave collar, I have to suspect something amiss. The Declan I know would never be collared willingly."

Declan looked away.

"I must also assume you to be the odd-eyed pleasurer in the wanted posting? There is mention of a sword tattoo as well. When did you get a tattoo?"

He raked a hand through his hair. "I do not remember."

"I see. Ah laddie, you have got yourself into a heap of trouble."

Declan sat back down. "Please go and stay with the princess, Doctor."

In less than a standard hour, the *Stargazer* reached the *Claymore*. Blue and pink star clouds were splattered like paint on a black canvas all around the big ship's brilliant white hull.

Sitting in the pilot seat, Declan leaned forward and pressed the commlink. "*Claymore*, this is *Stargazer*."

"We have you, *Stargazer*," the ship's female communications officer immediately responded. "Medic team awaits in landing bay four, over."

Declan searched his memory but he could not remember the bay's location. "Port side?" he asked.

"Aft, sir."

"Affirmative, *Stargazer* out."

Declan drove his ship with expert ease under the warship's sleek belly and entered the landing bay from the back. He followed the landing strip lights to the last runway as if he had done this all his life and docked the ship in the cylindrical berth.

"We're in," he called back and quickly powered down systems. The ship did a *click-click-whir* before settling into a diminishing hiss in her berth. He stood, then vaulted over the black railing surrounding the pilot area. When he arrived at the back of the ship the doctor was securing the sleeper.

The princess lay pale and unmoving. Declan knelt beside her and nodded to the doctor. Reaching out, he stroked her cheek. "We're here."

"Where is here?" she murmured, sounding greatly fatigued.

"The Clan Douglas warship *Claymore*."

Her eyes cracked open. "So fast?"

"Yes, now hold still." Declan helped the doctor to detach the restraints holding the sleeper firmly to the deck, then he took up a position on the other side. The older man grasped the sleeper's carry handles, nodded, and said, "Let's go."

They lifted her and carried her to hatch. "Doc, I need to open the hatch. Set her down here."

They eased the sleeper to the floor and Declan stepped over and released the hatch. As it swung open, bright lights spilled in from the berth. Two medic technicians were waiting expectantly.

"In here," the doctor called.

Two men immediately climbed into the ship, took the sleeper between them with calm efficiency, and carried his princess back out of the shuttle. Declan followed right behind the doctor, who proved to be an agile man despite his age.

"Hang on, lassie. I'm going to give you something more for the pain."

The princess nodded bravely.

"Let's go." The doctor waved and they started off at a brisk pace, with the technicians carrying the sleeper between them.

"Declan, please do not leave me," she rasped.

Gently, he grasped her bandaged hand. "I'm right here."

"Declan, I want you to keep her awake," Dr. William called over his shoulder, then turned to one of his technicians. "Give me a blasted commlink."

The man handed the doctor the small circular

device. Immediately, he began giving orders into it.

Declan heard the doctor say something about "traumatic pneumothorax" and "air entering the pleural space," and "not enough pressure." There was also a mention of "depersonalization disorder," "identity theft," and "possible psychiatric impact."

He understood "traumatic pneumothorax" to mean a collapsed lung due to injury. But the disorder and psychiatric impact, he guessed, had to do with him. Soon, they entered a white corridor filled with black uniforms and headed for the turbo lift.

When they entered the lift, he squeezed her hand. "How are you doing?"

"My chest feels heavy."

He could hear her struggling for breath and nodded that he understood. The lift began to ascend, taking them to Medical, but it was not fast enough to suit him. "Can you hang on a little longer?" he asked.

She nodded. "As long as I have to."

Doors slid open with a whoosh and they exited into a crisp white corridor. The doctor turned to his technicians. "Get her prepped for the emulsion tank. I will be right there. Declan with me."

Declan squeezed his princess's hand. "I'll be right back."

"Declan, I do not want to go into the tank."

"You have no choice. I'll be right there with you."

She searched his face, her eyes gone hollow.

"You need to let go of my hand. I'll be right back. I promise."

She released him and turned her face away.

Although her response gave him more cause for concern, Declan followed the doctor through a set of large white doors while the technicians disappeared with his princess down the corridor.

"Doctor, why did we come in here?"

"This is the main part of the science lab and I need to double check the emulsion tank's startup readings for your DNA."

"I'm not going into the tank. What are you talking about?"

The doctor looked up from his computer. "Do you remember this place?"

Declan glanced about the cavernous space. Numerous computer printouts plastered the walls and two black examination tables stood in the center. Behind the tables, an ominous black cylindrical machine spanned half the length of the room. "No," he replied.

"Verra well. The emulsion tank I ordered readied for the princess is back here."

The two-ton glass emulsion tank stood off to the side,

shrouded in lavender light, a ghostly specter from Fallon's childhood nightmares. In the tank's center, a cone of gelatinous bubbles would develop, rising endlessly to the surface, over and over, again and again, until finally sinking away, their jelled life spent in healing.

The old nightmare took hold of Fallon's memory, eroding her good sense.

In the small white room, she could taste the metallic sweetness of the healing fluid, feel the cold liquid chill her skin, see the gray darkness of approaching death.

"Princess Fallon," the blond technician leaned over her, "we must remove your clothes."

Fallon blinked, returning to the present, and pushed at the technician's hands. "Stop."

"Princess, nonorganic material impairs the tank's healing ability. We need to remove your clothes."

Her panic increased and she shoved at their hands.

"Don't touch her." Her savior burst through the doors, causing the technicians to back away quickly, their hands held high.

Declan came to her side. "Hey," he said simply.

Fallon grabbed the front of his jacket with her bandaged hands. "I do not want to go into the tank."

"Princess, calm down."

"I am calm," she wheezed in his face.

"What's wrong?"

"I do not like emulsion tanks." She stared up into

silvery-blue eyes, hoping he understood the desperation growing inside her, and let go of him.

He frowned faintly and glanced at the red and blue veins skirting the bottom of the tank. They crackled with an electrical current. He turned back to her and Fallon saw understanding light his eyes. "Are you afraid?"

She nodded, shamed to her core, and grabbed his jacket again. "I cannot go in there."

"No reason to be afraid," the doctor said with firm conviction from their right. "Declan, I want both of you in the tank. Strip down. I have programmed the tank for both of you. Now, laddie. Her left lung has collapsed. I've stabilized her but I want her in the tank immediately."

My lung? Fallon squeezed her eyes shut. It felt like one of those fat brillbears from Planet Glyndwr was sitting on her chest, restricting her breathing.

"Fallon?"

She looked up at Declan through a watery blur.

"You need to let go of me, honey." She had not realized she was holding on to him. He squeezed her hand and freed himself, as she was incapable of letting go. "Doc, do you need these technicians?" he asked.

Out of the corner of her vision, Fallon saw the doctor peek around the control panel at the two young men standing quietly nearby. "Edward, Daniel, wait for me outside."

The two technicians turned and left, leaving the three of them alone.

Fallon looked back at Declan. The drugs Dr. William had given her were finally taking effect. She felt light as air and curiously displaced as she watched Declan undress. First, went the jacket. Next, the ribbed knit sweater came flying off, revealing a muscular torso.

"Laddie, does the slave collar come off?" the doctor called from behind the control column.

"No." He removed the pulsar gun from his waist and laid it on the floor within easy reach.

"And about the tattoo . . . I know you said that you doona remember getting it. Perchance, do you remember if the tattoo is synthetic or organic flash ink?"

"I have no idea," he replied.

"Verra well."

"Declan, the controller is in my thigh pocket." Fallon struggled to reach for it.

"Lie still, I'll get it in a minute."

He unwove the bandages from her hands.

The doctor moved from behind the column of controls into her peripheral vision again. "I will have to make a few additional calculations to compensate for the collar, Declan. Emulsion technology and nonorganic material doona play well together, as you know. If the tattoo proves to be formed with nonorganic flash ink, you may lose it."

"Not a problem," Declan said.

It was a problem for her. Fallon liked the tattoo.

The doctor leaned over a small screen on the tank. "I have already loaded the program to compensate for your biomated matrix, Declan. What materials is that collar made of?"

She frowned. "What is biomated matrix?"

Declan straightened, the silver in his eyes suddenly shadowed. "I don't know what the damn thing is made of, Doc. Code it synthetic."

"That's not too helpful, laddie."

"I'm sure you'll figure something out."

"I find your confidence in me most inspiring."

"You will be going in the tank with me?" Fallon rasped and tried to rise up on her elbows.

"Yes. Lie down." He pushed her back down, then turned and pulled off one of her boots. Declan's reassuring presence and the dulling affect of the drugs in her system were doing wonders for her panic. "Are there system alerts for drowning?"

"The oxygen coil." He paused and looked up. "Is that what happened to you?"

"When I was four years old, I nearly drowned."

"That will not happen here, Princess."

He yanked off her second boot then opened the pocket flap containing the controller.

"Don't touch it," Fallon whispered urgently, coming to her elbow.

"I have no intention of touching the damn thing."

With a quick snatch, the hated device tumbled from her pants' thigh pocket and hit the floor in a muffled thump. Wrapped still in the piece of red silk sheet that Declan had given her, it looked small and harmless. With the tip of his boot, Declan coaxed the device over to the emulsion tank.

"Doc," he called.

Dr. William lifted his head and looked over.

"On the floor," Declan directed. "Be careful with it when you remove the cloth, and don't push any buttons."

"Ah, the collar's controller." The doctor carefully picked the controller up and removed the red silk. He tossed the silk in the corner and put the controller in the front pocket of his lab coat. "I will be keeping it safe for the princess, then." And once more he disappeared behind the tank's control column.

"Declan?" Fallon asked very seriously. "You trust that man to hold the controller? We hardly know him."

"I don't know why, but I feel strongly that we can trust him and so far my instincts have proven true."

"But the controller."

"It'll be all right. Besides, the less synthetic material in the tank the better."

With curious detachment, Fallon lay back and watched him finish undressing. Lavender light from the tank reflected the sinewy strength of him. Before long, he stood there completely unclothed, except for the collar. And what a fine body he had, she thought. In her drugged state, she voiced thoughts she would normally keep silent. "You remind me of a warrior god from one of my books."

He chuckled, shaking his head and coming to her. "You say the oddest things, Princess." He pulled the pants off her easily. Next, he began to cut her out of the top part of her uniform with a slim ultrasonic cutter. "I'll try and make this quick. Doc," he called over his shoulder, "do I carry her in?"

"Bring the table to the tank's entrance then lift her."

"Got it."

Fallon tried to swallow but her mouth had gone dry. The feeling of displacement increased. "Declan, I feel strange."

"Hang on." He pulled the transport table with him as he climbed the black ring platform surrounding the emulsion tank.

CHAPTER THIRTEEN

THEY WERE BOTH naked.

Fallon felt chilled and clung to Declan with faltering strength. It felt weird, this druglike numbness making her body heavy and making her mind slow. Burying her face against his neck, she tasted salt and potency, and sought the safety of him to ward off the fear. Her arms tightened around his neck, pressing into the stiff control collar.

"Princess, you're choking me again."

Fallon loosened her death grip with a soft apology, her fingers curled around the silken waves at his nape.

He shifted her in his arms. "There is nothing to fear here," he reassured her.

Yet, despite the drugs, she could not stop this new inner quaking.

"Princess, you need to ease up a little on the hair."

Fallon murmured another apology and released his hair.

They stood at the entrance of the tank, the transport

table behind them. "We are on the platform," Declan called over his shoulder.

"Doors opening," the doctor called back.

In front of them, the emulsion tank's glass doors slid sideways, filling the air with metallic sweetness.

"Be careful when entering," Dr. William warned. "The steps may be slippery."

Fallon closed her eyes and held on while Declan cautiously climbed down the five steps leading into the tank.

"How are you breathing?" Declan said gently against her temple.

"The doctor's drugs make it easier."

"Good. You can open your eyes, you know."

Reluctantly, she opened her eyes to a strange, tranquil environment. They were bathed in lavender light and surrounded by thick glass. Azure waves lapped softly at the edge of her vision, offering a calm pool of healing. She glanced down. The warm blue healing fluid, heavier than water, came to Declan's thighs and was quickly rising.

"Secure seals, Doctor," Declan called. "We're in the tank."

Behind them, the glass seals locked with a single click, leaving only the sounds of moving fluids and the soft whir of the tank.

"How are you doing, Princess?"

Fallon looked up. "All right."

"Do you have any objection if we move into the healing bubbles?"

Without her answering, he carried her to the center of the tank. Gelatinous bubbles rose in columns all around them. She knew they were weapons against infection. Electrical currents were pulsing in the curative fluid, forming a dynamic interface with the elements of hydropathy. She knew all this in her mind, but still could not shake the panic.

"Not cold?" Fallon tilted her head sideways to view the whole tank.

"I believe the tank is regulated to the occupants' warmest body temperature."

Fallon's gaze snagged on the red and blue veins wiggling like glowworms along the lower part of the tank.

"Tank looks different," she said, keeping a tight rein on her fear.

"Yes, it does. I'm going to lower your legs into the fluid now."

Fallon tightened her hold on his neck. She looked up at the blur of him through glassy, dilated eyes.

"Princess, I want you to stand in the healing bubbles while I retrieve the oxygen coils. Can you do that for me?"

She nodded.

Gently, he lowered her legs into the column of bubbles. She gripped his wrist for balance.

"You're doing well, Princess."

The blue fluid felt warm on her skin, rising to her waist.

"I need you to let go of me. Submerge your injured hands in the healing fluid."

Fallon glanced down at the gelatinous bubbles streaming vertically. They were like living creatures slithering up and down her body.

"Fallon," he spoke with infinite calm, "you need to release me and put your injured hands in the healing fluid. I'll be right by the back wall. I'm not going anywhere."

Fallon forced her fingers to uncurl. She let go of Declan and dropped her hands into the fluid. Almost immediately, they tingled with icy warmth.

She concentrated on breathing, knowing instinctively that she should remain tranquil against the threat of terror, and watched Declan back away.

"You're doing great," he said.

She wanted to do great. She wanted to be rid of this confounded fear crippling her.

He reached for the oxygen coils behind him. They would allow them to breathe while their bodies healed in the fluid. Fallon's gaze dropped to the coils. They reminded her of small black octopi with gripping tentacles.

Declan inspected the coils, turning them over in his hands and adjusting the straps. It seemed to take him forever.

He looked up just then and must have seen the question in her gaze.

"They're fine. I'm just refreshing my memory on how they work. Each mask contains a commlink so the tank's operator can tell us what is going on."

He tapped the tiny red light on both masks. "See? They are both active."

Fallon eyed the masks warily. Her heart rate increased dramatically. The red light on her father's mask had been lit too, yet it had not worked properly. The old childhood terror took hold and all she could think about was getting out of the tank.

The commlink clicked above her head.

"Declan," the doctor's voice crackled from the commlink above, "calm your princess."

She was *trying* to be calm.

An arm slid around her waist. "Easy." He pulled her back against his chest, sending waves through the blue fluid. Warm lips touched her temple but her gaze remained riveted on the oxygen coils in his other hand. "Do you fear me?" he asked.

Fallon shook her head. "Not you. The tank suffocates me, Declan."

"The oxygen coils will give us air," he said reasonably, but there was nothing reasonable about the situation, in her estimation. She shook her head.

"You need to stay calm," he insisted.

No, she had to get out and she strained against him, throwing her head back.

"Fallon, you're panicking." Gently, he nipped her ear and Fallon gasped in surprise.

Dropping the oxygen coils into the fluid, he cupped her jaw, holding her in place. The coils slid down her legs and landed at her feet.

"Dangerous, Princess," he spoke against her heated cheek. "When a man nibbles your ear, you do not pull away." With the tip of his tongue, he traced the tender shell of her ear.

Fallon gripped the forearm holding her in place.

"Calm down," he purred seductively against her throat. "For this to work, we both need to be peaceful. The doctor told me your right lung is fine and can support you. You are not in any danger. Nod, if you understand."

She nodded.

He licked her ear, nuzzling his way to her nape. "I love the way you taste, Princess."

All thoughts of pain and the tank slowly slipped away. She heard only his breathing and the sound and echo of the moving liquid. A floating sensation and numbness came into her limbs.

"I love the scent of you, like morning roses dripping with raindrops. Clean and innocent."

"I am not innocent," she rasped low.

"Yes, you are. I've had my hand inside you and felt the veil of your virginity."

His lips slid down her throat, leaving a trail of moisture to her shoulder.

"You are the most beautiful creature I've ever had the pleasure to lay eyes upon."

Fallon closed her eyes, lost in the blurring of drugs and sensations bombarding her system.

"How are you breathing?" he asked softly.

"A little difficult."

He slid his hands down her back to her hips, carefully avoiding her wound. "You need to listen to me. Concentrate on my voice. I am going to retrieve the oxygen coils lying at our feet." He pushed her hair aside and kissed her nape. "You are doing fine. Do you know the courage quote from the author Mary Anne Radmacher?"

"Courage doesn't always roar," she whispered.

"Yes, that is the one. 'Courage doesn't always roar. Sometimes courage is the little voice at the end of the day that says, "I will try again tomorrow."' Perhaps you can tap into that well of courage inside you and try again for me today."

Fallon opened her eyes. He came around to face her, but his features were indistinct, blurred from medicines and anxiety.

"Can you do that for me, Princess?"

She nodded that she would, and he dropped below

the surface of swirling bubbles.

But he did not release her.

A strong hand followed the curve of her body. His palm opened over her belly to keep her steady.

She felt him against her leg, one hand grasping the black oxygen coils at her feet. His face grazed the curve of her hip. He kissed the tender place above her auburn fleece.

He licked and kissed his way up her body.

His head emerged from the pale blue surface of the healing fluid, puffs of hot breath warming her breasts.

She grabbed his shoulders and stared into eyes mirroring a strange, tormented intensity. Blue teardrops glittered on shiny black lashes.

"*Álainn*," he murmured in the Old Irish. Beautiful.

His head dipped. Warm lips caressed her cheek. "You are so beautiful."

Fallon felt lost in the blending of her body's hurt and her heart's awakening desire. One strong arm came up; a hand splayed, supporting her back.

His mouth found her jawline.

He sucked on her chin.

"Close your eyes for me. Good, let's see if we can help your breathing a bit. No, don't pull away. Concentrate on me, Princess. Listen to my voice. Feel my touch, my breath, my lips."

A warm tongue stroked her ear. A single calloused hand cupped her cheek. He kissed the edges of her parted mouth. "Open wider for me," he commanded huskily.

Her lips parted, expecting his kiss.

Instead, the oxygen coil's hard mouthpiece slid into her mouth. Fallon pulled back in surprise.

Reality crashed in. She pulled at his thick wrist.

"Don't fight me." Soft lips pressed to her temple. "I'm here. I'll not leave you. Our oxygen coils are linked so I'll know if there is a problem and Dr. William will monitor us. Trust me."

Fallon eased her grip on him and nodded into the pitch darkness of the coil. She trusted him.

"That's it, my brave princess." He fastened the coil over her face and secured the tentacles behind her head. "Breathe for me. Nice and slow. The doctor is giving you a special breathing mixture."

Fallon bit down on the metal piece and dragged the mixture into her lungs. It definitely felt easier to breathe.

"You are doing well, lassie." The Douglas doctor's voice crackled over the coil's commlink behind her ear. "I have altered the oxygen mixture for you to . . ."

Declan lifted her.

Fallon lost track of the doctor's words.

Wet sensitive skin slid erotically against wet sensitive skin.

Declan's mouth nuzzled at her breasts, sending a thrill down to her toes. Hot lips latched onto her left nipple, starting a wild ache.

Fallon buried her fingers in his hair to keep from falling or to hold Declan in place—she wasn't sure which. Air seemed to enter her chest cavity, a continuing relief from the strain. A hand kneaded her right breast. Waves of aching pleasure began to consume her drugged body. Gently, he arched her back into the fluid.

She couldn't think beyond the touch and feel of him in her arms. He released her breast and Fallon felt him throw his head back, heard him inhale deeply, pulling air into his lungs. Then he latched on to her other breast and brought them both under the surface of the healing fluid.

She held on to his shoulders, arching against him in wanton pleasure, her legs sliding against his. He suckled her, heating her blood, his tongue lapping her nipple. Then suddenly he withdrew, reaching for his own oxygen coil. Fallon held on to him, feeling his movement, feeling a lessening of stiffness in her left side. It took only a moment to fasten the coil into place over his face. Tentacles clicked, locking behind his head.

She heard the new flush of bubbles as the coil's air reached his starved lungs.

"His oxygen coil has been activated," Dr. William's voice said in her ear, then silence followed. She knew the Douglas doctor now spoke directly to Declan.

She held on to Declan's shoulders. Erotic pleasure seeped away, replaced by the tank's healing warmth. Her lungs no longer hurt and she began to drift. Large hands caught at her waist and nestled her close, his body shielding hers—protective and powerful. Fallon gave in to the pull of a dreamless oblivion, her trusted clan trader ever close.

Twenty-four hours later, Declan lay sprawled on his back while the healing fluid slowly drained from the tank. Consciousness came gradually, leaving behind his distorted perception of self.

He remembered the hollowness of his existence.

He remembered the wants that were his destroyers and the guilt and shame that came in their wake.

His name was Declan de Douglas.

Douglas Savage.

Bastard and soldier.

Trade negotiator.

Defender of Clan Douglas.

The feeling of depersonalization disappeared.

He had gone to the space station to protect Lachlan and his family. Fought and killed kidnappers. Made a misjudgment and got bashed in the head for it. The kidnappers had sold him to Balan, the slaver.

Declan's hands clenched. Memories of pain and restraints that cut his flesh filled his mind. He pushed aside the really awful ones. He remembered Balan's ancient emulsion tank smelling of mold. The bastard stole his identity. The partial healing had left him disoriented and weak, too weak to fight the slave collar they'd slapped on him, too weak to fight Balan's demonstration of the pain modes. Later that night, they had shackled his wrists and brought him to his first patroness.

Princess Fallon MacKendrick.

Betrothed to Lord Tomaidh Henderson.

Enemy.

A small hand flexed on his shoulder, fingers curled in his hair.

Princess.

Was she part of Lord Henderson's failed attempt to kidnap the Douglas twins? He felt a terrible rent inside his soul at the thought of it and put his hand on her slender arm.

He could not progress beyond that thought.

The tank finally emptied, leaving him chilled and nauseous. Shivers racked his body as he adjusted from a liquid to an air environment. A light mist coated his sensitive skin.

The weight of a slender leg rested across his hips.

"Declan, lad, be you awake?" Dr. William's voice crackled near his ear.

Declan propped himself up on his elbow. He felt a small tug at his scalp. The princess's leg slid off him.

"Do you remember?" the doctor inquired, a calm

voice entering his darkness.

Declan's teeth clamped down on the coil's mouth-piece. He gave a curt nod to the man who had saved his life and made him other than human. He remembered.

"Good. You can remove the oxygen coil now," Dr. William directed. "Remember to move slowly. The effects of the healing fluid take time to wear off."

Declan knew it firsthand. With unsteady fingers, he tugged the coil free and tossed it behind him.

Throwing his head back, he inhaled deeply, filling his lungs. It felt good to breathe in regular air instead of the refinement of the oxygen coil. He licked his lips and tasted the metallic sweetness of the healing fluid. His eyes opened to a world of blue spray and unfocused shapes.

A smaller form, lying pliant beside him, shifted.

Fiery-red tresses fanned under his forearm.

"Dr. William?" he called, with lips that still felt a bit numb.

"Here." The doctor's voice piped in from the tank's overhead commlink.

"Is the princess unconscious?"

"Aye, she still sleeps."

Declan closed his eyes and focused his thoughts. "Warn Lachlan on a secure channel. I foiled a kidnapping plot to snatch the twins on Io's space station. There could be another. Clans MacKendrick and Henderson are suspect. Lord Tomaidh Henderson is behind it, but

I don't have proof. Advise caution."

"Give me a minute."

Declan opened his eyes and stared down at his very naked princess. He could hear the murmur of voices over the commlink as Dr. William relayed his message to Braemar Keep on planet Mars, the Clan Douglas stronghold. If the Clan Douglas First Family was not there, Braemar Keep would know where to find them.

When the doctor signaled that the message had been sent, Declan gently removed the black oxygen coil from his princess's face and let it slide to the side in a thick tangle of black tentacles. Her skin, no longer tinted blue, appeared pale and translucent. "Time to wake, Sleeping Beauty."

Her eyelids fluttered, then opened. "I feel nauseous," she blurted out, "and you look like a white blob."

Declan regarded her steadily, a smile playing about his lips. "The nausea, chill, and unsteadiness will pass."

"What about the blob?"

"It takes a few moments for your eyes to adjust. How do you feel otherwise? Your lungs? Can you breathe?"

She inhaled deeply and exhaled. "Yes."

He kept his gaze on her face. "Any pain?"

"No. Is it raining in here?"

"Healing spray."

"Feels good," she squinted at him, "like the warm rain back home."

"You like the rain, as I recall."

She blinked. "I like wild things."

Declan glanced down her creamy slenderness, desperately trying to ignore the familiar stirring deep in his belly. "Let me check you." Carefully, he inspected her side and found no mark of the wound under her left arm. Lifting her left hand, he explored tapered fingers.

"Wiggle your fingers for me."

She did, awkwardly.

He lifted her right hand. "And the right."

She wiggled those fingers, too.

"Dexterity returns shortly after awakening," Declan reassured and put her hand down. "Everything looks fine, Princess."

She laid a soft hand on his arm. "Your scar is gone, Declan."

Declan glanced down at his forearm. Gone were the marks of injury upon his body. Gone was the innocence the identity theft had given him.

"I remember," he said simply, not looking at her.

"What do you remember?"

"Who I am." He tried to keep his unease in check.

"Was it amnesia?"

A muscle flexed in his jaw. "You are perceptive, Princess. It was a bungled identity theft spilling over into other areas of my memory." Declan stared at the gentle swell of a white satiny belly.

"I am glad you remember."

"I am not."

She sat up and gently cupped his cheek in quiet possession.

Everything inside him went still. "Don't, Princess." He knew she didn't understand, could never understand, what he was, a matrix abomination. In the silence following, fingers slid into his hair. Before he knew it, she pulled him down. Tasting him as he had once tasted her.

Declan could not hide his surprise and groaned in need. His mouth crushed hers in a kiss of smoldering passions and frustrated desires. His tongue swept inside her mouth, tasting her and the metallic honeyed remnants of the healing fluid.

He held her, her soft body pressing into his with seductive promise. His kiss grew deep and languorous, tasting the very essence of her being.

He hungered for her.

Needed.

Wanted.

Nothing could hold him back from taking what she offered, what belonged to him. Her warmth replaced the matrix coldness and the violence living inside him, a blessing he could never have comprehended until this moment.

He wanted her under him, meeting his thrusts, accepting his seed in her womb.

His mate.

Desire seared his blood, taking him beyond redemption, and his mouth feasted on hers like that of a starving man.

The overhead commlink in the tank buzzed with noise, then . . . "Ahem," Dr. William said, and cleared his throat with discomfort.

Declan jumped back. "Saints almighty." His back hit the wall of the emulsion tank. His vision grayed and flickered about the edges. Sliding down the slick wall, he landed hard on the bottom of his spine. Legs bent, he buried his face in trembling hands. "Bloody hell."

"Declan?"

His lids cracked open. He watched her roll carefully to her hip and knew her world tilted as precariously as his own did.

"No sudden moves, Princess," he warned while his own world continued to waver before his eyes.

She crawled to him then eased down beside his leg.

Declan held still while she openly admired his length. He had never met anyone like her. Perhaps he had always been a little bitter, given the circumstances of his birth, and a little pessimistic about people, but her loyalty and trust both confounded and amazed him.

"You should stay on the other side of the tank, Princess."

"Why?"

A grunt of disbelief locked in his throat. "Are you that naive?"

"I am not naive," she retorted with a touch of temper.

It made him want to smile. The gentle patter of the tank's falling rain ended, replaced by a silvery-blue mist.

"Don't you understand? I almost . . ." He ran a hand through his hair. "What was I thinking?"

"What were you thinking?" she whispered.

He examined her from beneath lowered lids, a drenched faerie with lips the color of ripe peaches and dark eyes that stole away the coldness of his existence.

She tilted her head, unmindful of her nakedness, unaware of what she did to him.

"You need to stay away from me," Declan murmured.

"I cannot stay away," she said quietly, moving closer, her hand coming to rest on his shin. "I love you, Declan."

"No." He grimaced, pulling his leg away from her touch. "No. You don't know what I am."

"What are you?"

"Princess Fallon?" the doctor prompted overhead and the princess jumped. Covering her breasts, she peered over her shoulder, trying to see outside of the tank.

That's right, Peaches, we are not alone.

"Lassie, if you would please move to the doors. Your healing is complete."

"What about Declan?"

"He needs a little more time in the tank. Come now, lassie. The sooner you are out of there, the sooner I can finish with him."

Her gaze settled back on him, her features turning solemn. "I will wait for you outside, Declan."

He nodded but she did not move.

"May I see your back?"

His mind blanked. "My back?"

"Yes, I want to see if the sword remains."

He showed his back and caught a glimpse of her smile.

"It is there," she said, and he felt unexpectedly warmed by her delight.

"Yes," he murmured, "organic flash ink." The tattoo was meant to last through any emulsion healing that he might require in the future.

"What does it mean?"

"A sword symbolizes warrior honor and strength."

"Why did you get the tattoo?"

He gave his standard answer. "To honor those who lost their lives in the war." *Because of my father.*

"Is that your full reason?"

Damn her perception. "No."

"Lassie, if you please," the doctor's voice filtered over the commlink.

"You need to go." He gestured to where the doctor waited outside the tank.

"What is the rest of it, Declan?"

He blew air out of his lungs. He did not want to bare his soul, but the truth would not remain silent this time. "As I said, to pay tribute to those who have died in the war and . . . to remind me to be better than my father. To do this, I need the honor and strength of a warrior, if I am to make things right."

She nodded. "It is both burden and homage."

Yes, he thought and felt a sense of relief at sharing a thing that was buried so deep inside him.

"You are a good man, Declan."

He had no response for that. All he felt was guilt and remorse.

"I will await you outside."

He watched her crawl on wobbly knees over to the tank's sliding glass doors where the doctor waited. The older man assisted her to the black platform surrounding the tank and wrapped a robe around her. The doors whooshed closed behind them, leaving him alone in the tank. God help him. Declan dropped his head in his hands and managed a tight smile. His princess loved him.

The doctor took her to another area of the ship. Holding the white cup to her lips with shaky hands, Fallon drank the chamomile tea slowly, letting the liquid warm her chilled body. She sat in front of a massive desk littered with paper piles, the scent of bitter chocolates wafting in the artificial air.

Hardcover books were scattered about the floor, marks of a brilliant mind confounded by neatness. The range of topics included physics, regeneration, biology, DNA studies, behavioral patterns, and other scientific endeavors that she found extremely boring.

She looked up. The Douglas doctor was watching her from behind the desk. With his oversized white lab coat and spiky white hair standing on end, he looked disheveled, his appearance of little concern to him. She found his study of her very disconcerting.

"How do you feel?" he asked and popped a piece of dark chocolate into his mouth.

"Tired and a little unsteady."

"Those are the aftereffects of the healing fluid. It will pass. Are you hungry? I can send for some food. Or would you prefer a piece of chocolate?"

"No, thank you." Fallon could not think of food right now. She set the cup down on the corner of the massive desk and looked around.

Computer printouts lined the gray walls to her left.

"I have never seen so much paper," she remarked.

"Computer screens hurt my eyes."

Fallon shifted around and glanced right. Two black examination tables stood before a large cylindrical machine, which spanned half the length of the laboratory, if it was a laboratory.

"What is this place, Dr. William?"

"The Matrix Science Lab."

Fallon brought her attention back to the doctor. "Are you going to tell me what this has to do with Declan or are you simply going to stare at me?"

"Pardon me." The doctor straightened. "I needed to think a wee bit." He rested his forearms between the piles of papers. All amusement fled his face. "I have a question for you."

"Only one, Doctor? I have many."

"Princess Fallon MacKendrick, do you love Declan de Douglas?"

Fallon looked him squarely in the eye. "Beyond measure."

The doctor folded his arms across his chest and sat back. "I believe you do, lassie."

"Tell me what it is you need to say."

"Declan is different."

She huffed in agreement. "I know. A wild and reckless man, he refuses to trust anyone. Stubborn, arrogant, he follows his own code of conduct. Behind the insolent stare, I think, lives an idealist who wants to believe in honor and integrity and goodness, but something happened to him in his past. He never lets his guard down. Never lets me in."

"Lassie."

"Yes?" Fallon looked up.

"You doona know about the difference I speak of."

Her brows knitted together. "Oh."

"No one knows outside these walls except my lord and his lady wife."

"Tell me, what is this difference?"

"Do I have your word that what I say here remains only between us?"

"Yes, Dr. William," Fallon said slowly. "I give you my word as the MacKendrick Princess. What you tell me stays here."

"Good enough." The doctor nodded with an un-hurried thoughtfulness. "In war, there is always the inevitable casualty."

"Death is a constant companion of war," she added.

"Well said." Dr. William pulled out a hidden shelf from under his desk, revealing a gray keyboard. "Are you squeamish?" he asked without looking up.

"No."

"Good." His fingers played about the keyboard as if it were a musical instrument. "Activate holographic displays," he said loudly.

Fallon lifted her face to four holographic displays that appeared behind the doctor. Long mathematical equations began to roll down them in endless lines of scientific data. Too rapidly for her to read, she watched one formula overlay another, numbers upon numbers, symbols upon symbols. In the top left corner of the screen, a tiny file notation read "DLT Journal One: Matrix."

"Do you recognize any of these equations?" the doctor asked patiently.

She shook her head.

"These formulas are based on the journals of Doctor Damien Logan Townshend. They show some of his theories on quantum physics, chromosome counts, DNA and RNA replication, regeneration, and others. These are matrix robot formulas."

She recognized the name, Damien Logan Townshend, the matrix creator. "Dr. William, the High Council outlawed the matrix robot data years ago. It is illegal to study them."

"True enough." Straightening in his chair, Dr. William prepared to give the same speech he once gave to Lady Kimberly, Lachlan's wife. "Science is poorly understood."

"Will this be a long speech, Doctor?" Fallon interrupted. "Because I really would like to skip this part." She gestured to the holographic displays. "Please tell me what this has to do with Declan."

Dr. William struggled not to show his displeasure. "Details are important, lassie."

"I understand, but science and I never got along."

"All right, we shall simplify it. Can you briefly tell me what you know about the matrix robot theories?"

"What do the matrix robots have to do with Declan?"

"Indulge me, lassie. We must start from the same page."

Fallon took a deep breath. *A common start.* All right, she understood that. "The High Council forbade the use of the matrix robot theories since before the war of the clans. No robots exist today."

"Continue."

"The matrix robots were female, imprinted to a single master. They were killing machines composed of an alloy from the moon Io and were nearly invincible. That is all I know."

Dr. William nodded. "Like my lord's lady, you know just enough to get into trouble."

"I beg your pardon?" Fallon said indignantly. "You asked what I know."

He chuckled. "I did, didn't I?"

"Dr. William," she said, studying him with a sudden and terrible insight, "Are you one of those matrix scientists?"

He nodded and her stomach nearly dropped out.

"Does it make you feel uncomfortable?" he asked.

"Yes," she answered honestly. This man knew secrets beyond her comprehension.

"Doona feel uncomfortable. In your own words, can you tell me what is human reality?"

She frowned at the unexpected question. "Self-awareness, I should think."

"Good answer. In laymen's terms, the matrix process creates an alternate reality, an alternate self-awareness."

"What alternate reality?"

"Declan de Douglas died at the end of the war."

"Died?" Fallon's heart hurt. She clutched the robe under her chin. "Then who . . ."

"Physically, that is," the doctor quickly reassured. "Breathe, lassie."

"I do not understand."

"As long as you keep breathing, I'll continue with the explanation."

Fallon forced air in and out of her lungs.

"I believe you said you were not squeamish. Best to get this over with," he grumbled, fingers working over the keys of the keyboard. He lifted his head and spoke clearly, "Show Transference Two file."

A single holographic image formed.

Fallon stood up in horror.

Declan lay on a black examination table with a blood-splattered hole in his chest.

"This was before the transference," the doctor said.

Fallon covered her mouth at what she saw next, tears welling in her eyes. "Oh, God."

"This is after the matrix transference."

Shackled to a black examination table, another Declan, hearty, whole, and very naked, cursed and fought two technicians trying to inject a hyperneedle into him.

"As you can see, the matrix alloy in Declan's new chemical makeup adds an instinctive aggressive behavior to his responses. It is unfortunate, for he never had that kind of violence in him before. It is a behavioral trait he must always struggle to control now."

Fallon turned to the doctor, not quite understanding. "You said he died."

"He did in a manner of speaking. But the essence that is Declan did not. Sit down, lassie, before you fall down."

"Essence?" Fallon plopped down, her body trembling in shock.

"His soul."

"He is a matrix robot then?" she heard herself ask.

Dr. William shook his head tolerantly. "Nay. I used the metal alloy of the matrix and altered the process."

"Metal alloy?"

"The matrix metal alloy of the moon Io changes the cellular structure of living tissue. There are special crystals from the planet Glyndwr that I use in the transference and . . . needless to say, Declan is human but with a different genetic makeup."

"How different?"

"The theory of mind energy and transference is difficult to explain, so let me make it simple."

"Yes, please do. Is he human? Are we compatible?"

"Although certain properties of his body have changed, he is human and, aye, you are compatible."

"What is different?" Fallon glanced up at the holographic image again. The technicians had finally managed to inject him with something. It must have been a sedative because he had lost consciousness.

"He has improved strength, agility, and other things. Unfortunately, weaknesses were inadvertently introduced as well. Let me explain. The composition of the existing body, the location and speed of every molecule is recorded and combined with the matrix alloy, then completely reassembled down to the cell structure. Of course, I altered things a wee bit. His chest cavity was all but gone. And due to some incompatibility issues with his DNA structure, I borrowed a short sequence from his half brother, Lachlan."

"This is all very confusing. How can you borrow someone else's DNA?"

"It is a complicated explanation, lassie. Needless to say, Declan is unique."

Fallon covered her face with her hands and took in great gulps of air.

"Are you all right?"

"I am not sure. How long has he been like this?" She looked up.

Dr. William rubbed his chin in thought. "About eighteen standard months. He died on the last day of the war."

"I find all of this extremely complex."

"I suppose you would. I call it the Genetic Transference Process."

Her gaze lifted to the image. "Declan is human."

"In every sense of the word."

"What weaknesses?" she prompted, warily.

"Ah?"

She regarded the doctor through a watery blur. "You said weaknesses were inadvertently introduced."

"He has no tolerance for alcohol."

"I do not perceive that to be a problem." She swiped at her cheek. "What else?"

"Well, I doona know if you would describe this as a weakness, but as I mentioned before, the matrix alloy introduced an element of aggression and rage into his behavioral makeup. His first instinctual response will always be toward violence."

"I do not find it to be so."

Dr. William nodded. "Good. Good. He is learning to control it."

"There is something else concerning me."

"What is that?"

"His right ear bleeds and he collapses sometimes."

Dr. William's white brows furrowed together. "What do you mean?"

"I don't know, his ear just starts to bleed sometimes and perhaps collapse is the wrong word to use. But it almost seems like he runs out of energy and his body shuts down. He definitely collapsed in my arms at the brothel. But sleep appears to rejuvenate him."

Dr. William's cheeks reddened a little at the word *brothel*. "Sleep is probably a temporary solution," he murmured.

"What do you mean?" Fallon asked.

"I suspect the bleeding ear and *collapsing* are signs of a growing problem. Unless Declan comes to terms with his altered existence, his soul will reject his new body and he will die. Make no mistake of it."

"He will die?"

"Aye, lassie. He must accept what he is. He must want to live. And I want *you* to make him want to live. That is . . ." the doctor paused, "that is, if you still love him."

Fallon looked down at her hands. *Do I?*

CHAPTER FOURTEEN

DECLAN STAYED IN the emulsion tank another two standard hours while warm blue spray coated his skin, but it still wasn't enough to satisfy the good doctor.

They placed him in a goddamn sensory unit to stimulate his senses. For what purpose, he could not fathom. He hated the damn things. The white capsule was large enough for two, the faint hum providing more of an up-front irritation than a background sound. He supposed the doctor's decision to place him in the unit was a precautionary measure because he was not entirely human. He blew air out of his lungs to relieve some of the stress. He lay naked on his back in a warm womb of white gel, the slave collar a foreign thing around his neck. Gel globs slid down his body as he shifted, trying to get into a more comfortable position. It was hopeless. He smelled the burning of the electrical current, shut his eyes, and locked his jaw.

He hated . . .

. . . being alive.

Hated wanting *her*, and never having.

Because he was not good enough.

Because he was no longer human.

Fallon stood quietly outside the double gray doors marked *Sensory Unit 1A*, searching her feelings. *Do I love him?* she wondered, and the answer came immediately within her. *Yes, more than life itself.*

He had been given a second chance. *So very precious. How could he refuse it?*

Dr. William had said Declan carried demons inside him—guilt and blame for wrong choices made during the war. Choices based on his need for a father's love, a father so undeserving of his son.

She placed her hand on the smooth gray door and took a deep breath. What she did here, she did of her own free will. Declan's refusal to embrace his altered humanity put him at high risk. His soul could eventually reject his altered body and end his life.

Fallon could not imagine her world without him and came to a fateful decision. What better way to reinforce Declan's sense of self-worth than to make love?

Dr. William had choked on his coffee earlier this morning when she had suggested it. But how could she not? She loved Declan. She would do anything to help him. Yet even as she suggested it, she knew there were complications. Being the MacKendrick Princess meant responsibility to clan above self. Would Declan accept her and agree to be her consort? Would her people accept a Douglas lord as chieftain? Though they lived in the new worlds, the old ways and values of Ancient Earth were very much with them.

Fallon pushed through the gray doors and entered the blue antiseptic room of the sensory unit.

Cool air caressed her face. Several paces in front of her stood the horizontal white capsule called the sensory unit. Streaming blue and red veins pulsed in the capsule's gelatinous skin with low-level electrical currents.

She moved quietly to the corner. Dr. William stood at the front end of the capsule, adjusting the settings on the control panel.

Above their heads, two spotlights bathed the capsule in blue light.

For three standard hours, Declan had rested within the sensory unit capsule. It was time to release him.

Fallon watched a female technician place white towels with gold threads on a black table against the far wall. She knew those specialized towels helped minimize electrical current when wiping the gel from the skin.

She looked left, to the large blue doors. Beyond them, the unit showers waited, for when the towels were not enough.

Dr. William motioned the technician to leave before he turned to her. "Are you sure? There be no going back once we start."

Fallon nodded. "I am sure." She finished plaiting her hair into a thick braid down her left shoulder. She wore nothing under the red robe except her heart and her passion.

"Do you know how the sensory unit works?" the doctor asked.

"It heightens sensory inputs."

"Good enough."

Fallon's gaze slid to the capsule. It was larger than most. The gelatinous outside skin would be sticky to the touch.

"Doctor, can the sensory unit affect the slave collar he wears?"

The doctor looked up from the control panel with a thoughtful frown. "It should not. All indicators show the collar is inactive."

"When can you remove it from him?"

"Soon. The proper tones to deactivate it still elude me."

"What tones?" Fallon prompted, stepping forward.

"According to my research, a sequence of tones deactivates the failsafe feature and disengages the lock."

"I see." But she really did not.

The doctor continued to regard her with uncertainty.

"Do you still wish to go through with this?"

Fallon gave him a heart-wrenching smile. "I love him, Dr. William." It had been love at first sight for her, a heady infatuation flowing in her heart and veins, hot and constant.

"All right then." The doctor checked the settings of the capsule once more. "I have negated the eFlame effect on him, but his sensitivity will still be heightened. He may be a trifle difficult to handle in this state."

"Doctor, I believe Declan has always been a trifle difficult to handle."

Dr. William chuckled in agreement and came to her. He reached for her hands and said very seriously, "Lassie, if he rejects you, I ask you not to press him."

Fallon kept her smile in place, touched by his concern. "Do you think he will reject me?"

"Since the transference, Declan avoids all kinds of intimacy. He keeps his feelings locked away."

Fallon kissed the doctor's ruddy cheek. "That is the reason we are here, Doctor, to help him accept who he is, to help him feel again. Do not worry. We shall be all right."

A faint reluctance showed in his face and she decided to take the first step. "Shall we begin?"

He nodded, letting go of her hands. "No one will disturb you. I will be in the main lab, just down the hall. All you need to do is call out for me."

"All right."

"I will leave you then."

"That might be prudent, Doctor."

His cheeks turned a bright crimson. "All right. I am down the hall," he repeated.

"I understand. Down the hall." Fallon indicated the door.

The doctor gave a quick nod and left. But it was obvious he had a few misgivings, and now that she was alone, so did she.

Fallon chewed her bottom lip, her confidence slipping.

The low rumble of the big warship's engines filled her ears. She looked around. Not exactly a romantic place to lose one's virginity, she mused. Her gaze returned to the sensory unit. Blue and red veins throbbed in the capsule with a low murmur of life, his life.

"Dim lights to twenty percent," Fallon said, following Dr. William's suggestion. Shadows crossed the pale blue floor and formed behind the capsule. It was not candlelight, but it would have to do.

Holding the red robe closed, Fallon climbed the three steps to the black platform housing the white capsule. The black plastic flooring felt cool beneath her bare feet.

She knew a little bit about sensory units and their concentrated effect on the senses. According to Dr. William, Declan's threshold had been lowered. He would never be more susceptible to her charms than he was now.

"Computer, drain gel," she commanded in a steady tone.

"Gel draining," the capsule's computer responded and the veins along the unit altered into a different and throbbing rhythm, one that mirrored her own misgivings. Fallon waited, a hundred thoughts running through her head, none of them reassuring.

When the capsule had emptied, the computer's voice said, "Gel draining completed."

"Open capsule." Fallon loosened her belt and let the robe slide off her shoulders. It dropped to the floor behind her. Goosebumps formed over her naked flesh and she could feel the tingle of electricity in the air.

The top part of the capsule cracked down the center like the shell of an egg, sides sliding below a concave bottom. She peered in.

He was most profoundly naked.

Globs of whitish gel dotted the surface of his skin.

Fallon watched Declan grab the edge of the capsule with his right hand and pull to a sitting position. His right leg bent for balance and he used his left hand to support and push himself up. When he looked up, he froze . . .

She froze, too. Her heart went right into her throat. She wondered what he saw. Wondered what he thought when his face looked like that, and took a measured breath to calm her inner quaking.

He sat slowly back, the muscles in his body taut with tension. The fingers of his right hand dug into the capsule's gelatinous inner skin.

"Hello," she whispered.

His nostrils flared in return.

Keeping her courage close, Fallon climbed inside the capsule and placed her foot near his left ankle. Slipping a little on the surface, she regained her balance, if not gracefully, and knelt beside him. Her gaze moved down the muscular length of him, drawn by his locked stillness. His manhood was erect and her stomach did a decided flip-flop.

He smelled male, a delicious musky scent somehow enhanced by the white gel and the electrical charge of the sensory unit. She shifted into a more comfortable position and looked up. Wet hair spilled into his eyes. They appeared oddly alien to her, a silvery shade of blue moonlight and impenetrable intensity that betrayed no emotion. Clan MacKendrick needed a strong warrior chieftain for the future. An alliance with Clan Douglas would bring strength to her clan, just as Declan brought joy to her heart.

He was her choice and she would never regret what she was about to do.

Increased breathing echoed in the capsule and in her ears, a battle of needs and wants she knew he would never allow himself to have.

She eyed him guardedly, a novice when it came to this seduction.

Raising her hand, she gently cupped his roughened chin. Her thumb traced the full shape of his bottom lip.

He did not like it and pulled back, eyes smoldering.

Fallon took a deep breath and tentatively touched the muscular steel of his left arm. Slick gel wetness coated his golden skin.

His left hand clenched and he pulled his arm away from her touch. She tried not to let the rejection hurt, and shifted closer to him. If he was to accept her, she could not give up.

With her heart in her throat and her knee pressed into his thigh, she watched the rapid pulse beat at his neck.

"Declan?" she murmured and met his gaze. "Do you not want me?"

His left hand locked around her nape and she found herself dragged on top of him in a rough embrace. His mouth took hers, his tongue thrusting inside, exploring and tasting every crevice of her being.

Heat flashed in her blood and her heart soared. Her fingers dug into gel-covered shoulders. She had tasted his kisses before but nothing prepared her for this desperate need. He consumed her, a furious and turbulent hunger threatening and demanding her acquiescence. She kissed him back, breathless and fearful of this new experience, her body melting into his. Fallon held on to him, following where he led, desire raising the temperature in her blood.

It was madness.

Declan locked her to him.

Wanting her so much that it hurt to breathe.

The honeyed scent of her filled his lungs.

The touch of smooth skin beneath his hands.

The sweet taste of her passion in his mouth.

The sound of her heartbeat in his ears.

All his enhanced senses focused on her.

It maddened him. Too long denied, his body pulsed with lust and fever, ready to mate. He had to have her for his own.

He deepened the kiss, taking her air.

She started to protest his demands, small hands pushing against him.

He rolled, positioning her under him while he continued feasting on her mouth. He could not get enough of her. His hands curled in the damp silk at her temples, anchoring her head, arms braced to hold his weight above her. He pushed her white thighs apart with his knee. Hunger raged rampant through his system, making him aggressive.

She shoved hard at his chest and Declan pulled back from the brink, a moment of sanity in the torment.

"My love, please go slow."

It took him a moment to understand her plea. *Go slow. Slow down.* He clamped down on his primordial needs, on the violence inside him. Nodding, he slowly tasted the flesh of her neck.

Declan nipped at her collarbone, taking control of the frenzy inside him, slowing down and placing her needs above his own. He licked her skin, tasting salt, and gel, and a virgin's untried desire.

A measured touching.

An unhurried tasting.

Building a firestorm within her.

His princess threw back her head, lost in her body's sensual initiation.

He tasted his way down her body, leaving a trail of moisture and current.

His princess pulled his head down to her breasts. "Please," she said huskily.

He complied, suckling first one peach nipple then the other, giving each equal attention.

She moaned with impatience, her hands gripping his hair, fingers digging into his scalp.

The gel coated his skin.

It coated her skin.

Sensations became more acute, almost hurtful in

their intensity.

His princess grabbed his wrist and guided his hand down a silken belly, down to where she ached for him.

Wetness, heat, pleasure, all gathered under his hand.

She tossed her head, pressing down to relieve the desperate ache forming inside her womb. "Please, Declan."

He nipped her shoulder, wanting to see her eyes when they became one in the firestorm.

Lashes fluttered open. Dark eyes captured him in their depths . . .

Fallon stared into eyes of molten silver.

He rose above her, large and powerful, a male of enormous strength locked in passion. He gripped her, hands holding her hips, his manhood pressing into her, probing, teasing, testing her wetness. Fear raced through her, a moment of indecision then . . .

He thrust between her legs, taking her maidenhead and making his claim.

Fallon cried out in surprise, instinctively pulling away. But he would have none of it. Cupping her bottom, he held still while a great stretching pressure centered in her womb.

He drank of her whimper while slowly moving deeper, deliberate strokes asserting his ownership.

Between her thighs was a liquid burning, hurtful and yet not. Tears seeped from beneath her lashes and her womb convulsed with something other than discomfort.

Warm lips brushed hers in tender reassurance and a different cadence began between them. It wrung free a new and desperate ache. Heat built and swelled through her womb. Fingers raked his back in demands she did not know she made. She could not think beyond the raw intensity bringing her to some terrifying unknown brink, her body his collaborator to nature's ancient mating dance. And in that next desperate breath, when he entered her whole and full, pleasure burst, funneling through her.

Declan held on to his sanity by a thin thread.

Her little cries echoed in his ears, in his blood, in his soul. Every sense, every movement was attuned to her pleasure. She jolted under him, a virgin's first taste of ecstasy and in the next instant . . . the slave collar popped open, hitting the underside of his chin.

He froze, embedded deep within her and stared with disbelief at the hated device resting across her pale shoulder.

"I freed you," she whispered huskily.

It hurt to look upon her.

It hurt deep inside, where feelings were kept carefully chained.

"Fallon," he rasped her name, unable to say more. Gritting his teeth, he shuddered in torture, in misery, and in joy, spewing seed into a virgin's womb.

Then the merciful calm came.

Foamy waves, soft and caressing, quieted the chaos within, a soothing in muscle, in limb and in bone—a reclaiming.

Human.

Blissful and ignorant of the battle before.

He collapsed beside her, a trembling heap of male flesh. Shoving the open collar aside, he tucked his face into her shoulder. "How?"

"As we made love, I envisioned you free then it just happened."

He held her close. Eyelashes fluttered closed and his soul found some semblance of peace, but it was not to last long.

"Declan?"

He lifted his head and stared into large brown eyes framed by glistening lashes. He lay half on top of her and dimly realized that he must have fallen asleep. His arm and leg were pinning her down into the soft tissue of the capsule.

"The gel," she said, shifting beside him.

"The gel?" he repeated blankly, his brain a mash of oatmeal.

"It itches."

Declan glanced down and his brain kicked into gear. They were both covered in globs of the white gel. "The goddamn gel," he muttered. "Hold on." He stood up, scooped her up, and climbed out of the capsule onto the black platform.

"How long has it been itching?" he asked and jumped down. He slid a little on the blue floor and quickly regained his balance.

A soft cheek pressed into his shoulder. "Not long."

"Goddamn eFlame effect."

"Dr. William said he negated it."

"Not enough, obviously." Declan shoved through the shower doors.

"What about the towels?"

"The towels cannot reach up where they need to."

He stepped into a black tiled room with four stalls and turned right. A single amber light in the ceiling kept each stall in shadows.

"Stall A. Water On. Set to body temperature," he commanded loudly and moved into the right stall. Water jets clicked on, spraying them from every direction.

"Does the water need to be so cold?"

"Our bodies are overheated. The water is set at a comfortable level and will relieve the itching."

He slid his arm from under her legs and helped her stand in the center of the stall.

"Careful, the tile is slippery." He positioned her over a spray shooting up from the floor. "Spread your legs, so the water can reach you."

His princess positioned herself carefully over the circular jet, letting the water spray.

"Are you itchy?" She looked up at him, her gaze clear and direct.

"No." Even covered in globs of gel, she was so incredibly beautiful to him that it almost hurt to look at her. He stepped back and pushed strands of hair out of his eyes.

"Fallon, how do you feel? Is the water helping?"

"I am a little sore down there but it is helping."

His gaze dropped to white thighs dotted with blood then to his own bloodstained manhood. He took her virginity, aggressively, and without thought of her discomfort, and she in turn, freed him from the collar. Shame washed over him. "Why, Fallon?" he asked in an agonized tone.

"Why what?"

"Why did you offer yourself to me?"

"Because I love you, Declan. Because you needed me to."

She said it so matter-of-factly that he felt his insides quiver. It occurred to him that he probably loved her too, but he quickly squashed the thought. Loving her would destroy him. He could not afford to love her. He knew she waited for him to voice his devotion in return but nothing came out of his throat. And the more she watched and waited, the thicker his breathing became. Mist deepened in the stall and the gurgling sound of running water filled in the awkward silence.

"Are you not going to say anything?" She blinked the water from her eyes.

"Did I hurt you?" he inquired instead, side-stepping the whole love and devotion issue.

"I am told it always hurts a little the first time."

"I should have been gentler with you. It was your first time and I am sorry."

"Dr. William said he enhanced the sensory unit's effects." She rubbed the gel from her skin. "I believe your immediate state prevented any rational thinking."

Declan muttered an oath under his breath regarding the good doctor's ancestry.

"Do not curse him, Declan."

"All right, my mistake."

She gave him a small smile and he became lost once more in the sultry call of her. "Thank you," he said hoarsely.

Pink tinted the cheeks of his sweetly shy and bold princess before she flinched when the water stream caught her wrong. Her hurt jarred him. "Princess, I am sorry. I never meant to hurt you."

"You did not hurt me. We made love, Declan."

"That was not making love, far from it."

"What was it then?"

Their gazes locked and Fallon stilled. In the silence following her question, he came to her, all seething darkness and strength, making her feel very small and very feminine.

He touched her right cheek, fingertips caressing her skin. "I'll show you what making love is, Fallon."

His head lowered, soft lips taking hers in gentle possession.

She thrust her tongue into his mouth and he pulled back, chuckling with pleasure.

"What?" she demanded.

He caressed her face. "You make me feel alive." He pressed a finger to her lips to silence her. "I've shown you lust, Princess. Now let me show you passion."

"I want to," she breathed, looking into his eyes. He had such beautiful eyes.

He kissed the seam of her bottom lip. "I know you are sore. Can you trust me in this? I will not hurt you again."

"I trust you."

He started with her delicately formed chin, taking his time, tasting every texture of her sweet flesh. "Guide me, Princess."

Fallon tilted her head back, giving him better access to her throat and shoulder. He was a quick study and suckled the curve of her neck in a way that made her legs buckle.

He caught her and pressed her back against the cool black tile. Water sprayed hard into her back.

"Can you stand for me?"

She could only nod helplessly as he knelt in front of her. "What are you doing?"

"Introducing you to passion. Tell me what feels good."

He nuzzled the underside of her left breast, taking his time, making her tremble all over once again. Fallon gripped his hair, and he chuckled deep in his throat, before his hot mouth took her nipple, his tongue doing decadent things to her flesh. She moaned and his left hand splayed against her back, lending support, while he laved and teased her flesh with his mouth. Her hands fisted painfully in his hair but she could not let go of him. "Oh, God." She buried her fingers in his silken hair and when he suckled her right breast, she nearly came off the floor. Her knee smacked him square in the chest but he did not seem to notice. He shaped her breast with one hand, while the other slid down her hip and kneaded her bottom. She squirmed against him, a kind of torture quickening both their blood. He released her breast and licked his way downward. "What are you . . ."

"Shhhhh."

Fallon gasped when she felt warm lips kissing her down there.

"Spread your legs for me. I wish to taste you."

Fallon banged her shoulders and the back of her head against the tiled wall while strong hands pressured her thighs apart. "Oh, God."

"Not God, Princess. Say my name." He pulled her hips forward, tasting her deeply. Licking her with long deep strokes and sending waves of excitement streaming to her core.

"My name, Princess." He nipped her inner thigh.

Fallon took in great gulps of air, her body vibrantly alive.

His mouth returned to the ache he had started. What he did to her was corrupt, indecent, and immoral—but she never wanted him to stop. Intense pleasure licked at her womb, fire raced through her blood, an inferno of need and desire, wants she'd never known the true meaning of until him. She held on to his hair, anchoring him to her. She was riding a fire-blazing comet into the blanket of space. And when the world exploded into a thousand meteor showers and she screamed his name, she fell into the vortex of the night and into his strong arms.

CHAPTER
FIFTEEN

IN SPACE, DAWN is always a black sunrise, Declan thought, *except for the stars; they shine eternally bright, oblivious to the dark shroud around them.*

In the early morning, he had walked the corridors of the warship, the scents and sounds of the crew giving the vessel a living presence. A turn down the corridor and he had headed for the star room. Pushing through the big doors, he had not realized that what he had been seeking was solitude, until he had arrived in the room's dimness. Solitude, it was a condition new and startling to him, a remembrance perhaps of a forgotten human self. He walked across the expanse of the room, his boots silent on the pitch-black carpet. To his right, the large viewing window filled his field of vision, a great screen into space and time. To his left lay a span of blue wall. His gaze moved to the private alcoves at the end of the room. They, too, were empty at this early hour. He was alone, a matrix abomination experiencing inner peace because a spirited princess saw into the deepest recesses of his soul and did not pull away. He took up a position in the right corner of the massive viewing window and braced his hand upon the smooth black frame. He had left his disheveled princess sleeping soundly in his quarters and hugging pillows to her perfect breasts. She occasionally snorted in her sleep. It was a delicate sound, tiny, and so very feminine that he had listened for it. It made him smile. She was in his blood now, part of the human self lost over a year ago and suddenly found once more, unexpectedly.

Found.

He had never thought to feel human again.

Never dared to hope.

He exhaled loudly and focused on the moving star trails. Dots of light and splendor passed in a soothing white blur on their way to nowhere. He thought of his earlier decision. At his request, *Claymore* was rendezvousing with *Saltire*, another Clan Douglas warship. Named after the St. Andrew white cross appearing on the flag of Scotland, the *Saltire* carried his black stealth freighter in her holds. He had almost not made the request. But he wanted the *Black Ghost* for what he intended to do. It was a purely personal choice and once he arrived at the decision, he had felt better. The *Saltire* would retrieve his black freighter from Braemar Keep and bring it to him.

The *Black Ghost* could pass for a freighter; her ship signature registered as a freighter, and she was not recorded with Clan Douglas. He did not want any Clan Douglas ships near or in MacKendrick space. He did not want to provoke an incident. Clan Douglas was vulnerable, a condition he was trying to rectify, except . . . somehow, he had lost momentum, misplaced in the tones and textures of a young woman.

He could still taste her in his mouth, hear her little sexy-as-hell cries as he thrust into . . .

"Blood and ashes, I want her again." He ran a hand down his face, struggling for balance in a world and place he no longer understood. He looked out, once again. The matrix rage in his blood had cooled to a distant memory. It would rise again, a promise of anger always within him, but not at this moment. In this time, peace and calm reigned inside him. He'd almost forgotten how it felt. He took in a deep breath. In the distance, a globular cluster of blue light caught his attention, fluorescent colors and layers unwound, a stunning image of more than a million stars. The cosmos was infinite to him, the universe complex, like the soul of his princess. He could not fathom her loyalty and love. He tried searching for an inner perspective, a reason behind her devotion to him, and found none within reason. If this devotion was infatuation, she would eventually get over him. But would he ever get over her? He lifted his gaze to the frosty white ice clouds. Beyond was a battered moon and glowing gases thrown off by a nebula.

Since the matrix transference, he had never dared to listen to his heart. He was afraid the roar of rage would deafen his mind and make him insane like his father. But he was different now.

Human. And yet, not human.

Separate. And yet, part of Clan Douglas.

He locked his hands behind his back, spread his feet in a subconscious warrior's stance, and contemplated life's journey with a skeptical chuckle. Certainly nothing had ever prepared him for this dilemma. He wondered what his guardian, Second Commander Winn de Douglas, would have said about an infatuated and spirited princess had he lived through the clan war.

Declan tilted his head to the sound of heavy footfalls. His other, self-proclaimed guardian approached, bringing the bitter scent of chocolates along with him.

"Good morning, Dr. William," Declan said softly.

The Douglas doctor appeared by his side, cheeks a ruddy color and white hair standing straight on end. *Pillow hair*, Declan thought, and, it appeared, a bad humor to match.

The doctor shoved his fists into the front pockets of his white lab coat. "Morning to you, then," he grumbled and perused the large window.

"The blue and white star clouds are majestic this

morning." Declan attempted to open the conversation in a polite manner.

"I dinna notice. I understand from the captain that we are to rendezvous with the *Saltire*."

"Yes, we rendezvous with *Saltire*."

"For one who wears a Clan Douglas uniform without rank or insignia you command our fleet with authority."

Declan's silvery blue eyes narrowed at the doctor's uncharacteristic accusation. "You question my loyalty?"

"Never that. I know your war record, laddie. Your loyalty is unquestionable, and during the war it was to High Council, as it should have been. What I question now is your refusal to wear a Clan Douglas commander's rank. I question your refusal to take your proper place and stand beside Lord Lachlan. Your half brother needs you to stand with him."

"When I am worthy, I will."

The doctor rocked back on his feet, showing his displeasure. "When might that be?"

"When I am worthy," Declan repeated tightly.

"Payment for past sins, it is then. You will never forgive yourself for taking your father's side as any son would have done."

"I almost killed Lachlan and Kimberly."

"No, laddie, your father almost killed Lachlan and Kimberly. You saved them."

Declan turned away, uncomfortable with the doctor's

words. Toward the end of the war, his choice had almost cost Lachlan his life and damned an innocent clan into annihilation. He wanted redemption from Lachlan. He was bound by a vow of loyalty to Clan Douglas, a vow he would never break. "Let it rest, Doc. Tell me, how is Thorn doing?" He deftly changed the subject.

"Ah?"

Declan looked back at the doctor and urged softly. "Thorn, my wee-gadhar companion. Remember? I left her in your care back on Braemar Keep."

"Doona get your back up with me. That poodlefly abandoned me soon after you left."

"Abandoned you?" Declan retorted. "Where is she?"

"Took one look at the handsome Kite and fell in love. She life-mated to Lachlan's wee-gadhar and should be in the family way soon."

Declan's lips curved in both relief and amusement. "Good for her. I knew her time approached. She was restless on our last trip and insisted upon sleeping on my throat."

"They do that when their mating cycle approaches. The heat and pulse in our necks attracts them."

"I'm glad she found her mate."

"So am I," the doctor agreed. "Now on to the matter of another mate."

He fought back a grimace. "Must we?"

The doctor rubbed his chin. "I will come right to

the point."

"That would be nice."

"How do you feel?"

Declan raised a dark brow. "You tell me."

"Identity restored?"

"Yes."

"Injuries healed?"

"Yes," he answered and frowned. "How long is your list of questions?"

"Depends on the answers. Any aftereffects from that blasted slave collar?"

Declan looked away for a moment. "None." He hated the animal he had become when in a lust stage.

"Any residual effects?"

His cautious gaze slid back to the doctor. "Such as?"

"Intimate feelings. Emotions."

"I feel . . ." He tried to describe it and failed miserably. A momentary tension rifled through him and he looked back to the window, seeking sanctuary. "The damn thing ripped me open." He did not want to discuss this new vulnerability, this new capacity to hurt. "Where is the slave collar?"

"I burned it. Controller and collar are in ashes."

"Good."

"That brothel owner should be vaporized."

"Agreed. I shall pay Master Balan a visit sometime soon and see that the punishment fits the crime. What else bothers you, Doc that you had to seek me out?"

"You dinna answer my summons to come to the science lab?"

"After I finished here, my intention was to come by. I just needed some down time."

The doctor's white brows furrowed in a frown, then eased. "I dinna give you much time, did I?"

"No," Declan agreed, "not much."

The doctor gave a quick look over his shoulder and scrutinized the room for occupants. "Since we appear to be alone, I will discuss what I need to discuss here."

"All right." His guard went up.

"Declan, your body's degradation appears to have stopped, at least for the moment, but I remain a wee bit concerned because . . ."

"I could have lain with anybody if I knew that would stop the degradation."

The doctor glared at him. "You know as well as I that a simple physical intimacy would not work in your case. Other factors are involved. The sooner you accept it, the better."

"Accept it?" he mocked. "Do you know what I have done?"

A smug grin spread across the doctor's face and Declan's jaw stiffened with irritation.

"Aye, I know what you have done. You have fallen in love. It happens to the best of us, you know."

"I don't know what I feel." Declan glowered at the doctor. "The woman confounds me."

"'Tis a good start."

"A good start to what? Never mind. Don't answer." He moved to another panel of the window. "Is that all, Doc?"

"Nay. I assume the *Saltire* has retrieved the *Black Ghost* from Braemar Keep?"

"Yes," Declan answered, maintaining a civilized tongue. "I want my own ship under me when going into a possibly volatile situation. I'll not have one of our warships in MacKendrick space."

"Good plan," the doctor rejoined.

Declan glared at the older man, who returned his look with barely suppressed enthusiasm.

"Ah hell. Out with it. What else do you wish to discuss with me? I know that you will not leave me in peace until you have said what it is you have come to say."

"Well, it is true I be wanting to check on you. But I have a verra important issue I need to discuss."

"Obviously." He had a sense that something bad was coming. Hundreds of images flashed in his mind.

"Princess Fallon is pregnant."

His jaw dropped in shock. That was not what he had expected.

The doctor rocked forward on his toes, a wide grin spreading across his face. "You have impregnated a princess. Congratulations, laddie."

"Not funny."

"Nay, not funny at all," the doctor replied in all seriousness, except his lips twitched, giving away his thoughts.

"You are telling me Fallon is pregnant?"

"Aye, I am."

Declan tunneled a hand through his hair. He did not expect to feel this elation sweep through his whole body.

"Ah, I see it pleases you."

He felt like grinning from ear to ear. "Doc, are you sure?"

"Am I sure?" He blubbered in mock outrage. "What kind of a question is that? The current state of emulsion tank and sensory unit technology maps every human function, including conception. I'm verra sure, laddie. You caught her well and good the first time. The same way Lachlan caught Kimberly." He chuckled proudly. "'Tis the Douglas virility, you see."

Declan looked blankly out the window, the unaccountable joy warming him. "I thought the sensory unit was off."

"The gel drained, but the unit was on and set for one. That is why she suffered a little of the eFlame effect."

Declan pressed his hands against the cool window glass. The joy he had felt only moments before dissipated and was replaced by a sudden cold, hard reality. His gaze dropped. "Will the babe be normal?"

"What do you mean by normal?"

"I'm not precisely human anymore, Doctor."

The doctor gave a significant snort. "What are you then?"

His gaze met the doctor's in full challenge. "You do not make it easy."

"Do you consider your nephews normal?" Dr. William countered and spread his hands wide. "Lachlan is matrix like you. His twin sons carry the matrix influence in their DNA."

"They appear human." Declan wasn't precisely sure what defined human anymore.

"They are, trust me. Now, we must talk of your princess, something you need to be aware of."

"There is more?"

"Aye, as you know, the sensory unit was on. Although set to one occupant, it picked up a strong telekinetic mind signature, so the rumors about the lassie are true. I know for a fact that you have no such mind ability."

Declan's eyes narrowed at the doctor. "My mind works just fine."

"Debatable."

He chuckled in amusement. "You are in rare form this morning, Doc."

The older man rubbed his belly. "Aye, I could not

find any chocolates in my lab so I will admit to being a wee bit cranky."

"Ship stores?" he prompted battling a smirk.

"The lads have not yet filled my request."

"That could be described as a catastrophe," he said with a twitch of his lips, feeling unaccountably light-hearted.

"Aye," the doctor replied with a steely glare. "Now back to your princess."

"I will deal with her," Declan said and experienced a sudden sense of uncertainty.

"I doona know whether she will pass her telekinetic gift on to the babe."

"I guess we will have to wait and see." He looked out the window once more, struggling to get ahold of his emotions.

"I also picked up something else in her mind signature, but it is too faint to be measured and so I would not worry about it."

Then why mention it? Declan pushed off the window and focused on the present. He was going to be a father. "This complicates things," he murmured. "Someone threatens the First Family of Clan Douglas and I'll not rest until I eliminate the threat. But neither will I subject my princess to danger."

The doctor shoved his hands into his pockets. "It is only as complicated as you choose to make it."

"What do you mean?"

"The older I become, the simpler life becomes. It goes without saying that you will protect our First Family to the best of your ability. As to the other, you have two choices, laddie. If you doona wed the princess, Clan MacKendrick will undoubtedly cause trouble for Clan Douglas. Whether it will lead to war, I doona know. However, if you do wed her, now therein lies the problem. You will have to admit you are human."

Declan looked out the window again. "My loyalty is to Clan Douglas. I'll do what needs to be done."

The white pillow smelled like him, a lingering of a light tantalizing masculine scent that called to her nature. She took it into her lungs as she had taken him deep inside her body. Fallon opened her eyes to a world of white walls and the low murmur of ship engines. She stretched lazily, a slight ache dwindling between her legs. She was alone in Declan's quarters, sleeping in his bed, and huddled beneath white sheets and warm blankets of Douglas gray plaid. Pulling the covers back, she swung her legs over the right side of the bed. Her toes landed in a soft medallion rug with a green salamander and orange flames in the center.

Tugging at the white bedclothes she had gotten from

ship stores, she leaned over her knees to better inspect the interesting weave. Unbound hair tumbled over her shoulders in an untamed mess and she shoved it back. "Odd badge," she murmured, studying the green salamander.

"Perhaps. But the Clan Douglas heraldic badge is quite old and the clan is rather attached to it," Declan replied in quiet explanation from where he sat in the corner.

Fallon looked up in surprise. "I did not hear you come in."

"You were asleep. Pleasant dreams?"

His voice sounded odd. In a corner chair of blue, he looked every bit the regal warrior, with long legs outstretched and crossed at the ankles. His elbows were braced on the chair's arms, large hands bracketed in front of him. She frowned at his subtle cast of disdain. "Why did you not wake me, Declan?"

"You looked too peaceful."

She searched his face, sensing his return to aloofness.

"What is your badge?" he asked.

"A dexter hand holding a star argent surmounted by a crescent."

"A noble badge," he remarked.

"Our motto is *Sola Virtus Nobilitat*."

He took a moment to translate. "Virtue Alone Ennobles, a noble motto."

"Yes." Fallon pushed the tangled waves away from

her face for a second time. "The MacKendrick are a noble people."

"I agree."

She waited for him to say something more, feeling uncertain and peculiar with this awkward quiet and distance between them. His glorious eyes always made her feel queer inside, except now she knew him intimately, or at least as intimately as he allowed himself to be known. "How do you feel without the slave collar?" she asked.

He tilted his head before answering. "Strange."

"Strange good or strange bad?" she inquired.

A long silence came and went, and in his face she saw a brief surge of regret before the mask returned.

"I am unburdened," he answered, a small telling of his true feelings.

"Unburdened is a most odd answer."

"From the rage," he clarified.

They no longer spoke of the slave collar but of other things, of the horror that had come before. With three fingers, she twisted the folds of the blankets. "I know how you died."

"Do you?"

"Yes."

Darkness spread across his features. "Then you know what I am?"

"I know."

He chuckled darkly. "'I died with disgrace and

shameful cowardice, it is the most infamous and harmful of all.'"

"I believe you quote from Polybius and that is not true."

"Yes, I quote from Polybius." His sensual lips curved, mocking the turbulence inside him. "What do you know about me, Princess?"

Fallon took a moment to compose her answer. "Nathaniel Hawthorne of Ancient Earth once said, '. . . the truest heroism is to resist the doubt; and the profoundest wisdom, to know when it ought to be resisted, and when to be obeyed.'" She held his gaze, falling deep into the burning of smoldering silver. "On that long, last day of the war, you served as second commander aboard the High Council warship *Necromancer.*"

"I was on *Shadowkeep*, the Clan Ramayan warship," he corrected with a tilt of his head.

"Yes. You left *Necromancer* to join Commander Lin Jacob Rama on *Shadowkeep*. Commander Rama attacked Braemar Keep. You were part of his invading force, tasked to place planetary bombs, but you did not set them to explode."

A muscle ticked in his jaw. "I did not."

"Why?"

"I came to understand Rama's obsession with Lady Saph-ire de Douglas, his need for vengeance, and his desperate madness."

"You stepped in front of Commander Rama's

weapon and used your body to shield Lord Lachlan and Lady Kimberly."

His gaze narrowed to slits. "You make it sound heroic."

"Rama fired point blank into your chest, Declan. You died."

"But I'm here now," he said in a strange bitterness.

"Yes, thanks to Dr. William and Lord Lachlan. I saw what was left of your body on the holographic displays in the science lab."

"Dr. William gave you a tour of his science lab and an explanation of his Genetic Transference Process then?"

"He showed me." She gripped the edge of the bed. If only she could reach the emotions seething below the surface of him.

"No one must know of it, Princess."

"I gave my vow of silence to the doctor." She curled her toes into the rug. "I would never break my vow, Declan."

"I know," he added in a barely audible voice. "Does it not offend you, Princess?"

"Offend me?" She did not understand.

"What I am."

How could he think that? she wondered. "I knew who and what you were before I entered the sensory unit, Declan."

A moment of silence passed between them, a remembrance of sharing their bodies in the heat of passion.

A small smile tugged at his sensual lips. "And a most splendid entrance it was, Princess Fallon MacKendrick."

"Declan, I love—"

"Will you marry me, Fallon?"

The soothing tone of his voice did not match the flat expression in his eyes.

"I am betrothed to Lord Henderson."

"Not anymore."

She searched his face. It was uninterpretable, cast in shadow and weariness. "You ask from the heart, Declan?" That peculiar slanted smile made her heart ache.

"I do not want a war with Clan MacKendrick."

With his response, her heart plummeted into a sea of hurt. "There will be no war," she whispered. He asked out of a sense of obligation, not love.

"Clan MacKendrick follows the olden ways of Ancient Earth. I took your virginity, Princess. Believe me, there will be some sort of confrontation, especially with tensions being what they are. My clan cannot afford any type of conflict right now."

She lifted her head, feeling miserable, and reached for the self-possession her beloved mother had given her. "I will tell my father I threw myself at you. He already knows of my *infatuation* with you." How she hated the word, infatuation. It made her feelings sound so ugly.

"Whether or not infatuation is the accurate word in this situation, I do not know. But I will tell you this.

There will be no conflict because you will consent to marry me."

The light inside her soul darkened even more. Hurt seeped into every cell of her body. She slid from the bed, and headed for the facilities room to the right. It never occurred to her that one could fall in love and not the other.

"Princess, I need an answer."

Fallon stopped in the doorway. She stared at the gray floor, at the design of blurry etchings. "Declan, there will be no war because I will agree to a handfasting with you."

"Handfasting?" he echoed suspiciously.

"Yes." She gave a fleeting look over her shoulder and straightened, a royal princess in full control of her emotions, if only for this moment. "It is the trial marriage of our ancestors," she explained.

"I know about our goddamned ancestor's handfasting ceremonies," he grumbled, not at all pleased.

"Well then, you must also know handfasting was the way to test a bride's fertility and guarantee an heir. If no heir was born within a year, the clan elders revoked the trial marriage and chose another bride. The royal line must continue. Honor and duty must be upheld. There is no dishonor to the bride or the bride's clan." Fallon paused, her heart in her throat. "You will offer for me. I will accept and agree to handfast with you. But I will not share my body with you again, Declan of Clan Douglas. After a year, when no child is born, the trial marriage ends. Honor and duty served."

"Honor and duty served," he repeated with a peculiar amusement around his lips. "I am at your mercy, Princess."

Fallon frowned at his quick acquiesce. "A war shall never begin by a MacKendrick hand, I will not allow it."

"I know."

"I wish to go home." She attempted to stare him down.

"I know that, too."

"Now." She laced her voice with imperial command.

A brow arched as he considered her arresting tone. He came swiftly to his feet and approached.

Fallon turned away, presenting her back. But it was no use. She felt him in her bones.

Warm breath puffed upon her bare shoulder where the gown had slipped down her arm.

"Do you trust me?" he asked in a voice of quiet shadow.

A shiver ran down her spine and she gave him a civil nod.

"Good. For I trust you with my life. Remember, Fallon. I trust you."

She bit her lip. When she looked back, he had gone. She was alone. Crossing her arms to hold herself, she leaned against the doorframe, her body weak and trembling. Deep down, she knew Declan followed his own code of conduct. He did not give his trust easily, but once given, he was bound by it.

She had won his trust.

It was a beginning, and her heart took comfort in that one achievement.

CHAPTER
SIXTEEN

IT HAD BEEN two days since he had spoken with his princess.

Two days of cold emptiness in his chest.

Two days of yawning need.

Now, she was here.

And he wished she were not.

Earlier in the morning, *Claymore* had retrieved the *Black Ghost* from *Saltire*.

Soon after that, the princess arrived for a stately inspection. In Fighter Bay Four, where white steam surrounded them in opaque specters, Declan stood motionless, his heart locked in longing.

His princess circled the *Black Ghost* for the second time, her face turned upward with interest. She moved gracefully in the Clan Douglas black uniform, all fluid female motion that made him ache. A single braid of captured flames fell down her slender back. She ignored the twenty fighters lined up in static display to their right. Her full concentration was on his ship and he wondered at her thoughts.

There was a part of him willing to sacrifice honor to claim her for his own. But he knew he never would; he would never go beyond the point of no return. Rather than torture himself more, he moved into the stream of amber light on the walkway and paused under his ship's right wing, waiting for her to notice him.

When she spotted him, he nodded in greeting. "Princess."

She turned away, giving him a royal cut, and walked to the front of the ship. "Do I see the inside of the ship this time?"

"Yes."

"When?"

He gestured to the hatch. "Now, if you're ready to leave."

"Leave now?"

"Yes, the sooner we leave the better. I'll not have an unauthorized Clan Douglas warship in MacKendrick space when I go to meet your father."

"Agreed, we should remove all possible causes for provocation." She touched the ship's smooth hull. "What is the *Black Ghost*'s classification?"

"Freighter Class," he answered carefully.

"So not a freighter," she countered impudently and he silently agreed.

Declan locked his hands behind his back to keep

himself from reaching for her. He felt miserable. "What is she then?"

The princess shrugged.

"Your thoughts matter greatly to me."

"My thoughts are my own, Master Trader," she said in majestic reprimand, a defense against the hurt he detected.

Declan ran a hand along the hull of his ship and approached her.

"True. Your thoughts are your own." He stopped beside her. "I wish only that you share them with me."

"Why?" She lifted her face to him. "Tell me why I should share them with you."

Declan swallowed hard. *Because I lo . . .*

"What is this? A lover's quarrel so soon?" Dr. William walked around the front of the freighter and joined them, his timing impeccable.

"Dr. William," Fallon greeted warmly.

"Hello, lassie. Are you keeping our fine Douglas lord on his toes?"

"I'm not a lord," Declan complained, never once looking away from his princess.

The doctor scoffed. "Whether you like it or not, Declan, you share the same birth mother as our Clan Douglas chieftain."

His princess contemplated him briefly and he knew she had made the connection of his birth. "Their mother is Lady Saph-ire de Douglas?" she questioned.

"Yes," the doctor replied.

The princess waited for him to elaborate.

Declan could not, he could not reveal the name of his father, the madman who had started the clan war—Commander Lin Jacob Rama. The wounds still cut deep, even after all this time, and he turned to the older man for respite. "I'm taking the princess to MacKendrick."

"Nay, laddie. The captain asked me to find you."

In response, Declan quirked a brow and tapped the commlink on his chest.

"Your commlink is not working," the doctor noted.

He pulled the device from his chest and inspected it.

"Lachlan sent a message requesting you and Princess MacKendrick join him on the silver base at Io."

"After I visit with the MacKendrick." Declan tossed the defective commlink into the red trash canister along the maintenance wall, opposite his ship.

The doctor shoved his fists into the pockets of his white lab coat. "Change in plans, laddie. It seems an angry Lord MacKendrick has requested High Council to consider an act of aggression against Clan Douglas for the kidnapping of his daughter."

"I was not kidnapped," Fallon protested. "My father would never make such an accusation unless given proof."

"According to someone named Lord Henderson, you were taken by force off his ship," the doctor explained.

"Henderson," Declan said irritably, but then something else slammed into his thoughts. He looked hard at Dr. William. "Where are Lady Kimberly and the twins?" he demanded.

"Lady Kimberly?" The doctor blinked at him, thrown off balance by the quick change of subject.

"Just follow my lead here, Doc. Where are they?"

"Lady Kimberly and the boys remain home at Braemar Keep."

"I don't like this," Declan said low and raked a hand through his hair.

Fallon and the doctor both glanced at each other.

"Declan, what is wrong?" His princess moved to his side.

He held his hand up to stop her next question. "Princess, give me a moment to work this through in my mind. Doc, is Lachlan already on Io?"

"Aye. The High Council sent a ship to bring him to the silver base and he went on good faith. He took several of our guardsmen with him."

Declan turned to Fallon. "When Henderson shackled me in the *Pict*'s cargo hold, he spoke of oligonucleotides. Do you know what they are?"

"Strands of DNA?"

"Good answer, Princess. I need you to think. Does he have any DNA synthesizers? They are large machines, not easily missed."

"I think I have seen four of them. I am sure he spoke of them but I never paid attention to his boasting. I am sorry."

"Don't be. The synthesizers, I'm guessing, are set for biological bullets." Declan walked over to the wall commlink on the maintenance wall. He punched the red button for the bridge.

"Bridge here," the female voice of the communications officer piped through the wall commlink.

"Declan here. Get me the captain," he commanded.

"Yes, sir. One moment."

The commlink went silent for what seemed an interminable time to him, but in truth it was only a few seconds.

"Liion here."

"Go to Alert One, Captain," Declan ordered. "I have reason to believe an infectious agent is going to be introduced to Braemar Keep. Lady Kimberly and the twins are the main targets, but the whole clan is in danger."

"Understood."

"Have the defense interceptor satellites been deployed into Mars' orbit yet?"

"No."

"All right. I want you to get Dr. William to Braemar Keep with all speed. No ships are to enter our space. No cargo drops."

"Do you know where the threat comes from?" the captain asked.

Declan glanced at his princess. "Clan Henderson,

possibly Clan MacKendrick, too. But it could be any ship. I want *Saltire* to go to Io with all speed to give assistance to Lord Lachlan, if needed."

"Yes, sir. I'll inform *Saltire*. Do we have permission to fire?"

"Permission to defend only. By God, I do not want to start another war."

"Agreed. Should we alert Lord Lachlan of the threat?" the captain asked.

"No. Dr. William will inform him once plans are set."

"Very well."

"Liion, it goes without saying that you must keep your ship secure."

"Understood. No crew communications in or out."

Declan met the doctor's steady gaze.

"I will be speaking privately with Lachlan, laddie. No one will know who should not."

Declan nodded and leaned closer to the commlink. "Liion, Princess MacKendrick and I are taking the *Black Ghost* out."

"To Io, I presume?"

"Yes, Lord MacKendrick believes I kidnapped his daughter. I need to meet with the High Council and douse this blaze before it engulfs us in another war. As soon as I'm deployed, get moving."

"Will do."

"Godspeed, Declan out."

"Liion out."

Declan grabbed his princess's upper arm and looked meaningfully at the doctor. "Screen everything, Doc. Do not let them eat, drink, breathe, or touch anything you have not personally cleared."

"Right!" Dr. William turned on his heel, white lab coat flaring out, and ran back through the maintenance area.

Declan tugged Fallon with him, pulling her to the *Black Ghost*.

"Declan, my father would not attack Clan Douglas without just cause."

"Shall we prove it?" He turned to his ship. "*Ghost*," his command cut through the air, "Open hatch."

The black hatch swung open under the wing. White hull lights clicked on.

"Into the ship, Princess." Declan wrapped an arm around her slender waist and brought them both up into the cool confines of the ship. He set her down safely and turned to the hatch. "Hatch close and secure."

The black hatch swung closed with a double click, locking them in the cool blue-gray interior of the ship.

He pointed right. "My quarters are down the corridor, Princess. You'll be safe there. Cargo holds are empty and off limits." He headed in the opposite direction.

"My clan is innocent." His princess ignored his instructions and followed right behind him.

"I hope they are."

"I want to help prove it."

Declan frowned at her over his shoulder. "Have you any combat experience?"

"No, but my father made sure I knew my way around ship systems in case of an emergency." She followed close on his heels. "Please, Declan, let me help."

They entered the bridge of the ship.

"All right, take the copilot seat, strap in, and don't touch anything."

He vaulted over the black railing and sat in the black pilot seat behind the command console.

"Engines online," he commanded and secured the black strap across his chest. The console lit up and the engines came online in a low growl.

She hurried around the black railing and took the copilot seat to the right. In front of her, digital displays and tactical monitors came to life.

Declan grasped the pilot controls and the *Black Ghost* rose silently under his hand. He guided her past the fighters to their right, out of the hangar, and into the airlock. Release codes activated and soon they were out in space. As the ship's wings swept back for space travel, he felt the powerful lurch of speed. They quickly left *Claymore* behind, a magnificent white dot in space.

Declan headed for the MacKendrick jump gate at full speed. Configuring navigation, he punched in the codes that would bring him to Planet Jupiter and her large moon, Io, where the silver base, the High Council, and Lord MacKendrick resided.

He did not look at the princess.

Time seemed to go by interminably before she spoke.

"Do you believe Clan MacKendrick guilty?" Fallon asked.

"I believe the threat to Clan Douglas comes from Henderson," Declan replied as he verified jump end coordinates. "I look at Clan MacKendrick because of association." He positioned the ship to enter the jump gate. "Navigation set. Jump gate lock executed. Hold on, Princess."

The ship lunged forward into a sea of black space.

"Jump gate accessed," he said.

"Yes, I can see that." Fallon held on to the edge of the console. Tactical monitors noted the change to black space by the loss of all data readouts. "My clan has nothing to do with this and Lord Henderson is not powerful enough to attack another clan on his own."

"Agreed. There is someone else working with him."

In front of her, Declan adjusted the ship's speed then turned to her. "Do you have any ideas?"

Fallon tapped her chin in thought. "We need to find out who he does business with. Someone with a vendetta against Clan Douglas."

"Do you have someone in mind?"

"Let me think on it."

"Don't take too long, Princess."

"A princess never takes too long."

In the dimness of the ship, she could just make out the amusement crossing his features.

"I stand corrected," he answered and turned back to the pilot console.

A surge of inner silence beset her as she mulled over her father's acquaintances. Fallon stared down at her lap, trying to remember. Although encumbered by limited experience, she realized most of the clans who dealt with her father were distrustful of Clan Douglas. And that was the problem. She wished she could point to someone in particular, but the truth was, no one stood out. Clan MacKendrick looked guilty by association with Henderson. She was still not entirely convinced of Henderson's involvement. The man was not that bright. She looked out the window and said plaintively. "I cannot think of any names to offer you."

"Very well."

"How much longer must we travel in this blackness?"

"Check your console; we're approaching the jump end coordinates now. It may get a little bumpy, so hold on."

They left the black space of the jump gate and slid across ripples into normal space. Data streams returned to the ship's screens.

Fallon looked outside, eager for the first sight of the planet Jupiter, the prototypical gas giant. The planet came into view, gleaming like a yellowish pink luminescent ball, its great red spot a region of cyclonic coldness.

"So this is the failed star," she murmured in observation, her hand resting on the console.

"The space station and Io are starboard," Declan directed, bringing the ship about.

Fallon's gaze settled on the silvery space station. The massive wheel-like structure did not interest her. Io did. One of the four large Galilean moons, so named for their brightness, Io looked like a bruised orange. From this distance, she could just make out the starfish structure of the silver base and the white dome of the expanding town.

"Dr. William said Io is the home of the matrix robots. This is where you were reborn, Declan."

"I was reborn on the *Claymore*, in Dr. William's science lab."

"What I meant to say is that the matrix alloy that is part of your DNA came from Io." Her fingers closed over the console and she looked left. "Declan, do you see that ship? Is it another one of the Douglas warships?"

"No, that is the Clan Ramayan warship *Shadow-keep*."

Weapon tracking clicked on in front of her and Fallon looked down, feeling slightly agitated. "Her gun ports are locked on us."

Declan punched the commlink. "This is the *Black Ghost*. We are in the High Council air space. Remove your weapon lock."

The commlink went silent for the breath of a heartbeat before a male voice answered. "I know who you are, *Black Ghost*. This is the Clan Ramayan warship *Shadowkeep*. Hand over the MacKendrick princess."

He turned to her and said in hushed urgency, "Princess, can you scan for the *Saltire*? Is she near?"

Fallon nodded and did a quick scan as he requested. "She is docked at the space station," she whispered.

"Good. *Saltire* will protect Lachlan. We will deal with *Shadowkeep*." He turned back and pressed the commlink. "By what authorization do you make your demand?"

The voice on the other end of the commlink chuckled darkly. "Come now, pleasurer. You go by so many names I do not know what to call you. Let us see, Second Commander of the High Council warship *Necromancer*? No, you resigned your commission to serve Clan Douglas after the war. A stupid decision, in my opinion. You no longer go by Townshend, your mother's clan name. Nor do you go by Rama, your father's name. Your choice appears to be Lord Declan de Douglas and I do find that perturbing."

"Declan?" Fallon edged to the end of her seat and leaned forward.

Declan held up his hand for silence.

"Identify yourself," he ordered.

The voice chuckled again, this time with heavy irony. "Do you not know me, Declan?"

"You have me at a disadvantage," Declan replied.

Fallon hardly knew what to make of this exchange, but quite obviously, it was not good.

"Come now, pleasurer, play the game. Guess."

"Guess?" she muttered and Declan glanced sharply back at her, warning her to silence.

"Do you need a hint?" the male voice taunted.

"You sound very much like Commander Lin Jacob Rama."

"I am impressed by the acuity of your senses, Declan. My name is Lin Derek Ramayan. I am the commander of the warship *Shadowkeep* and the bastard son of Lin Jacob Rama."

The tension in the ship spiked, and Fallon's stomach churned.

A long silence passed before Declan answered. "So am I."

"I know, little brother. But somehow you've become something more. Douglas Savage is what they call you now. How very unique."

"Give me safe passage to deliver the princess to Io and I will return so we can speak."

"No, that is not how this is going down. Surrender

the MacKendrick princess, then we speak."

"Not happening." Declan slammed the ship's controls forward and the *Black Ghost* veered to starboard. "Hang on, Princess. Shields up," he said loudly.

The shields of the *Black Ghost* activated just as the *Shadowkeep* fired a warning shot.

"How dare they?" Fallon said indignantly. She bent to try to configure the pulse cannons to return fire.

"What are you doing, Princess?" Declan demanded, glancing at her sideways.

Fallon lifted her gaze to his. "Returning fire?"

"No. There is one captain per ship and I'm it. I will not fire upon another clan's ship and give them an excuse to start another war against Clan Douglas."

"Oh, I never thought of that. What shall we do?"

"Outmaneuver them and hope the space station or Io is monitoring the situation." He banked the ship and ducked under *Shadowkeep*. "The only problem is, Clan Douglas's stolen energy crystals fuel *Shadowkeep*, so I cannot outrun them."

"Clan Ramayan never returned the crystals after the war?"

He glanced at her in disbelief. "Are you serious?"

"Yes. It is only proper."

"Nothing in war is proper." Declan inverted the ship and dove for cover behind the space station.

In the next instant, five blue star defenders blasted

out of the space station.

"Look out!" Fallon cried.

"Stay calm."

"How can I stay calm? We are under attack from a warship, hiding beneath a spinning wheel posing as a space station, and about to collide with a star defender!" Her stomach took a nauseating dip.

The commlink crackled loudly. "By order of the High Council, you are to cease and desist."

Two blue defenders took position on either side of them and Declan righted the ship. "This is the *Black Ghost*," he replied into the commlink. "We await your direction." He glanced at her. "Princess, you look a little green."

"I am all right."

"The facilities are down the corridor to the left. Throw some cool water on your face. You'll feel better."

Fallon took his advice, unstrapped from her seat, and went to find the facilities. Closing the narrow door behind her, she leaned over the tiny silver sink, turned the cool jet on, and splashed water onto her hot cheeks. Closing her eyes, she waited for the queasiness to ease.

"Princess?" Declan's voice came through the commlink on the wall.

She opened her eyes, straightened, and wiped her mouth with the back of her hand.

"Princess, if you don't answer me, I'm coming down there, and damn the High Council directive."

Fallon pressed the wall commlink. "I am fine," she lied, her stomach still distressed.

"Fine, as in what?"

"Blast it, just land the *Ghost*. Fallon out."

Declan released the commlink, glad to hear the royal impatience back in her voice. He held the *Ghost* immobile between his escorts while the *Shadowkeep* headed for the space station. The big warship slid alongside one of the tubular spokes into Space Dock Eight. A shuttle would be dispatched to take the ship's commander and his party to an assigned sector on the base.

He had to get his head on straight. Commander Lin Derek Ramayan was his brother, another complication in his already complicated life. He was not the only bastard Rama had left behind. Declan wondered how many of his father's seed littered the universe. He thought he had been the only one. Instinctively, he knew there would be no brotherly affection between himself and this commander. This one sounded too much like their deceased father.

The commlink clicked.

"*Black Ghost*," the lead defender called, "by order of the High Council you are to accompany us to the silver base, over."

Declan leaned forward and pressed the commlink in response. "Lead on, defender. *Black Ghost* out."

Keeping up with his escort, Declan turned the *Black Ghost* into Io's shiny atmosphere. From this distance, the silver base looked like a starfish with many arms radiating from a central disk set against a bruised orange surface. A massive white dome hid the town. His gaze swung back to the console. He did not tell his princess, but he suspected the moment they landed on the base, he'd be placed under arrest for kidnapping. He was not looking forward to the coming turmoil and pressed the commlink. "Princess, we will be landing soon. I will await you outside the ship."

"Yes," she answered and he cut communications, wondering how she was doing.

Fallon felt the ship land. She continued to lean over the small sink and took her time rinsing her face in the cool water. When she straightened, she caught a glimpse of herself in the oval mirror above the sink. No longer was she a sheltered girl but a young woman caught in the pull of reality. The seeing and feeling of life could never be experienced in books. It must be lived. The few weeks with Declan had taught her much about love and heartache. She did not regret it. With a deep sigh, she reached for her determination. To prevent a war, she would handfast with him. Then, after a year, he would be free to leave and she would go on. Life would obstinately go on. She turned away and gave her sleeve a hard tug. Fallon opened the narrow door, entered the gray corridor, and headed for the open hatch in the back of the ship. The amber lights on the floor were dimmed, marking a ship in berth. She held her head high. The heels of her black boots clicked loudly in her ears. Taking a fortifying breath, she paused at the open hatch and peered out.

She could not believe what awaited her.

Four gray-uniformed guardsmen had Declan on his knees. His hands were locked behind his head as if he were a criminal.

"What is the meaning of this?" she demanded, outraged at this welcome. She jumped down and approached the group of men in front of the ship.

"It's all right, Princess Fallon," Declan reassured.

Fallon stomped forward in fury. "By no means is this all right." She saw the tip of a pulsar rifle graze Declan's cheek, a warning to remain still. It infuriated her. "Remove your weapon from him this instant or so help me, you'll be sorry you ever lived."

"Daughter!"

Fallon turned at the sound of the beloved voice.

"Father," she cried in relief and ran into his outstretched arms. "I am all right," she reassured, holding tightly to him. "This is all a grave misunderstanding."

Lord Henderson stepped out from behind her father. "He kidnapped you, Princess Fallon!"

"He did not kidnap me!" she snapped back.

Her betrothed winced at her sharp tone but refused to cower. "He set fire to my ship!"

She pulled out of her father's arms. "He set fire to biohazardous material in the cargo area of your ship where you shackled him like a dog. Perhaps you should be more concerned with explaining your actions than proliferating lies, Lord Henderson."

His cheeks turned red with instant denial. "I do not know what you are talking about."

Fallon dismissed him and turned back to her father. She did not expect to find his face unforgivingly hard.

"Father, Declan did not kidnap me," she explained. "I went with him willingly."

"Lord Henderson says differently, Fallon."

"Lord Henderson is an arrogant imbecile and I am not going to marry him," she proclaimed loudly, clenching her fists.

"Princess, perhaps we should discuss this more privately," Declan spoke from behind her with the voice of reason.

"I agree." She smiled sweetly at him, letting all know, including her father, where her loyalty lay.

Declan sent her a warning look and Fallon fought the impulse to go over and hug him with both her arms.

"Ahem," an older man with ornamental brown robes cleared his throat rather loudly. From the man's regal stature and fancy attire, Fallon surmised him to be a member of the High Council. The man stood to the left of her father. A tall, blond warrior with silver armguards flanked him.

"Fallon," her father guided her forward, "Let me introduce you to High Councilor Jared-lynn. High Councilor, this is my daughter Fallon. Fallon, this is High Councilor Jared-lynn."

Fallon faced the learned man. "I am honored to meet you, sir."

"As am I, Princess Fallon." The councilor bowed his hooded head to her, a smile tugging at his lips.

Fallon liked him instantly. "I do believe Declan served as second commander aboard your warship."

"Yes, my *Necromancer*."

"A fine ship."

"As ever there is." The councilor grinned and turned to her father. "Your daughter will make a fine ambassador, Lord MacKendrick. Already she woos me with her gracious tongue."

"Thank you, Councilor." Her father bowed beside her, obviously pleased with her manners.

But Fallon already looked beyond the councilor to the blond warrior who stood apart and watched her intently. He wore the black uniform of the lord commander of Clan Douglas and his blue eyes were . . .

"Ah, Commander Ramayan, how good of you to join us," the Councilor said from beside her.

Fallon spun around to meet the approaching man. Commander Ramayan looked nothing like his half brother, Declan. He was rangy, with white-blond hair, and his eyes appeared so pale they could easily be mistaken for those of a blind man.

"I see the charismatic pleasurer is caught," Commander Ramayan said smugly, coming up to her. He took her hands in his and bowed. "I hope he did not hurt you, Princess Fallon."

She pulled her hands free of his, recoiling from his sweaty touch. "Declan would never hurt me. This is a misunderstanding, Commander Ramayan."

The commander straightened. "I am sure it is, Princess."

There was an odd darkness written all over his face. It made her guard go up even as her father squeezed her waist. "Fallon, I would like to introduce Commander Lin Derek Ramayan of the proud warship *Shadowkeep*. He was kind enough to offer his assistance in trying to find you."

"Was he?" she disputed softly. She held the commander's pale gaze. "Why would you do that, sir?"

"Chivalry, I suppose."

Her eyes narrowed with suspicion. "More like the possibility of a large reward, I'm thinking."

"Fallon," her father corrected angrily. "The commander tried to help. The least you could do is be grateful."

"I am grateful. To Declan."

CHAPTER
SEVENTEEN

FOLLOWING PROTOCOL, DECLAN allowed his hands to be shackled behind his back. Four guardsmen escorted him from the docking bay to the private living area of the councilor. It was located at the far end of the base, with a small courtyard shaded by two medallion gardens, one reminiscent of Dr. William's blue garden room on *Claymore*.

When they came to an ornate black door with the seal of Ancient Earth upon it, the first guard ordered him to hold while another removed the shackles.

Declan remained where they positioned him and rubbed slightly reddened wrists. The door to the counselor's quarters opened.

"We will remain, outside. Please enter, sir."

He nodded and stepped inside a dimly lit foyer. The doors closed behind him with a soft whoosh. A console table of replica mahogany with ball and claw feet stood to his left. The scent of sweet-smelling brandy came from an old-fashioned lead crystal decanter shaped like an oversized spin top. It reminded him of a child's toy.

Moving down the hallway, he paused beside the entryway to a spacious library of old fabricated woods and ancient books.

"You have changed, Second Commander." Councilor Jared-lynn walked around him and entered the room, heading for a green monstrosity of a chair in the corner. When the learned man had settled himself comfortably, he looked up and said, "Join me."

Declan entered. The green chair overwhelmed the space with its gothic trefoil design and griffin jacquard fabric. It was a chair fit for royalty and he positioned himself at attention in front of it. "Sir, I resigned my commission," Declan replied. "I am no longer a second commander." He kept his gaze glued to the bookcase on the back wall.

"Yet you still remain at attention in my presence."

"Yes, sir."

The older man exhaled with a sigh. "I was greatly disappointed when you resigned from my *Necromancer*, Second Commander. You do not mind if I call you second commander? Old habits are hard to break."

"No, sir. I do not mind."

"At ease."

Declan spread his legs for balance and locked his hands behind his back.

"I had plans for you to command your own warship

one day."

"Yes, sir."

The counselor bracketed his hands in front of him. "But you went heroic on me and died."

Declan could not hide his surprise and saw a knowing smile light the other man's craggy features. "Sir?"

"Dr. William conferred with me when Lachlan died. Your rebirth posed more of a problem for him since some of your DNA proved, let us say, problematic."

Declan studied the bookcase once again. "I would not know."

"You carry the royal marker in your eyes."

"I always had blue eyes," Declan countered firmly.

"So you did, but with larger irises now, a mirror image of the Clan Douglas lord. Due to the infusion of Lachlan's DNA into your own, you are of royal blood now. More of the matrix rage and strength too, I would imagine."

Declan shifted uneasily.

"The Clan Douglas lord trusts you, Declan. What do you make of it? Are you worthy of his trust?"

Declan locked gazes with the man. "Yes, sir. I am worthy."

"I think so, too. You have a soul of honor and integrity. Your childhood was unfortunate and you lost your way for a time. But I never doubted you would find your place in the world."

"Sir. I'd rather not reminisce. There are more important matters to discuss."

"Patience, Declan. It is not every day I see a living miracle born out of madness and destruction. If I had my way, Dr. Logan's matrix robot records would have been destroyed long ago. But then neither you nor Lachlan would be alive today, and I could not envision that." He paused, prolonging the moment. "I see you are uncomfortable. Very well, shall we talk of the spirited MacKendrick princess?"

"Yes, sir."

"Lord Henderson charges you with kidnapping the MacKendrick princess from the Dove Inn. Kidnapping her again from his ship. Setting fire to his ship. Altering his ship's navigational computer . . ."

"Lord Henderson is . . ."

"An arrogant imbecile, I do believe is how the princess put it."

Declan bit back a smile. "Yes, I believe that is exactly how she put it."

"A very fiery young woman."

"You have no idea."

The councilor's lips curved in a quick smile.

"Permission to speak freely, sir?"

"Granted."

"It is my belief that Lord Henderson is synthesizing and selling made-to-order pieces of DNA."

Jared-Lynn waved his hand in dismissal. "Smidgens of DNA are individually benign. What would he use them for?"

"They can too easily be made into a pathogen," Declan countered in challenge, "a virus aimed at Clan Douglas."

The councilor eyed him skeptically. "You speak of dangerous things, Second Commander."

"Yes, sir. Dangerous things, which need your attention."

"Explain, start from the beginning and leave nothing out."

"Yes, sir. I would like Lachlan to hear this as well."

"I'll send for your chieftain after I hear your words and make my judgment. Pull up that red chair and talk with me."

Declan pulled the chair over. He perched on the edge of it, leaned forward, and started from the beginning. He left nothing out. It would take him most of the night to explain and strategize a line of defense with both the councilor and Lachlan.

Clan MacKendrick was given quarters in the red sector of the base and asked to wait. It was nearly dawn.

Fallon had not slept.

She sat stiffly in a red paisley chair in the small parlor of her quarters. Her father paced in front of her. Back and forth he moved between her tasseled chair and the oval table, without a word shared between them. He had dressed in the regal green finery of Clan MacKendrick and silent condemnation set his shoulders in a stiff posture. Red hair, with nary a gray strand, lay in a single braid down his back.

Her father stopped and faced her. "You have disgraced me, Fallon."

Fallon met his icy accusation with calm. "I would never disgrace you, Father, or our clan."

"Did the Douglas Savage kidnap you?"

"No," she replied.

"Speak up."

"No," she stated more firmly, sitting straighter in the chair.

"What were you doing in a brothel?"

"I went into town for the evening."

"Into town, alone? Where was the good Lord Henderson?"

"The good Lord Henderson was attending to his business interests. He never told me where he was going. He just left. I took two guards from the inn with me."

"And then what?"

Fallon composed her words. "I met a woman. She was friendly to me and we both knew the Douglas

Savage. She told me of a pleasurer who looked like him and showed me the location of the brothel."

"This infatuation with the Douglas Savage must end."

Yes, Fallon thought. *But I love him.*

"The guards from the inn did not caution you of this place?" her father asked.

"I bribed them to leave me alone," Fallon stated flatly.

He rolled his eyes in familiar distress. "Why does this not surprise me?"

"I am sorry." And she truly was.

"Continue."

Fallon chose her words carefully. "When I arrived, I purchased time with the pleasurer. I never intended to bed him; I just wanted to see what he looked like. But it turned out to be Declan. He wore a slave collar against his will, and that vicious little man, Balan, had hurt him." Fallon's voice rose. "I could not leave Declan there. He needed my help, so we broke out. We ended up at the Bloodgood bar where Madam Cherry helped us."

"Madam Cherry? What kind of a blasted name . . ."

"Madam Cherry is the proprietress of the Bloodgood bar," she said quickly to stop her father's prejudiced outburst. "She helped us and gave us a room to rest." Fallon glossed over that part. "We were not long at the room before Balan and his men found us. We escaped the bar and traveled to a place outside of town where we hoped a collar master would help us to remove Declan's slave collar. It turned out to be a trap set by Lord Henderson. We escaped that one, too. But then he and his guardsmen caught up with us at this air vent."

"Let me understand this," her father interjected with quiet fury. "Lord Henderson found you on our moon, Orrin, but you did not wish to go with him. Then he forcefully brought you to his ship."

"Yes. He shackled Declan in the cargo hold and held me prisoner in his quarters."

"Understandable. A warrant for arrest had been issued against the pleasurer. I cannot believe we are having this discussion. Lord Henderson told me you set fire to his ship and stole one of his shuttles. Is this true?"

Fallon kept her tongue civil under the hard accusation. "We did not set fire to his ship. Declan torched dangerous biohazardous containers in the cargo hold."

"I doubt Henderson's property posed any danger. You must have misread the label."

Dread clutched at heart. He did not believe her and nothing she said was going to change his judgment of the situation. In his mind, she was the one at fault.

"Continue. I wish to hear all of it."

"We returned to Orrin." Her voice reflected the dark void widening inside her. "Declan found Dr. William in the landing area, or rather he found us, and here we are."

"Fallon," her father warned. "You be telling me all of it?"

Fallon regarded him with quiet dignity and a daughter's injured heart. Age lines creased his once-handsome face. Shadows rimmed blue eyes, gleaming with censure and anger.

"Father, whatever I say to you seems to hold no worth. You have already judged me." And in his next response, he proved her suspicions right.

"By your foolishness you have jeopardized relations with Clan Henderson and Clan Douglas. Do you realize I had asked High Council to declare an act of aggression against Clan Douglas?"

"They had nothing to do with this."

"So it seems." Her father scowled deeply and turned away. "Lord Henderson sent me a note. He still wishes to honor the betrothal."

"I do not wish to honor it."

"He wishes to honor the contract even if you are soiled, Fallon. We need Clan Henderson's alliance. I gave my word. Do you know what giving your word means?"

Fallon paled, her stomach queasy. "I know."

"I am glad you remember some things your mother taught you."

"Do not bring my mother into this."

Her father looked at her with impatience. "I am glad she is not around to see how far her daughter has fallen."

"So am I," she whispered but for different reasons. If her mother had lived, she would not be used to further

her father's ambitions.

"Now tell me, did the Douglas Savage lay hands on you?"

Fallon looked down at the floor, mortified to her very soul.

"Answer my question, Daughter."

"Perhaps you should ask me, Lord MacKendrick." Declan strode into the dimly lit parlor and met the brunt of the father's fury.

"You dare show your face in here."

Declan presented himself to his princess, ignoring the irate father for the moment. He looked down upon her bent head and made a little bow from the waist.

"Forgive my delay, Princess," he stated formally. Indecently long lashes of red-tipped lace rested on cheeks leeched of all color. "I needed to speak with Councilor Jared-lynn and Lord Lachlan de Douglas in order to clear up this confusion."

"Confusion," she whispered, not looking up at him. "You could call it that, I suppose."

Declan straightened and faced the father, whose cheeks were flushed a bright, heated red.

"Savage, how did you get past my two guardsmen positioned outside?"

"By right of the High Council," he replied with controlled calm.

"So, the High Council has released you?"

"Yes." The disgust in the older man's tone sent a flash of rage through his blood. But he was careful to keep his own emotions in tight lockdown. "Sir, will you withdraw your request for aggression against Clan Douglas?"

"Did you kidnap my daughter?" MacKendrick countered sourly, his question full of consequences.

Declan held the older man's gaze with cool restraint. "What does your daughter say?"

"My daughter says she found you in a brothel wearing a slave collar and that you needed her help. I find it difficult to believe."

"She speaks the truth."

"How did you become a piece of flesh in a brothel, Savage? You, who are noted to be a warrior weapon of no divergence."

"Father, please do not do this."

"It's all right, Princess," Declan tried to reassure her before facing the father's irrational hatred. "I got bashed in the head while trying to protect the First Family of my clan. After that, I did not remember much else. I have since recovered."

The father snorted with disgust. "Given your reputation, I find the event unlikely."

"I may have done questionable things in my life, but being a liar is not one of them," he answered.

Lord MacKendrick waved his hand in dismissal and

turned away.

"Lord MacKendrick," Declan commanded, pitching his voice as if speaking to a first year crewman.

The father stopped in his tracks.

"Any transgressions you perceive against Clan MacKendrick, I will answer to personally. I ask again, will you withdraw your request for aggression against Clan Douglas?"

"Did you lay hands upon my daughter, Savage?"

"Yes."

The older man's neck flushed bright red before he nodded. "I will not punish an innocent clan for my daughter's misconduct." He walked over to the wall commlink, which was opposite where his daughter sat with her head bowed low. Declan listened as the MacKendrick spoke briefly to the High Council's secretary and withdrew his request for aggression.

He should have felt a sense of victory, but the single tear spilling down his princess's pale cheek nearly undid him.

Lord MacKendrick sidled over to the small liquor cabinet and poured himself a tall drink of Scotch. "I rescinded my request."

"I heard. Thank you, sir," Declan said.

"Do not thank me, Savage."

Another battle was unfurling and it was one he intended to win, as well. He locked his hands behind his back and threw the first salvo. "Your daughter helped me escape. She saved my life."

MacKendrick slammed his glass down and faced him. "My daughter, Savage, has shamed herself, her clan, and her father."

"There is no shame aiding one in need," he replied, studying his adversary, reading all the nuances in the man's lined face.

"I am made to look the fool."

You are more the fool to sacrifice your own daughter's happiness, he thought. "No one can make you look the fool." *Except yourself.*

The princess stood up.

In her eyes, Declan saw a deep wounding. He had to fight the urge to draw her into his arms.

"Father," his princess said with a slight nervous quiver in her voice. "Am I to understand Clan Douglas is no longer under threat of attack from us?"

"You heard me, Fallon."

"Yes, I did."

She walked up to him, a grave and serious princess about to destroy the possibility of a future.

"Lord de Douglas, the need to handfast with you to prevent a war, or an act of aggression, is no longer necessary."

Her father exploded with outrage. "Daughter, what handfasting? I authorized no . . ."

"I extracted a promise from Lord de Douglas to handfast with me," she inserted. "Given the volatile situation, it seemed the only way in which neither Clan MacKendrick nor Clan Douglas would lose face. But it seems this extreme measure is no longer necessary."

"Princess," Declan said softly, but she was not listening to him.

"The needs of my clan must come before my own, Lord de Douglas. Clan Henderson is an ancient kinship; my father's word cannot be broken without serious repercussions. I cannot allow my clan to suffer because of my foolishness."

She lifted her chin, ready to surrender for the good of her people, a stupid, idiotic, and gallant notion.

"Father, I shall honor the betrothal, if that is your wish." She turned away with false fervor.

Declan felt himself go queer inside, as if someone was cutting a piece of his heart away. "Fallon, you will not do this."

"I must," she said in a desperate whisper.

"Quiet, Savage. You have no say in this. Henderson wants her, soiled or not."

"I have a say." Declan brushed a single finger against her soft cheek.

She shook her head, a denial accompanied with a dampening of her eyelashes. She would not look at him and so he slipped his palm over her slightly curved stomach in an act of possession.

"Take your hands from her this instant!"

MacKendrick bellowed, stepping forward, ready to defend what he owned.

Declan met the furious gaze of the older man, but it was nothing compared to the rage rising inside him. "She is mine and carries my child," he countered and the older lord stilled.

"Child?" she whispered. Confusion darkened her features before small hands covered his where they pressed softly against her stomach.

"Yes." Declan felt a firestorm of desire arc through him and replace the matrix rage in his blood. He wanted her in his life and was willing to battle for her.

"How do you know I am pregnant, Declan? I do not feel . . ."

"You would know and soon," he spoke gently to her. "Dr. William confirmed conception."

"Oh," she said low and looked away.

But he was not done yet, not by a long shot. He lifted his face to engage the silent and enraged father, and took the first step toward redemption. "I would ask for Fallon to be my bride."

The older man did not answer.

CHAPTER
EIGHTEEN

It TURNED OUT to be a fine day on Io with the sky cast in the colors of ginger fire. Above distant mountain peaks, the red curve of the planet Jupiter could just be seen.

With the announcement of the wedding, word spread quickly through the silver base and settlement of five hundred. Io did not have a place of worship large enough with so many of the residents planning to attend, so the High Council decided the nuptials would take place in the red sector's observation room at nine the following evening. Once the decision was made, notices were posted throughout the base.

It would be the first royal wedding ever to take place on Io and many planned to attend. Who the many were, Fallon could not begin to fathom.

In the afternoon of her wedding day, she went to view the finished decorations in the observation room. Pausing in the entranceway, Fallon stood in awe beside a fluted stone urn with an ivy cone. The decorations were startling in the vast openness of the room. Before her, a red carpet flowed outward to the picture window on the opposite end, bisecting the large rectangular room. Along the room's perimeter, tables and seating were arranged for the wedding guests. White votive candles with pewter knot necklaces graced the center of every table. To the right, a stainless steel sword etched in gold hung above the long bridal table, representing some ancient clan tradition, no doubt. She had no clue.

Fallon walked into the center of the room and inhaled the cool fragrance of the vanilla-scented candles. A tinkling sounded about her head and she looked upward, mesmerized by the many thousands of crystal spheres, stars, and snowflake ornaments. Made of handblown glass, the ornaments hung from the white ceiling on strands of tiny pink crystal beads. The many facets on the beads refracted the light upon the white walls. She had never seen anything so magical. It felt like a holiday, but none she had ever participated in. Her gaze followed the red carpet to its end. At the massive picture window stood a dais of fabricated cherry wood flanked by two stone urns with ivy cones. A makeshift altar was decorated with white ribbons and pomegranate wreaths. She did not know where all these lovely things came from. Perhaps Clan Douglas brought them in, for certainly her father would not offer to do so.

Her chest tightened with anticipation. She knew

Declan wished to marry out of duty, because she carried his child, because honor lived in his blood. She suspected he cared for her on some deep, subconscious level, for he was not the kind of man to be forced into doing another's bidding. Yet he was unable to admit or recognize this love. For so long, he had pushed his emotions aside, keeping them under tight rein. She knew it would take time to reach his heart but she remained hopeful that someday he would let her in. She touched her stomach tenderly. A miracle grew in her womb, a child who would have a proud name and her love. She took comfort in those thoughts as her future unfolded before her.

She moved to the expansive observation window and gazed out. The rocky landscape was bathed in the orange hue of an ending day, a luminescence comparable to none. A large moon of spent volcanoes and sulphur-dioxide snows, Io had mountains twice as high as Ancient Earth's Mount Everest. In Io's sky of bright and dark, the planet Jupiter climbed the sky, sharing its majestic presence of reddish brown clouds.

Fallon looked down. In her hands, she carried a simple wedding dress, a gift from a town tradeswoman. It was ivory and she thought of it as her faerie dress.

The cape of floral lace appliqué would rest upon her bare shoulders. The silk jacquard dress would glide down her body into a double flounce at the hem, ending at her ankles. Fallon inspected the lettuce-edged hem, awed by the fine details.

"The wedding dress, I suspect."

She looked up in surprise. "Commander Ramayan." She touched her chest. "You startled me."

"I did not mean to, Princess."

"What are you doing here?" she asked, feeling a bit uneasy at this unexpected encounter.

Locking his hands behind his back, he joined her by the window and looked out to the landscape.

"You are incredibly beautiful, Princess. Henderson is a fool to have lost you."

"He never had me," she answered carefully, wondering at the commander's intentions. He was not a man to be trusted, of that she was sure.

"Yes, I can see. You have too much fire and spirit in you to be tamed by the fat lord." A slow smile curved his mouth. "Many of the matrix robots had a like fire in them."

What did matrix robots have to do with her, she wondered, and when he turned and studied her with those pale eyes a warning chill enveloped her.

"Would you care to tour the matrix facilities with me?" he asked.

She held his gaze in consternation. "I thought the matrix facilities were forbidden."

"To some, but I have access."

Fallon shook her head and took a cautionary step

away from him. Above their heads, glass ornaments swayed in newly disturbed air, chiming and tinkling against each other in response to her sudden unease.

The commander looked up. "Your telekinetic gift shows itself, Princess. I have often wondered if the rumors about you were true." He tilted his head back further, his expression flat, and his voice lowering in oddly curious tones. "These ornaments remind me of defense satellites, subservient to their controller and master. Do you not think so?"

Ornaments reminded him of defense satellites? He made no sense. There was something terribly not right with Commander Ramayan and she answered, "No."

He chuckled. "Perhaps not."

His gaze returned to her and Fallon suspected he was examining her for some awful purpose.

"Princess, come with me to the matrix labs and let me show you magic like you have never seen before."

"No." She held tight to her wedding gown and her courage.

His lips flattened. "Are the MacKendricks cowards?"

"No. But neither are they foolish."

He nodded, his gaze glinting with a hint of admiration. "Bright, as well as beautiful. I can see why he wants you."

"Who?" Did he mean Declan?

"Are you not curious about the matrix facility resident below us?"

"I am, but not during the hours before my wedding."

His focus rose above her head and an odd tightness came to his features before he faced the picture window once again. "Your groom is charming and smart, but beware of what lies below the handsome surface. When you tire of Declan's placid bed sport, find me, Princess. There are other experiences to explore. Other things that only I can teach you." His voice seemed to come to her from very far away. "I will teach you things no female could ever imagine."

Fallon had the distinct feeling of something dark and ill-conceived living within his flesh.

Her instincts took over. It was time to go. "I must take my leave of you, Commander," she said in a rush, then turned and hurried from the room, glad to be gone.

From the shadows, Declan watched his princess go.

"Spying, little brother?" Commander Ramayan taunted, after the princess had left.

"Stay away from her," Declan warned.

"A threat? Are we on opposing sides so soon?"

"As you wish it."

"She is a weakness, little brother, a wicked allure not meant for such greatness as you and I."

Declan made no response, but within his soul, he disagreed. Fallon would be his strength.

"The matrix robots were great, do you not think so?"

the commander said all too quietly.

"You need to get help, Ramayan."

The commander lifted his head and squinted at the ornaments hanging from the ceiling. "The princess has an uncommon spirit in her, just like the matrix robots."

"Listen to me carefully," Declan said with barely restrained ferocity. "Stay away from her or you will not survive my anger."

"Is that a threat, my brother?"

"Take it as you will and leave."

The commander gave a brief nod, turned on his heel, and left.

The older man's sudden acquiesce surprised him. Declan scanned the decorated room for possible threat. When he found none, he returned to his quarters. Once there, he stripped down to his breeches. Rage beat at him and he punched the gray parlor wall, lashing out. The pain in his hand was not enough to quench the bloodlust and he punched the wall again.

They had given him quarters in the blue sector, beside the Clan Douglas lord commander. He would have preferred to be placed in a sector by himself, away from everyone.

The buzzer sounded outside.

Someone was requesting entrance and he had a damn good idea who it was. He ignored it and punched the wall again, giving into the primitive force consuming him.

Declan heard the door to his quarters whoosh open. Sucking in his breath, he struggled to get ahold of his rage and present a calm exterior. He faced the entryway just as the Clan Douglas lord commander strode into the small parlor, all golden and perfect and formed of honor, as he was not.

"Lachlan," Declan greeted.

Lachlan looked at the wall, then back at him with an odd touch of humor curving his lips. "Does punching the wall work for you?"

"At the moment, it fills my need." He turned back to the wall and spread open palms against the cool flat surface. "What are you doing here?"

"Checking on you. Nice warrior tattoo, by the way."

He gave a brief nod.

"I suggest you deal with those bloody knuckles."

He had other things on his mind than bloody knuckles. "Ramayan followed the princess into the observation room."

"I know. But she is unharmed."

He pushed off the wall. "The bastard spoke about matrix robots and wanted to give Fallon a tour of the facility."

"What does Ramayan know about matrix robot technology?"

Declan wiped the sweat from his brow. "I don't

know. But our infamous father knew. Why would his eldest son not?"

"I am not following you."

A harsh laugh burst out of him. "Apparantly, Commander Ramayan is my older half brother."

"You are serious?"

"Yes. Same father, different mothers, obviously," Declan explained.

Lachlan looked away, a surge of fury crossing his features. "Rama captured and transformed Kimberly into one of those matrix robots."

"I know," Declan murmured. At the end of the clan war, Commander Lin Jacob Rama had captured Kimberly and altered her into a deadly matrix robot. It was only Dr. William's controversial retransformation process that had saved her.

"By the way, how is your lady wife?" he asked quietly and a slow smile replaced the fury in Lachlan's face.

"Beautiful."

Declan chuckled, walked over, and squeezed Lachlan's shoulder. For an instant, their gazes locked and the matrix influence within each of them tuned into stillness. It was an acceptance of fate. Declan squeezed his half brother's shoulder once more then moved to the window and braced his hands against the frame. He dropped his head down between his shoulders and asked, "Have the defense interceptor satellites been deployed into Mars' orbit yet?"

"No, twelve hours to launch."

"You'll be leaving then?"

"Yes, right after the wedding ceremony. Braemar Keep and our outposts are on high alert, *Claymore* is in orbit, and Dr. William is supervising several virus detector teams. Kimberly has briefed the squadron leaders and we have round the clock rotating patrols both on the surface and in orbit. If anything unusual approaches Mars, our combat pilots will be on it."

"Good." His gaze fell to the floor. "I still feel like we are missing something, Lachlan."

"I know it."

Declan pushed off the window frame. "We must be sure to negate all threats, whether temporary or permanent. It is the only way to protect ourselves."

"Agreed, but there will be time for battle, Declan. The next hour is for your wedding. Go and clean up those knuckles and get dressed."

He put his hands on his hips, tilted his head back, and sucked in some air. "Fallon is pregnant."

"Yes, Dr. William told me."

He gazed at his half brother with surprise. "The doctor told you?"

"Yes, he told me. Get dressed. I would prefer not to face an irate princess when I escort the groom late to his own wedding."

For the first time, Declan noticed the prestigious dress uniform adorning Lachlan's frame. "Nice uniform. Did you get the rings?"

"Of course."

"I'm not wearing a blasted kilt," he grumbled.

"The dress uniform of the *Claymore* waits in the bedroom. Get moving."

Declan headed for the air shower, intent upon washing off the stink of the matrix rage and cleaning up his bruised knuckles.

"Declan."

He stopped and looked over his shoulder.

"We make our own destiny. The sooner you realize this, the sooner you can move on with your life. Your father's mistakes were his own. They do not require your blood."

If only it were so, he mused darkly and turned away to clean up.

People he did not know, dressed in all forms of Ancient Earth finery, packed the observation room and spoke in soft whispers. His bride-to-be was already late.

On the dais, High Councilor Jared-lynn stood beside his attendants, adjusting the sleeves of his white robe for a second time. *Not a man used to waiting*, Declan mused.

"Brides are always behind schedule," Lachlan offered from behind him.

Declan nodded to his best man and locked his hands behind his back. Both he and Lachlan wore the dress uniform of the Clan Douglas warship *Claymore*. Two Clan Douglas guardsmen stood at Lachlan's back. Other guardsmen from their warship *Saltire* mingled throughout the room, ever watchful for threat.

Declan wondered at her delay, wondered if she changed her mind. A hush descended and he turned once more to the entranceway. Immediately, he understood. Fallon walked alone, unescorted. The father, making his disapproval known to all, had chosen not to give his daughter away. *So be it*, he thought.

She paused before entering, her face very pale.

He held his hand out to her. "Come to me, Fallon." *I will not let your father ruin this day for us.*

The wedding music started, a lilting bridal chorus filling the air with hope.

A brittle smile played about her lips but she held her head high, and pride welled in his chest. Eyes bright with unshed tears, she walked to him in an ivory dress, holding a bouquet of white lace and red roses.

Declan kept his hand extended, palm up, waiting.

She came, a bride's walk to her groom.

Her small hand slid into his. Brown eyes lifted and his heart sobered. His princess hurt.

He pulled her gently to him, damning the father for his selfishness. The music dwindled to a few simple notes of magic, the glass ornaments tinkling above their heads and the scent of vanilla candles sweet in their lungs.

They turned together and knelt before High Councilor Jared-lynn.

"Never have I waited for a more beautiful bride," the councilor announced loudly. He leaned forward for their hearing alone, "Your father is a fool, Princess."

Fallon nodded once, trying desperately not to break into tears. It was far worse. Her father had disowned her. She was no longer the first daughter of Clan MacKendrick, but a nobody without title, alliance, or a means to support herself. She clutched her bouquet of roses with trembling hands. Presenting her best face, she focused on the ornate gold book the councilor held and took comfort from Declan's strong presence beside her.

High Councilor Jared-lynn looked around. "Teilhard de Chardin, a twentieth century priest and scientist of Ancient Earth, once said, 'By the love of man and woman, a thread is woven, stretching to the heart of the world.'" He paused, his gaze lowering to the wedding book. "Let us begin. We gather here for a Christian wedding ceremony," he said, "to join Lord Declan de Douglas of Clan Douglas of Clans Scotland to Princess Fallon MacKendrick of Clan MacKendrick of Clans Scotland in holy matrimony . . ."

Fallon went through the motions, the councilor's craggy voice a murmur in her mind, her body deadened with cold and shock. A simple gold wedding band slipped over her ring finger. She did the same for Declan and sometime later answered, "I do."

Silence filled her being and the councilor said, "You may kiss the bride."

Her new husband's warm lips slid over hers, sharing heat, fire, and promise.

Fallon held on, wanting to crawl inside him . . .

Someone cleared his throat.

She pulled back, embarrassment flooding her cheeks.

Declan's silvery-blue eyes gleamed triumphant. A joyous roar shattered the silence and he turned away, accepting congratulations.

They were married.

She felt breakable.

Fallon looked around at the people attending her wedding. Not one did she recognize. She stood in a room full of strangers amidst faces marked with envy and faces bright with joy. It was not the wedding she had imagined, as she had once dreamed—with Clan MacKendrick banners blowing in the breeze, her father's castle decorated in white lace, friends and family all in attendance. No, it was not as she had once dreamed.

Her gaze dropped to the roses. The flowers looked wilted.

"Fallon?"

She turned to her new husband.

"May I introduce the lord commander and chieftain of Clan Douglas, my half brother, Lord Lachlan de Douglas."

Fallon extended her hand and met the lord commander's gaze. "I am honored to meet you, Lord Lachlan." She found herself staring into the same large silvery-blue eyes as her new husband's.

The lord commander smiled indulgently and took her hand in his. "We look alike, Declan and I."

She nodded, completely at a loss for words. The lord commander had golden hair to Declan's raven black. There were other differences, but they were minor to the overall picture of handsome warrior brothers.

"You are staring, Fallon." Her new husband laughed quietly beside her.

Fallon blinked, regaining her composure. "Forgive me, Lord Lachlan."

"I hope you will not hold it against me." He bowed and kissed her hand. "Welcome to the family, Princess Fallon."

"Thank you." She returned his smile, warmed by his gentle manner, and decided she liked him very well.

"May I borrow your husband for a moment?" the lord commander of Clan Douglas asked.

She nodded and stepped back to give them privacy.

"High Councilor Jared-lynn," her husband called to the clans' leader on the dais. "Would you keep my bride company for a moment while I speak with Lachlan?"

"Of course, I'd be happy to." The councilor handed the wedding book to his younger attendant and came off the dais in a flurry of quick steps and white robes. "My dear."

Fallon smiled up at the learned man. "It was a lovely ceremony."

"You lie well. We did the best we could on such short notice." He took her arm and guided her around the dais. "I do not know where all these people have come from."

Fallon laughed softly. "Neither do I."

"I'm not sure we have enough food to feed them all."

She glanced at the buffet tables. "Probably not."

But it did not seem to matter to anyone. In the air, the sweet ancient melody of Pachelbel's *Canon in D* played, coaxing the people into small groups of celebration.

Fallon allowed the councilor to guide her to where the remaining twelve-member council waited. She searched the crowd in a desperate hope that her father had changed his mind and decided to join in his daughter's wedding celebration. But that was not the case. In her heart, Fallon realized she must accept her father's decision for now. Perhaps after a time he would feel differently. She did not want to start her new life with tears and so struggled to calm her upheaval. While the councilor spoke with another one of his attendants, she took the time to look around at all the new faces. Her gaze settled on Lord Henderson and his gangly companion, Commander Lin Derek Ramayan. These two she knew, although she would have preferred it if they were not at her wedding. They were in a heated conversation in the right corner of the room, oblivious to all around them.

Fallon watched them, unaccountably intrigued. They seemed to know each other well enough to argue openly, a familiarity she found strangely disturbing. Commander Ramayan crossed his arms; his mouth curved in a twisted smile, which caused Lord Henderson's face to turn beet red. *Pitfalls for the sin seekers*, she mused, knowing Lord Henderson's lust for riches.

Her husband came up behind her and touched her elbow.

"Thank you, sir," Declan spoke to the councilor.

"Come to claim her, have you?" the councilor teased. "About time."

"Yes, sir."

"Lord Lachlan returns to Braemar Keep?" the counselor asked.

"Yes, sir."

"Understandable, given the current situation."

"Yes," he replied and bent to speak quietly to the

councilor.

Respectful of Declan's wish for privacy, she turned away, once more seeking to watch the exchange between Ramayan and Henderson. The secretive verbal skirmish appeared to be ending. But from the look of the fat lord, she doubted he had come out the winner.

"Fallon, is something wrong?"

"What?" She looked into Declan's face.

"You were gazing off into the distance." He looked to where she'd been staring and Fallon glanced back. Both Lord Henderson and Commander Ramayan were gone.

"I guess I am a trifle overwhelmed," she whispered, looking down at her bouquet of wilted roses.

He slid his arm around her waist and pulled her close to his side.

"Hungry?" Fingers tenderly touched her cheek.

"I am a bit hungry," she admitted. "Except, I have an overpowering urge for garlic pickles and ice cream."

He laughed. "That's a bit of a cliché."

"Is it?" she replied in all seriousness and quickly altered her request. "Maybe a small bowl of vanilla ice cream then?"

He continued to grin and guided her through the crowd of congratulators to the bridal table.

Fallon found herself quickly seated. Three ornamental gold plates befitting a royal bride were placed in front of her, one of green pickles, one of vanilla ice cream, and one of roasted poultry and mixed vegetables in steaming butter sauce. A gold goblet of orange juice came next, followed by a glass of milk.

She touched the glass of milk and looked up at him. "Declan, I cannot eat all this."

"We'll share." Her handsome husband walked around the table and took his seat by her side. He very carefully positioned the plate of poultry and vegetables in front of her.

Fallon laid her bouquet of roses on the empty seat beside her. Lord Lachlan was to have joined them, but it seemed he needed to return home immediately. She understood clan obligations quite well and her heart saddened with thoughts of her father.

All around them was the hum of voices as guests settled down to partake of the fine meal. Everyone seemed to be enjoying themselves, enjoying any chance for celebration. To her right, the twelve members of the High Council had already taken their seats and were sharing laughter for the first time in a good long while. Children smiled at her, their faces smeared with desserts and delight.

Fallon returned their smiles, glad to be the bridal sponsor of this joyous gathering. There were too few good things in life not to grasp and hold tight when one crossed your path. She glanced at Declan then reached for a thin green pickle. She dipped one end of it into the ice cream, and took a small bite. It tasted heavenly. She took another bite and reached for the glass of milk.

"Perhaps some protein?" Declan prompted. He held a slice of the white meat between his index finger and thumb.

"There are utensils for eating, Declan."

"This is more fun. Open."

She opened her mouth.

His thumb brushed her lips as the succulent piece of meat landed on her tongue. Somewhere deep inside her, butterflies awakened and danced in her stomach. Another piece followed, then a tiny juicy carrot, and always the touch and taste of him remained on her lips. He fed her this way, in front of all these strangers, branding her as his own. It was their first meal together as husband and wife, and Fallon felt special despite her father's condemnation.

"I could get used to this," she murmured between mouthfuls.

"I know." He grinned and placed the glass of milk within reach.

Fallon settled in for a wonderful wedding feast.

By the time the festivities ended, dawn was approaching and Declan's lovely bride had fallen asleep at the bridal table. Gently, he scooped her up in his arms and stood.

She snuggled against him in slumber, her nose tucked into his neck.

Walking around the bridal table, he left the remnants of the celebration behind. As he headed for the exit, he nodded his farewells to those few remaining guests unwilling to leave.

His bride was light in his arms and he carried her easily through the hall to their quarters in the blue sector. Everything was quiet, the sound of his boots the only echo. When he arrived at their quarters, the door whooshed open and he headed directly for their small bedroom. Declan placed her on the white blankets of the simple bed and straightened. He was rather surprised to find her watching him intently.

"I thought you were asleep, Princess."

"This is my wedding night; I have no intention of sleeping." She kicked off her white shoes, knelt on the bed, and faced him. "You belong to me now, Declan."

"Do I?" he teased.

"Oh, yes." She slid the ivory cape off her shoulders in a seductive shrug. With the release of a single button, the wedding dress glided down her body like a living thing, leaving her bare, except for ivory stockings.

Declan made no move, but allowed his spirited young bride the freedom of her seduction. She tugged on his forearm and he placed a knee on the bed beside her, inner thigh to slender hip, and waited for her next move.

Fallon tugged again and suddenly found herself beneath him, in a position of submissiveness, her legs caught in the folds of the confounded wedding dress.

Her new husband braced his arms on either side of her head, his lustrous eyes glinting with male enjoyment. This was a side of him she had never seen before. A playful spirit had replaced the cynical and jaded man. It was unbearable and agonizing and wonderful to have him in her arms like this, to be free from the burdens of life, if only for this one special night.

He kissed her forehead and gently nuzzled her temple. "My pampered princess bride, what do you want of me?"

I want. I want. I want. The quote from the prize-winning author flickered briefly in her mind and her eyes closed. "Much," she replied, passion unfurling. "Kiss me."

He obeyed with a leisurely touch of supple lips plied to her own. Slivers of heat engulfed her and she gripped his biceps in frustration, fingers digging into flesh with her needs.

"Patience." His tongue skimmed the silken dampness of her bottom lip in an unhurried caress. She strained up against him, losing all semblance of control. She was helplessly in love with her new husband and wanted . . . her teeth caught on his lower lip and held. Tonight was not a night for patience. Tonight was for tangled limbs, gasping breaths, and a whirlpool of sensations.

Blue eyes cracked open, revealing slits of smoldering

passion. Lean hips slowly surged against her in response.

She released him.

"I know what you want, my impatient one. I know," he breathed huskily. Large hands fisted in her hair and he took her mouth in the hot fevered kiss she had been yearning for. Fallon's eyes fluttered closed to the roar of his claim.

It was ecstasy kissing him like this. She kicked her legs free from the dress and arched up against him, her body straining to join his. In the next moment, he pulled free from her and came off the bed.

Fallon pushed up to elbows and watched as he shoved off his uniform. "Please hurry," she said, shivering with anticipation and excitement.

He arched an amused brow before blanketing her body once more. The feel and scent of him was dangerous and wild to her senses. She liked him like this, barely under control. Hot kisses trailed down her body, from her mouth to her toes. He ministered to her ankles, stirring up squeals of delight from her before he worked his way back up her calves to her thighs.

"You are so beautiful," he murmured.

She lay quivering before him, her hands clutching the bedcovers at her sides as he sampled every corner of her flesh. She felt consumed by him, and when he pulled her thighs apart, leaned forward, and kissed her intimately, her violent gasp locked in her throat. He settled there, his mouth demanding waves of pleasure from her. Large hands cupped her buttocks, kneading the supple flesh, and pleasure intensified, impaling her. She writhed under his hot mouth, struggling for an urgent completion, struggling, pressing down, gasping loudly . . . then she ignited, a shattering of blood and soul into a thousand brilliantly lit stars. Lights danced and dwindled behind scrunched eyelids as her womb flooded with the liquid warmth of her release. It claimed her fully and she tumbled back to earth in a blur of radiance and sensitivity.

"Ready for me?" he rasped and covered her body once more with his own.

"Yes." She gripped sweaty shoulders, pulling him down. His hips settled between her thighs and with a single thrust, he penetrated her wet core. Pleasure spiked and her world narrowed to him.

He moved with a deep grinding, his body demanding an urgent closure within hers. Tenderness and hunger were all tangled together, and she tasted her release upon his lips. He was breathing heavy and a second rekindling formed and quickly consumed her. She panted in the ecstasy of it and in the next moment his breath hitched. A marking of the silent agony of his own taunting release seized hold and carried over him. While he quaked above her, she pressed kisses to his throat and in human redemption once more asserted, took his seed into her womb.

He collapsed on top of her in a trembling heap, a final willingness to let go and embrace his altered humanity.

She held him close. Calm euphoria settled in her blood and settled in his blood.

Fallon lay content under him, stroking his strong back, her fingers unknowingly following the lines of his tattoo. He shifted off her; his face nestled into her neck. One arm flung possessively over her waist while their legs remained entangled.

In her arms, he continued to quake with little aftershocks of spent passion even as sleep rose and claimed him. He smelled of her desire as she did of his, the sweet, rich fragrance of wantonness. His large body kept her warm, made her feel secure, made her feel wanted.

Fallon sighed and her eyelashes fluttered closed. *The burdens of tomorrow would come soon enough*, she mused, as the peace of slumber and the warmth of her true love cradled her.

A new day crept up upon them, though neither noticed. For six hours they slept deeply, locked in each other's embrace, replenishing body, spirit, and soul—and then . . .

. . . Fallon's dreams shifted to a horrific darkness.

The nightmare pulled her down into fear and death.

She knew she was dreaming, but could not wake up. An invisible weight confined her and a warning cry locked in her throat.

Above her head, frilly satellites moved in a twilight sky then exploded into frosty red clouds. Blood rained down upon the people, peeling away skin, until only standing skeletons remained.

She screamed in terror and battled her way up to consciousness.

"Fallon, wake up."

Fallon awoke to find her husband holding her. She clung to him, her eyelids scrunched closed, tears streaming down her face. "Oh, God. Oh, God."

"It was only a bad dream," he reassured.

No, it was not a dream. She shook her head, dragging in great gulps of air and pulling away from him. Fallon clutched her sides and began to rock. "They all died. Their skin peeled away until nothing was left but parched bone."

"Fallon, look at me."

She looked up through her misery and tears. "They are all dead, Declan."

"Who is dead?"

The moment stretched on and on before she could answer, before she could name the planet where death would come. "Mars," she whispered, not knowing why.

Her husband's large hands slid to her wrist and held

her. "I know you have the gift of telekinesis. But do you experience premonitions as well?"

She stopped rocking, afraid to answer, afraid he would draw away. She looked down at their tightly held hands, his so much larger, quietly confident in their touch . . .

"Fallon, are you all right?"

Her mind flashed back to yesterday, to the crystal-clear moment after she had taken her wedding vows.

In the back of the room, Lord Henderson and Commander Ramayan were arguing.

Lord Henderson's face turning red . . .

Commander Ramayan's twisted smile . . .

Sin seekers, they were.

Sin seekers was what she had called them.

Fallon looked up, the meaning of her nightmare suddenly so appallingly clear. "It is in the satellites, Declan."

He searched her face. "What's in the satellites?"

"A virus, Declan. It is in the defense satellites."

CHAPTER
NINETEEN

DECLAN MOVED CLOSER to his young bride and pushed the sheets between them aside. "Fallon, am I to understand that a virus is in the defense satellites of Mars?"

"Yes." She wiped her eyes and clutched the sheet to her naked breasts.

"Please tell me how you know this."

"Before the wedding, I went to the observation room to see the wedding decorations. Commander Ramayan joined me there. I was surprised to see him. He is such a strange man that I . . ."

Declan touched the sheet covering her thigh and found her trembling. "Go on," he said gently.

"Commander Ramayan said the ornaments hanging from the ceiling reminded him of defense satellites. His white eyes glazed over as he said it. Then he made the strangest comment, something about being subservient to their controller and master."

Declan sat back. "I did not hear that piece of it."

"I don't understand."

His gaze met hers in apology. "I followed you."

"Why?"

"With Ramayan about, I needed to know that you were safe."

She shoved hair off her forehead. "Ramayan said defense satellites are subservient to their controller, Declan. He knows about your clan's satellites."

"But why do you make the association of the viruses in our satellites?"

She moistened her lips. "After our wedding vows, you left me to speak with Lord Lachlan. As I walked beside High Councilor Jared-lynn, I saw Lord Henderson and Commander Ramayan in the back of the room in a heated argument. Lord Henderson's face turned very red. It only gets that red when financial discussions do not go his way. And then Commander Ramayan looked up and saw me watching them."

"They could have been arguing about anything." Declan tried to calm her, but a terrible suspicion had taken root inside him.

"No, you must believe me." A frightened wildness shone in her eyes and she took a deep, uneven breath. "I have had dreams about terrible things before they happened."

"You have precognitive abilities?"

She nodded, terrified he would look at her differently, but she would not let Clan Douglas die. "These dreams happen rarely and I cannot control them," she said in a hushed and battered voice. "Once when I was young, I dreamed of my mother falling down a lacework of clouds and the next day she fell down a staircase."

"Only one dream?"

"There have been others. They are infrequent, but have always come true. These dreams make me unwell. I feel like a cracked mirror, all fractured up inside into tiny bits. I cannot describe it any other way. Declan, I feel cracked inside again, like that broken mirror."

Declan knew his bride had psychic talent, a special and unique gift. But this? "If Ramayan blames Clan Douglas for the death of his father . . . our father," he corrected and felt lost to the pull of that miserable day.

"Declan?" His bride touched his arm, drawing him back from the guilt. "You must believe me."

For a long moment, he could only look at her, then said softly, "I believe you." He had to deal with the present and put the past behind him, once and for all. Now was the time to do it, this day, when another threat grew. "If Ramayan blames Clan Douglas for the death of Rama . . ." he murmured his thoughts aloud.

"Yes."

He met her gaze. ". . . what better way to destroy the hated enemy than with an untraceable and lethal virus?"

"He would need access to the satellites, Declan," she

offered and he saw fear in her eyes, fear for him, and for his clan.

He looked away, striving for an answer. "Access," he echoed. "How would he gain access?" And then he had his answer. "Contact the defense satellite manufacturer and say you were interested in the purchase of satellite technology. You'd have access then."

"Lord Henderson could have supplied the virus," she added.

"Agreed." He leaned over and kissed her squarely on the mouth. "Get dressed."

They both climbed from the bed and dressed.

Moments later, they bolted out the door into the vacant corridor of the blue sector. Bright lights momentarily blinded Fallon before she took off after Declan at top speed.

Hastily dressed in the black uniform of the *Claymore*, jacket unbuttoned, hair in wild disarray across her face, Fallon struggled to keep up with her husband's fast pace.

"Declan, wait," her urgent call echoed in the cool air.

He skidded to a halt, one hand touching the white wall for balance, and doubled back. He grabbed her right hand and hauled her with him down the corridor.

"Should we notify the High Council?" she gasped between breaths.

"No, too risky."

"Why?"

"If there is an informant among the leadership ranks, I don't want to chance it."

They came to the end of the blue sector and turned right down a short recess. It looked like a service corridor to Fallon, all musty and gray. He released her hand and headed for a set of red double doors.

She followed, her lungs hurting, her chest heaving. "I thought . . ." she took a moment to catch her breath, ". . . we were going to the *Black Ghost*."

"Yes."

She came up beside him and laid a hand on his arm. "This way?"

He did not answer but continued to inspect the access console.

"Declan?"

"This leads to the bay."

"The doors appear to be locked. I do not suppose you know the code to open them?"

"Possibly. During my service as second commander, I created a few backdoor and override codes. One of them might still work." He touched the screen on the console to activate it.

"Console ready," a metallic voice said in response.

"Computer, access code MIABK20."

"Access denied."

Declan grimaced.

"Try another code," she offered.

"Computer, access code RGG90," he prompted.

"Accepted," the computer said and the red doors slid open with a burst of cold air.

Trepidation dissolved and Fallon stared into the amber glow of the dank cavernous ship bays of the blue sector. Waiting only a moment for her eyes to adjust, she entered, walking beside Declan. The air was much cooler here. Dotted lights illuminated gray walkways, which serpentined through several bays. The place was empty as they made their way toward the shadow of the freighter gunship. It felt surreal, as if they were the only people left alive on the moon. Her husband came to an abrupt halt and so did she.

"What is wrong?" Fallon flung tangled curls out of her face. "The *Black Ghost* is there." She pointed.

"It does not smell right," he said deliberately.

"It smells like fuel, metal, and cables, a typical ship bay."

"That is not what I smell." He stepped forward.

Clasping her hands in front of her, she looked around and sniffed. "What do you smell?"

"I smell men and fear."

"What would men fear in this secured bay?"

"Exactly."

He turned to her with a quicksilver flash in his eyes, a marker of his matrix difference. "Stay behind me, Fallon."

She nodded and followed at a short distance.

Declan approached the *Black Ghost* with extreme caution.

His ship stood alone, a sleek phantom shrouded in a cast of dim light and gray shadow. A single amber spot-light illuminated her closed hatch. Walking under the forward-swept wing, he lifted his hand and touched the cool hull. "They've been here," he murmured angrily.

"Who?" she prompted, coming up behind him.

He shook his head. A sharp surge of alarm washed over him, his instincts kicking into high gear.

"Fallon, stay here."

"Why?"

"Please don't argue. Just stay." He turned back to the ship and gave the order. "*Ghost*, open hatch," he commanded.

White lights clicked along the hull, bringing the ship to life. The hatch swung upward and he moved closer, the inside greeting him with . . .

Silence.

Emptiness.

Breathing.

His wife.

"I thought I told you to stay back," he said angrily without looking at her.

"This is back."

Declan grabbed the handhold and swung up into

his ship. His feet landed with a thud on the metal floor. The *Ghost* smelled of intruders. He could detect the trace of bitter sweat.

Behind him, he heard his wife climb aboard and tried not to lose patience.

"The ship has been compromised," he said low and harshly.

Her eyes widened. "Are you certain?"

"Yes, remain here. I mean it, Fallon."

She nodded, her gaze locked on him.

"Don't move," he ordered in a scathing tone, which probably only infuriated her princess sensibilities, but he did not care. Besides his clan, her safety was of utmost importance to him. He went down the corridor ready to do battle, but what he found was emptiness. He checked the ship's engines and the energy crystal chamber first, before moving into the other vulnerable engineering areas.

When he returned, he knew he had been gone a long time.

He did not expect his wife to fling herself into his arms the moment he returned.

"Engines appear fine," he reassured quickly, masking his surprise. "Crystal chamber seems intact. Engine and Delta system compartments appear okay as well. Cargo holds locked and empty. Let's check up front. Are you all right to do this?"

"Yes."

He slipped his hand in hers and led her forward. "*Ghost*, close and secure hatch," he called over his shoulder. The black hatch swung closed behind them, locking them in the cool blue-gray interior of the ship. They headed for the bridge.

The *Ghost* smelled of men. Yet, he could detect nothing out of order. He hardly knew what to think. His insides continued to clamor out warnings, but he was running out of time.

"What do you want me to do?" she asked.

"Look around for explosive devices. If you find any, don't touch, just call me."

"All right."

They meticulously inspected every area. Declan checked in all the obvious places, and the not-so-obvious ones.

"I cannot find anything, Declan."

He looked down to where she sat on the floor beside the navigation console.

"I was afraid of that. It looks clean. I don't like it."

"Could your senses be wrong?" she asked in a small voice.

They had served him well over the years. Never had he been wrong.

"Declan, we are running out of time. If we can, we must go."

"I know. Get up and sit in the copilot chair."

He strapped into the pilot seat beside her. "*Ghost*, engines online," he commanded. The command console lit up. Powerful engines came online with a low growl.

"Are you strapped into your seat? This may be a jarring trip."

"Yes." She pulled the gray belts across her chest and secured them.

Under his expert hands, the *Black Ghost* lifted from the deck, a black smudge moving in shadow. He guided her to the airlock doors at the far end of the bay and hoped for the best.

"Declan, do we need authorization to leave Io?"

"Yes."

She cleared her throat delicately. "Do you have authorization?"

"No." Declan focused on the closed airlock doors just outside the ship's window. He could blast the doors open or he could breach their computer system.

He chose the latter and quickly interfaced with the base's computer network.

"What are you doing?"

"I am acquiring authorization, sort of."

"Oh."

The lights on the silver doors turned white, seals released, and the doors slid open on their glides.

Declan piloted the ship into the airlock. Moments later, they left the silver base behind and entered the skies.

Immediately, the ship's commlink crackled with requests from the silver base for identification.

Declan ignored them.

"Declan, should we not answer them?"

"No."

They entered space with the planet Jupiter full and brilliant in the ship's windows. All of a sudden, a red tactical warning light blinked on Fallon's console, accompanied by a rapid series of loud beeps.

"Weapon lock," Declan stated sharply.

"From the base?"

"No."

"Look out!"

"I see them." He banked hard to avoid a stream of pulsar cannon fire. "*Ghost*, shields on," he commanded loudly.

Ship shields activated. Three streamlined cruisers came in behind them from Jupiter's dark side.

"Who are they?" Fallon demanded.

"I have no idea, possibly pirate cruisers." Declan rolled the *Ghost* to port and felt the stealth ship hesitate. "I goddamn knew it," he snarled. "Hold on!"

An explosion rocked inside the ship, throwing both him and his princess bride forward against the straps in their seats. The bridge went black before the power backups kicked in and red emergency lights switched on.

"Fallon?" He glanced over at his disheveled copilot.

"I am fine. What happened?"

"It looks like they rigged the first cargo hold to blow the moment I turned to port. I'm going to eject it."

The ship lurched under them as he released the fire engulfed hold.

"*Ghost*, report status," Declan quickly demanded.

"Communications out," the metallic voice of the ship's computer replied in a flat tone. "Power flow compromised. Shields down. Oxygen levels dropping." They knew just where to hurt him.

"Fallon, can you stabilize oxygen levels?" He had his hands full, fighting and dodging the attacking cruisers. Without full power and shields, they made an easy target.

Out of the corner of his eyes, he saw her bend over several control consoles. "Reroute the flow of oxygen through the undamaged pathways," he explained. "You told me your father had trained you for emergency ship situations. I hope the training was good."

It took her a few moments, but then his magnificent bride did exactly as he requested.

"Oxygen levels stabilized," the computer said.

"How about communications?" he asked, not looking at her. "We have to warn Lachlan about the virus in the defense satellites."

In the confines of the bridge, he could hear the frustration in her breath.

"Fallon?"

"I think this will . . . Got it!" his princess bride said

proudly.

The *Black Ghost* roared back to life under his hands.

"Power flow at one hundred percent," the computer said in response.

"Good girl, what about communications?"

"I do not understand the readouts for the communications or the shields."

"It will have to do." Declan took advantage. With a single burst of speed, he left the slower cruisers far behind, not wanting to waste any more precious time.

"Keep working on communications."

She focused on the streams of data then shook her head. "My father taught me how to restore environmental systems and reroute power in times of ship emergencies, but these readouts are beyond my comprehension, Declan. I am sorry."

"Don't be. You got us up and running. We'll just have to do this the hard way." He had several choices. He could set the ship on autopilot and fix ship communications, which would, no doubt, take hours and leave them vulnerable for attack from those cruisers.

"What exactly is the hard way?" she asked with worry.

"Give me a minute." Or he could ignore the problem with ship communications entirely and pilot through the dangerous Moukad Nebula. The nebula was unpredictable, and with a damaged ship under him the chances for survival dropped exponentially. *No*, he thought, the only option left was the jump gate. "We are going through the jump gate. It is the fastest route to Mars." He headed for the jump gate at full speed, a litany of prayers in his heart.

They made the jump into black space an hour later.

Fallon gripped the console as the *Black Ghost* roared into Mars' orbit. Declan's home world was a planet in transition. Her father had told her that the atmospheric equipment worked to remake the fretted terrain, scarred crevasses, gullies, and glacial features into a landscape of abundance and life. To her, saving the planet was worth sacrificing everything.

"Declan, we cannot respond to your planet's requests for identification."

"I know. Our only hope is they recognize the *Ghost*'s ship signature."

Fallon looked up from the console and saw what looked like four silver butterflies coming into view on the port side.

"Are those the satellites?" she asked. They clustered together, a glittering of metal and menace.

"Yes. They have not yet reached their placement above the planet."

Fallon sat perfectly still as the terrible reality pressed

heavily down upon her. "Which one?" she whispered and heard Declan swear.

"I don't know. It could be in all of them."

She stared at the satellites. "Can you destroy all of them?" she asked quickly.

"Would an exploding satellite destroy the virus or release it into the planet's atmosphere?" he countered. "I don't dare chance."

Fallon glanced at him, and for the first time uncertainty shown in his eyes. She looked back at the satellites again. "Bring the satellites into the *Ghost*'s remaining cargo holds."

He did a quick calculation then shook his head. "With cargo hold one gone, I can only carry three of them and it would be an exceedingly tight fit. They're just too damn big."

A light flashed on the console between them. "What is that?" she asked.

"Satellite four has dropped out of orbit and is reentering the planet's atmosphere. That's the one."

"How can you be sure, Declan?"

"Instinct."

Fallon held on as Declan brought the *Ghost* directly behind satellite four. Beyond the satellite, a great big ship loomed into view just as the red tactical warning light blinked on her console. "Oh, no," she whispered, her concern lost under the rapid series of loud beeps.

"Weapons lock," she stated louder, wishing she were not having to become familiar with this particular part of his ship.

"Yes, it is the *Claymore*. Standard procedure for un-authorized ship arrivals." He reached behind him at a rather awkward angle and Fallon frowned.

"What are you doing?"

"Setting the hull lights to pulse in sets of threes, a se-cret recognition code between Clan Douglas ships when communication is down."

"Oh."

"Let's hope *Claymore* sees it."

"Yes, let us hope."

Outside the *Ghost*'s window, satellite four moved into the planet's upper atmosphere and began shedding its silver skin like a moth. It was incredibly beautiful, panels outspread like insect wings, leaving behind a trail of glitter in the darkness.

Beside her, Declan's hand trembled above the trigger of the *Ghost*'s pulsar cannon.

Fallon looked at the satellite, looked at Declan, then looked back at the satellite. This is what her father had meant by a crisis situation—a choice of life and death. Now, she understood. Now, when all rested upon her. Unstrapping from her seat, she stood and walked over to the ship's main window. "Do not fire. I shall hold the satellite intact."

"What are you talking about? Fallon, you have a low five rating. You do not have that kind of psychic strength."

"I am stronger than a five rating. You must trust me in this."

"How strong?"

She envisioned blood sores and peeling flesh, horrible things that made her want to shrink back in terror . . .

"Fallon! How strong are you?"

"Strong enough." She turned around in the small space and met the fear in his gaze. She knew he saw it there in her eyes, the pulse and power of her gift.

"Bring the *Ghost* around," she said firmly. "I shall put the thing into one of the cargo holds. You seal it."

"Fallon, I don't . . ."

"Trust me, my love. I am stronger than you know. I can keep the satellite intact."

"God, help me." He gave a brisk nod. "I trust you."

Fallon turned back to the window. She felt it starting, the shivering and the shuddering inside, the fear. She knew what she had to do, knew she had the strength to do it, deep down, untested, and waiting. Innocent lives were at stake. Death waited to happen and only she and Declan stood in the way.

But it was up to her now.

Only her.

Pressing her palms against the ship's cold window, she focused on the shedding satellite and the splintering sounds that were not heard in space but only in her open mind.

She watched the outer skin unraveling like a patchwork of silver quilts.

Gripping the window handholds, her world narrowed to the terror and horror of what lay within that silver machine. She saw herself dying, blood spurting from skin wounds ripe with the virus.

Her heart picked up a rapid beat.

A trembling twisted inside, a grieving for what could be lost. Her jaw tightened with dread and anguish. Tears shimmered in her eyes. The trembling intensified, growing, expanding until she could not breathe. She gulped back a terrified sob, then the anger came.

The full rage of it fueled her gift.

Crackling burst inside her and her mind splintered. Power released.

Fallon reached out with her gift and felt every layer, every molecule, every atom of the deadly satellite and virus.

She fused them together by sheer force of will.

A frozen mating.

Metallic binding.

Virus and satellite and death.

The brutal force of the effort threatened to rip her

apart. In the far reaches of her mind, a part of her erected a mental shield to protect her unborn child. She prayed it was enough. She had no choice but to give all her life energies to save what must be saved.

Fury fueled her power. Tears of wrath blurred her sight.

She fought the satellite's code for discharge, its rain of hell and damnation. She would not let Mars become barren of life, no matter the cost. No matter the cost.

"Hang on, honey," Declan called from somewhere behind her.

My one true love.

I love you.

Tears streaked crimson down her cheeks. Fallon dug her fingers into the window holds, battling the shedding silver monster with her mind, gripping it closed with the very essence of stubbornness and will.

Her mind became cloudy.

The *Ghost* moved under her.

Give peace in our time, Oh Lord.

Cargo doors slid open.

Ashes to ashes and dust to dust.

Focus.

To have and to hold from this day forward.

Focus.

It hurts.

Focus.

Focus.

Focus.

Fallon drew the toxic satellite nearer to the ship.

Slow.

Steady.

Closer.

Her body burned. She bit back a moan.

To love and to cherish until death do us part.

Focus.

Will thou . . . forsaking all others.

She held on through the pain, through the blood red tears, through the terror of failure, keeping the virus locked within the satellite.

So long as you both shall live.

Her heart pounded painfully in her chest, a loud drumbeat in her ears. Space became wavy.

Satellite.

Virus.

Satellite.

Virus.

Death.

Life.

Her child was still with her, a desperate clinging of life within her womb.

"Satellite in. Doors closed and sealed!" Declan

yelled urgently. "Fallon, by God, let go."

Fallon let go of the rage and fury, let go of the terror, and shuddered. She closed her eyes and welcomed the unforgiving darkness. It cleaved her into a thousand more pieces of that cracked mirror and she fell into her husband's waiting arms, unconscious.

CHAPTER
TWENTY

Braemar Keep, Home to Clan Douglas
Planet Mars

ANOTHER NIGHT INTRUDED, an unwelcome shroud upon the land and black waters of the crater lake. Declan turned from his bedroom window. He walked back across the light wood floor and carpets to the four-poster bed where Fallon slept.

For two days he had watched her sleep, watched her breathe, so small and still in his bed, covered in white blankets. She was disengaged from self, unresponsive and unaware. A single fiery braid fell down her right shoulder across her breast. They had dressed her in a violet sleeping gown with satin trim on the neckline and long sleeves.

He gripped the bedpost, his knuckles turning white.

"Fallon," he whispered achingly. "Do not leave me."

Dr. William named the condition coma, a bihemispheric dysfunction with no physical trauma noted. He did not want to use an emulsion tank in this case and insisted that all she needed was bed rest.

Declan swallowed hard as pain expanded in his chest. He turned and dragged a wingback chair closer to the side of the bed. Tossing a small gold pillow to the floor, he sat down on the chair, his eyes gray and hollow. Behind him, night seeped into the room, an unwanted guest, a marker of another day passing. In the marble hearth across from the bed he kept the fire burning, a bright light, should she need to find her way back to him.

Declan reached over and smoothed the soft bedcovers across her stomach. Their unborn child continued to develop in the warm safety of her womb, unharmed by the events that had stolen her from him.

His gaze moved to her face. Her mind had retreated to some faraway haven to heal from the psychic wounds. Auburn lashes rested on pale cheeks the color of virgin snow. Her eyes were responsive to light. A good sign, Dr. William had reassured him earlier. Give her time.

Time she would have.

She had saved Clan Douglas.

She had held the poisonous satellite together by extreme telepathic force, giving him time to contain it safely within the *Ghost*'s holds. Hours later he'd ejected the damn thing into the old nebula. The *Claymore* had monitored the situation and destroyed the satellite, and the deadly virus it contained, without a trace.

Flames crackled in the hearth, shooting sparks of orange and blue light across white walls.

"I'll wait, my love." He blinked away the moisture in his eyes. "Take all the time you need to heal."

Fallon stirred. She felt a heavy pressure resting across her hips, not a good thing when one's bladder was full. She opened her eyes slowly, her mind sluggish from a receding haze. Shafts of pink morning light spilled from the window into the large butternut-colored bedroom, across the wooden floor, to the large bed and her.

She lifted her head slightly and looked down her nose at the offending weight.

Declan held her in slumber, in an odd and uncomfortable position from the look of it. He half sat in a sumptuous gold chair. The rest of him lay heavily atop the bed and her. He wore a wrinkled white shirt with the sleeves rolled up and brown form-fitting breeches. One arm was flung over her upper thighs, the other held close and under her, hugging her hips. His head rested on her stomach, his face was turned to her. A ragged beard shadowed his strong jaw and lent an air of ruggedness and mystery to him.

Her lips curved in a tender smile. Fallon knew he loved her, even if he was unable to admit it to himself.

On his right shoulder blade, a tiny white movement caught her attention. Strands of Declan's blue-black hair were shoved aside.

"Woof."

"Shush, Thorn," Declan murmured sleepily.

Fallon blinked rapidly to clear her vision.

The tiny creature watched her with worldly, iridescent eyes. Gossamer wings of silvery white unfolded from its slender back.

"What's that?" she inquired in a stunned voice, "a tiny poodle with wings?"

Her husband jerked upright, unsettling the tiny beast from his shoulder.

The beast flew over her head and settled on the night table. It sat and wagged its tail, showing pearly white teeth and a red tongue.

Fallon turned back. "Declan, what in the Lord's name . . ." her voice faltered at what she saw in his face.

He watched her, his gaze hooded from sleep, his emotions sharp and obvious. The wrinkled white shirt fell open to his waist, giving her an enticing view of a muscular chest.

"Good morning," she murmured with a smile and pointed over her shoulder. "What is that tiny creature?"

He swallowed hard. "A wee-gadhar."

"A wee dog?" she translated, her brows gathering in curiosity.

His lips curved in relief. "Yes, a wee-dog. We call them poodleflys. How do you feel?"

"My mind feels a little drifty." She glanced back at the poodlefly, who continued to regard her with uncommon zeal. "Does the poodlefly have a name?"

"I call her Thorn. She travels with me sometimes when the mood strikes her." He gestured to the poodlefly. "Thorn, meet my lady wife, Princess Fallon. Princess Fallon, meet Thorn."

"Woof." Thorn stood and wagged her tail.

"Hello, Thorn," Fallon returned the greeting. "You are quite lovely."

"Woooof."

Apparently the poodlefly agreed, and Fallon laughed softly. But the laughter was not meant to last. Rather unexpectedly, the poodlefly and all the room began to blur into waves of blue light. Her smile wilted.

Painful memories washed over her and she sat up abruptly, touching her temple with trembling fingers.

"Fallon?"

Declan sounded far away.

She had kept the satellite fused and whole.

No matter the cost.

She'd focused and held tight.

An icy pain had spread in her mind.

It had hurt to breathe, yet she held on.

Light had converged into darkness, overwhelming

her senses until she could not see, or hear, or touch the outside world.

Her legs had begun to shake, strength ebbing with each passing moment.

And still she had kept the satellite together. Never would it release its deadly cargo while she lived.

And above all else, above all else, an instinct strong and true, her hastily erected mental shield had protected her unborn child until she lost consciousness.

"Fallon?"

Her mind flashed back to the present.

Her husband sat on the edge of the bed, fingers caressing her cheek with concern.

Her voice caught in anguish, hands covering her stomach. "My babe."

He leaned forward, sheltering her small hands with his. "Our child is unharmed. You are safe. You are both safe."

"My babe is safe," she said quietly.

"Yes."

Deeply shadowed eyes watched her, his face worn and haggard. A swift horror constricted in her chest. "Clan Douglas?"

"Safe," he answered. "All are safe. Lie back down if you please." He pushed her gently back into plush pillows.

"What happened to the satellite?"

Thorn jumped up and barked enthusiastically.

"Yes, Thorn." Declan chuckled, turning back to her. "I ejected the cargo hold containing the satellite into the Moukad Nebula. The pulsar cannon of the *Claymore* vaporized it. The other three satellites checked out clean."

Fallon felt the tension ease out of her body. "I thought the nebula unsafe for travel."

"Not to Clan Douglas. We know how to navigate it."

"Oh."

He smiled down at her, his eyes kindling with warmth and relief.

"Do you know who sabotaged the satellite?" Fallon asked.

He shook his head. "I have my suspicions. Lachlan is looking into it."

She struggled to sit up, her body demanding she find a facilities room, and soon. "Where is this place?"

He shifted back to give her room. "You are in my quarters on Braemar Keep."

"Are there facilities near?"

"Yes." Standing, he pulled the white blankets back and reached for her.

"What are you doing?" Fallon looped an arm around his neck and held on as he lifted her.

"Taking you to the facilities."

He smelled of black coffee.

Thorn took flight in front of them, wings beating at a swift tempo.

"Shall you help me in there, too?" she demanded indignantly.

"If you need me to," he answered, quite serious, and she believed him.

He walked around the bed. Pushing open a white door with his shoulder, he carried her down a short corridor to a warm, ivory-tiled room with old-fashioned dentil molding. It was a combination of the very old and the very new.

"Are all Clan Douglas facilities rooms this big?"

He shrugged. "I never gave the matter much thought."

In front of the triple sink lay a white rug in the shape of a shield. He settled her feet lightly upon the thick weave.

"Towels to the right," he said. "Air shower, water shower, and bathtub are at your disposal. Lavatory to the left."

He stood above her, his face consumed by turbulent emotions. She had never seen him like this, nearly undone. "It's all right, Declan," she soothed, touching his arm.

His gaze settled on her lips and Fallon knew he was going to kiss her.

He leaned down, his kiss featherlight, an aching brush of tenderness, relief, and need. He drew in a deep breath and moved away from her.

Fallon watched his retreat, watched him pause at the door, his hand resting upon the frame. Strangely, he seemed to be trembling.

"I would die without you, Fallon," he said softly and turned to her. "Do not ever do that again."

Fallon said not a word, completely overwhelmed. She just stood there, her heart full, watching him, her face alight with compassion and love.

Thorn landed on his shoulder. The tiny poodlefly rubbed her head against his throat, offering comfort that he seemed unable to accept.

"I love you, too. It's all right," she said quietly.

Thorn made a low woof in the accompanying silence and Fallon smiled patiently, understanding his inner battle. "Declan, my heart, my only love. If you do not give me some privacy, I fear a puddle shall form under me."

"I will be outside," he said gruffly.

"Yes, thank you." She gave him a bright smile.

Declan used the air shower in the empty quarters next door to clean up and tried to get hold of his emotions. He could not go on as he had, living in the past, seeking redemption for his father's sins, for wrongful choices based on a son's need for love. Fallon had become the calming strength to his matrix rage. She was everything to him, compassion, bravery, tenderness, and joy. He didn't know how or when it had happened, but somewhere along the way he had fallen hopelessly and desperately in love with his spirited young wife.

He stepped out of the shower, grabbed the towel he had brought with him, wrapped it around his hips, and punched the commlink on the blue wall. "Medical," he ordered.

The commlink crackled. "Medical here," Dr. William answered. "Is the lassie awake?"

"Yes, finally."

"I expected as much. It has been my experience with induced comas of this nature that the body heals itself."

"I wish you had told me this before," Declan said.

"I did," the doctor replied smugly. "Keep her warm, rested, and fed. I will have the kitchen send food, including the garlic pickles and ice cream."

"Thanks, Doc."

"Expect me later in the evening to check on her. If you need anything, let me know. William out."

"Declan out." He headed back to his quarters to get dressed and stopped short just inside the bedroom.

Thorn hovered a hair's breadth from his nose.

She gave a deep throaty growl of reprimand and bared her teeth.

"I did not forget you," Declan argued with a grin.

"Woof."

"Yes, my little one. I'm grateful for all your support. My wife is going to be fine. Please return to your handsome Kite. There is no need for you to remain here any longer."

The poodlefly tilted her head, her iridescent gaze uncertain.

"Yes, I'm also all right."

Thorn licked the tip of his nose and he laughed softly. "Thank you, pet. I adore you, too."

With shimmering silver wings, she turned and flew down the corridor. His heart warmed at the delicate beauty of her. All quarters in the Keep had a tiny door through which the wee-gadhars could fly in or out. He always left the tiny door to his quarters unlatched so Thorn could come and go as she pleased. The wee critters were intensely loyal to the humans they imprinted on, and Thorn had stayed by his side since he had brought Fallon in. Her mate, Kite, came to visit often to check on things, but otherwise remained close to Lachlan. It complicated things a bit, but they would figure it out.

Declan had turned to the bedroom when a knock came at the front door. Dr. William's food delivery had arrived. It took him only moments to greet the young man, show him where to leave the tray of steaming plates in the morning room, escort him out with a thank you, and head back to his bedroom.

When he arrived, pink morning light was spilling into the large space and he tossed the towel from his hips onto a chair. With a worried glance at the facilities, he walked over to the large closet on the other side of the hearth . . . not once noticing his wife. From there, he dropped a white shirt over his head then slipped on a pair of brown socks and breeches.

"Do you have anything for me to wear, dear husband?"

He turned around and Fallon pressed her lips together in a smile. She held the damp ivory towel to her breasts, pondering the covetous desires of the flesh. The taste for life was strong in her blood. Surviving a near-death experience made colors and sounds sharper, life infinitely sweeter, and love exceedingly more precious.

He said not a word, his gaze one of silent possession.

"'Thou are that,'" she referenced an old quote.

"Really?" he prompted in bemusement.

"Oh, yes."

He slanted her a smile. "Saucy princess." He pulled out a monstrous blue robe from the closet. "Here, put this on." He held the large robe up for her.

Fallon let the towel drop. Walking over to him, she swung her hips provocatively, all the while enjoying the glint of devilish enjoyment across his face. She turned her back to him and slipped her arms into the sleeves. Gathering the soft robe closed, she made a purring sound of appreciation.

"I have orders to keep you warm, rested, and fed." He pulled her back against him, tied the belt around her waist and tenderly pulled her damp curls from under the robe.

Fallon wiggled up against him while he plaited her hair.

"You are making this extremely difficult."

"I hope so."

He chuckled. His hands slid down her arms and around her waist. "Is it your intent to drive me insane?"

"Definitely."

In one swift move, he scooped her up in his arms and headed down a corridor.

"Mmmm, something smells good." Her nose twitched in appreciation as she nuzzled his ear.

"Dr. William sent some food over."

"Good, for I am ravenous. Where are we going?"

"To the morning room."

Fallon looked over his shoulder. "Where is Thorn?"

"She returned to Kite, her mate. She will be back later to check on you, I'm sure."

They turned the corner and Fallon saw a pale yellow morning room with a roaring fire in a great stone hearth. To their left stood a set of rose arched glass doors, and beyond was a sprawling loggia filled with potted plants and black wicker furniture.

"Could we sit out there on the stone terrace?"

"It's a bit cool this morning."

"All right. Here will be fine."

He walked across the pale gold carpet and carried her to the hearth.

Several paces from the roaring fire stood a black table littered with breakfast plates.

Using his foot, he pulled out a high-back chair from the table and eased her onto the padded seat.

"Oh, there is such a thing as too much food," Fallon said. In front of her, steam rose from an assortment of meats, cheese and vegetable pies, strips of bacon, cuts of cooked sausage, eggs, and other dishes, plus one plate of garlic pickles and one plate of vanilla ice cream. When she saw the pickles and ice cream, she covered her mouth and giggled.

"Compliments of Dr. William." Declan tucked the blue robe under her, making sure her feet were covered, and pushed the chair in.

Fallon pulled the vegetable pie closer and sampled it. The cooked fare tasted light and wonderful. Facing death made one appreciate all the little things life offered. She felt alive with sensations. Everything felt new, from the crackling fire's heat at her back and the delicious food smells under her nose to the sounds of a new morning. Placing the blue silk napkin on her lap, she took another helping of vegetables and finished off the crispy piecrust.

Her warrior husband seated himself at the head of the table, rested his chin in his hand, and watched her with a grin.

It disconcerted her a bit, this sudden close scrutiny.

With utensils in hand, she peeked at him through lowered lids.

His smile only broadened and he pushed a plate of steaming sausages under her nose.

"Eat, Princess."

Fallon put a forkful of sausage into her mouth and found the meat deliciously spicy. She reached over and sampled some of the buttery bread while her husband slid a glass of orange juice closer to her plate.

"Thank you," she murmured and took a sip. "Are you hungry, Declan? The food tastes delicious."

"No, thank you." He gave her another one of those sideways smiles, a seductive tilt full of meaning.

The room grew quiet. Fallon tried valiantly to concentrate on the breakfast foods spread out before her, but he was making it extremely difficult. "Why do you look at me this way?" she prompted evenly.

"Because I have come to understand that I will love you to the end of my days."

Her heart did a decided thump in her chest. Fallon carefully placed her glass of orange juice down beside her plate and took a deep, fortifying breath. She hardly knew whether to cry or laugh with happiness. "I never thought to hear you say those words to me."

He rested a powerful arm on the table, his palm spread across her wrist. "I know. I can be a bit dense sometimes."

She looked down at the long blunt fingers stroking her skin, her body humming to the call of his passion.

"Are you still hungry?" he asked with a familiar emphasis in his tone.

"No." Placing the napkin on the table, she shoved the chair back.

Her warrior husband grinned. "I am." Unfolding his large frame from the chair, he took her hand and led her back into the bedroom.

EPILOGUE

Planet Mars, Home of Clan Douglas
Standard Year 3213

ON THE FIRST day of the new year, Declan gazed out upon their new home. His right ear no longer bled and he felt hearty and whole in a way he had never thought possible.

The setting Sun of late afternoon changed the sky to misty purples. He stood on a warm hilltop beside his lady wife. Their son, Rowan, slept secure and peaceful in his arms.

Declan gazed down at the nearly completed castle base, Thornhill Keep. Clan Douglas was constructing it on the far side of Mars, utilizing all of its resources and building it in record time. The new keep proved to be a good morale booster, as well. It was the foundation for new plans for a new future, creating instead of destroying. Declan's thoughts turned to his meeting with Lachlan last night.

Both he and the lord commander agreed there were sound reasons to continue to prepare for a possible attack. Strength meant peace to them. It always would.

The new castle base was the first item in their plan for an ensured victory, no matter what scenarios they would encounter in the future.

Commissioned by Lord Lachlan and Lady Kimberly, Thornhill Keep was a wedding gift, another sentinel set against danger. It would house several thousand. *A good beginning*, Declan thought, *a very good beginning indeed*.

Beside him, his lady wife turned her face into the warm breeze, her hand shielding her eyes, a long blue gown billowing at her booted ankles.

"Mmmm," she whispered, "our living quarters look like a grand manor house from Ancient Earth." Four white stone towers reached for the heavens, set against a hilly countryside of green-gray woodlands and frothy ponds.

"Agreed. But the castle base is much more," he replied, his thoughts occupied by what the future held for them and Clan Douglas.

"I know." She pulled a stray curl out of her eyes. "Fueled by our energy crystals, her power source is completely independent. Simulations have proven we will soon have a fully functional castle base, an excellent stronghold against attack," she mimicked his words of the previous night.

He smiled. "Does it please you?"

"Yes, my love. It pleases me well. We shall bring love and warmth to live within her fortified walls."

Declan gazed down at their son, a small weight

sleeping against his chest and heart. Behind them, the engines of the *Black Ghost* hummed low and familiar, their son's favorite lullaby. He inhaled deeply, his gaze scanning the rolling landscape. "It must be a peace without victory, then."

She looked up at him. "Commander Ramayan has disappeared?"

"He has taken a leave of absence from his post as commander of *Shadowkeep*. No one knows where he has gone."

"I think the best strategy is for us to wait, then."

"Do you?" His gaze moved over her face.

"Yes," she replied, "we must focus on preparation and when the enemy returns, you and Lachlan will be ready."

Declan chuckled. "Know me well, do you?"

"I do."

He could not help but grin. He felt gloriously human, made of flesh and blood and full of life's experiences, both the good ones and the bad ones.

A rustling sound came from behind them, followed by a loud meow.

"Your kitty calls, my lady wife."

His wife glanced over her shoulder into the open hatch of the ship. "In a moment, Gray. You are a most impatient kitty."

"Like her mistress." He looked at her sideways.

A glint of royal fire flashed in lovely brown eyes. "I

am not impatient."

"No, my love. Just magnificent."

She laughed under his steady gaze.

Though they did not speak of it, Declan knew she had lost her gift, burned and gone, a sacrifice he suspected she would willingly make again to protect the innocent. He got down on his knees every night and thanked the Lord for bringing her into his life. There was quiet and peace in him these days, as if the matrix rage had burned and gone out, too.

In the past year, he had negotiated treaties with seven other clans while Lachlan continued talks with the High Council on the highly volatile energy crystal issue.

Distrust still shadowed them, but that, too, would change. Clan Douglas would prosper because they fought for, and stood for, a common future peace.

Declan looked out upon their unfinished home. "Did your father respond to the missive you sent?" he asked.

"No, he cannot forgive me for marrying you. I do not think he ever will."

"Give him time. Your father carries the stubborn Scottish pride in his blood, but he cannot deny the alliance of our marriage and the benefit it brings to Clan MacKendrick."

"I know. I hope you are right. I only wish it was sooner, rather than later. He has already missed Rowan's birth."

Declan touched his wife's cheek with a gentle caress. "All will be well, my love." He pulled her close to his side, careful not to disturb his sleeping son. "Come, let Rowan and me show you your new home."

"Yes," she whispered. "Let us go home."

And they did.

~ the end ~

GLOSSARY

TERMS:

Álainn—beautiful

Beagán— a little

Bíodh an diabhal agat—you go to hell

Dia duit—hello

Jamais Arrière—"Never Behind," the clan Douglas motto believed to be of French origin

Péitseog agus uachtar—peaches and cream

Spéirbhean—beautiful

Slán leat—farewell to the person leaving

Slán agat—farewell to the person staying behind

Slán a fhágáil ag duine—I bid you farewell

Wee-gadhar—tiny dog with wings

CONVERSION MEASUREMENTS:

1 centimeter = 0.4 inches

1 meter = 3.3 feet

1 kilometer = 0.621 miles

CLANS OF ANCIENT EARTH,
A SHORTENED LIST:

CLAN DOUGLAS:

Lord Declan de Douglas—hero

Lord Commander Lachlan de Douglas—Declan's half brother

Lady Saph-ire de Douglas—Declan's and Lachlan's mother

Lord Commander Drumlanrig de Douglas—Lachlan's father

Doctor William de Douglas—matrix scientist

Second Commander Winn de Douglas—Declan's adoptive father

High Councilor Speaker Jared-lynn—ally to Clan Douglas and matrix researcher

CLAN MACKENDRICK:

Princess Fallon MacKendrick—heroine

Lord Dughall MacKendrick—Fallon's father and chieftain of Clan MacKendrick

Lord Tomaidh Henderson—Fallon's betrothed

CLAN SPAIN:

Commander Lin Jacob Rama—Declan's father

Commander Lin Derek Ramayan—Declan's half brother

Castles and Bases:

Braemar Keep—Clan Douglas home base located on planet Mars

MacKendrick Keep—Clan MacKendrick home base located on planet Forest

Silver Base—located on Jupiter's moon, Io; home of the matrix robots

Ship List:

Ambassador Class
(Compliment of twenty crewmen)
Pict—Lord Henderson's ship

Freighter Class
(Compliment of six crewmen)
Black Ghost—Lord Declan de Douglas's gunship

Gazer Class
(Compliment of five crewmen)
Stargazer—commissioned on Clan Spain warship

Starship Class
(Compliment of fifty crewmen)
Edinburgh—Clan Douglas starship

Warship Class
(Compliment of one hundred and fifty crewmen)
Claymore—Clan Douglas warship
Necromancer—High Council warship
Saltire—Clan Douglas warship
Shadowkeep—Clan Ramayan warship

AUTHOR NOTES

THIS QUOTE APPEARED around the Internet, and although I was unable to locate the original source by the time I handed this book into my editor, I found it fitting for *Redemption* and wished to share it with you:

> "Life is too short to wake up in the morning
> with regrets, so love the people who treat you
> right, and forget about the ones who don't, and
> believe that everything happens for a reason . . .
> If you get a chance, take it.
> If it changes your life, let it.
> Nobody said life would be easy, they just prom-
> ised it would be worth it."

Darkscape: Redemption continues the saga of the Douglas clan with a hero who is haunted by the choices he had made in a war.

Like *Darkscape: The Rebel Lord*, *Redemption* was one of my first books and has been completely revised for my publisher, Medallion Press. I hope you enjoyed it.

Where possible, I updated celestial references impacted by the decisions made in the International Astronomical Union meeting in Prague in 2006. I also tweaked the technology in the book to fall in line with recent advancements. But as development is ever ongoing, I must accept the possibility of my references becoming obsolete.

Look for *Darkscape: First Heir* to be released next year. For information about my books, please visit my website: www.rgarlandgray.com and, as always, thank you.

Blessings,
Garland

R. GARLAND GRAY

DARKSCAPE

THE REBEL LORD

Lord Lachlan de Douglas, a noble warrior lord, is heir to a Clan of Ancient Earth. Bold, rebellious, possessing strength and passion, he defends his clan from annihilation against a wretched war of masked vengeance and treacherous shadows. Until one day, a sudden horror alters his being, condemning him to a world of private anguish and torment.

Kimberly Kinsale, a diplomat's daughter, is a rare beauty motivated by honesty and integrity. Serving as a lieutenant in an elite combat fighter group aboard a war ship, she governs her life by the intrigue and lies of her commanding officer. A moment of lunacy and folly, a secret revealed, and Kimberly stumbles upon an unspeakable deception.

Now she must decide. Maintain her loyalty, or betray her Clan and ship for a Douglas enemy lord who can prove the truth—never knowing the battle for justice will take her through Lachlan's nightmare, a rage so deep, a suffering grounded in shame and pride, even when peace shines in sight.

For theirs is an unexpected passion, born in the fires of a shared need and desperate struggle. Kimberly must fight the sinister legacy of the matrix robots and trust the handsome enemy lord with her life, her heart, and her very soul. But as time slowly runs out, even an exquisite love may not be enough for salvation.

ISBN# 978-193383648-5
US $7.95 / CDN $8.95
Sci-Fi Romance
Available Now

Coming in December 2010 by R. Garland Gray
The third installment of Ms. Gray's Darkscape series.

Darkscape: First Heir

A special presentation of Darkscape: First Heir

Schooled in the unconventional ways of the crystal mystics, Isabo Gyllenhaal must settle for work a servant. When she becomes ensnared in the lies of a deceitful princess bride who refuses to obey her father's wishes, she finds herself waiting in a moon garden, a reluctant imposter about to deliver a bride's rejection to a fiercesome off-world lord. Never does she imagine the danger and passion waiting for her.

Lord Drumlanrig de Douglas is the Prince Regent to Clan Douglas, an Ancient Earth clan trying to escape a tarnished past. An assertive leader, he seethes with rage and resentment for the stained heritage he shares with his symbiotic twin. But unlike his twin, he wants the normal life that fate has denied him. When a respected clan makes an unexpected bridal offering, he is intrigued and decides to go and meet her.

But the young woman is not what he expects. And their meeting takes an unexpected turn, plunging them into the sinister world of space pirates and vengeance, where capture means a living death for Drum and slavery for Isabo. With time running out, they struggle to escape, struggle to trust, but there are far worse things stalking the Douglas prince, a horrific nightmare waiting to engulf him –

And as their attraction grows out of control, Isabo will risk all to save the prince's soul, even sacrifice her future, if only he can accept her love...

ISBN# 978-160542076-9
US $7.95 / CDN $8.95
Sci-Fi Romance
December 2010

Susan Gourley

The Keepers of Sulbreth

With elfin blood in his veins, talented swordsman Cage Stone is an indispensable half-breed with a special purpose. He must save Futhark from the monsters that detect growing evil in society and threaten to destroy the human race. Blessed with miraculous enhancements, Cage is the only man who can prevent the annihilation of the world. He is the chosen one—a savior in need of his soul mate to complete his mission.

Long ago, these precious elves created a powerful magic to imprison the demon beings. Now acciptors, cave boas, and gordragons have emerged from their sleepy cavern to torment their victims with malilcious relish. Before abandoning Futhark forever, the elves entrusted only a few Keepers of the Gate with the knowledge and ability to restore the supernatural spell that holds their enemies captive. With the passage of time, these fragile scales have weakened, putting humanity at risk.

Sabelline is a Keeper with a tremendous burden. She must renew the seals with a selected Marshal at her side. Only she can create the mystical union with Cage that will enable them to descend into the depths of hell and drive these horrid creatures back into oblivion. But will their mysterious, spiritual bond surpass the daunting obstacles on the way to Kingdom's Gate in time to rescue Futhark from destruction?

ISBN# 978-160542065-3
Mass Market Paperback / Fantasy
US $7.95 / CDN $8.95
JANUARY 2010

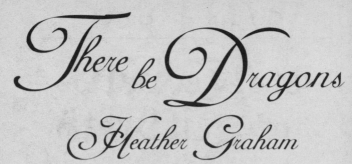

There be Dragons

Heather Graham

Illustrated by

Cherif Fortin & Lynn Sanders

Bonus CD produced by

Reuven Amiel

Nico d'Or was a kind and gentle man who lived in the age of dragons. Through a simple twist of fate, Nico married the lovely Princess Elisia, and the couple were blessed with a beautiful daughter, Marina. Would they live happily ever after?

Well, not quite. The neighbor's wife, Geovana, was neither sweet nor lovely, but a devious sorceress who spent her time casting dreadful spells, devising vile tricks, and mixing powerful potions with eye of newt and the horn of a toad.

Geovana used one of her favorite spells—strategically hurling rocks through windows to smash into the heads of her victims—tragically killing both Nico and Elisia, and leaving the beautiful Marina all alone. To make matters worse, Geovana became Marina's guardian and, greedy for power, arranged a marriage between Marina and her own evil son, Carlo Baristo.

But Marina was in love with someone else. And as Christmas Day approached, Marina was faced with a terrible choice: save her land and her people, or follow her heart and believe in the magic of Christmas and true love.

ISBN# 978-160542071-4
Hardcover Adult / Illustrated Romantic Masterpiece
(Includes bonus audio CD)
US $25.95 / CDN $28.95
Available Now

WILD
MAGIC
ANN MACELA

Irenee Sabel is a witch—a good witch, a sophisticated beauty, a member of Chicago's old money elite, and a Defender of an ancient code of ethics that prohibits the indiscriminate use of power attached to magical possessions. As a Sword, Irenee is responsible for confiscating and destroying hidden relics of the sorcery realm still employed by practitioners of the craft for self-centered reasons. Her present target: an aging warlock.

While attending a gala party at Alton Finster's Gold Coast mansion, she burglarizes his safe in search of an item of mystical mayhem. Irenee doesn't anticipate Jim Tylan interrupting her break-in. From the moment they meet, she knows this is no ordinary man.

With an undisclosed search warrant from the Department of Justice and Homeland Security, Tylan enters Finster's office to obtain covert financial records. There he finds a glowing handbag and an overpowering attraction to the benevolent sorceress holding the luminescent purse.

This mysterious encounter launches an escapade to expose pieces of the legendary Cataclysm Stone, an evil object of interest for the Defenders since the fifteenth century. In the heat of the chase, Irenee discovers that her real object of interest isn't the famed stone, but the undercover agent destined to be her lover . . . her soul mate.

ISBN# 978-193383699-7
US $7.95 / CDN $8.95
Paranormal Romance
Available Now

NEW
DAWN
RISING

SCOTT GAMBOE

Captain Arano Lakeland and his wife, Alayna, must save Rystoria from the threat of a Bromidian totalitarian regime. Their unusual partnership is not a typical romance. This ongoing quest for freedom led by the Rystorial Liberation Front is a treacherous mission in outer space, a terrifying hell that threatens to end their lives. Bombs, terrorists, and spies create an intergalactic obstacle course only the strongest will survive.

As the elite Avengers infiltrate the New Dawn uprising, every precious disclosure of information could determine the future. Freedom is at stake. Losing sovereignty to the lethal Bromidians means the end of the world as they know it. Until Arano and his army have overthrown the illegitimate government of Gorst IX, Rystoria will never regain its liberty. No longer a given right, independence is a privilege of the past. Peace will be impossible to achieve in a dangerous empire controlled by unstable forces of evil.

Trapped in a deceptive realm where no one can distinguish between friend and foe until loyalties are revealed, every perilous assignment may lead to death or prolonged agony. The Avengers must determine who is faithful to this overpowering insurrection. In the hands of an enemy skilled at torture, every moment is a critical turning point. Escape or die.

ISBN# 978-193383695-9
Trade Paperback
US $15.95 / CDN $17.95
Science Fiction
Available Now

Be in the know on the latest
Medallion Press news by becoming a
Medallion Press Insider!

<u>As an Insider you'll receive:</u>

• Our FREE expanded monthly newsletter,
giving you more insight into Medallion Press

• Advanced press releases and breaking news

• Greater access to all of your favorite
Medallion authors

Joining is easy, just visit our Web site at
<u>www.medallionpress.com</u> and click on the
Medallion Press Insider tab.